INVASION

ROXANNE BLAND

BLACKROSE PRESS
BALTIMORE, MARYLAND

Invasion

Published 2017 by Blackrose Press
Book and cover design copyright © 2017 by Blackrose Press

Book interior design by Vyrdolak, By Light Unseen Media

Perfect Paperback edition
ISBN 13: 978-0-9967316-9-0
ISBN 10: 0-9967316-9-5
LCCN: 2017914526

A Blackrose Press Original

Blackrose Press
P.O. Box 18402
Rosedale, Maryland 21237
www.blackrosepress.com

Other Books by Roxanne Bland

The Moreva of Astoreth

The Underground

For My Parents,
Ronald and June Bland

CHAPTER 1

For the second time in less than six months, Kurt, vampire regent, and Master of Seattle was terrified.

Fear turned to anger. *This cannot be happening to me.*

He stood in the dark before a wall-sized, plate glass window on the top floor of his office tower in downtown Seattle. Turning, he stepped over to a small lamp on his sculpted steel desk and switched it on. In the low light, the plate glass reflected everything in the room—except him. Baring his teeth, he swept his arm over the desk, sending the lamp crashing to the floor. His office was plunged into darkness again.

Kurt glared at the shattered lamp. *It's inexplicable. My powers are supposed to strengthen with age, not weaken.* Yet here he was, losing the powers he'd nearly died twice to obtain.

His first indication that something was wrong happened about a month ago while dining at Harrow, his flagship restaurant. He and a client, Jack Hewitt, had been lunching in one of the restaurant's private dining rooms. It had been a celebration on Kurt's part for having closed a deal for a complete renovation of one of Hewitt's sprawling luxury hotels to the tune of thirty-five million dollars. His thoughts drifted, remembering.

"A perfect lunch, Kurt," Hewitt had said. He put his fork down on his now-empty plate.

"Of course. I wouldn't have it any other way." Kurt had popped the last piece of filet mignon into his mouth, chewed, and then tried to swallow. He choked, instead. Gagging, he curled over the table, his throat muscle spasming. "Urk. Uurrk!" After several seconds of coughing up, he'd felt the meat shift toward the back of his mouth.

"Kurt? Kurt," Hewitt had shouted. "Oh, my God!" He'd leapt from his seat and ran around the table to where Kurt sat. Kurt had waved him away, but Hewitt hadn't seemed to notice. Hauling him out of his seat, Hewitt had proceeded to perform the Heimlich maneuver, not knowing that the technique would be useless. Kurt had managed to dislodge the piece of food on his own and spat it into his napkin.

Back in the present, he shivered as if to shake off the humiliating memory. Now, the only human foods he could manage were clear soups and wine.

Lips pursed, he reached for a bottle resting near the edge of the desktop and poured some of its contents into a large, heavy crystal goblet. Upending the cup, he drained the murky liquid, its slightly viscous texture coating his tongue and throat. When the cup was empty, he set the goblet back on the desk and fixed it with a baleful stare. "Nothing like a pint of blood to ruin a perfectly good wine," he muttered.

From the day of his lunch with Jack Hewitt, his losses had only worsened. He had a near-constant need for blood. A vampire regent need only feed once or twice a year, but now he had to feed every day. *Stealing blood from my own blood bank, hiding my tracks…no one's caught on, but how long will it be until someone does?* He used the stolen blood to make his bloodwine, mixing the concoction himself, and then stashing the bottles in a wine cellar he had built in the deeper recesses beneath his nightclub. *And when the hunger comes, I sneak away to my cellar and drink like a secret alcoholic until I can face a live human or zot without attacking him. It's embarrassing, is what it is.*

Kurt started pacing. *And then there are the other powers I've lost. I can't read minds. I'm no longer telepathic. I can still go out in daylight but I have to stay out of the sun because I don't cast a shadow.* He shook his head. For every day that passed, it was getting harder and harder to maintain the lie that, for him, it was business as usual.

He stopped in his tracks and clapped his hands over his face. *And what's so maddening is that I don't know* why *this is happening.*

Dropping his hands, he walked back to the window and stared at the dark construction cranes guarding their sites like skeletal sentries. He traced a perfectly-manicured fingernail over his cheek. *Could Balthus Coven have put a hex on me?* It was possible. Vampires are not immune to magick. He thought about it, then dismissed it. *No. It would take a coven of mages to hex a regent like me. Balthus only has one mage—Garrett. And she wouldn't dare. She has just as much to lose as I do.*

He pursed his lips again. *Could I be ill? I've never heard of it happening to our kind before. But there's always a first time. Maybe…* Then he grabbed his head in both hands and gritted his teeth, knowing he was grasping at straws. "That's simply absurd. I'm getting the vampire equivalent of senile, not catching a damned cold."

His jaw relaxed, but he didn't let go of his head. Whether senile or something else, his diminishment could cost him dearly. *I deal with humans nearly every day. Before all this—whatever it is—started, it was impossible for anyone to guess I'm a vampire. But now…if any human figures out what I am, I'll be permanently dead in short order.*

Kurt let his arms fall to his sides. His—infirmity—could cost him in other ways, too. He was of some renown among his kind for having attained his full regency at two hundred years old, a comparatively young age for a vampire. But if word of his disability got out, who knew how many of the undead would try to topple him from his Seattle throne?

And Seattle was a prize any would-be Master or Mistress would covet. Kurt had been among the city's founders. He was the reason Seattle had become a place where zots could live and work relatively free from human molestation. But his influence went far beyond his control over the city's zots. Through his human servants, he pulled most of the strings in the city and county governments. Washington's lieutenant governor was one of his human servants. He had influence in the state legislature and even held influence over the state's delegation to Congress. As far as he knew, no other vampire in America wielded that kind of power.

I'll have to defend my domain against all comers, just like I did almost six hundred years ago. His jaw tightened again. The prospect didn't cheer him. That never-ending chess game had been fun while he'd been a prince among the living but now that he was dead, he'd no appetite for it. *And I'm not fool enough to think my zots would help me keep what's mine. They hate me, and right now they hate me even more because of that damned revolution last June.* He sighed. *I really should have paid closer attention to those so-called college students. Those idiots…burning my city. Equal rights for exotics is all well and good but that won't happen as long as humans outnumber us by thousands to one. All those morons managed to accomplish was nothing.*

Kurt returned to his desk and decanted the rest of the bloodwine into the goblet. Narrowing his eyes, he stared at the cup for a moment and then poured the foul concoction down his throat. His face knotted. "Ugh." Giving the goblet another evil glare, he grimaced and set it on the desk. Then he started pacing again.

If the tryst had worked the way Garrett said it would... His lips tightened. *It isn't her fault.* It had been the mage's idea to combine her own formidable talent, Kurt's regent's powers, and the extraordinary psychogenetic strength of her werewolf ex-lover, Parker, by casting a magick spell to create a tryst. When they'd joined forces last June, they'd planned to use the tryst to cast a second spell that would have erased human Seattleites' fear and hatred for zots. *She couldn't have foreseen the revolution. And the conditions under which we had to work...'less than optimal' would be an understatement. The only thing the spellcasting accomplished was to stop the rioting.*

A thought struck him. *Could whatever's happening to me now be because of the tryst?* He thought about it for a few minutes and then shook his head. *Can't be. It's been over five months since we cast that spell. If the tryst was behind this, I'd have noticed something long before now, wouldn't I?*

He stopped his pacing, returned to his desk and sat in his black leather executive's chair. Leaning back, he gazed at the ceiling. Wasn't there any way he could stop his deterioration? A moment later, his jaw set and he bolted upright in his seat. *No. There's a reason why this—cancer—is happening to me, and I'm going to find out what it is. And then I'm going to beat it.*

He nodded once and stood. Then he dissolved into mist and flew across the city back to his Last Chance nightclub.

CHAPTER 2

While Kurt paced his office downtown, Parker Berenson, alpha of Seattle's werewolf pack, lay sprawled on the outdoor chaise he'd dragged from his house's rear patio into his backyard. A full tumbler and a half-bottle of Jack Daniel's rested on a small stand bolted to the side of the chaise's sturdy metal frame. Next to the Jack was an ashtray with a half-smoked joint. Fingers laced over his stomach and his face pointed toward the stars, Parker's dreamy expression made him look like any other stargazer lost in contemplation of heaven's mysteries.

He closed his eyes. *The problem with being in love with a space alien is that if you break up, the only people who can sympathize are usually locked up in the loony bin.*

Opening them, he unlaced his fingers, sat up, and reached for his drink. He stared into the tumbler's night-blackened depths for a moment, then tossed back a healthy slug of whiskey. Lowering the glass, he slowly traced his index finger along its rim. "Melera's been gone three months, one week and five days," he said in low voice.

His beast stirred inside his mind. *Been counting, have you?* he growled. *You counting the hours and minutes too?*

Parker set the now half-empty tumbler on the stand. He picked up the joint and concentrating a moment, torched it with his pyrokinetic ability, a rare trait among *weres*. Inhaling once, he lay back and settled into his earlier position. "Like you haven't been doing the same thing, fuzzbutt?" he exhaled in a cloud of smoke.

By now, this exchange between Parker and his *were*, a gargantuan man-wolf eight feet tall had become familiar. Since the day Melera had left them for Maqu, her home galaxy, they'd camped here in their backyard on as many of the few clear nights they could, their shared eyes scanning the heavens for a sign of her return with the desperate fervor of shipwreck survivors scanning the horizon for signs of rescue. Unlike shipwreck survivors, he and his wolf had no idea what they were looking for. But they'd know it when they saw it. At least that's what they kept telling each other.

Look…I-I'm sure she's okay, his wolf growled. *Think of it this way. She's on the mother of all road trips. She's probably been doing it since she was a cub.*

Parker took another hit from the joint. Reaching for the ashtray, he stubbed out the roach. Then he re-laced his fingers across his stomach. "Except the road out there goes on forever and there aren't any gas stations along the way."

Man and wolf watched the sky in silence. Despite the ambient glare from the city's lights, he could see well enough, with his wolf-sight, to spot anything that moved. So far they'd seen a bunch of birds heading for wherever, a few jetliners heading for wherever else, and a slew of satellites heading for nowhere. But they'd seen nothing that looked like it might be a spaceship heading for base in the South Pacific.

"What happened?" he whispered. "Us and Melera…we were so good together. God, we loved her enough to leave Earth and follow her to her galaxy, even if it meant dying in that crazy war she's fighting over there. And then…I don't know. It's like some kind of switch got thrown, and then we were fighting all the time—about what, I can't even remember—and then she was gone. Why?"

Uhrrm. Maybe us being assholes had something to do with it?

He ignored the question. "Those things we said to her just before—"

We? You had our body that last time, remember? I didn't say jack.

Parker rolled his eyes. "Okay, those things *I* said to her just before she left. Happy?"

His wolf didn't answer.

Reaching for his drink, he picked up the tumbler of Jack and drained it. "The look on her face…for a second I thought she was going to kill us." He refilled his empty glass and knocked back another slug. "And then she skipped through the Void. Disappeared. Poof—just like that."

You're forgetting about her chewing us a new one first.

He snorted. "Yeah. In Xia'saan, or however it's pronounced." He smiled a little. "Those five voices of hers…I don't know what Melera said, but from the way it sounded, I'm pretty sure I don't want to know."

Me neither. Though learning some new cuss words might have been fun.

Behind them, the sound of a door opening cut off further conversation. Parker sensed a pair of lupine eyes focused on the back of his head. "Maybe you should take up astronomy," a woman's warm, contralto voice said.

Parker said nothing. He didn't move, either.

The silence lengthened. Then he heard the sound of bedroom slippers slapping across the patio and then swishing through the late fall grass. A large, red shape appeared in his peripheral vision. "Parker," the woman said in a tone that demanded acknowledgment.

He rolled his head toward the sound. Mandy Stewart, the mayor of Seattle's chief of staff, stood over him. A handsome blonde by anyone's standards, her brown eyes looked angry.

"Yes, Mandy?"

Dressed in only a thin silk robe, Mandy seemed impervious to the November chill. She took a breath and the look in her eyes softened. "Park, when you chose me for your freya last August, I accepted not because I thought you loved or wanted me, but because our pack needed me. So I agreed to all of your conditions. You will not father my cubs. You will not allow me to live with you. Other than the times when the pack needs to see us together, we are freyr and freya maybe once a week."

She dropped to her knees beside the chaise and gazed at him, the look in her brown eyes almost pleading. "You know a freya is committed to serving her pack, Parker. She must be everything they need her to be—mother, sister, friend or lover. She is committed to serving her freyr—her alpha—with as much, if not greater, devotion."

Parker watched Mandy's lips descend until they were only inches from his. "Parker, I am yours. I promised you that I will be whatever you want me to be, whatever you need me to be, whenever you wish me to be." She stared into his eyes and suddenly kissed him with fiery passion.

A white-hot burst of pain seized the right side of his face. Parker jumped. "Argh!" he grunted. He tasted blood.

Bitch did not just do that! his wolf howled, and surged to the forefront of his mind. Without thinking, Parker slammed his will against him and held firm as if trying to keep a monster from exploding out of the closet.

He looked up, blood dribbling down his chin.

Mandy towered over him. "But the one thing I will not be is ignored," she said in a voice as hard as marble, matching the look in her eyes. She glared at him a moment longer, then turned and stalked toward the house.

Parker watched her go while wiping the blood from his lip with the sleeve of his sweatshirt. After Mandy had disappeared inside, he picked up his glass and took a swig, wincing a little when the alcohol passed over the wound she'd made. Returning the glass to the side table, he pinched the remains of his joint between his thumb and forefinger, torched it, and took a deep drag. Stubbing it out, he popped the now-cooled roach into his mouth. Then he lay back in the chaise and stared up at the sky. A moment later, he laughed.

What's so funny?

"You. Me. Mandy. Melera," he said between chuckles. "God, think about it. A sexy, willing blonde waiting for us in our bed, and we're out here—"

Waiting for the impossible, his wolf finished for him.

His breath caught. His look turned bleak. "Yeah."

Neither one said anything for quite a while. Parker looked at his watch. Ten minutes had passed since Mandy had bitten him. Enough time for him to salvage his dignity as alpha wolf, but not enough time for Mandy to think he was disrespecting her again. Swinging his legs to his right, he planted his feet on the ground, lifted his muscular, six-foot six-inch frame off the chaise and stretched. Dropping the ashtray into the chair, he picked up the now-empty tumbler and the near-empty bottle of Jack in his right hand, grabbed the chaise with his left and dragged it across the yard, releasing it once he'd reached the patio.

Hand on the sliding door panel, he'd been about to step over the threshold when a wave of vertigo hit him. The tumbler and bottle slipped out of his fingers and smashed on the paving stones. Swaying like a drunkard, he staggered around the patio until he tripped over the chaise. He tried to get up, only to fall on his knees and then flat on his face. Gasping, he managed to rise up on all fours.

"What the f—" he started but that was as far as he got when his stomach clenched into a fist. Pain exploded through him. He would have screamed but he couldn't get enough air into his lungs. He rolled onto his side and curled into a fetal position, desperately trying to breathe.

The spasm ended as abruptly as it had come. Now he felt nauseous. Managing to raise himself on all fours again, he crawled across the patio and made it to the edge just in time to throw up the Jack Daniel's and the remains of his late-night snack on the grass. Turning, he crawled deeper into his yard. When he could go no further, he closed his eyes and rolled over onto his back. He felt weak as a newborn cub. With effort, he lifted his arm, wiped his mouth on his sleeve, and let his arm drop to the ground.

An eternity later, his vertigo vanished, only to be replaced by an acute sense of dislocation as if his body was in three different places at once. Now he understood what was happening to him. He slowly opened his eyes. It was just as he'd expected. He had trifocal vision. Three different views showing three different scenes superimposed on one another. One view belonged to Kurt and the other to Garrett, he knew, but the only one he could be sure of was his own—the view of the stars overhead.

The tryst…Garrett said the spell hadn't worked well enough to keep us linked together. Did she lie about that, too? Anger welled up in him but he squashed it. No point in getting pissed off. That could come later. Right now there was nothing he could do but wait and hope this nightmare ended.

Watching, he noticed one of the two appeared to be in a darkened office downtown, on a high floor and looking out of a window at a bunch of construction equipment below. He could feel the springiness of the carpet's deep pile through a pair of shoes he wasn't wearing. The other view…he frowned. To him, it looked as if someone was tearing apart an animal by hand. It was impossible to tell what kind of animal it had been since it no longer had a head. He could feel the hard, cold earth digging into his knees as well as the unfortunate beast's slick blood covering his hands and lips.

At least Parker now knew which view belonged to whom. *What the hell is Kurt doing?* The vampire was an asshole but a cultured one, and he was pretty sure disemboweling small animals barehanded wasn't his style. But he was positive it couldn't be Garrett. Her Witches' Credo forbade her to harm a living soul. *But what's she doing in an office building downtown at this time of night?*

Then as suddenly as the spell had come over him, it was over. Now he was looking through only one pair of eyes—his own—and his body felt whole again. He struggled to sit up. Expecting to feel wasted, he was surprised that other than feeling a little tired, he felt fine. He looked at his watch and was amazed to see that only six minutes had passed. It had seemed like six hours.

Human, we have got to figure out how to stop this shit, his wolf snarled. *I don't know about you but I'm not spending the rest of my life puking my guts out and seeing triple.*

"Quit calling me 'human'. And I'm with you. I'm calling Garrett and Kurt first thing in the morning." Then he cocked his head. "Huh. This is the first time something like this has happened to us. I wonder if anything's happened—"

Don't you think they would have told us if it had?

Parker curled his lip. "Those two? No. Especially not Garrett." Picking himself up off the ground, he returned to the patio and crossed it, his feet crunching on the broken glass. Stepping through the open sliding glass door, he entered his kitchen. Then he slid the door shut and locked it.

He walked through the kitchen into the great room and reached the stairs moments later. On the second floor, he made a stop at the bathroom. After what had happened to him in his backyard, he needed to shower and brush his teeth.

Ten minutes later, he was out of the bath and heading for his bedroom.

I wish Melera was here, his wolf blurted. *It just isn't the same.*

Me, too, pal. And I know.

Pausing in the bedroom's doorway, his hand slid over the hallway's wall until he found the light switch and turned the light off. He stood in the darkness for a moment, then let out a tiny sigh. Reluctantly pushing thoughts of Melera aside, he stepped into his darkened bedroom where Mandy waited for him.

He sighed again.

Duty time.

CHAPTER 3

The following afternoon, Kurt had just returned the telephone handset to its cradle when the door to his office beneath his Last Chance nightclub was flung open.

Annoyed, he looked up to see Parker storm over the threshold and slam the door shut. He looked furious. "Listen, Kurt. I'm not your damned servant anymore. The tryst took care of that, remember? What gives you the right to tell me to haul ass down here from a job just because you say so? And——"

"On the contrary, dear Parker," Kurt said in a voice like smooth velvet. "The alpha of the wolf pack is required to serve me in exchange for my saving the pack from annihilation in nineteen twelve. That debt remains outstanding and will not be satisfied until I say it is. So far, I haven't said." He raised his brow. "Surely you couldn't have forgotten about that?"

Parker glared at him but said nothing.

Kurt dipped his head. "Yes, the tryst severed our psychic connection but that changes nothing between us. You are still my servant." His lips stretched into a knowing smile. "And you're obviously used to obeying me. After all, here you are, hmm?"

Parker's bright green eyes narrowed. "Fuck you, asshole."

Kurt almost laughed. That was one of the wolf's favorite terms of endearment for his master. Then his expression hardened. "In any event, I didn't *ask*"—he gave Parker a pointed look—"for you to come down here to argue with me." He pointed to a plush, velvet-covered chair positioned a few feet away from his desk. "Sit. We need to talk."

Parker remained standing. "About what?"

Kurt pursed his lips. "You telephoned me this morning to say you'd had an…episode, with the tryst's magick resurfacing. Has anything happened since then?"

"No, but—"

"Did you ever get hold of Garrett?"

"No. That's why—"

"Let me finish, please. You didn't talk to her because she seems to have gone missing."

Parker's angry and distrustful look melted into incredulity. He sat hard in the chair. "What?"

"I called the Stohlman Theater and they said she'd taken a leave of absence for an unspecified period. Something about an aged relative in Ireland. I naturally assumed she was referring to someone belonging to her first coven. But there's just one problem. She didn't go to Ireland. She went to France."

"France?"

"I've tracked her as far as Montpellier. Beyond that, nothing." He nodded at the telephone. "I'd just hung up with the city's Mistress when you arrived. Her vampires hacked into the networks of all the airport's transportation companies and found no record of her hiring a vehicle, whether a car, a cab or anything else. So maybe she got in touch with the local coven and they sent someone to pick her up." He shrugged. "Or something like that."

Parker gave him a skeptical look. "Since when are you vampires so cooperative?"

Kurt's lips curved into a tiny smile. "Mistress owes me a number of favors."

Parker rolled his eyes. "Yeah, I'll bet." Then he frowned a little. "But why France?"

"Because that's where her answer lies, hmm?"

"Make sense, Kurt."

"I'm talking about the answer to the tryst's magick. I think Garrett's had an episode, too. You told me that last night you saw, through your trifocal vision, a view from the window of an office building downtown and another of someone ripping apart and eating some kind of small animal." He paused. "Parker, the view from the office you saw was mine."

Parker laughed. "Oh, come on. Garrett a killer? No way. It had to have been you."

Kurt cocked his head. "You remember Garrett's cat, don't you?"

"Mr. Squiggles? Sure. He hates me."

Kurt opened the top drawer on the left-hand side of his desk and took out an opaque plastic bag distended by a couple of small bulges. "When you called and told me what you'd seen, I sent one of my servants over to Garrett's house to take a discreet look around the grounds. She'd already left by then. But Gordon came back with this." He tossed the bag to Parker.

Parker undid the bag and gasped. Then he looked up, saucer-eyed. "Mr. Squiggles?"

"What's left of him. His head, part of a leg, and his tail." Kurt sat forward and rested his elbows on the desktop. "Now you tell me—why on earth would I want to kill Garrett's cat?"

Parker handed the bag to Kurt, then fell back in his chair and let out a low whistle. "Damn."

Kurt nodded. "Indeed. She's broken her Credo—'an' it harm none'. Everything she stands for."

Parker snorted. "Except for the night she tried to kill Melera."

"Exigent circumstances, dear Parker. Melera was about to kill me, remember?" He raised his brow. "Or are you saying she should have just let Melera run that laser knife though my brain?"

"All I'm saying is— "

Kurt waved his hand. "Enough. We were talking about Garrett."

Neither man said anything for a long while. Then Parker looked up. "Kurt…have you—has anything happened to you?"

He said nothing and leaned back in his chair. How much should he reveal? He knew from past experience that the wolf was highly intuitive and he was no dummkopf, either. But he also knew that Parker hated him. If the latter guessed correctly, who knew what the wolf would do with his new-found knowledge that the Master was anything but the Master? And if Parker and Garrett were having problems, he couldn't very well say he wasn't. They'd never believe it.

Kurt stared at the wolf a moment longer. "Yes, Parker. I've had some—difficulties, shall we say. It started about a month ago. I didn't link it to the tryst's magick until you called."

Parker's eyes narrowed. "What kind of difficulties?"

Kurt's stare didn't waver. "Difficulties."

The other man shifted in his chair but said nothing. A minute later, a slow smile spread across his face. "You've lost all your special powers, haven't you, Kurt?" he said in an amused tone.

Kurt gazed down at his desktop. Once again, Parker had taken the barest of hints and somehow hit upon the truth. *No point in denying it, now.* He looked up. "Not quite. But close enough."

"Okay…so since you're not the biggest, baddest dead man in town these days, are you still the Master?"

"Unless the title is wrested from me, yes."

"I take it that would be pretty easy, huh?"

"Most likely."

Parker gave him a wolfish grin. "Now, how about that? Maybe I'll be free of you sooner than I thought."

Kurt smiled a little. "Parker, are you familiar with the vampire law of succession?"

"Sure. You guys in the colony duke it out until somebody comes out on top."

"No. Only a regent can rule a colony." Kurt rose from his leather executive's chair. Stepping away from his desk, he clasped his hands behind his back and began to pace. "It's like this. When a Mistress or Master's position within the colony weakens, we vampires have a ritual similar to your wolves' death-match. We call it a contest of wills." He paused but didn't stop his pacing. "Anyway, the victor in a will contest inherits the former Mistress or Master's entire estate. Real property, money, influence…all of it."

By now, Kurt was back at his desk. He sat on its edge and looked down at Parker, who still sat in his chair. "That includes accounts receivables, Parker—the favors and other debts owed to me." He watched the other man's eyes widen a fraction. "Oh, so you're beginning to understand, hmm?" He smiled again. "That's right, wolf—you and your pack are one of my accounts receivables." Kurt looked up at the ceiling. "I can think of three regents off the top of my head who'd kill to be first in line for a will contest over my Seattle estate. If I lose…" He looked down again, this time with a mirthless grin. "You will have a new Master, Parker. And believe me—compared to those three? I'm a veritable saint."

Vampire and werewolf stared at one another. Then Parker let out a little snort. "So I guess I'd better keep my mouth shut, right?"

"I think that's advisable." Kurt stood and then walked around the desk to his chair and sat. Elbows on the desktop, he laced his fingers.

Parker looked at him. "So what do we do in the meantime?"

"I'll keep looking for Garrett but I'm not hopeful. Exotics in the Languedoc-Roussillon are pretty close-mouthed and I also happen to know that neither Mistress nor anyone else in Montpellier knows who the local coven's witches are. All we can do is wait for Garrett's return."

There was a moment of silence. "Well, I hope she finds something and soon," Parker said. He gave his head a little shake. "God, if I have another tryst attack like that last one while I'm in the middle of a job, I'm gonna be in deep wolf shit. Somebody'll call an ambulance and they'll take me to the hospital and you can bet they'll do a genetic screening test to find out whether I'm zot or human. And when they find out I'm a zot, I'll disappear."

Kurt looked down at his hands. That possibility had occurred to him too, and the last thing he wanted was Parker's execution. The wolf might hate him but the feeling wasn't mutual. Far from it. But if Parker were caught, there'd be nothing Kurt could do about it.

Neither one spoke for a long while. "Is that it?" Parker broke the silence.

"Isn't that enough?"

Parker blew a heavy sigh and stood. He looked at his watch. "I need to get back to work. I'm supposed to wrap up this program job in a couple of hours." He turned and headed for the door.

"Parker," Kurt called.

The wolf looked over his shoulder.

"I'll keep you informed."

Parker stared at him without expression. "Yeah. You do that." Then he left the office.

Kurt sighed and leaned back in his chair, thinking on their conversation. He and Parker weren't the only ones in danger. Garrett had allied herself with a vampire and a werewolf, which the witches' Millennium Agreement with humans forbid. The punishment for doing so was to burn at the stake. And Garrett had obviously absorbed some of

Parker's *were* traits. If she was caught by humans or her coven mutilating small animals—or worse, mutilating humans—before the three of them could figure out how to counter the tryst's magick, they were all dead.

Then something occurred to him. *I wonder if Garrett absorbed any of my regent's powers?* He raised his brows. *Parker, too…and what traits have I absorbed from him?* He thought about it, then gave a little shrug. *Well, it hardly matters at the moment. The important thing is that we find some way to reverse the spell. And right now, I've other things to do.* Kurt sat forward and pulled the computer keyboard to him. Checking the monitor to see where he'd left off, he resumed going over Last Chance's quarterly financial report.

About an hour later, a spasm wracked his body. Panting, he felt blood sweat leaking from his pores. Then he began to shake. Kurt knew what was wrong. He hadn't had any bloodwine since this morning. He needed to feed—*now*.

Yanking open the desk's large, lower right hand drawer, his trembling hands pulled out the magnum bottle of bloodwine which he kept inside. It was empty. "Damn," he whispered. Searching the top drawer, he located the key to the wine cellar. Pushing himself back, in one fluid move, he leapt from his chair and sailed over the desk. He hit the floor running and almost barreled into his office door. Grabbing the knob, he flung it open and then ran along the hallway until he reached his cellar. By now his hands shook so much he could hardly get his key into the lock. When he did, he threw the door open and then slammed it shut, barely remembering to lock it behind him.

Kurt grabbed the nearest bottle of bloodwine and popped the cork. Lifting it, he guzzled its contents. Then he opened another magnum and did the same. And another.

Finally sated, he set the third bottle down on the little wooden table in the room's center and fell into the matching chair. Then, bending forward, he rested his elbows on the tabletop and put his head in his hands. *Three bottles in one sitting.* His need was getting stronger. *I don't care what I said last night. This is intolerable. I don't know if I can hold on much longer.* But he knew he had no choice. Not if he wanted to keep his city.

He sat that way, face hidden in his hands, for a long time. Then, feeling every second of his six hundred and four years, Kurt rose from his chair, left his secret wine cellar and returned to his office.

CHAPTER 4

Fifteen hours after Parker left Kurt's Last Chance nightclub, Garrett Larkin, mage of Seattle's Balthus Coven, stood before the wooden door of a medieval cottage perched on a rocky outcropping. Though morning, it was still dark in the mountains in the Languedoc-Roussillon region in southern France and the kerosene-lit iron sconces on either side of the door shed little light.

She stared at the aged wood with trepidation. Behind that door lay one of two things—salvation or damnation. The only question was which.

A shiver ran down her back.

Garrett banged the heavy iron knocker twice. *Will he even see me? The last time I saw him, I—*

The old door creaked open. She looked up, her eyes wide with fear and uncertainty. A cocoa-skinned man with white hair, not much taller than her five foot three inches, stood in the doorway. His jaw dropped. "Ma Déesse...Garrett! What are you doing here?"

Her jaw worked, but no words came. "Feodor," she cried after she'd regained her voice. Then she burst into tears.

Feodor, her mage mentor when she was his young and headstrong apprentice, stepped forward and enveloped her in a warm, comforting hug. "Oh, ma cherie, I understand." He held her while she sobbed on his shoulder. When her tears subsided, he released her and stepped back. "Come inside, cherie. Seattle is a long ways from here and I know you must be hungry. We'll talk after we get you something to eat."

Gazing into Feodor's kind brown eyes, Garrett felt a ray of hope. "Th-thank you, Feo," her voice hitched. "I was afraid—"

"Non. Eat first, talk later." Feodor picked up her suitcase and then stepped aside to allow her to enter. He set her bag on the foyer's stone floor, then turned and beckoned. "Come."

Garrett smiled for the first time since leaving Seattle and followed Feodor into the cottage's ancient kitchen. She looked around. It was just as she'd remembered it—its massive fireplace, the stones blackened after centuries of use, and the iron cooking pots hanging on hooks nearby. From experience, she knew he only used the fireplace for magickal brews that required heating with either coal or wood. Otherwise, the kitchen had most of the modern conveniences and electricity was supplied by a generator outside that ran on witch-power.

Feodor indicated a chair at a scarred, rectangular table made of thick wooden planks. She sat and watched as he put the kettle on for tea. Then he went to the refrigerator, took out a number of items and set them on the counter. Reaching to his right, he selected a medium-sized knife from a nearby rack and got busy.

Her smile widened. Slim and spry, Feodor hadn't changed a bit from the first time she'd met him over thirty years ago. Now she understood why speculation over his true age was such a hot topic. Magick workers aged slowly, but they rarely lived beyond one hundred and twenty years. Feodor had left his youth far behind when Garrett had first arrived those many years ago and from what she'd heard, by now he had to be at least a hundred and sixty years old. But whatever his age, Feodor was believed by many of their kind to be the most talented mage alive—"an entire coven unto himself," she'd heard another witch say. Garrett considered herself lucky that he'd accepted her as his apprentice, especially since she'd been only twelve years old when her first coven in Ireland had sent her to him.

Then it dawned on her. "Feo, how did you know I came here from Seattle?"

Feodor stopped slicing the apple he'd taken from the bag lying on the counter beside him and turned. "I've been following your career, just like I do all my former students. You're quite an accomplished actor. I'm proud of you." He grinned.

She smiled back. "Thanks. I worked hard for it."

Something in the quality of Feodor's grin changed. "Yes, you did, cherie." He returned to his slicing. Garrett frowned a little, wondering what he'd meant. But she said nothing.

After finishing his preparations, Feodor set a platter laden with assorted cheeses and fruits on the old table and then picked up the whistling teakettle from the stove. He poured the boiling water into two mugs he'd retrieved from the cupboard earlier, dropped a tea bag into each cup and returned to sit across from her.

At that moment, Garrett realized she was ravenous. She said a quick prayer to Goddess and then fell upon the food, devouring it in silence. After she'd had her fill, she looked up to see Feodor giving her an amused look. Embarrassed at making a pig of herself, she looked at the ceiling, her lips twisted into a crooked smile.

The two mages sat in silence for a few moments. Then she took a deep breath. "Feo, I'm sorry for—"

Feodor reached over and grasped her hand. "No need to be sorry, cherie. You did what you did because it was what your heart told you to do. I should have respected that." His look turned grave. "But that is also why you are here, non? You tried to make the tryst, but it didn't work out so well. And you've been experiencing its after effects. What happened?"

Garrett looked into her lap. "I…I killed Mr. Squiggles last night," she said, her voice low and heavy. "My cat." Her lower lip trembled and then the tears came streaming down her cheeks again. "Mother, I tore him apart with my bare hands and then"—her voice hitched—"I ate him." She squeezed her eyes shut. The memory of the metallic taste and slick feel of her beloved cat's blood in her mouth made her want to throw up. Swallowing her nausea, she forced herself to continue. "When I realized what I'd done I fell to my knees and prayed for forgiveness but Goddess didn't answer." Garrett paused. "Huh. Not surprising, I guess. Not after that." She opened her eyes and looked up. "I'm scared, Feo. I came here because I know that if there's anybody in the world who can help me, it's you."

Feodor didn't speak for a while. "Is this the first time it's happened?"

"I think so. I mean, this was the first time I'd woken up with blood all over me."

Feodor nodded once. "We'll just say that it is. What of the other two—your vampire regent and grand *were*?"

"I don't know. If they've been showing aftereffects, they haven't said anything to me about it."

"And even if they are, they may not know enough to ask." Feodor pursed his lips and gazed into his teacup. Then he looked up. "Garrett, making a tryst is a kind of dying. Each trystant's persona is merged to create a single, tripartite entity. It means their individual minds—the knowledge of who they are and what they are—is erased. Once the trystants are of one mind they are as dead to their former selves as they are to those who knew them. That's why trystants have to agree to work the magick of their own free will. In doing so, they are agreeing to die."

He paused. "That's a lot to ask of anyone, whatever the reason. And that is why there have been only two instances of a mage, a vampire regent, and a grand *were* making a tryst in the last thousand years." Feodor fixed her with a level stare. "Your regent and *were*. Did they understand what you were asking them to do?"

Garrett threw up her hands. "I don't know. I mean, there wasn't time to tell them much of anything. The riots in Seattle last June..." She let out a heavy sigh. "Feo, we did it to save our kind from being massacred."

"Yes, I heard about your riots in America. And according to the news, the violence was not confined to Seattle." Feodor shook his head. "Terrible." He leaned forward. "But let me rephrase my question. What did you tell your regent and *were* about the tryst so they'd agree to work its magick?"

She hesitated. "I told them our powers would be pooled and we could draw from each other whenever we wanted."

"So you told them a half-truth and maybe not even that much. That's no different than a lie, cherie."

Garrett started in her chair. "But we had to..." Then she sat back and closed her eyes. "Yes. I see." Her voice shook.

Neither mage spoke for a long while. Then Feodor took her hand. "I understand why you wanted the tryst so badly. As a child, to see your family butchered...I would have wanted the same thing, to create a safe haven for our kind. And the tryst is the perfect vehicle for it. But your dream turned into an obsession. I could see that twenty years ago and that's what I was trying to warn you against, Garrett. As a means to save your city or to make a haven for zots, your willingness to sacrifice yourself to the tryst is commendable. But lying to convince others to sacrifice themselves is murder. You, obsessed with your noble heart's desire, couldn't see that. For your sake, thank Goddess your magick didn't work."

Garrett said nothing. Head bowed in shame, her tears dripped onto her woolen skirt.

Feodor released her hand. "Look at me, Garrett."

She slowly lifted her head. Even with her blurred vision, she could see the old mage's look was stern. "Goddess is merciful. But you have much to atone for, Sister."

Garrett squeezed her eyes shut and then knuckled them to clear her vision. "I know, Feo," she said, lowering her hands to her lap. "That's why I need your help. I have to undo what I've done." Staring into Feodor's brown eyes, she felt her lower lip tremble. "Will…will you help me?"

Feodor's expression didn't change. "As far as I know, there is no counterspell for a tryst."

Her heart beat faster. "What?" she whispered.

"Didn't you realize? The tryst is a one-way street. Once the trystants have merged it isn't so easy to separate them. It's like trying to separate the crêpe batter you've just made back into milk, egg, and flour. Your tryst magick hardly worked at all, but it's obviously worked enough for you to absorb *were* traits."

Garrett sagged in her chair. It had never occurred to her there wouldn't be a counterspell. Twenty years ago, she'd been too impatient in her fiery zeal to save whatever corner of the world she could than to do more than the most cursory magickal research into the tryst spell after she'd discovered it in an ancient book in Feodor's library. After that, she'd been so focused on her frustrating search for two zots like Kurt and Parker to tryst with her that she'd never thought to go back to the books to learn more.

Oh, Mother…I'm damned. She blinked a few times. She wanted to cry again but couldn't. She had no more tears.

"Now, now, cherie," Feodor said in a soothing tone. "All isn't lost. That your spell worked so poorly might be the key. It means the magick must have a few 'holes' in it, so to speak. If we can find those holes, we may be able to figure out how to use them to dissolve the rest of the spell."

Garrett heard Feodor's chair scrape against the stone floor and looked up to see him standing over her. "Come. You look worn out. Why don't you go to bed? The sun will be up soon, but I bet you'll sleep until lunch." He gave her a broad smile, his white teeth gleaming in the kitchen's overhead light. "You can even have your old room if you want."

She was too upset to smile back. "Okay." She rose and followed him out of the kitchen and back into the foyer. He grabbed her suitcase and started up the cottage's stone stairway, with her on his heels. At the top of the stairs, he turned right and walked along the hallway until he reached a wooden door recessed into the wall. Holding her suitcase in one hand, Feodor grasped the knob with the other and pushed the door open. "Here we are." He flipped a switch and stepped through.

Garrett walked inside and stopped. Swiveling her head, she took in her old room, with its heavy furniture and ornately carved canopy bed. It looked the same as it had when she'd left twenty years ago.

"I won't wake you for breakfast. Just sleep until you feel like getting up," Feodor said from behind her.

Garrett turned and gave him a tight hug. "Merci, Feo," she whispered. "For everything."

Feodor kissed her forehead. Letting go, he headed for the door. After reaching it, he turned and gazed at her, his face somber. "I must tell you, Garrett. We will certainly try to dissolve the tryst, but I don't know how successful we'll be. Maybe we'll find something that'll work. Maybe we won't." He paused. "But whatever we find, you need to be prepared to live with it, cherie. Vous comprenez?"

Without waiting for her reply, he stepped over the threshold and was gone.

CHAPTER 5

Two days after Garrett showed up at Feodor's cottage, Melera, Shen'zae of Xia'saan and fugitive from the Akkad Protectorate, returned to Dirt.

Her sleek, space corvette hovered before a barren rock mountain surrounded by an endless blue sea almost six thousand miles southwest of Seattle. The czado—shadow—warrior, sitting in the bridge's command chair, reached for the secondary instrument console above her and threw the disruptor's switch. She watched, unblinking, as a huge section of the mountain's exterior dissolved. The disruptor was a device that scrambled the molecular structure of anything at which it was aimed, causing it to disappear. A force field held the surrounding rock in place and once she was safely inside, that part of the mountain would rematerialize.

She slowly steered her spaceship through the opening. The mountain closed behind her. Hovering a few feet above the enormous artificial cavern's smooth floor, she turned her craft around until it was parallel to her campsite about two hundred feet away. Then, with her long, slender fingers, she drummed a quick tattoo on a dark square panel on the primary instrument console. The whine from the corvette's support pylons lowering into position echoed in her ears. After making sure the supports had locked into place, she gently set her ship on the ground and then shut down its four drives.

"Kyle," she said, her quintuple voices sounding peeved. "Those pylon motors—what's going on with that? I thought I fixed them."

"Yes, Shen'zae." The five voices belonging to her corvette's artificial intelligence module filled the small bridge. "You did. But the tertiary relay has shorted out again."

She frowned. "Was it me or the flow tubes Qarli's shipyard sold me?"

"The flow tubes, Shen'zae."

Her lips twisted into a grimace. "Jakkers."

Melera rose from the command chair and stretched, thinking about the Akkadian javelin jockey with whom she'd battled in a fierce dogfight and who had turned her ship into a pile of space junk. "You're a jakker too," she muttered.

Turning, she walked a few paces and then stepped onto the lift that would take her to the main deck. With a jerk, it began to descend. She narrowed her eyes. Something was wrong. The lift shouldn't have jerked like that. Her lip curled. *Had to be the luckiest shot in the whole jakkin' universe.*

"Kyle, find out what's wrong with the lift and see if you can fix it."

"Yes, Shen'zae."

On the main deck, a few steps aft brought her to the ship's airlock. She placed her hand on the controls and paused. "One more thing, Kyle. You can stop calling me Shen'zae. Xia'saan…home…" A look of anguish passed over her face. She swallowed the lump in her throat and tried again. "Xia'saan is just an asteroid belt orbiting binary stars, now," she said, her quintuple voices sounding husky. "I'm the Shen'zae of nothing."

"Yes, Shen'zae."

Melera knitted her brows but relaxed once she understood the why of Kyle's insubordination. She smiled. Artificial intelligences were literal and for a solitary starfarer like her, it was easy to forget that an AI like Kyle was nothing more than an incredibly sophisticated computer program. Her brows knitted again. *Though sometimes I wonder about Kyle.* Shaking her head, she opened the airlock's two hatches and exited the ship into the mammoth cavern.

Melera halted and swiveled her head. *Feels weird to be back.* When she left, she'd no intention of returning. Yet, here she was.

She started across the cave's smooth floor, her boot heels echoing. *Nothing's changed. But then, why would it?* She looked around. The four heavy-duty generators hummed in the background. Glowing power cables festooned the cavern's uneven walls and smooth floor. Straight ahead was the seven-by-four-feet replicator which could produce just about anything she needed. To her far right was the commcen, which she used to communicate with the Vst—the rebel faction battling the Akkad—with its tall, column-like quantum transmitter and receiver.

The arc lamps suspended from the huge grid attached to the cave's ceiling burned with fierce intensity. Between those and the power cables, the interior was lit almost as brightly as the day outside.

Reaching her sleeping couch, she stood over it and surveyed its pockmarked surface. *Still looks like the back end of some misbegotten moon.* She looked up. *The ceiling looks just like my bed.* Out of long habit, she slept with her plasma pistol under her pillow. In the throes of one of her frequent nightmares, while shooting at an enemy she often shot at the ceiling. Loosened by the plasma's extreme heat, the superheated rocks would fall, sometimes barely missing her.

Sitting on her bed, she leaned forward and rested her elbows on her thighs. *And after the nightmares come the seizures.* She stared at the polished stone floor and thought about the seizure that had brought her and Parker together. She smiled a little. *When I was with Pawkher, I didn't have nightmares. Along with everything else, I guess I forgot to have them.* Then she sighed. She fell backward onto her couch, tucked her hands beneath her head and closed her eyes.

We should not have come to back to Dirt, her czado's cold, four-toned voice echoed in her mind. Her czado was the conscious remnant of a twin she'd absorbed while in their mother's womb.

Melera shrugged. "Where else were we to go? All of our usual planetside hideouts were compromised. You saw that."

We could have found another uninhabited planet. Even if it could not support our bioform, we could have always stayed aboard ship.

"This is much more comfortable, don't you think?"

No. With Kyle's holosensory projections, you could have chosen any enviro you pleased.

Melera shrugged again. "Maybe I like Dirt." Then she frowned a little. "You know, I really should start calling this planet by its real name. Earts."

That is not this planet's name.

"Oh, come on. I can't help it if I lisp when I speak hu-man."

Then you should not try to speak it.

Annoyed now, Melera opened her eyes. "What the jakk is the matter with you? We would've had to come back to this star system anyway. The Xia'saan battle fleet is around here somewhere, and besides, I haven't—"

Now that we are back, you will go to your Dirtwolf. That would be a bigger mistake than the one you have already made.

She bolted upright. "Who said anything about going to See-at-tell?"

I am your twin. I know you.

Melera took a deep breath. "Then listen, twin. I'm here to do a job. No different than an assassination run for Tarq or the Vst. When I finish breaking our father's code, I'll make the transmission and the fleet's AIs will show me where it is. Then I'll herd it to Maqu and deliver it to the Vst. I'll have kept my ka promise to Tarq and I will be done with the Vst and this jakkin' war."

And if your solution to the code is incorrect?

She narrowed her eyes. "Don't even think it."

Neither one said anything for a long while. *If it makes you feel better, once the fleet has been delivered, then you can return to your Dirtwolf.*

A pained look crossed her face. "I doubt he'd want to see me again. Not after the things I said…" She made a small grimace. "If we were home, I'd be genchai."

Yes, but the Dirtwolf does not understand our tongue.

She chuckled. "He doesn't have to. I think it was pretty obvious, don't you?"

Her czado didn't answer.

Melera rose from her couch and stretched. "And whether he understood or not doesn't matter now, does it?" She shook some of the kinks out of her muscles and then blew a breath. "I'd better get the siitheer set up. I've got a code to break and the sooner I get it done, the happier I'll be."

Walking over to the commcen, she retrieved a rectangular object from a holster tacked on to the side of the translator. Staring at it, she pursed her lips. "Let's see…I'll need three of them for this." She tapped out a short series of commands on the remote's fingerboard. Then, aiming it to the right of the nearest generator, she pressed a small, round indentation on the side of the unit. Three of five hauler drones, their green fire-hydrant bodies scratched and dented from heavy use, trundled forward on flexible treads and stopped a few feet in front of her.

She tapped out another series of commands. After transmitting her instructions, the mechanical mules spun around and rolled towards the ship's lowered boarding ramp.

While the drones were busy, Melera stepped over to the quantum transmitter and receiver. She picked up a set of glowing cables, knelt on the floor and reconnected them to the machine. Lifting her head, she watched the receiver's opaque gray column bloom into a mass of swirling colors spanning the rainbow. The maelstrom soon settled into bands of different colors of varying widths, most of the bands corresponding to a frequency used by the Vst to communicate with her.

She stared at the column. *If it was up to me, I'd let the Vst lose this jakkin' war. No difference between them and the Akkad, anyway. Both are despicable.* But she'd given her ka promise to her father that if something happened to him, she would carry out his pledge to deliver the Xia'saan battle fleet to the Vst. Tarq was dead. And if she didn't help the Vst, her ka would drive her insane.

"Jakk them," she muttered, speaking of the Vst and the Akkad. She stood and looked toward her ship. One of the hauler drones was pushing her siitheer across the floor on the instrument's retractable wheels. The second carried the flat-screen, three-sided monitor that sat on top of it and the third carried the ornately carved audio box. By now the drones were about fifty feet from her little camp. After reaching it, she watched them skirt her sleeping couch and proceed until they were about fifteen feet behind it. Then they quickly assembled the siitheer. Once finished with their assigned tasks, the three robots trundled back to their places by the generator.

Melera replaced the remote in its cradle, walked over to her siitheer and connected several glowing cables into the ports located on the instrument's rear. Straightening, she stepped around to its front and slid onto its built-in bench. She thumbed a small switch and was rewarded by the siitheer's quiet hum.

She looked up. The three-panel screens showed where she'd left off trying to crack Tarq's symphonic code. Without looking at the instrument's seven rows of twenty-five blue buttons, she played a series of runs to limber up her fingers. Finishing her warm-up, she closed her eyes. *Thank the Dark I'm almost done with this.*

A minute passed before she opened them again. She stared at the screens for a moment. Then, with a small sigh, she bent over the siitheer's keyboard and went to work on her father's musical puzzle.

Several hours later, Meleras rose from the bench, stretched, and then headed for a medium-sized round table made of clear resin. Along the way, she decided to make a stop at the smaller replicator first. *I need a drink.* She programmed the machine for a bottle of Stk, a potent brew banned by several galactic sectors in Maqu. When the machine had fulfilled her order, she grabbed the bottle. Opening it, she stepped over to the table and sat in one its matching contoured chairs.

Staring into space and taking an occasional swig from her bottle, she lifted one foot onto the table and let her thoughts drift until they settled on the last night she'd spent at Qarli's shipyard. She'd been putting the finishing touches on the repairs she'd made to her corvette when she realized she'd left the set of nanopliers she needed below, on the drive deck. Stepping on the lift, as soon as her head had cleared the supply deck, she saw she wasn't alone. In the low light, a figure with seven lopsided appendages and no discernable head had opened the door to the cabinet where Kyle's brain was housed and seemed to be fiddling with the AI.

Melera had leapt from the lift without thinking and was on the deck's far side in two bounds. But by the time she got there, the intruder was gone. She had raced around the drive deck, searching, but found nothing. Returning to Kyle's cabinet, she'd grabbed a small electronic tablet from a nearby hook and switched it on. After the heads-up display appeared, she'd run a diagnostic on the AI. Scrolling through line after line of colorful symbols, the only thing she'd discovered was that Kyle's programs were intact.

Shifting her foot on the tabletop to a more comfortable position, she took another swig from her bottle. "I know I saw the jakker," she muttered. "But how did it get off my ship? Or aboard, for that matter?"

It could not have skipped through the Void because we would have seen the flash, her czado said.

"Not to mention being flash-frozen after it ripped through the universal fabric. Br-r-r," she shivered. Then she plopped her other foot onto the tabletop. "I don't know. Maybe—" She raised her brow. She'd just remembered something. "It was holding something in its lower left pincer just before it disappeared. A black polyhedron-looking thing. No lights. You remember?"

Yes.

"There's got to be a connection." She pondered it, her thoughts circling like a rok chasing its tail. A minute or two later, a possible answer dawned on her. "Listen. This would've been about five standard years ago, but do you remember that scagg in the Fourth Sector who claimed he'd proven teleportation was possible? He said he was working on a project that could generate something like a personal wormhole on demand. And remember how the rest of those theoretical types went after him, saying he was either a fraud or insane? And in the middle of it, the scagg and all of his research just vanished."

I do.

Melera licked her full lips. "Well, what if he was right?"

She felt her czado hesitate. *That would explain why the scagg disappeared. And how our visitor did the same.*

"Mag Beloc," she said through her teeth. "The jakker's probably got him locked up in one of his prison ships." She snorted. "And I know what that's like." An unpleasant memory surfaced. Once again she was inside the box, a coffin-like contraption filled with needle-like lasers. Strapped inside, the lasers slowly burned tiny, deep holes into her flesh. It had been agony.

She shoved the memory aside. "All right, let's assume the scagg perfected his teleportal and Beloc has it. And that's how that sept got aboard. But while we were at Qarli's, you shifted me every time I had to leave the ship. If I never wore my natural form outside, how would anyone know who I was?"

The corvette's design is distinctive. There are not that many drivers in Maqu who own one.

"Yeah, but half of those who do own one are outlaws like me."

But how many limp into port looking like they had been attacked by a wing of javs? A jav's cannon has a distinctive scoring pattern. Anyone familiar with Akkadian ordinance would recognize it at once, including Qarli's personnel.

"Mmm. So if someone at Qarli's sold me out to the Akkad, then I guess we know what the sept was doing there." She tightened her lips. "Splicing a tracking code into Kyle."

A reasonable assumption.

She shook her head. "Well, it didn't get a chance to finish the job before I surprised it. I found nothing in the diagnostic. So there's nothing to worry about."

Setting the bottle down, Melera removed her feet from the table and stood. "I'm going to bed. It's all speculative, anyway. I don't know that Beloc kidnapped that scagg. I don't know that he developed his wormhole generator. All I know is that some sept somehow got aboard my ship and disappeared before I could kill it."

She walked over to her pock-marked sleeping couch. Removing her pistol from its thigh holster, she started to slip it beneath her pillow. She paused and then lifted the pistol to her face and stared at it. *Should I leave it in the holster?* She thought for a moment. "Nah." Shoving the pistol under her pillow, she stripped and flopped down on her bed face first.

Lifting her head, Melera reached to her right and grabbed the controls for the cavern's interior lighting from its cradle attached to the couch's frame. She dimmed the lights until the only illumination came from the glowing power cables. Dropping the remote back into its cradle, she rolled over onto her back, stretched out her six-foot, two-inch frame and closed her eyes. "The Dark be merciful. Please, no nightmares," she whispered.

Her body relaxed and sleep stole upon her almost immediately. "Nothing happened to Kyle," she murmured. Just before she slipped into oblivion, she heard her czado's reply.

You had better hope so—for both our sakes.

CHAPTER 6

Four days after Melera had docked her ship inside her island hide-out, a vast, truncated tetrahedron settled into a stationary orbit on the far side of the moon. The prison ship's stealth shields covered every micrometer of its bulk, so as not to be visually or electronically detected by Earth's space-borne surveillance equipment. And with the main and most of the auxiliary drives shut down, their exhaust signature was nearly invisible.

Mag Beloc, Jahannan warlord of the Akkad Protectorate, stood on his hoverdisc inside the immense, cave-like disembarking station aboard his spacecraft. His executive officer stood beside him on her own hoverdisc.

"Are they ready?" he said without looking at her.

"Yes, sir."

Beloc swept his gaze over his starlegion contingent. Seven hundred legionnaires stood in orderly ranks below him. Hand-picked for this mission, he'd chosen only the most human-like bipedal species under his immediate command. Even so, most of them had to undergo surgery on their hands, feet, and faces. In many cases, the replication was far from perfect but his 'bot surgeons had done the best they could.

The legionnaires were dressed in Earth clothing. From his research, he learned that Terrans—as they styled themselves—called the current season on the northern hemisphere of the planet "winter," and that it was cold. His men, women, and in-betweens were dressed in sweaters, long pants, and heavy, hooded jackets. The hoods, he hoped, would help protect them from discovery. Their clothes were also worn, with the pants frayed at the cuffs and the shoes so stained it was impossible to tell the original color. They would be "the homeless," which Beloc understood to mean they lived outside on the streets or, at times, in dedicated shelters. He also understood that to those who were not homeless, they were usually invisible. That was exactly what he needed.

His people would go to a place called New York City. "New York," as the Terrans called it, consisted of five separate sections called boroughs. For this experiment, they would go to the borough called "Manhattan." He'd divided Manhattan into seven hundred sectors, one for each legionnaire. Implanted with a chip that could detect Melera's brainwaves in every direction for five hundred feet, they would patrol the sector assigned to them. Some of the structures in the city, he knew, were far taller than five hundred feet. But his legionnaires were equipped with standard-issue personal stealth shields and should have no problem getting into those buildings.

He would not be going with his troops—this time. He would stay with the ship and monitor his legions' progress. Besides, with his blue skin and three eyes, he needed surgical attention himself.

Beloc tightened his thin lips. *I'm not sure my plan will even work. But I know Melera is here. There's no place else for her to go.* He blinked. *Over seven billion people…a small planet. Still, looking for one person in just a fraction of that number will be dicey at best.* He'd thought about using the drones but soon realized that was out of the question. Stealth shields would hide the spacecraft from Terran eyes but they couldn't hide the drones' heat signature or the drive noise. And he didn't want to alert the Terrans to their presence. Not yet, anyway.

Damn that tracking program for corrupting. I would have had her by now. He wondered if Melera had found the program in her ship's AI and destroyed it. Or maybe her AI destroyed it on its own. It didn't matter now. He'd lost her and now he had to find her.

He looked over the contingent again. "Legion. You have your assignments. This is a test and you are the rok. Be as invisible as you can. Do not engage the Terrans under any circumstances. Go."

Beloc watched his troops head to the conveyer in orderly rows. The conveyer was a means of transporting personnel to a planet's surface without using landing craft. Transporting his legionnaires from here to Earth would be stretching the conveyer's capabilities, but he knew from past experience it could be done.

The legionnaires were gone in minutes. He turned to his executive officer. "Meet me on the bridge at twenty-eight hundred hours. We will monitor their progress from there."

"Yes, sir."

Beloc turned his hoverdisc and descended to the deck. He strode out of the disembarking station and into the ship's wide corridor. A small smile played on his lips. Then he grinned, showing jagged brown teeth.

The hunt for Melera was on.

CHAPTER 7

A week after arriving at Feodor's, Garrett woke feeling almost like her old self again. She hadn't had another incident since killing Mr. Squiggles and though she'd never forget what she'd done, the horror of it had receded in her mind until it felt mostly like a bad dream.

The early morning sunlight fell across her face like a warm caress. A minute later, she climbed out of her high bed—it even had steps—and throwing on a loose robe, walked into the adjoining bath.

Inside, she stepped up to a sizeable copper tub and twisted the single spigot until water poured forth in a steady stream. She cupped her hand under it. Drawn from a subterranean pool deep beneath the cottage, it was ice-cold. She smiled a little. Very few, if any, mundane household plumbing systems would have been capable of drawing water up from a source so far underground. But a magickal plumbing system could do it just fine.

After the tub had filled, she dipped her finger into the water up to the second joint and murmured a few words. In moments, the water began to warm. Twenty seconds later it was piping hot, just the way she liked it. She threw off her robe and stepped into the tub. Tipping her head backward until it rested on the tub's edge, she thought about what she and Feodor had accomplished in the past week.

The first day after her arrival, Feodor had presented her with a little basket of fruit, cheese, and bread for her lunch. Then he'd shooed her out of the cottage. "You need fresh air, cherie. Walk and explore like you used to and don't come back until the sun is halfway behind that ridge," he'd said, pointing towards a line of cliffs on the far side of the valley below. The second day, they'd entertained each other with the kind of easy magick tricks that had delighted her as a child, like the small, glowing butterflies that flitted about and sometimes settled in her hair before winking out of existence. As the week progressed, the magick they wrought became more and more complex until they'd reached that which required mage-level talent.

"Mmm," Feodor had said yesterday. "Not good. Your talent has degraded more than I would have liked." Then he'd planted a quick kiss on her forehead. "But hopefully we can fix that."

Rising to her feet, Garrett stepped out of the tub. She dried herself off and put on her robe again. Then, turning back to the tub, she whispered another spell and watched the water evaporate almost instantly. That was the beauty of magick. There was a spell for just about everything one might need to do, like getting rid of seventy-five gallons of water in a tub with no drain.

Returning to her bedroom, she was surprised to see Feodor sitting on one of the three tapestry-upholstered chairs, dressed in a robe similar to the one she wore. He smiled at her. "We're going to do something a little different today, cherie. It means no breakfast, I'm afraid. But we'll eat when we're finished." He stood and headed for the door.

She followed. "Where are we going?"

"You'll see. Come."

Feodor led her to the library, with its books and manuscripts neatly arranged on shelves. Halting before a bookcase on the far side of the room, he chanted something that she recognized as a type of locking spell, but it wasn't one she knew.

The bookcase swung open to reveal a stone archway. From where she stood, she could see a few steps leading down into the darkness. Her jaw dropped. "Feo, I never—"

He looked at her over his shoulder. "None of my students did. You're the first." Then he turned and stepped through the stone archway. "Lumina brilho." The stairwell immediately lit up with witch-light, almost as bright as the day outside. She trailed Feodor through the entrance and down the steps. The stairs were a little steep but using the rough rock wall for support, she soon found her rhythm.

After ten minutes, her leg muscles cramped. Five minutes after that, she was sure she'd die.

They finally reached the bottom. The stairway opened out onto a medium-sized chamber, the rock seeming to sparkle in the witch-light. Garrett understood. The Languedoc-Rousillon region was famous for its extensive network of caves and Feodor's cottage obviously sat atop one of them. She looked around. Judging by the length of time it had taken them to get here, she was pretty sure they had to be at least two hundred feet underground.

Feodor started for an unlit entrance on the chamber's far side. She sat on the steps. "Feo," she called. "Could we rest a minute? My legs are about to fall off."

He gave her a surprised look. "Oh! I'm sorry. I didn't think. I'm used to it," he said, waving a hand at the stairs. Then he cocked his head, a sly smile on his lips. "But you could have just floated down here, you know."

Now it was her turn to look surprised. "What?" A moment later, she laughed. "Of course. A float spell. Why didn't I think of that?"

"You've fallen back into your role as my student. As the master does, so does his apprentice." Feodor walked over and sat next to her.

She laid her head on his shoulder. "Speaking of apprentices, did I ever thank you for giving me a home here after the Kilkenny City coven kicked me out?" She lifted her head and looked at him.

He frowned. "What do you mean?"

"Oh, come on. I stole all that stuff from the Temple and then had the nerve to try and sell it back to the coven? No wonder they sent me packing after just a few weeks." She grinned. "And you, Feo. You should've just turned me over your knee and given me a good spanking."

He returned her grin. "I didn't because I knew it wouldn't have worked." Then his brows knitted. "But cherie, the coven didn't kick you out. Didn't they tell you why they sent you here?"

"No."

He frowned a little. "Garrett, the coven asked me to take you because they realized you were something almost unheard of among magick workers—a child with mage-level talent. And the coven didn't have a mage. The witches could have taught you a great deal but they couldn't teach you the most important thing you needed to learn—how to control your talent. Without proper training, you would have been a danger not just to them but to yourself."

She goggled at him for a few moments, then laughed. "Well, I'll be. And here I thought it was because I nearly destroyed the Temple's kitchen trying out a cooking spell after I was told not to."

Feodor laughed with her. "Not at all." Then he sobered. "But I wonder why they didn't tell you?"

He chuckled. "Oh, I think I know why. They didn't want to give a certain mage-level street punk any ideas."

Feodor laughed again and then stood. "Are you rested, cherie? It's not much farther, I promise." He held out his hand. Garrett's legs still hurt but she took his hand and let him help her up. "This way." Letting go of her hand, he walked toward a darkened archway and halted at the entrance. "Lumina ofuscante." The interior immediately lit with a soft glow.

He stepped inside. She limped in after him. A quick glance around told her this chamber was even larger than the one they'd just left. But she didn't see any more archways. Apparently, this cave had only two rooms.

She hadn't gone twenty feet further when she stopped in her tracks. She stared, saucer-eyed. Before her lay an irregularly shaped pit, about eight feet across, with delicate tendrils resembling blue smoke spiraling up and down into its depths. "Is…is that what I think it is?" she said, awestruck.

Feodor grinned. "It is."

Her pain forgotten, she stepped closer and peered at the blue tendrils snaking around each other. "A vortex," she said, her voice full of wonder. She looked up. "What are we going to do?"

"I need to find out exactly what happened after the three of you cast the tryst spell. The spell I will cast now uses the vortex's energy to take your memories of that night and project them. To me, it'll be like watching a movie through your eyes but I'll also be able to see the magickal forces the three of you brought forth." He paused. "Now. Give me your robe and step inside the vortex."

Garrett glanced at the pit's inky depths and looked back at her mentor. "Uh, Feo? The pit…um, it looks…bottomless."

Feodor smiled. "No, cherie. It has a bottom. I just don't know where it is."

She opened her mouth but Feodor spoke first. "Don't worry, Garrett. The vortex is strong enough to keep you from falling in."

With trepidation, she removed her robe and handed it to Feodor, who draped it over a nearby rock. She stepped over the edge of the pit and into the vortex. The soreness in her legs disappeared. She laughed. "It feels like I'm standing on a springy mattress."

"Are you ready?"

"Yes." She watched Feodor lift his face to the ceiling and spread his arms wide. Then he started chanting in a singsong language like nothing she'd ever heard. The words sounded something like "deen a carason gir la maen." Feodor upped the pace of his chanting, singing faster and faster until she could barely distinguish the words. She felt the vortex's energy swirling around and through her, holding her upright. Her limbs grew heavy. Moments later, her vision began to dim. Then she fainted.

When she came to, she had been dressed in her robe again and was lying on the roomy sofa in Feodor's library. It seemed to her that she'd been unconscious for only a minute but right now it was dark outside. *That spell must've done a number on me. We went down to the cave this morning.*

Pushing herself into a sitting position, she swung her legs over the sofa's edge. The sound of the door to the library opening off to her right made her look up. Feodor entered, bearing a tray with a large bowl of lightly steamed vegetables and a small carafe of juice. Her mouth watered.

"Bon." He set the tray on the low table in front of her and stepped back. "You're awake. How do you feel?"

"Starving." She picked up a small plate and a fork and began spearing the assorted vegetables. After filling her plate, she poured herself a glass of juice, then sat back and started to eat. She looked up to see that Feodor had retreated to a wing chair across from her. "What did you find out?" she said around her mouthful of food.

Feodor didn't answer immediately. "I found out that you are either a very brave woman or a very foolish one." He gave his head a little shake. "Attempting the tryst spell completely unprepared. Not even a mandala…it's a wonder any of you survived." He paused. "If I'd been in your position, I don't think I would've done it."

She looked down at her plate. "Brave, foolish, or both—it doesn't balance out the lies I told the others, does it?"

"No."

She sighed and started to put her plate back on the tray. Suddenly she wasn't hungry anymore.

"Eat, cherie. The spell has sapped much of your strength. You have to build it back up."

Obeying, Garrett pulled her plate towards her and resumed eating but somehow the vegetables didn't taste as good as they had earlier.

Feodor nodded. "Now. I examined your magickal auras closely after the three of you had awakened from the tryst spell. Each of you has been affected but it's very uneven. Your grand *were*—he is a wolf, non?—has captured some of the talent you lost. His magickal aura is bright green, shot through with veins of bright blue, which is your aura. His aura also contains large splotches of red. That belongs to your vampire regent. So if the wolf has experienced anything, it's probably the spell's trifocal vision stage and maybe the tri-tactile stage, too. Since his aura has so much red, I'd say he's probably acquired vampire powers, perhaps the power to dissolve into mist. Your aura shows plenty of green and we already know you've been affected by *were* traits. It also contains some red but so far you haven't shown any vampiric tendencies."

He frowned a little and tapped his upper lip with an index finger. "But it's your regent that concerns me most. He has a great deal of your blue—almost certainly enough to manifest magickal talent. He also has your grand *were's* green but probably not enough to show those qualities. What's alarming though, is that his aura shows several black streaks as if it had been torn." He paused. "I'd guess he's lost most or maybe all of the powers that mark him as a vampire regent." Then his expression turned grave. "But there's more. I take it your regent is Seattle's Master?"

"Yes."

He blew a heavy breath. "The spell has left him crippled. If another regent learns of it, he or she will kill him to become the new Master. If that happens, I have no idea how you and your grand *were* will be affected."

Garrett's throat tightened. She squeezed her eyes shut and fell against the sofa's back support. "Kurt...oh Mother, what have I done?" she cried.

Silence reigned for a minute or two. "You are in love with your regent, non?" Feodor said, his voice quiet.

She nodded, feeling miserable. "I know the Millennium Agreement forbids—"

"No, cherie. Unlike the head, the heart knows no rules."

She opened her eyes. "Feo, do you think it's possible Kurt and Parker—he's the wolf—haven't experienced any aftereffects?"

"Anything's possible. But if you've experienced aftereffects, then they most likely have, too."

She swallowed, hard. "So what do we do now?"

Feodor smiled a little. "Now we go to the books and try to figure out a way to separate your auras. We can start as soon as you're ready."

Determination straightened her spine. "I'm ready."

"Then come with me." He led her to a long table situated in front of the library's huge fireplace. Garrett sat in the chair at the table's foot. Reaching up, Feodor pulled two thick, leather-bound tomes from the top shelf of the nearest bookcase and handed one to her. Then he handed her a ruled notepad and a pen. "We'll take the obvious route first. Flag every spell that has anything to do with auras. We can sort them out later." He sat in a chair nearby and opened his book, his notepad, and uncapped his pen.

She eyed her pad and pen. "Wouldn't using a computer be faster?"

"Probably. But I don't have a computer, much less two."

Garrett nodded. She'd forgotten Feo's skepticism of most modern technology. Opening her tome, she began reading the first spell.

It was going to be a long night.

CHAPTER 8

While Garrett and Feodor toiled in the cottage's sun-drenched library, Parker trudged along a shadowy, deserted street in downtown Seattle, his mind in a fatigue-induced fog. He'd spent the entire day and much of the night debugging his client's database software and it had been a nightmare. At one point, he'd felt like giving up in despair. But he'd kept going and now the program was working fine. Even better, his client had promised him a hefty bonus for his hard work. Best of all, he'd snagged two new clients over his lunch hour, each of whom insisted on keeping him on retainer. He'd even had time to deposit their checks before the bank closed. Between his bonus and his new clients, his bank account was fattening up just in time for Christmas. But right now, all he wanted to do was go home and sleep.

I gotta have something to eat first, his wolf growled. *I'm starving.*

Me too. We had those three foot-long subs couple of hours ago. He paused. *Well, we still have three of those big cowboy steaks in the fridge. How about it? Maybe with some vegetables?*

Vegetables, yuck. Let's just have the steaks.

He let out a quiet chuckle. Heels thumping on the pavement, his mind turned to the tryst. *I wonder if Kurt's been able to find Garrett yet. It's been a week since she disappeared.*

The wind strengthened and he turned up the collar of his black wool coat. The weather had turned arctic while he'd been inside working but he wasn't cold. He was hot—hot enough to feel the puddles of sweat under his arms leaking through his suit. For *weres* like him, the energy that enables transformation meant his body temperature, like his metabolism, was way off the charts. Tonight, he could've gotten by with a medium-weight jacket. Still, he had to keep up appearances.

"Hey, buddy—can you spare a few bucks for some food?" a scratchy voice sounded from his right. Deep into his reverie, Parker twitched, startled, then turned to look. A homeless man—a human—sat under a blanket in an alley next to an office building. By the light of the streetlamp, Parker could see the man's unshaven face, hollow cheeks, and bloodshot eyes. *He'll probably just spend it on booze. But maybe not.* "Sure." He dug his pocket for his wallet.

He was in the act of taking out his wallet when a red haze clouded his vision. Vertigo descended upon him. He staggered backward. *What the hell?*

"Hey, are you all right?" he heard the homeless man say. His voice sounded faint.

Then, as suddenly as it had appeared, the red haze and the dizziness were gone. In its place was a maddening thirst that insisted on being satisfied *now*. He stared at the homeless man. His wolf's laughter—a rumbling snarl—echoed in his brain. They were hungry for blood and here was their food.

Parker smiled. "I'm okay. Just a little too tired, that's all." He paused. "When's the last time you ate?"

"I dunno. Couple, three days ago."

His smile broadened. "Tell you what. I could use a sandwich. Let's go to that all night place around the corner and I'll buy you one, too. Then I'll give you some money. Sound good to you?"

The homeless man struggled to his feet and grabbed his blanket. "Sounds good to me. Let's get going."

"What's your name?" Parker said after the homeless man had stood up.

"Ralph."

Parker stuck out his gloved hand. "Pleased to meet you, Ralph. My name's Parker."

Ralph took his hand, pumped it once and turned toward the street. He'd taken a step when Parker, calling on his *were*-strength, punched him from behind. He heard Ralph's spine crack. The other man cried out and crumpled to the pavement. Parker hauled him to his feet and clapped his hand over Ralph's mouth, reducing his cries to mewling sounds. Then he dragged him deeper into the alley, to a spot where human eyes couldn't see.

He held Ralph against the wall with one hand still clamped over his mouth and the other pressed against his chest. Ralph's eyes bulged in terror. "Make another sound and I'll rip your lungs out," Parker growled. Ralph quieted. He tore open the homeless man's coat, tearing his worn sweater and t-shirt in the process. Seeing all that exposed flesh sent him into a frenzy. Before his wolf's teeth had fully emerged from his gums, he lunged and sank his fangs into Ralph's throat. Blood spurted. He clamped his jaws over the red fountain and drank. Within seconds, he'd drained Ralph to a husk. He looked up, his mouth stained with the homeless man's blood and laughed.

The blood-madness disappeared in mid-chuckle. Parker stared in horror at Ralph's body and dropped it to the ground as if it had burned him. *Oh, God—what did I just do? Have I gone crazy?*

Crazy or not, we'd better get out of here, his wolf growled.

But we can't just leave him. I mean, look at him. Somebody'll find him and they'll know a zot did it. It might spark a pogrom.

We can always throw him into the Sound. The weresharks will finish him off.

No. Too far. I don't want to drive around with a dead guy in my trunk any longer than I have to. We'll take him Underground.

So you'd rather take the chance of somebody seeing you hauling a dead guy out of your trunk in the middle of Pioneer Square?

Oh, come on—we'll be in an alley.

Uhrrm. But there's lots of homeless people about. And they hang out in alleys. Like Ralph, here.

Yeah, but it's…good point. Okay. We throw him in the Sound.

We should walk around the block so we won't have to walk past the diner.

That was the plan.

Wiping his mouth on the sleeve of his coat, Parker then lifted Ralph's lifeless body and threw it over his shoulder. He started walking, fast. In seconds, he'd left the alley and was hurrying along the street. Rounding the building's corner, he saw a trio of humans stumbling towards them, their raucous laughter assaulting his ears. "Shit," he muttered. "Let's hope they're not curious drunks."

In moments, they were abreast of each other. "Hey—wha' happened to him?" one man slurred, pointing to Parker's burden.

He didn't stop walking. "Too much partying. I'm taking him home. Boy, is his wife gonna be pissed."

The two men and one woman laughed. "Maybe you'd better hang around so she doesn't kill him," one of the men said. "Or worse," said the other. The three laughed harder than ever.

Parker forced a chuckle. "Maybe I should. Well, have a good night," he said over his shoulder.

He walked two more blocks and turned another corner. By now he was closing in on his car. He quickened his pace, almost running. After reaching it, he swiveled his head left and right. There was no one around. Fishing in his pocket for the car keys, he pulled them out and pressed a button on the key fob. The trunk popped open. He shoved the body inside. Then he walked around to the driver's side and got in.

He started the engine and blew out a heavy breath. "Okay, okay… just keep calm. The last thing I need is to be stopped by the police for doing something stupid." He pressed the accelerator but then stepped hard on the brake. The car rocked on its tires. "Like not having my seat belt on," he muttered as he buckled himself in. Secure in the driver's seat now, he slowly pulled away from the curb and after circling the block, proceeded north along Geiser Avenue. Keeping his gaze straight ahead, he drove through the streets while his peripheral vision kept track of what was going on around him. Maybe it was his imagination but the police seemed to be everywhere tonight. And they seemed to be watching him.

Parker soon left downtown behind. Still driving north, he headed toward the fishing wharves. When he'd reached them, he switched the car's lights off. He didn't want some night watchman to wonder what a car was doing here this late at night. He wasn't worried about someone hearing the engine. Unlike his old Caprice, which had been burned during the rioting last June, his new Crown Vic ran quieter than a whisper. He coasted along, looking for a place that wasn't well lit. Just when he was about to despair, he found one. Though fenced, it looked abandoned. Not a light shone anywhere.

Perfect.

Parker drove up to the gate and got out of the car. The fence was about six feet tall. Getting over it wouldn't be a problem. Inspecting the gate, he saw a rusty-looking lock holding the two halves in place. He could have broken the lock with little trouble but decided not to do so. Just because the old complex was abandoned didn't mean someone didn't come up here from time to time to make sure everything was all right.

He walked back to the car and popped the trunk. Pushing the lid up, he hauled Ralph's body out, tucked it under his arm, ran to the gates and threw him over. Then he climbed into the compound. He picked up the dead man and jogged to the edge of the wharf. Reaching it, he lifted Ralph high overhead and calling on his wolf-strength, threw him over the edge. The body crashed into the Sound about thirty feet out, and soon sank beneath the waves.

Parker ran back to the gate and climbed over it. Hopping into his car, he started the engine and drove away, again with his headlights off. He didn't switch them on until he had gone quite a ways south. Driving as carefully as he had earlier, so as not to draw attention, he made his way home.

Arriving at his house, Parker pulled the car around back rather than in the driveway. He didn't want any of his neighbors who might be still up at this hour to see him. Unlocking the gate to his eight-foot privacy fence, he stepped through and locked the gate behind him, thankful he'd left the patio light off. He sprinted across the grass to the back door and let himself in. With the patio light out, the kitchen was almost too dark for him to see, even with his wolf-sight, but he dared not turn on the overhead.

Feeling his way to the basement door, he opened it and switched on the light. From here, the light's glow couldn't be seen outside. Closing the door behind him, he clattered down the steps and headed straight for an old, dusty, full-length mirror. He dragged it out of its corner and positioned it under the bare bulb. As far as he could tell there was no blood on his collar or tie. His coat had protected him from Ralph's life-force pumping from his neck.

Parker shrugged out of his coat, stripped off his clothes, and stuffed them into a large, dark green plastic bag, including his belt and shoes. After what had happened tonight, he knew he could never wear them again without remembering. He'd set the bag out for the city trash pick up tomorrow.

He ran up the stairs and let himself into the kitchen. Hurrying across the tiles, Parker entered his great room. He tried not to think about what had happened tonight but it was no use. He kept seeing his hand clamped over Ralph's mouth and the look of terror on the other man's face. He shuddered.

In the bath, he took a quick shower. Then he ran into his darkened bedroom. Parker crawled into bed and hid his head under the sheets.

He didn't sleep a wink.

CHAPTER 5

Early the next morning before going to work, Parker walked along the hallway beneath Kurt's nightclub, headed for the vampire's office. Since being pressed into Kurt's service a year ago, this was the first time he'd voluntarily come to see his Master.

The irony wasn't lost on him.

He stopped in his tracks about sixty feet from Kurt's closed office door. The hairs on the back of his neck stood up. *You smell that?*

Yeah, his wolf growled. *And it don't smell too good, either.*

He sniffed. *I'm sure it's a vampire. But I've never known any vamp to smell like that.*

And just how many vamps do you know?

Parker ignored him. Then he felt his wolf hesitate. *Don't laugh, but to me it smells…corrupt. Not like the grave, but——*

I ain't laughing. Come on.

He jogged along the hallway until he reached Kurt's office, flung the door open and stepped inside. "Hey, Kurt," he said, hoping he sounded nonchalant.

From the corner of his eye, he caught sight of someone and turned. His eyes widened a fraction. Standing by the chaise was one of the loveliest women he'd ever seen. A lavishly embroidered, deep fuchsia silk jacket with a stand-up collar and matching trousers complemented her flawless, pale gold skin. Her black hair had been swept up into a large bun, held in place by two exquisitely jeweled chopsticks. She gave him a warm, inviting smile.

Her smile made his skin crawl. It was her scent he and his wolf had picked up in the hallway. There was no question this china doll was almost as powerful as Kurt—or at least, almost as powerful as Kurt had been. Though the Master didn't appear to be threatened at the moment, the odor of his visitor's malevolence seemed to be growing by the second. *If she tries anything, I'm going to torch her. Never thought I'd say it but I need Kurt dead and walking.*

Barging into Kurt's office the way he had, he thought he should say something. "Oh. Sorry. Uh...I'll come back later."

Kurt gave him a small smile. "Not necessary." He nodded at the Asian woman. "Li An was just leaving. Weren't you, Li An?"

Li An had been staring at Parker since he'd walked in. "Yes. I was." She didn't take her eyes from him. "But Kurt—surely you wouldn't be so rude as to let me go without introducing us first?"

He dipped his head. "Ah. My apologies. My servant and I have urgent business to discuss. Li An, this is Parker Berenson, alpha of my city's werewolf pack." Then he turned to Parker. "Parker, Li An, one of vampiredom's oldest regents."

Li An shot Kurt an annoyed look and stepped forward until she stood only inches away from him. "What a pleasure to meet you, Parker," she said in a silken voice. She was so tiny, she had to fully expose her throat just to look into his face. "Kurt has told me much about you and how invaluable you are to him. I would love to get to know you...better."

He shivered a little under her black stare. "Uh, thanks. Likewise, I'm sure." Get to know her? Right now he wanted nothing more than to be twenty miles from this undead bitch.

Li An's jaw dropped a little.

"Li An!" Kurt's voice cracked through the silence. He turned to see Kurt standing next to him. Kurt took a step toward the female regent, who took a step back. She looked uncertain. "You dare to abuse my hospitality like this?" He jerked his head at Parker. "The wolf is under my protection, just like everyone else in Seattle. Your power means nothing here." He glared at her. "Get out, Li An. Do not return to my estate again or I will pound a stake through your heart. Is that understood?"

Li An tightened her beautiful lips. Without another word, she dissolved into mist and was gone.

Vampire and werewolf were silent for a minute or two, staring at the spot where Li An had stood. Then Parker turned and raised an eyebrow. "Invaluable?"

"I said no such thing." Kurt walked over to the velvet chaise where Li An had been sitting, then plopped down on its cushions.

Parker frowned a little. "So what was that all about?"

Kurt looked up. "You saving my miserable life."

"Huh?"

"Li An tried to lay a stasis on you. It didn't work."

"Why?"

Kurt eyed him. "Only regents can lay stases. No one is immune, except other regents and those under their protection. Li An couldn't take over your psyche, meaning I was protecting you. Except, I wasn't."

Parker slowly sat down in the velvet upholstered chair across from Kurt. "So she tried to immobilize me," he said. He looked up. "Now it makes sense."

"What?"

"I was talking with a bunch of people at work yesterday when I turned into a statue for about three, maybe four seconds. When it was over, they were looking at me like I'd just flown in from Venus, so"—he shrugged—"I told them I'd had a brain fart. Nothing to worry about."

Kurt stared at him, a smile playing about his lips. "A brain fart. How…original."

"All I could think of at the time. And it sent them into hysterics—exactly what I needed to take their minds off of it." He paused. "So how do you control this stasis thing, anyway?"

Kurt pursed his lips. "Usually, you might think of it as throwing a blanket over someone's head. But—"

"Like this?" He threw a mental blanket over the vampire.

Kurt frowned. "Like what?"

Parker gave him an innocent look. "Oh, nothing."

"As I was saying, in your case, I don't think that's true. Apparently, the only one you can put under stasis is yourself."

Parker shook his head. "Great. With your stasis power, I bet one day I'll find myself playing statue in front of a speeding bus."

Kurt's brows twitched. "Or worse. A policeman."

"Yeah. God knows what the humans would do to me before my execution." Neither one said anything for a moment or two. Then Parker gave him a curious look. "Kurt, what was Li An doing here? Does she know about you?"

"Don't be silly. Li An doesn't know a thing. Someone made a shrewd guess about how I was able to stop the rioting so quickly last summer. Garrett, you and I aren't the only ones in the world who know what a tryst is, what it can be used for and how many ways it can go wrong. And among regents, word travels fast."

Parker stared at his shoes. If Li An had thought the tryst might have left Kurt severely weakened, how many other regents thought so too? After this morning's demonstration, would Li An spread the word that the Master was just as formidable as ever? Or would she guess the truth?

"Parker, why are you here?" Kurt interrupted his thoughts. "Surely it's not for the pleasure of my company."

Parker looked up. His unease over Li An blossomed into fear. "Kurt, I…I think I'm a vampire."

"Nonsense. You're alive."

"No, listen. I killed a man last night. I was walking to my car from a job and there was this homeless guy sitting in an alley. He asked me for a few dollars and while I was pulling out my wallet…" He told Kurt what had happened.

"What did you do with the body?"

"I managed to get him to the car and then I drove to the north side and found an abandoned warehouse. I climbed the fence and dumped him in the Sound."

Kurt stared at him. "An abandoned warehouse? You saw it?"

"Yeah, why?"

"That's Balthus Temple. It's under an obscuring spell. Only the witches can see it."

"Well, I saw it."

Kurt slowly shook his head. "You really can break through a witch's spell."

"Isn't that what you told me last June? When most of the doors to Underground had been warded against anybody getting in?"

"Yes, but—"

Parker shrugged. "Okay, so I can break through witch's spell. That's not important right now. The important thing is what I'm going to do about being a vampire."

Kurt gave him a curious look. "How do you feel right now?"

He ducked his head. "Hungry. A little bit."

Kurt opened a drawer in his desk and pulled out a bottle. "Here. Try this."

Parker popped the cork and took a sniff. "What is it?"

"Bloodwine. It will help."

He upended the bottle and nearly spit. His throat tightened in revulsion but he managed to swallow his mouthful. He gave the bottle back to Kurt. "God, this stuff is nasty."

"I know. But it's how I'm getting along."

"So does this mean I'm a vampire?"

"No, but I want to try something."

"What?"

Kurt rose from the chaise. "Stand up. Take off your jacket and tie. You can take off the rest of your clothes if you like—the fewer clothes you have on the better, at least in the beginning."

Unpleasant memories of being naked with Kurt surfaced. He shook them off. "I'll keep them on just the same, thanks." He blinked and stood. "What are we going to do?"

"Turn you into mist. It's something every vampire can do, even the youngest of us. All you do is will your body to discorporate."

Parker concentrated for a minute. Then he felt himself dissolving as if his body was separating into its cellular components. It was a weird feeling.

Kurt pursed his lips. "Well, you definitely have vampiric tendencies. Look down."

He did. His clothes had pooled around his feet. He lifted his arm. All he could see was a swirl of mist. Panic shot through him. *How do I turn back?* he mentally shouted at Kurt.

Kurt didn't respond. Then he remembered that the vampire was no longer telepathic. *Okay, calm down. Kurt will tell you what to do.*

"Well, I suppose this little experiment is over," Kurt said, looking thoughtful. "Will your body whole again."

Parker did and a moment later, stood naked in the middle of the room. He dressed, fell into his chair and dropped his head in his hands. "Oh, God…what now?"

"We go see Garrett."

"But we don't know where she is."

"I do. Come on." Kurt held out his hand.

"Kurt, I really don't like that misting thing—"

"Then how do you suggest we get there, hmm? Air France? Come on. I'll lead you."

With a heavy sigh, Parker took Kurt's proffered hand and instantly felt his body dissolve. As vapor, they slipped under the office door and floated along the hallway. Moments later, they arrived at the nightclub's back door and slid under it. Then they were flying high above Seattle and soon left it behind. Kurt picked up speed. Parker looked down at the cities and towns flashing by beneath them. He realized that except for the weird feeling of being without a body, misting wasn't all that much different than mundane air travel.

And it's a lot faster, he heard Kurt think.

Thought you weren't telepathic anymore, Parker thought back.

Everybody's telepathic when in mist form. Even humans.

Oh. So how do you keep your clothes on when you mist?

It takes practice. But Parker, being able to mist isn't so bad. It can be useful, as you can see.

They flew on in silence. Parker saw the eastern shoreline growing closer and closer and then they were over the Atlantic Ocean. Sparkles of sunlight winked in and out on the murky blue waters. On and on they flew, with no land in sight. He'd never been overseas and was awed by the ocean's vastness. When he saw the day steadily giving way to night, he knew they were close to their destination.

An hour or so later, they were flying over Languedoc-Roussillon. Slowing their speed considerably, Kurt descended until the two were skimming over the mountaintops. For the moment, Parker forgot about his discomfort with mist travel. Even though it was night, with his wolf-sight he could see the mountains and the towns in the valleys. It was exciting.

He and Kurt finally re-materialized at a hoary-looking house perched on a rocky outcropping. Dropping Kurt's hand, he shook himself. Now that they were on the ground, he felt relieved at having a physical body again. He looked around. "Where are we?" he whispered.

Kurt banged the iron knocker on the oaken door twice. "This is

Feodor's cottage. He's a mage. As a matter of fact, he was Garrett's mentor. And I have it on excellent authority that she's here."

Parker frowned. "Whose authority?"

"Feodor's."

The door creaked open and he found himself looking down at a brown-skinned man not much taller than Garrett. "Kurt," Feodor said warmly, taking the vampire's hands into his own. "I was afraid—"

Kurt gave him a cocky grin. "Nonsense, Feo. You know me better than that. Nine lives, remember?"

The short brown man turned and looked up at Parker. "And you must be the grand *were*. Parker, isn't it?"

"Yes. Nice to meet you."

"Likewise. But please, come in," Feodor said, stepping back. Inside, the old mage showed them into the library. He waved his arm. "Sit anywhere. I'll get us some wine. It…might make things a little easier." He started for the large archway but stopped and gave Kurt an inquiring look. The vampire nodded once. "Trés bien," Feodor said with a grin. "I put in a case of your favorite merlot."

Kurt laughed. "Feo, you are far too good to me."

"Of course I am. Garrett will be down shortly." Then he left them.

Kurt took a seat in a plush wing chair across the room from a huge, age-blackened fireplace while Parker sat on a large sofa nearby. "How do you know Feodor? You two seem pretty friendly."

"Dear Parker, in six hundred and four years, you meet a lot of people. Some of them you even come to like. Why do you ask?"

He shrugged. "Well…I just never thought of you as having friends."

"What do you mean?"

"Well, you're—"

"Wolf," Kurt said through his teeth. His blue eyes blazed with anger. "Just because you think I'm an asshole doesn't mean other people do, too."

Parker held up his hand. "Whoa, whoa…I didn't mean it that way. I just meant—"

"I strongly suggest you shut up because you're only digging yourself a deeper grave, hmm?"

The library door opened and Feodor entered with a bottle of the promised merlot and four wine glasses on a silver salver. "Everything all right?"

"Yes," Parker and Kurt said at the same time.

Feodor chuckled. "No, it isn't." He shook his head. "All the more amazing." Parker wondered what he'd meant, but kept quiet. The old mage set the salver down on a low table. Straightening, he glanced around. "Where's Garrett?"

"Here I am," a soprano voice rang out. The three men turned as one. Garrett, dressed in a white robe—a color Parker knew the Craft permitted only mages to wear—entered the room, her light brown hair bound in a single braid that reached her waist. Head held high, she made her way to a wing chair across from where Parker and Kurt and sat. She looked from one man to the other but said nothing.

Feodor filled the four wine glasses and passed them around. Then he settled on the sofa. "Mes amis. Let me propose a toast." He paused a moment as if thinking. "To Garrett, Kurt, and Parker—three of the bravest souls I have ever had the honor of knowing, for they dared the impossible…and survived."

Lifting their glasses at the same time, Parker shot a sideways look at Kurt. Returning his attention to his glass, he took a sip of wine and raised his brows. He wasn't much of a wine drinker but this one was quite good. He set his glass on the table and looked up to see Garrett take a second sip from her glass and set it on the low table not far from his own. Then she sat up straight. She looked from one man to the other.

"Kurt, Parker—it's time I told you the truth about the tryst."

CHAPTER 10

After Garrett finished her narrative, silence fell in the library. She took a sip of wine and adjusted her robe.

Parker leaned forward in his seat. "Let me get this straight. If the tryst spell had worked, we wouldn't have been able to tell each other apart at all? We'd move, act and speak as one?"

She gave him a steady stare. "Yes."

He stared back and then rolled his eyes. "Oh, that's just great. The triplets from hell." Parker shook his head. "Look. We cast the tryst and the Eall Tholia spells last June to keep Seattle from being burned to the ground. It worked, sort of. But Garrett, did you ever once stop to consider the other side of this spell business? That night in Kurt's party room, you said the Eall Tholia would change how humans feel about us. Well, what about changing how zots feel towards humans? Humans might hate us but we don't exactly like them, either. And then there's the different zot races. Sometimes I think we hate each other more than we hate humans. If your spell didn't change that—"

"Your utopia of sweetness and light would be anything but," Kurt broke in. "The main reason zots behave now is because they don't want to attract human attention. But without that inhibition, it'll be zots constantly fighting each other and don't be so naïve as to think humans won't get caught in the cross-fire. And did you think that except for you witches, elves, and a few other types, the rest of us zots are predators and humans and other zots our prey? What do you think would happen if the *weres* ran wild among humans? Spell or no spell, don't you think they would eventually retaliate?"

She shook her head. "The spell would have taken care of that, too. It would've brought peace between and among zots and humans. There would be no need for you to prey on humans or zots. For vampires, there'd be more than enough willing donors and as for *weres*, you could do what you do now—hunt deer or whatever—except there'd be no consequences if you were discovered." She looked from one man to the other. "I'm surprised you haven't figured it out already. We stopped both sides from fighting, remember?"

Parker nodded once. "Okay, so why didn't you tell us that zots would be affected by the spell, too?"

Garrett shrugged. "You two might not have agreed to the tryst, if only for the sake of the pack"—she nodded at Parker—"and the colony. She looked at Kurt. "I couldn't take that chance."

The library went quiet for a few minutes. "All right, Garrett," Kurt broke the silence. "Since you seem to have all the answers, answer this." His eyes narrowed. "Who gave you the right to decide Parker and I should die so you could have your tryst?" he said, his voice tight with anger.

Garrett took a deep breath. "No one. And before you say it, yes, I've broken my Credo. Time and time again." She lowered her eyes and then looked up. "And don't think you're the only ones, either. You just happened to be the last in line." Her lips tightened. "I was only doing what I thought was right."

Parker leaned back on the sofa. "Speaking of breaking Credos… Garrett, when I fell in love with you, there was always a small part of me that wondered why it happened. I mean, you were a nice girl and all that. I liked our sex well enough but wolves aren't gentle lovers. I had to be careful not to break your bones or accidentally rip into you with my claws. The pack objected to my choosing you to be our freya because you weren't a wolf but besides needing a healer, I thought I was striking a blow for multiculturalism." He paused. "But when Melera came along, it was like my love for you just evaporated."

His lips tightened. "Wolves aren't like that, Garrett. When we mate, we mate for life. You were my lifemate yet I threw you over like yesterday's lunch." He stared at her, his bright green eyes cold. "Did you use a spell to make me fall in love with you?"

She folded her hands in her lap. "Yes. The spell held until you found Melera. That's how I know you do love her. Otherwise, the spell wouldn't have broken."

Parker's jaw set. "Uh-huh. So if I hadn't fallen in love with Melera, you were going to leave me twisting in the wind, still loving you, knowing you'd never come back to me because of Kurt, all so you two could keep trying to browbeat me into making this stupid tryst." He gave her a disgusted look.

"Who is this Melera?" Feodor said.

Parker turned. "It's a long story."

"But the short story is that you love her."

"What's that got to do with anything?"

"Maybe nothing. But a tryst involves one's being on every level, including the emotional." Feodor pursed his lips. "If we need her, can you get in touch?"

"No."

Feodor gave him a questioning look. "Why? Is she dead?"

"Melera's an alien, Feo," Garrett spoke up. "From another galaxy. She left last summer."

Feodor's look turned incredulous. He stared at Kurt. The vampire said nothing. Then he stared at her. She didn't say anything, either. Then his gaze settled on Parker. "You can't be serious."

Parker started chuckling, which quickly became full-fledged laughter. She glanced at Feodor, who now looked annoyed. "Feo—"

"No, that's okay, Garrett." Parker had managed to stop laughing but couldn't seem to help letting out a chuckle every now and then. "Sorry, Feodor. The look on your face is priceless."

Feodor still looked like he didn't believe him. "So you're in love with a space alien. And you seemed like such a sane young man." Then his expression turned stern. "But can we be serious, please? We have important work to do over the next few days if we're going to try and break the tryst."

Parker took a breath to say something but Kurt beat him to it. "Let it go, wolf. Melera's not here and hopefully, your feelings won't matter in whatever it is we're going to do."

Parker glared at Kurt. "I was going to say that as much as I'd love to hang out with you guys, I don't have a next few days. I've got a business to run, remember? I've got clients to satisfy. In fact, I shouldn't be here now. My client is probably going bonkers."

"I've taken care of that, Park," Garrett said. "I called your answering service and left a message that you're away on urgent family business. You'll be back in about a week or so."

He shot her a suspicious look. "You've got it all figured out, don't you? Again."

She blew an explosive breath. "Stop it. I'm not railroading you into anything."

"Sure feels like it."

"You want to stay trysted?"

"Of course not."

"Then it's settled," Feodor said. "Come." He beckoned to Kurt and Parker. "You two are hungry, non? You will eat and then I'll show you to your rooms."

The four trooped into the kitchen. Laid out on the scarred oaken table was a stack of raw steaks and a carafe filled with a dark red liquid Garrett knew was blood. The smell of all that extinguished life nauseated her. But she wouldn't leave unless Feodor did the same.

A small frown creased Parker's brow. "Aren't you two eating?"

Feodor shook his head. "We ate before you arrived. You go ahead."

Without another word, Parker dove into his food.

She watched the two men eat. Kurt behaved civilly, despite his obvious desire to upend the carafe and pour the blood down his throat. Using the goblet Feodor had provided, he filled and then drained it several times, never spilling more than a drop or two on his lips, which he promptly licked away. Parker ate like a starving beast. He'd morphed his hands into wolf paws, using his claws to cut, spear, and then gobble the bloody steaks. They disappeared so fast, it was as if he'd inhaled them. After he'd eaten, he licked his paws clean, then morphed them back into human hands. Watching, she was thankful—and not for the first time— for the restraint he'd shown when they'd been in bed together.

"Oh God, I needed that," he said and burped. "Excuse me. Thanks, Feodor."

"And you have my thanks too, my friend," Kurt said. Garrett noticed he looked a lot better than he had when he'd come in. His skin had lost its slightly waxy sheen and his blue eyes were brighter and more intense.

Feodor clapped his hands, making her jump. "And now to bed," he said in the tone of a schoolmaster. "We have much work to do tomorrow."

Kurt smiled. "My dear Feo. I may have lost most of my regent's powers but the need for sleep isn't one of them. I haven't slept in four hundred years."

Feodor smiled back. "I understand, mon ami. But the lack of whole blood these past months has taken a toll on you. You know what happens to vampires who don't get enough blood—the body begins to decay. I'm sure it's not far along in your case but if you've been depriving yourself like I think you have, you need to rejuvenate. And the best way to do that is through blood and rest. Whether you sleep is not the issue."

Kurt said nothing for a few moments. Then he laughed. "All right, Feo. As always, I defer to your superior logic."

Feodor turned and the four of them walked out of the kitchen, into the foyer and up to the second floor. The old mage halted. "This is an old cottage, mes amis. There are only three bedrooms, so someone will have to double up. Garrett is in that room," he pointed down the hallway, "and this one is mine," he said, pointing with his thumb behind him. Then he pointed over the two men's shoulders. "The room behind you is unoccupied."

"Oh, I think Parker and I will bunk together." Kurt cocked his head. "What do you think, wolf?"

Parker looked surprised and then alarmed at Kurt's offer. He glanced at Garrett before looking at Kurt. "Okay, but if you try anything I'll chomp you," he said in his wolf's growl.

Kurt chuckled. "I'm sure I'm much too tough and stringy for your tastes. Besides, I'm sated for the evening, so you don't have to worry. Come morning, though..." His look grew thoughtful.

Parker's eyes narrowed. "Don't you even think about it." He turned and stalked towards the bedroom.

Kurt smiled at the old mage. "For Parker and myself, goodnight, Feo. I do hope you sleep well." He looked at Garrett and his smile died. "You too, Garrett." Turning his back on her, he entered his and Parker's bedroom and shut the door.

The two mages were left in the hallway. Garrett stared at the door Kurt had just closed. "You'd better get to bed too," Feodor said. She glanced at him and nodded.

He kissed her forehead and stepped into his bedroom.

She watched Kurt's closed door for a minute. Then she walked to her room. Sighing softly, she opened the door and stepped inside.

CHAPTER 11

Almost a week later, Kurt stood at the window in the bedroom he shared with Parker, watching the sun rise over the mountains. Feodor had said the two of them had a lot of work to do to prepare for the tryst breaking, but for the past six days, all he'd done was to drink copious amounts of fresh blood, take long walks through the mountains, and read old books in Feodor's extensive library. *It's odd. I've never known Feodor to be this cryptic. But if there's anyone I trust besides Daniel, it's him.* The colony's executor appeared in his mind's eye. He knew Daniel would keep the colony running smoothly until his return.

A snuffling sound to his right made him look over his shoulder. Parker had awakened and now sat on the side of their shared bed. Kurt raised his brow. "You smell like blood." Five days ago, the odor would have driven him into a feeding frenzy. Right now, it didn't even give him a thrill.

Parker shrugged. "I ought to. I've been rolling in it all night."

"Out on the town, hmm?"

"Yeah. Once I told the local alpha I was staying with Feodor, you'd have thought I was a long-lost brother instead of a trespasser. Even though it's not a full moon, we went for a hunt and we brought down a couple of deer and then...yum." He stood and stretched. "I feel great." Then he turned to Kurt. "How about you? You're looking good."

"Why Parker, I didn't know you cared."

Parker shot him an annoyed look. "You know what I meant."

Kurt smiled and swiveled his head back to the window. "Yes, I feel quite well, Parker. Better than I have since we made the tryst."

A knock on the door made them both look up. Feodor stepped inside, carrying two brown woolen robes. "Good morning," he said, draping the robes over the back of a nearby chair. "After you get cleaned up, put these on. Kurt, I know you can't stand water anymore, so rub yourself down with these herbs." He pulled out a bulging linen bag from inside his loose, white robe. "Once you've finished, both of you come downstairs to the library." He smiled. "Today we try our grand spell, non?" Then he withdrew.

Kurt and Parker looked at each other. The vampire knew he and the wolf were thinking the same thing. *This had better work.*

The two men cleaned up and donned their robes. They left the bedroom and descended the stone steps, Kurt in the lead. Walking into the library, he saw Garrett was already there, sitting on the sofa. "Good morning, Garrett."

Garrett looked up. "Good morning Kurt." She looked at Parker.

Parker gave her a curt nod and mumbled something unintelligible.

An awkward silence settled over the large room. Kurt sat in the wing chair, while Parker sat in the chair across from him. It seemed as if the wolf wanted to keep as far from Garrett as possible without being conspicuous. If so, it wasn't working. He was as conspicuous as a screaming fire engine.

Kurt turned to Garrett. "Garrett, dear, do you know what the three of us are to do this morning?"

"Yes."

"Well then, would you mind telling Parker and me what that might be?"

"Sure. The three of us will cast a spell designed to—"

Parker raised his hand, his expression suspicious. "Hold it. This doesn't involve sex, does it?" He looked from one to the other.

Garrett smiled. "No. Sex-magick is a joining of energies to work a spell. We're trying to separate our energies and that's a different matter entirely. Anyway, the spell the three of us will cast is one Feo and I designed. Hopefully, it'll expel the parts of each other's auras trapped inside our own."

"Hopefully?" Kurt spoke up. "Do you mean there's no tryst counterspell? That the two of you had to make one up?"

She looked at him. "Yes to both. A tryst is permanent. Since ours isn't a complete tryst, Feodor thought we might be able to break it. To do that, we had to write chants of our own." A small frown appeared on her face. "Creating a spell is like composing a song. You don't know if it'll be a hit until you try it out."

Parker's expression turned angry. "In other words, if this doesn't work we're stuck being the way we are." His jaw clenched. "Garrett—" he said through his teeth.

Garrett's hazel eyes narrowed. "Cut it, Park. I fucked up big-time and fucked you over in the process, okay? Hate me all you want but at least I'm trying to do something about it."

He glared at her but said nothing.

She turned to Kurt. "Anyway, that's all there is to the spell. To save time, Feo will teach you the chant telepathically."

Kurt nodded once. "And what will Feo be doing while we are chanting?"

"Feo," said a voice behind him, "will be chanting another spell designed to use the vortex's energy to guide your misplaced auras to their correct bodies." By now, Feodor had reached them and stood beside Parker's chair.

Kurt's jaw dropped. "There's a vortex beneath this house? No wonder I—"

"Feel so peaceful? Yes, mon ami. The vortex's power realigns a body's energies so they circulate the way they're supposed to."

"But I'm dead."

"But you're still made of energy. That is the important work you and Parker have been doing over the past six days. Realigning your energies. Otherwise, you wouldn't be able to work the spell." Then he smiled. "Now. I will teach you the chant."

Kurt watched Feodor step over to Parker and place the first three fingers of each hand on each side of his head. The old mage closed his eyes and whispered something he couldn't quite catch. Seconds later, Parker's eyes widened and stayed that way until Feodor took his hands away.

Feodor peered at the wolf. "You understand?"

"Yeah. It's like I've known it all my life."

"Bon." Feodor stepped over to Kurt. "Your turn." He leaned over and did the same as he'd done with Parker. In a minute or so, Kurt too knew the chant by heart.

Feodor straightened. "Off we go." He crossed the library, the three of them trailing behind. Reaching the far wall, he mumbled a spell. A doorway-sized section of stone pivoted to reveal a darkened stairwell. "Lumina brilho," Feodor said. The stairwell lit up with witch light. The four of them entered and began to descend.

Twenty minutes later, they reached the bottom. Kurt looked around the natural cave and wondered how many others lay beneath these mountains. "In here," Feodor called. Kurt and the other two followed him into a second chamber and then he saw the vortex. He thought it rather pretty, with its blue, smoke-like tendrils spiraling and snaking around each other.

"Take off your robes and step into the vortex," Feodor said, bringing Kurt back into the moment. The three obeyed and stepped up to the blue smoke.

Kurt looked down with alarm. The pit appeared bottomless. He looked up to see Parker peering into the pit too. His expression matched the way he felt.

"It's okay," Garrett said. "I've been in it. The energies will hold you up. It feels like standing on a soft bed." As if to prove her words, she stepped off the edge and half walked, half bounced to its middle, the blue tendrils winding around her body.

Kurt and Parker looked at each other. The wolf took a deep breath and together they stepped into the void. He smiled. Garrett was right. It did feel like standing on a mattress.

"All right," Feodor said from behind him. Kurt turned. The old mage stood about ten feet from the pit's edge. "Stand facing one another, raise your hands, and touch fingers. Just like you did after making the tryst." They obeyed.

"Ready?"

"Yes," the three answered as one.

"Begin."

"Tre gaten raan dem evas," they chanted. After a few minutes, something tugged at Kurt from the inside of his body. A red glow enveloped him and flowed into the center of the triangle. His consciousness dimmed. He could no longer feel his fingers tapping out the complex rhythm, nor could he see Parker and Garrett's auras.

Then he was aware of nothing but the number one.

Feodor stood before the vortex, peering at his guests' auras as they flowed into the center of the triangle. *They're almost ready.* He took off his robe and laid it on the stone behind him.

As if on cue, the three lowered their arms to their sides and began a single word chant that sounded like "awn." Contrary to the previous chant, this time they sang in a slow monotone, sounding much like a single string plucked on a cello. Feodor began a chant of his own, "es capa zon lee a voor si," and clapped his hands in a complicated rhythm.

In response to Feodor's clapping and chanting, the swirling ball of red, blue, and green light slowly began to part. Tendrils of the vortex's energy filled the spaces between the colors. The auras pushed against the walls created by the vortex but the blue smoke held firm. Now Feodor turned his hands palms out and started making pushing motions while continuing to chant. The auras retreated from the vortex's walls until they each surrounded the body that owned them.

Feodor gave one more clap, lowered his arms and stopped his chant. Kurt, Garrett, and Parker also stopped chanting. The auric colors broke apart and swirled back into the three bodies. The old mage walked around the vortex, inspecting their auras. He shook his head. Each one's auric colors looked almost the same as it had before. He waved his hands and the three began chanting again. Then he started chanting and clapping, too. When he stopped this time, he could that see more of red, green, and blue auras had returned to their rightful owners but not by much. He tried it a third time. The result was the same. Feodor leaned back against the rock where they'd draped their robes and sighed. He and Garrett had done the best they could.

He clapped his hands twice in quick succession. The blue tendrils melted out of position. Kurt, Garrett, and Parker opened their eyes at the same time.

Feodor waited a few minutes. "How do you feel?"

Parker pinched the bridge of his nose between his thumb and forefinger. "I feel like I did after we made the tryst. I've got a hell of a headache."

Feodor leaned against the stone behind him and smiled. "I imagine so."

Kurt tried to hide his impatience but couldn't. "Can you tell how well your and Garrett's spell worked?"

"Listen, I know we're all anxious to find out whether the spell worked or not," Garrett cut in. "But Feo is just about worn out. Why don't we get him upstairs and comfortable before we start bombarding him with questions?"

Feodor shot Garrett a grateful look. Donning their robes, the four filed out of the cavern and into the smaller chamber. He felt Parker's hand on his shoulder. "Uh, look Feodor—I can carry you up if you want."

He shook his head. "No, Parker, that's quite all right. I think I have enough strength to make a float spell." He chanted a few words and then levitated. "See? Just fine. Now let's get upstairs."

Reaching the library, Parker exclaimed over the fact night had fallen. "We were down there all day? It sure didn't seem like it."

Feodor smiled. "It never does." He watched Garrett bustle about, making him comfortable on the large sofa. Then she left the room, obviously headed for the kitchen. He watched her go. *So different from the little hellion who arrived here thirty years ago.*

Within ten minutes, Garrett returned with a cup of tea. She handed it to him, then joined the others. The three pulled up chairs and surrounded him like expectant children waiting for a good story. They were in for a disappointment. He let out a heavy sigh. "The spell didn't work so well."

Kurt dropped his head into his hands and groaned.

Parker rolled his eyes and let out a soft growl. "Aw, shit."

Garrett seemed about to cry.

Feodor tightened his lips, looking at their crestfallen faces. "I'm sorry."

Parker grimaced. "Can't we do it again?"

He shook his head. "I doubt it would do any good. I cast the spell three times. There's been some change but not a lot. Still, some change is better than no change."

Kurt looked up. "What kind of change?"

Feodor turned. "You, mon ami, have more substance to your aura.

The tears have partially closed. I'd say you've gotten a little of your powers back. But you're still showing a lot of Garrett's aura. Perhaps enough talent to be a minor witch."

"That's hardly comforting."

He smiled. "Here, let me show you." He stretched his arm toward a low table in front of the sofa and pushed a mesh bowl of fruit off its mirrored base. "Take this." He held the bowl out to the vampire. "What do you see?"

Kurt took the mirror and stared into it. "Nothing."

"Now. Imagine you see your reflection. Concentrate on it. Now repeat exactly what I say and how I say it." Feodor took a breath. "Mira sjo meh," he intoned.

"Mira sjo meh." Kurt's face brightened. "There's my reflection." Then it fell. "Now it's gone again."

Feodor nodded. "It takes practice but these are the kinds of little magicks Garrett can teach you so you're not so vulnerable."

Kurt handed him the mirror. "Little magicks are all well and good but they won't fool another regent. Only mages can work that kind of magick."

"You aren't trying to fool a regent. You are trying to fool everyone else."

"Care to bet? I've already had one regent come sniffing around my domain."

No one said anything for several minutes. "What about me?" Parker broke the silence.

Feodor turned. "You have less red in your aura but not enough to curb your vampiric tendencies."

Parker let out another growl.

Then he turned to Garrett. "Your aura shows more blue but you still have enough green to manifest your *were*."

No one spoke. "So what do we do now?" Garrett said in a small voice.

Feodor took a breath. "Whatever traits the three of you manifest, you must teach one another to control them so they do not control you. Otherwise, humans may catch on to what you are and if that happens, you will disappear. And I don't know how much the death of one will affect the others."

The three gazed at the floor. Feodor felt a wave of compassion wash through him. He smiled a little. "Why don't we get some rest? You'll be leaving in the morning and all of us have had quite a day."

Parker stood. "I'm going for a run." He walked over to the window and seemed to gaze into the darkness. "Don't wait up." He shucked his robe, revealing his hairy, sculpted physique and opened the window. Cold air rushed in. Then he leapt through it, morphing into his wolf even as he cleared the sill.

While Garrett closed the window, Feodor turned to Kurt. "You have much to worry about, mon ami, but it is not all bad."

"Which of my powers do you think have returned?"

"I don't know. That is something you'll have to find out for yourself."

"Feo, what if we concoct another spell?" Garrett's voice sounded to his right.

Feodor nodded. "That's what I plan to do while you three are in Seattle."

Kurt sighed again. "Well, I'm going upstairs to rest. Thank you, Feo. Thank you for everything." He rose from his seat, bowed slightly, and left the library.

"And you, cherie?" Feodor smiled at Garrett.

"I'm going to bed. Like you said, it's been a long day." She stood, walked over to the couch and kissed his cheek. "And thank you for all you've done for us." Straightening, she turned and also left the library.

After she had gone, Feodor lay down on the couch cushions. He stared at the painted ceiling. He wasn't just tired. He was exhausted. *Ten years ago, today's magick would have barely affected me. It won't be too long before Goddess gathers me to her Breast.* His lips tightened. *But not before I free those three from their broken tryst. I must find a way to help them. I must.* He closed his eyes.

Before it's too late.

CHAPTER 12

The next day, while Kurt, Parker, and Garrett misted their way back to Seattle, Li An stood at her desk in her Shanghai office, staring at the huge silk tapestry on the opposite wall. Kurt had been on her mind since the day of her visit. "He is weak. I know it."

Mei, Li An's executor, gave her a questioning look. "Who is weak, Mistress?"

"Kurt."

"But he's one of the most powerful regents in the world—if not *the* most powerful."

Li An turned. "You know I went to see him. And I've told you how he is. He's vain and a show-off. Mirrors everywhere, eating in front of his guests, suggesting walks in the sun. This time there was none of that. The last time I was in his office, there was a huge mirror facing his desk. It's gone. And he didn't have a snack while I was there, or suggest we take a walk."

"None of that implies he's weakened. Maybe he didn't feel like showing off this time."

Li An glared at her. "Let me finish."

Mei inclined her head.

"But the two most telling things were that he offered me wine." Her look turned smug. "You do know I'm one of the few regents besides Kurt who can drink human wine, right?"

Mei dipped her head again. "Yes, Mistress."

Li An waved her hand. "Anyway, he was drinking when I arrived and opened a fresh bottle for me. He, however, was drinking bloodwine." She chuckled. "Why he thought I wouldn't smell it, I'll never know. Anyway, his servant—Parker, was it?—walked in. Kurt introduced him and I tried to throw a stasis over him but it didn't work. That's when Kurt kicked me out. But Mei, the power of that stasis wasn't coming from Kurt. It was coming from Parker. And Parker…" She frowned. "I'm not sure what he is. I could feel he's a werewolf but I also sensed vampire in him. The important thing is the only way he could have gotten those vampire traits was from Kurt."

Mei shrugged. "Those are interesting signs, I'll grant you—but it still doesn't prove Kurt is weak." She cocked her head. "What gave you the idea the Kurt is weak?"

"Oh…I suppose I forgot to tell you about the tryst."

"Tryst?"

"It's a magick spell that requires a mage, a top *were* and a vampire regent. I saw one once." She stopped her pacing and turned to Mei. "Didn't I tell you about that?"

"No."

"Well, those three were like one person. Not one of them remembered who they'd been. But get this—the tryst had made them greater than they'd been separately but those powers did not include what they'd been before. The regent was no longer master of his domain. The lion was no longer the king of his beasts. And of course, the mage was no longer the Father of his coven."

"So what happened to the regent's domain?"

Li An smiled. "I won all the will contests, so I became the Mistress of Shanghai."

"And the tryst?"

"They may have had unfathomable power but they were dead within a year."

Neither woman spoke for a minute. Mei peered at her. "So what does that have to do with Kurt?"

"You know about the Seattle riots in America, right? Well, I'd heard that he, a mage, and that werewolf Parker tried to cast the spell to stop the fighting. One thing about a tryst spell, Mei, is that when it goes wrong, it can go terribly wrong. And I think that's what happened here. I don't know how the three of them were affected but I'm sure the spell weakened Kurt to the point that he probably doesn't have much power left." Li An smiled again. It wasn't pleasant. "I think I'll challenge him to a will contest."

The office went silent again. Mei looked up. "Mistress, why do you hate Kurt so much?"

Li An's smile died. "A rebellion arose in my colony not long after I became Mistress. The vampire behind it wasn't a regent so he couldn't challenge me to a will contest. But he'd persuaded enough—more than half the colony—to challenge my rule. The fighting began and it was not going well for me. I asked Kurt for help and he refused." Her lips tightened into a line. "Mei, I almost lost that battle. It wouldn't have lasted nearly as long if Kurt had come to my aid. I vowed I would pay him back someday." Her face broke out into a happy grin. "And it looks like that someday is here."

"Why did they rebel in the first place?"

"They resented my taking over the colony after the contests. I defeated their favorite. Anyway"—she waved her arm—"enough of this ancient history. Now I have to decide who I'll get to challenge Kurt."

Mei cocked her head. "Mistress, all of what you've told me is thought-provoking but it still doesn't prove Kurt is vulnerable. What if you're wrong and Kurt wins the contest? Then you'd be right back where you are now."

"I'm not wrong," Li An snapped. Then her look turned thoughtful. "But I do see your point. What do you think is the best way of getting our proof?"

"A spy. Someone who can watch Kurt closely, track his behavior—things like that."

"Do you have anyone in mind?"

" No, but I've some ideas, though."

"Let's hear them."

"Well, first I'd suggest a human servant instead of a vampire. Even though Kurt will bite him or her, once a servant has been made it's impossible to remake him. At any rate, whomever we choose will ingratiate himself to Kurt in some way so as to be close to him. We only have to decide whether we'll send a male or female."

Li An stroked one cheek with a long-nailed, beautifully manicured index finger. "It doesn't matter as long as they're young. I've heard Kurt likes boys just as much as girls." She paused. "And they will have to be fluent in English, of course. But what excuse can we come up with to explain this new servant?" She frowned. "Not a college student. I read those riots in Seattle were started by college students. Kurt would be suspicious immediately."

"Surely he can't suspect every college student of being some kind of gangster. That would be absurd."

Li An's jaw set. "Absurd or not, a student is out of the question. We'll think of something. Right now, what's important is we find the right servant for the job. Come."

She walked to her desk and sat, positioning the computer before her. Mei, on the other side of the desk, made herself comfortable before a second computer. Li An looked up. "You start at the beginning of the roster and I'll start from the end."

The two vampires got busy.

Three days later, Li An and Mei had narrowed their choice to one. Li An tapped her chin with an index finger. "Zhang Wei. An actor, speaks and reads English fluently…he's a little older for the job than I would have liked but he'll have to do." She looked up. "Mei, find Zhang and send him to the receiving room."

Mei dipped her head. "Yes, Mistress." She left the office.

Li An rose, her silk dressing swirling about her. "Twenty-three years old," she muttered. "Hopefully, he'll look younger." She stepped out of her office and glided down the hallway to the receiving room. Opening the door, she walked inside and headed for a gilt chair that gleamed in the artificial light. She climbed the dais's three steps, then turned and sat.

Five minutes later, Mei entered the room with Zhang in tow. Li An looked him over. Zhang might be twenty-three but he looked to be about eighteen. That pleased her.

He walked to the dais and knelt before her. "My Mistress," he said, head bowed.

"Zhang, I have a job for you. It'll take all of your acting skills. I have reason to believe that Kurt, the Master of Seattle in America, has lost his powers. But I need proof of my suspicions. I have picked you to go to America because of your fluency in English. I hope you can speak without an accent." Li An raised her brow.

"Yes, Mistress, I can," Zhang said in perfect, unaccented English.

Li An smiled. "Good, good. At any rate, what you will do is get in touch with Kurt Masters, as he's calling himself these days. You will find a way to ingratiate yourself to him. He prides himself on the number of human servants he has, so if you make yourself indispensable, he'll most likely want to make you his servant. Since you are my servant, he can't make you his but you will act as if you are. And then you will spy on him. Understand?"

"Yes, Mistress. But how am I to get in touch with Mr. Masters?"

Li An gave her hand a dismissive wave. "I'm sure you'll find a way. Mei will help you get whatever you need." She paused. "And if you get me what I need, I will reward you with what you covet most—immortality."

Zhang's head snapped up. "Mistress, I'd be most grateful if—"

"But first you have to get me my proof."

He bowed his head again. "Yes, Mistress."

"Go now. And do not fail me."

Zhang stood. He and Mei turned and walked toward the receiving room's doors.

After they'd gone, Li An stroked the dragon's head finials attached to the chair's armrests. Her delicate lips curled into a smile.

Then she began to laugh.

CHAPTER 13

Four days after returning from France, Garrett stepped out of the elevator and into Kurt's penthouse. She took in the polished oak floors overlaid by thick rugs with abstract designs. A huge gas fireplace and conversation pit dominated the room. She smiled. "Some place you have here. Is this one of your hideouts?"

Kurt grinned as he helped her out of her coat. "No, this is where I entertain my…ah, human friends."

"Of the female persuasion, I suppose?" she said, trying to ignore her twinge of jealousy.

Kurt's grin widened. "Both." His grin subsided into a small smile. "Make yourself at home. Would you care for some wine?"

Garrett shook her head. "If I'm going to be spellcasting tonight, I need all my brain cells intact."

"Very well." He guided her to the conversation pit where he'd set up a small table for their use. She sat on the sofa on one side of the table. Kurt drew the other sofa forward until it was about a foot away and sat across from her. She gave him an inquiring look. "How do you feel? Have you been able to tell which of your powers has returned?"

"I've hardly had enough time to figure it out, Garrett." He pursed his lips. "But I did have two pints of whole blood the other day and I haven't had to take even a drop of bloodwine since. I'm just not hungry. That's a positive sign." He waved his hand. "But we're not here to talk about my vampire powers. Tell me again what it is we're going to do."

She drew a new deck of Tarot cards out of her purse. "Simple. You've seen this experiment before. I'm going to hold up a card and think about what I see and you're going to guess which card I'm holding." Garrett reached into her purse again and took out a small black eye mask. "Here—put this on."

"Why?"

"So we can be sure you don't see the cards I'm holding."

"But—"

"Just do it, Kurt. Please."

He put the mask on.

"Ready?"

"I feel rather silly, but I'm ready."

That was two and a half hours ago. Now, as Garrett shuffled the cards again, she heard Kurt's impatient sigh. She ignored it. After finishing her shuffling, she looked up. "Ready?"

"Must we do this again? This is what—the third time?"

"Yes, we must. I told you—I can't do this using magick. We have to figure out, the human way, whether you have any telepathic talent at all. That will tell me what spell I need to cast. Either I have to give you telepathic powers, or enhance what you already have. If I cast the wrong spell, it won't work."

Kurt sighed a second time. "All right," he said, sounding sullen. He readjusted the sleep mask over his eyes. "Get on with it."

With a pencil, Garrett drew a third column on the tablet before her. "Okay, let's start. What card am I holding?"

"King of Wands."

She made a mark in the column. "What's this one?"

"Three of Swords."

She made another mark.

"And this one?"

"Ace of Pentacles."

For over an hour, Garrett held up a card and sent her thoughts to Kurt, who then guessed the card she was holding. When she had his answer, she marked the column. "Last card. What is it?"

"Ten of Cups."

She made a mark. "Okay, you can take the mask off now."

Kurt ripped the mask from his face. "Thank the gods. So how'd I do?"

Garrett smiled. "Believe it or not, you are telepathic, Kurt. The first two times you got over ninety percent of the cards right and this last time it was almost one hundred percent."

"So how come I don't hear you?"

"Your conscious mind is blocking my thoughts. But your subconscious hears me." She paused. "At least I now know which spell to cast," she said and ran her hand through her hair. Then she peered at him. "You ready?"

"Cast away."

Garrett closed her eyes and concentrated. Her power gathered inside her, taking on weight in her solar plexus. She whispered a chant in the quiet of the large room. Five minutes later, she finished.

She opened her eyes. "All right. Let's test it." She stared at him. *What is your name?*

"Kurt."

"Very good. Now I'll go into the next room." She got up from the sofa and walked into the bedroom. *What is my name?*

"Garrett."

"Excellent." She returned to the living room. "Now we test the range. I'm going outside." Kurt helped her with her coat. Buttoned up against the cold, she turned to him. "See you soon."

The elevator doors whisked open and she stepped inside the cab. The doors shut. *Can you hear me?*

Yes, Kurt.

The elevator began its descent. She heard nothing for about a minute. *What about now?*

Yes, Kurt. I hear you. Listen, just talk to me, okay? That's all you need to do.

What do I talk about?

Anything you like.

Garrett heard nothing from him until she was in her car and driving. It was funny. She never imagined he could ever be at a loss for words. She'd heard Kurt talk like an expert on just about any subject— art, technology, medicine, and a host of other things.

Then he began to speak.

Kurt couldn't think of a thing to say. He leaned back on the sofa and closed his eyes. "Just relax," he muttered. "Something will come." He tented his hands over his stomach. Then his thoughts welled up inside him and burst through like a dam breaking. *I think about my darling Marguerite*

a lot these days. My wife when I was alive. She was Venetian. I wish I could talk to her. She was wise, for all her youth, and she always knew just what to say when times got rough. He went on about his marriage, his life as a prince in the Holy Roman Empire, the circumstances of his death, and his early years after his rebirth as a vampire.

Kurt, I'm downstairs, he heard Garrett think. His eyes popped open. It seemed like she'd left only moments ago. Kurt rose from his seat and walked to the elevator. Thumbing a small button beside the frame, he unlocked the mechanism. A few minutes passed. The elevator doors whispered open. Garrett stood in the cab, staring at him with an odd look on her face. He stepped back so she could enter.

"Well?" Kurt said as he helped her with her coat.

"I didn't know you were married."

He smiled a little. "It was centuries ago, my dear. Only the vampires remember."

"What happened to her?"

"Marguerite? She died in childbirth. Our son was born dead." He tried to keep the huskiness out of his smooth voice. Even after all this time, the memory still hurt.

"I'm sorry."

"Thank you." He was silent a moment. "So…how did it go?"

Garrett eyed him. "I think we should sit down."

"That bad? Well, maybe a glass of wine is in order. Would you care for some?"

"Yes."

Walking into the kitchen, Kurt selected a bottle of red sauvignon—Garrett's favorite—opened it, and poured the wine into two crystal glasses. Then he brought them to the fireplace. Garrett reached for the glass he proffered and took a sip. "Kurt," she said after he'd resumed his seat on the sofa. "I think Feo was wrong about you."

"How so?"

"He said that you had enough of my aura to be a minor witch. When I went out, I didn't just walk around the block. I got into my car and drove about five, six miles. I heard you clearly the whole time." She set her glass on the table. "Kurt, minor witches don't have that kind of range. Not even the major witches have it. Only mages." Garrett gave him a serious look. "You have mage-level powers. Maybe not enough to be a full-blown mage but what powers you do have…" She looked at the floor and then up. "It makes sense, really. You do have part of my aura."

For the first time since leaving Feodor's cottage, Kurt felt hope. "So you're saying—"

"You might not be as bad off as you think. You just need some help, that's all."

He took a sip of wine, sighed, and leaned back into his seat. "Well, that's good to know."

Garrett picked up her wine, took a gulp, and set it back on the table. "I'd like to try something."

"What?"

"Let's find out what magickal powers you have." She held out her hand. "We'll start with a ball of witch-light. It's easy—the first thing every witch learns." She seemed to concentrate and a moment later, a bluish-white glow filled her palm. She tossed it into the air, where it hung near the ceiling like a glowing balloon. "All you need to do is imagine the light in the palm of your hand, and concentrate on the image until it manifests."

"All right." Kurt held out his hand and stared at his palm. Seconds later, a laser-like shaft of blue-white light shot from his palm to the ceiling. A burning smell filled the air.

"Kurt, turn it off," Garrett shouted.

"How?" he shouted back.

"Close your hand."

He did so but the beam shot out from between the fingers of his fist. The burning smell grew stronger. Flames rose from the carpet. In his peripheral vision, he saw Garrett leap from her seat and stamp them out.

"Now what?" he yelled.

"Think of a light switch," Garrett screamed.

In his mind's eye, an old-fashioned toggle switch appeared with the toggle in the "on" position. He mentally turned it off. The light in his fist went out.

Neither one said anything for a few long minutes. Then Garrett returned to her seat. "That was…awesome," she said in a faint voice. "I've never seen anything like it. And witch-light isn't supposed to burn."

"Indeed," Kurt said, his voice just as faint. "I suggest I not do that anymore."

"Not unless you have to burn through a steel door."

"I'm not planning on robbing any banks."

Garrett finished her wine. "I should go. It's late." She stood, and so did Kurt. Walking to the closet, he opened the door and pulled out her coat. He helped her into it a second time, then escorted her to the elevator. The doors whispered open and Garrett stepped inside the cab.

She turned to him, her expression uncertain. "Kurt..." Then she swallowed hard. "Do you...do you think you could forgive me for what's happened?"

He stared down at her for a long moment. "Before we talk about forgiveness, let's see if I can survive, hmm?"

He pushed the button and the doors slid shut.

CHAPTER 14

The next night, Parker awoke to the sound of someone pounding on the back door to his house. He checked the bedside clock. It was three a.m.

Vaulting out of bed and not bothering to put on a robe, he ran downstairs to the mud room. He peered through the opaque curtains and could see a familiar figure standing under the patio light. Thumbing the deadbolt, he yanked the door open.

Garrett's small, willowy body fell into his arms. His brows shot up in surprise. "Garrett. What are you doing here?" It was the first time she'd been to his house in over a year.

She looked up. Tears streaked her gore-covered face. "I-I'm sorry, P-Parker," she stammered. "I didn't know where else to go, and you… you—"

"Get inside." He let go of her, closed the door and re-locked it. After flipping off the porch light, he closed the window blinds and turned on the kitchen lights. Then he stepped back and gave her a quick once over. She was covered with blood as if she'd been painted. A quick glance down showed him she'd gotten blood on him, too. He looked up. "Is any of that yours?"

Garrett shook her head. "I…no," her voice hitched. "Parker, I had another—"

His lips tightened in anger. "What did you kill this time? Never mind. That much blood, it had to be a human."

She shook her head again. "No. It was a big dog."

"Where were you?"

"In a junkyard. I don't know where."

"Well, that's good, at least. They usually don't have anybody on watch at night."

She gave him a pleading look. "Park, what am I going to do?"

He stared down at her without expression. "Go shower and meet me at the bar."

Garrett ran from the mud room. Stepping over to the kitchen sink, Parker wet a dishcloth with warm water, then picked up a bottle of dishwashing detergent and squirted a generous amount onto the cloth. He washed the blood from his midsection and arms. While washing, he noticed she'd gotten blood on his boxers, too. After turning off the spigot, he shucked his boxers, grabbed the cloth and threw both into the basement. Then he left the kitchen.

In his great room, he headed straight for the free-standing bar on the room's far side. Standing behind the marble counter, he picked up the tumbler he'd been drinking from earlier that night and poured it half full of Jack Daniel's. His lips twisted into a small grimace. *A damned dog. At least it wasn't a human.*

The sound of bare feet padding on the carpet made him turn. Garrett stood in the middle of the room dressed in one of his robes, her waist-length hair still damp from her shower. She walked to the bar. "Can I have one of those?" she said, inclining her head towards Parker's drink.

"You don't drink Jack."

"I do now."

Parker shrugged. He grabbed a shot glass from a storage rack and poured it full. He watched her toss it back and almost choke. "Wow," she said between coughs, "this stuff is strong." She coughed once more and patted her chest.

"You're just not used to it." He took the glass back and refilled it. "Here—just sip it." She reached for the glass and brought it to her lips. This time, she took only a small taste.

"Much better." She smiled a little.

Parker didn't smile back. Placing his elbows on the marble counter, he leaned against the bar. "Garrett, why didn't you come to me sooner? Tonight didn't have to happen. I could have helped you." He sighed and pinched the bridge of his nose between his thumb and forefinger. "Forget it. You're a wolf and so as alpha, you're my responsibility. I should've called you."

Garrett looked down. "I didn't think I…it'd been so long since I killed Mr. Squiggles, I thought maybe it wouldn't happen again."

He cocked his head. "Been having headaches lately?"

"Yes. Why?"

He leaned forward until his face was mere inches from hers. "That's your beast, trying to take control of your body."

She paled. "What?"

Parker drew back. "Right now your wolf's will is weak, like a newborn cub. You've been able to keep her in check with just your conscious mind, without even thinking about it. That's where the headaches come from. But at night, when your conscious mind is asleep, there's nothing blocking her way."

"So you're saying—"

"Yep."

"But if she's been out while I sleep, why didn't she kill?"

"Who says she didn't?"

"Because I didn't wake up with blood all over me."

Parker shrugged. "Maybe the other times she was just curious and wanted to check things out."

Garrett seemed to consider. "Okay. I'll buy that. But tonight isn't a full moon."

"And? Werewolves might be tied to the lunar cycle but that doesn't mean we can't morph at other times. Some of us can, anyway. You've seen me morph when it's not the full moon."

"But that's because…because…"

"Because what?"

She gave her head a tiny shake. "I don't know. I always thought it was one of the things that made you special. Like being pyrokinetic."

"No. Morphing's just a matter of will and control. The stronger the will, the more control you have over your beast. Will and control have to be developed, just like any other skill. We call it 'making friends with the wolf.'"

She gave him a dubious look.

"Okay, it's more like beating the shit out of her until she knows who's boss. Anyway, my mentor told me to think of my will as me sitting on top of a covered well while the beast is inside. The catch is that you have to put the wolf in the well. Once you do, that's where your control comes in. After the wolf figures out you're in charge, you don't have to worry about her coming out except at the full moon." He raised his brows. "Make sense?"

Garrett took a sip of her whiskey. "I think so." She set her glass down on the bar and closed her eyes. A moment later she opened them, her face troubled. "But Park, I-I can't do this. You said I had to hurt her. I can't harm another being, even if it's my *were*. My Credo—"

"Your Credo be damned, Garrett. You have to do it unless you want to be outed. Don't you understand that?"

She lowered her eyes. Then she looked up but said nothing.

He stared at her for a long moment. "Okay. Come on." He led her to the middle of the great room. "Take off the robe and sit. I'll be right back."

Garrett did as she was told. Parker headed for his study. Inside, he went to the closet. He reached to the back of its uppermost shelf and after feeling around for a second or two, drew out a length of large link chain which he wound in a loose loop around his shoulder. Extending his arm back into the closet, he again felt around for a bit and then took out a medium-sized box. He returned to the great room.

He watched Garrett's eyes widen when he reached her. "That chain is silver. How come it isn't burning you?"

"Only the purest silver burns while we're in human form. Too much copper and we don't. What's important is whatever the grade, if we're touched by silver while in human form, we can't change." He unlooped the chain from around his shoulder. "The links don't need to be this big, either. Something necklace-sized would've done just fine. I think whoever commissioned it had it made like this for its psych value." He paused. "An alpha inherits the chain when he wins a death-match. You could say the chain is a badge of office. Anyway, it's been around for as long as anyone can remember."

"So what are we going to do with it?"

"Chain you."

"Why?"

Parker gave her a long look. "So your wolf doesn't get out."

Garrett swallowed but said nothing.

He raised his brow. "Why the face? I thought you were into this kind of thing. Bondage, and all that."

"Yeah, but there's a time and place for it, you know?"

He loomed over her. "Well, sweetheart, this is the time and this is the place." Dropping to his knees, in a few minutes Parker had Garrett tied from her neck down to her ankles. He fastened the chain together with a good-sized lock that had been inside the box.

Parker sat beside her. "Remember what I told you? About will and control?"

She nodded.

"Call your wolf."

"How do I do that?" Garrett said, lying on her back.

Parker shrugged. "You have to figure that out for yourself. Everybody's different."

She closed her eyes. *How would I go about calling my beast?* She lay still, quieting her mind and relaxing as much as she could in her silver bonds. Her breathing deepened as she forced her consciousness down, down and down some more. Then she was there—in a self-induced hypnotic sleep. Images flew across her vision, images of her past, present, and possible future. She watched dispassionately as if the events they depicted had happened to someone else.

The pictures disappeared and she found herself in a wood. The trees were black and bare, their branches reaching up to the full moon like beseeching arms. She looked down. She was naked. Not knowing what else to do, she began to walk slowly and carefully so as not to trip over the tree roots.

She'd walked quite a ways when she came to a cave. Instinctively, she knew her wolf was inside. Cautiously, she entered. Dead leaves crunched beneath her feet. The moon's light didn't penetrate far inside and soon she was in pitch darkness. She conjured a ball of witch light and threw it toward the cave ceiling. In its glow, she saw herself at the far end of the cave—except this self was extremely hairy and had a formidable set of teeth and even more formidable claws. Her wolf let out a low growl and sprang at her. She tried to get out of the way but she wasn't fast enough. Her wolf's claws raked her thigh.

Garrett turned. Her wolf sprang again before she was ready for her. Clawing and biting, her beast knocked her to the cave floor. But she wasn't helpless. She'd spent years on the streets of Kilkenny City. She knew how to fight.

She elbowed her other under her chin. Her wolf let go. Garrett jumped to her feet and her wolf came at her again. Stepping into her beast's attack, she struck her other's face with the heel of her hand. She heard a cracking noise. She'd broken the beast's nose. Her wolf howled and tried to grab her by the waist. She danced out of the way and gave her a kick to the inner thigh. Her wolf faltered. She kicked her again in the groin.

Garrett's eyes widened. She'd expected her beast to be rolling on the floor in excruciating pain, but she wasn't. Her kicks had only made her beast angrier. Her beast's hands flew around her neck and tightened. She gouged her wolf's eyes with her thumbs. With a cry, her beast released her and covered her eyes with her hands. While her other's mouth was open, Garrett rammed her fingers down her wolf's windpipe as hard and as far as she could, withdrawing her fingers just before her wolf's jaws snapped shut. It worked. Her wolf fell to the floor. While her beast wheezed and gasped for air, she turned and ran for the cave's mouth, whispering a spell as she ran. The walls seemed to melt and flow toward the entrance.

Her wolf had apparently recovered because Garrett heard her beast's running feet getting ever closer. She ran faster. By now there was just a smallish hole in the rock covering the cave entrance. She leapt, feeling the wolf's claws rake her right foot. She tumbled through the hole, with only seconds to spare before it closed completely.

She hit the ground with her shoulder and rolled a few times. A minute or two passed. Still breathing hard, she looked up, leaves and sticks dangling from her hair. The cave entrance was solid rock. She couldn't hear her wolf's howls. She couldn't hear anything except the sound of her own panting. She lay in the leaves, her head in the crook of her arm.

After she'd gotten her breath, she tried to stand and almost fell on one knee. "Ugh," she grunted. Her right foot burned in pain. Twisting her face into a grimace, she managed to get to her feet. She looked around and spotted a branch a few feet away that looked sturdy enough to be a staff. Hopping over to where the stick lay, she picked it up and began limping through the woods, back the way she'd come.

As she walked, Garrett slowly rose to the surface of her consciousness. The woods and her stick disappeared, replaced by the montage of her life. That too faded away, and then she was awake. She opened her eyes.

Parker still sat cross-legged beside her, his face impassive. "Must've been a hell of a fight."

"How can you tell?"

"Look at yourself."

She looked down. Red welts covered her. Staring, she remembered every slash and bite her beast had inflicted. Her lips twisted. She'd managed to win their fight but she definitely got the worst of it.

"Did she submit?" Parker said, unlocking the chain.

Garrett shook her head. "I gave her one last punch and got out of there."

"You'll have to go back in, you know. You have to tame her."

"No, I don't."

He stared with raised brows. "Why not?"

"I walled her up in her cave. She's not coming out anytime soon."

"The bigger the opening, the more will it takes to hold the wolf inside."

She pulled her arm out of one of the chain's loops. "It's not my will holding it inside. It's magick. Times like this, being a mage can be pretty handy. Trust me—that girl isn't going anywhere."

Parker sighed. "You don't understand." He pulled the last of the long chain from around her body and looped it over his shoulder. She sat up, rubbing her wrist where the chain had chafed. "What don't I understand?"

"Your *were*—it's not like you're half beast, half human. She's an indivisible part of your whole. She has just as much access to your mind as you do, just as you have access to her mind. More than that, she's not stupid. She learns from you. And she learns fast."

Her jaw dropped. "You mean—"

"Yep. If there's a counterspell to the one you just cast, she can learn it on her own, figure out how it works...and use it."

Garrett fell back onto the carpet and stared at the ceiling. "Oh, Mother."

"And one more thing."

"What?"

"Your beast thinks you're a wuss."

"So?"

"So she knows that when she gets strong enough, she can come out anytime she wants and you won't be able to stop her. You'll be a berserker and there's only one thing to do with a berserker."

"What's that?"

Parker said nothing for a moment or two. "Kill her."

Her jaw dropped again. "What?"

"You heard me."

"What about the tryst? Feodor said—"

He shrugged. "Chance we'll have to take."

"But Park, you said if my wolf gets out, that means she..." The magnitude of her predicament dawned on her. "...knows how to use my powers. I'll be a berserker mage."

"And every zot in Seattle will be after you, including your coven. If humans get wind of it it'll spark a pogrom, too." He gazed at her, expressionless. "Still think you don't have to go back in?"

Garrett sighed. "Do I have a choice?"

Parker's response was to tie her up as he had before. "Okay. Go for it."

She closed her eyes and put herself into her deep trance. Touching down in the woods, she started walking. Reaching the cave, she stood before the solid rock entrance and looked down at herself. She was naked again. Her lips tightened. *I can't beat her like this. I've got to have some protection.* She thought for a moment. *And strength.*

She took a few minutes to decide on what clothes would give her the best protection. After figuring it out, she chanted a clothing spell. In seconds, she was dressed in black with a silver metal corset, a wide silver neck collar, a pair of silver braces on her arms, silver thigh guards, and silver-tipped engineer's boots. She frowned. *I need brass knuckles.* Looking at her hands, she chanted another spell and pair of the silver-coated weapons materialized on her fingers. Now she began chanting a third spell. Cold power flowed through her, settling into her bones and muscles. She kept chanting. A few minutes later, she stopped. Now she had the strength of her wolf, if not more. She nodded. *This should do it.*

Garrett walked up to the cave entrance and stopped about five feet away. She chanted the counterspell. As she did so, the rock melted and began to swirl like thick soup. Soon a small hole opened up in the rock and widened until it was large enough to admit a body. Then two bodies. After she judged it had widened enough, she stopped chanting. Taking a deep breath, she stepped toward the hole. A large ball of witch light appeared in her hand. Holding it before her, she entered the cave.

Her wolf was waiting for her. She leapt with a roar, her arms and claws out. Garrett threw the witch light in her face. Her wolf staggered, then turned and loped into the darkness. Garrett knew she hadn't hurt her. The beast was just temporarily blind. Summoning another ball of witch light, she threw it into the air, where it hung near the ceiling like a blue-white star.

Garrett ran deeper into the cave. Her wolf rushed her after she'd gone about fifteen feet. They crashed into each other and a burning smell filled the air. Her wolf howled. Before she could let go, Garrett kneed her other in her groin and then smacked her wolf's jaw with the metal knuckles. The blow snapped her wolf's head around and another howl cleaved the air. Her beast pushed her away and ran toward the back of the cave. Garrett's lips tightened into a line. Now she'd hurt her. The silver was doing its job. She threw another ball of witch-light towards the ceiling. Then, grim-faced, she ran deeper into the cavern.

Her wolf leapt at her from the shadows. Garrett fell. At the last minute, she raised her arm to protect her face and her wolf's mouth clamped over the brace. The beast screamed. Garrett rolled to her feet and with her magickally-enhanced strength, began beating her wolf mercilessly. Within twenty minutes, her beast cowered before her, whimpering.

Garrett lifted her wolf and half dragged, half carried her out of the shadows and into the light. Then she saw something she hadn't noticed before. There was a hole in the cave floor. *Perfect.* She dragged the mewling, bloodied beast over to it and shoved her inside, hearing a muffled thump when she hit the hole's bottom. Garrett looked around and spied a flat, stone slab about five inches thick. "That looks like it'll work." She hefted the rock and stepping forward, dropped it so that it covered most of the hole. "Now," she said in a loud voice, "you'll stay there until I tell you to come out, understand? You try and you'll get more of the same." She listened for a while but heard only silence.

Shoving the slab into place, Garrett walked to the cave's entrance. She looked up. She wanted to seal it shut but Parker's warning echoed in her mind. Shaking her head, she started walking. As she did so, her clothing seemed to melt off of her and then her feet left the forest floor. Higher and higher she rose, until she sensed she was back in Parker's great room.

She opened her eyes. He was staring at her. "You won, didn't you?"

Chained like she was, she nodded as best she could. "How do you know?"

"No fresh bruises or claw marks. So what happened?"

"Like you said, I beat the shit out of her and dropped her down a hole."

Parker smiled. "Good." Then his smile died. "Let's hope you don't have to do it again."

Her eyes bugged. "What?"

"Sometimes it takes more than once before the wolf figures it out." He started loosening her bonds. "I had to go in six times before my little asshole got the picture." He stood and began looping the chain around his shoulder.

"How will I know?"

"You'll get the headaches. And then we'll have to do it again. Let's hope your wolf learns faster than mine did." He paused. "Be right back." Parker disappeared into his study and returned without the chain. "Come on. Put the robe back on and I'll take you home." He hesitated. "Oh, wait. You don't have house keys. How will you get in?"

Garrett wound the sash around her waist. "Same way I got through your gate. I'll just spell the lock open. No problem."

He nodded. "Let me put some clothes on and we'll go."

After he'd gone, she stepped over to the bar, picked up her glass and drained what was left of her drink. It burned her throat but after what she'd just been through, it was welcome. She stared at the bottom of the glass and thought about her wolf. *I'm sorry I had to hurt you. But it was the only way you'd understand. At least, I hope you understand.* She closed her eyes. *Please, Mother. I don't want to do that again.*

"I'm ready," Garrett heard Parker's voice. She opened her eyes and swiveled her head toward the sound. "Let me warm up the car for you, and then we'll go."

"No need. I'll just cast a warming spell. I'll be fine."

"You guys got a spell for everything, don't you?"

"Pretty much." She gave him a weak smile.

"Okay, then. Let's go."

They exited the great room and filed through the kitchen. The car was out back, in the alley. Outside, Parker unlocked the gate and they slipped through the opening. He walked around the vehicle to the passenger side, unlocked it, and then opened the door. Garrett climbed in. Then he went around to the driver's side and slid into the seat. Starting the engine, he put the car in gear and drove off.

They rode in silence and soon reached Her house. Parker pulled up to the curb. She placed a hand on his shoulder. "Park, thanks for everything."

He just nodded.

Garrett exited the car. Stepping up on the curb, she walked along the path and then up the stairs to her front door. She murmured the unlocking spell and heard the tumblers click. Pushing the door open, she turned and waved. Parker waved back and pulled away.

Inside, she took off Parker's robe and laid it across the sofa. She'd give it back to him later today. Looking at the clock, she decided she needed a cup of tea but thought the better of it. "What I really need is sleep," she muttered. She mounted the stairs and walked along the hallway to her bedroom. As she entered, a wave of fatigue washed over her. She eyed her bed. It had never looked so good. She ran over to it, climbed in, and burrowed beneath the blankets. Staring at the ceiling, she thought about all that had happened tonight. *Thank the Mother no one saw me.*

She yawned. Too tired to think anymore, Garrett rearranged the bedclothes to suit her taste. Then she rolled over onto her side, tucked her hands beneath her cheek and fell asleep.

CHAPTER 15

Three nights after Garrett's escapade, Melera jerked awake to the sound of the commcen's loud chirping.

She pulled the pillow over her head, gritting her teeth against the irritating noise. "Jakkin' Vst," she muttered. "I told them I'm working as fast as I can." Clutching the pillow closer around her ears, the barrel of her plasma pistol pressed into her cheek as she willed the chirping to stop. It didn't. She threw the pillow aside and got up.

Sighing, she padded over to the commcen and checked the column transmitter and receiver. The deep red band was pulsing. She frowned. That wasn't a frequency the Vst used. That wasn't a frequency anyone used. Curious now, she turned off the alarm and placed her hand on the commcen's lit fluorescent-like panel. The machine measured her neural impulses. The panel turned orange and her hand sunk below its surface. Now neurally linked to the commcen, she looked to her right at a second, darkened panel that provided a heads-up display of messages received.

The message appeared. Melera's eyes popped and her jaw dropped. *Wha—what the...* She ripped her hand out of the lit panel, the pain from the abrupt neural disconnection barely registering. Whirling, she ran to her little camp and struggled into her clothes. She grabbed her pistol and rammed it into her thigh holster.

Melera raced for her ship.

Hours later, a faint line of shimmering, purplish-white light appeared inside Parker's great room. It grew longer and brighter until it stretched from floor to ceiling. Then it began to widen. More light spilled through, throwing the staircase into stark relief.

The universal fabric had been torn open. A figure stepped through the breach and into the room. The light vanished.

Melera stood at the foot of the stairs, shivering. Clad only in synskin and spikes, she was dressed for a planetside stroll through the dangerous part of town instead of skipping through the Void's abysmal cold.

Wear the collar next time, her czado said. *Its force field will keep you warm.*

That thing itches. Besides, the shakes don't last long.

As if on cue, her trembling stopped. She looked up. Judging from the familiar soft growling noises coming from the second floor, Parker was sound asleep. *Good. Makes it easier, if I'm fast enough. He won't know what's happened until it's too late.* Making no noise, she climbed the stairs to the second floor and then tip-toed along the hallway to his bedroom. Light from the streetlamp outside his house thrust its transparent fingers across the bed and bathed the room in a bluish glow.

She paused after reaching the doorway and frowned. *Pawkher isn't—*

A big black shape leapt from his bed. Melera dropped into a defensive crouch. When the shape was overhead, she reached out and grabbed two handfuls of its flesh. She stepped further into the room and using her attacker's momentum, swung it in a downward arc, then hurled it to the floor. Not giving her assailant a chance to recover, she jumped on its chest, whipped her pistol from its holster and pressed the barrel against the tip of the other's nose. She smiled. "Hel-lo, Mahn-dee. Me you remembuh, yes?"

Then she was grabbed roughly from behind, hauled her to her feet and thrown across the room. Crashing into the far wall, the gun flew out of her hand and clattered to the hardwood floor. Sitting amidst the broken drywall, Melera shook her head, the white plaster dust flying about her.

Parker loomed over her. "What the hell do you think you're doing?" he shouted, pointing to Mandy.

Her jaw set. "Mahn-dee," she shouted back, but that was as far as she got. She stared at Parker, wide-eyed. Then she glanced at Mandy and her shoulders slumped. She ducked her head as a tear formed in the corner of one eye. "Me sorry, Pawkher," she said without looking up. "Me go, yes." Melera got to her feet, not bothering to wipe the tear now trickling down her dusty cheek. She picked up her pistol and returned it to its holster. Lifting her head, she gazed at Parker's furious expression. "Goo-bye," she whispered.

Closing her eyes, she pictured in her mind the small, wooded island where her corvette waited for her, visualizing every detail until it seemed as real to her as the tears on her face. Her czado opened the portal leading into the Void. Its icy blast enveloped her like a subfreezing shroud.

Just as she stepped through the opening, Parker's strong arms clamped around her waist. Her mental picture wavered. She struggled to keep the vision in place. Without it, she couldn't skip them. They'd be trapped inside the Void, and without protection, its cold would kill them before she had a chance to re-visualize her destination.

In almost an instant, the cold disappeared. The two tumbled to the ground. Grateful for the relative warmth, she lay shivering in the grass. A minute later, she rose onto her elbows and glowered at Parker's head resting on her abdomen. "You c-cray-zee?" she shouted. "You maybe kill us b-bowts!"

He lifted his head. "I wasn't going to let you g-get away from me."

"W-what? Me you tsrow out, yes!"

"I d-didn't throw you out. You left."

She struggled to sit up. Parker's arms wrapped about her waist made it impossible. "Leggo," she said, pushing hard on his head.

"No. Not until you listen to what I have to say."

She pushed one more time and sighed. "Ohh-kay." She lay back in the grass and stared up at the cloudy sky. "Me listening."

He released her. From the corner of her eye, she saw him scoot up next to her and lie on his side, supporting his head with his hand. She sensed his gaze on her but didn't look at him.

Then she heard him take a deep breath. "I'm sorry I threw you into the wall. But you—"

"No 'splain. Mahn-dee jump me but her you defend. Why? She wolf. Pack come first always. Me understand."

"That's not why—"

"Is."

"Will you shut up and listen to me?"

She turned to look at him but said nothing.

"So first, let's get something straight. You're one of my pack. I made you one of us when you were here last and as long as I'm alpha, you're still one of us. Got that?"

Melera lowered her eyes. "Yes." A minute passed in silence and then she looked up. "Why Mahn-dee in you bed?"

Parker rolled over onto his back. "How do I explain this?" He shook his head and sighed. "Mandy's my freya, Melera. You remember what that means?"

"You sort of wife, yes."

"Yeah."

"Me tsought Gharrett fray-ya."

"Not anymore."

Another minute passed. "Mahn-dee you love, yes?" she said, her voice quiet.

"No."

"Tsen why she fray-ya?"

He sighed again. "I had to do it, Melera. You saw how we were last summer. Half of my pack dead in that revolution and after you left, three suicides. I had to save the rest of us from falling apart and the only way I could do that was to take another freya. I chose Mandy because I knew she was the best wolf for the job."

She said nothing for a long while. "Mahn-dee love you, yes?"

He didn't answer at first. "Yes."

"So you protect Mahn-dee 'cause she you freya and you tsink I kill her?"

"Yes. Weren't you?"

"No."

"Then why'd you pull your gun on her?"

She gave him an exasperated look. "Me her attack, Pawkher." She shifted position and stared at the sky. "Gun on lock, anyway."

"Okay…whatever. Even so, I'm sure Mandy smelled you when you stood in the doorway and given all the time you spent with the pack last summer, she knows your scent. She shouldn't have attacked you."

"So what you do about it?"

"Don't worry. I'll punish her."

Neither one said anything for a minute or two. "I thought I'd never see you again, Melera," he said, his voice soft.

She looked at him. "Me, too." Her voice was just as soft. Then she struggled to her feet. Parker did the same. They stared at each other, silent.

"So…why'd you come back this time?" Parker said, his voice still soft.

Melera said nothing at first. Then she stepped forward and gave his cheek a light slap, the Xia'saan way of showing affection. "Me love you, Pawhker. Me…need you."

He smiled and took her into his arms. He'd taught her some of Dirt's ways and knew what she'd done was wrong. "No, sweetheart. Like this, remember?" Lifting her chin, he gave her a deep, satisfying kiss.

When it ended, she stared into his startling green eyes. "But there be 'nother reason me come back."

He still smiled. "What's that?"

She took a breath. "Me tsink Beloc on Dirt."

CHAPTER 16

Dumbfounded, Parker's smile died. *Beloc? Here?*

"Take us back," he said after he'd found his voice. "Mandy needs to hear this."

"Why?"

"Because she's my freya, that's why. Let's go."

Melera's jaw set. "No. You and me. We leave Dirt. Now."

His eyes narrowed. "That's Earth. And no way. I'm not leaving our pack, and neither are you. You got us into this intergalactic mess and now you're going to help us get out of it. Take us back."

She stared at him.

He sighed. "Please?"

With a small smile, she took his hand and closed her eyes. In almost an instant, they were back in his bedroom. After his teeth stopped rattling from the Void's cold, he looked toward the bed. "Mandy's clothes are still here, so she must be downstairs. Come on." They left the bedroom.

The soft glow coming from the lights over the bar gave away Mandy's whereabouts. So did the smell of Jack. She stood behind the bar, bottle in hand, swaying. Parker walked over to her.

She blinked at him with glassy eyes. "Hey, Park. Wha' happened? You jus' disappeared into that funny light. Freaked me out." She took a swig. "An' now you're back." She giggled. "From outer space." She giggled again and took another swig. "Izzat where Melera went too? Outer space?"

"Mandy, how many bottles have you had?"

"Dunno. Din't count." She leaned in close. "Park, there's somethin' weird 'bout Melera," Mandy whispered. "Have you noticed? She smells funny. I don' like her." She burped in his face. Jack fumes filled the air. "'Scuse me."

Parker dropped into a squat. Judging from how many bottles remained in the case, she'd guzzled two of the jumbo-sized bottles and was working on her third. A werewolf's high metabolism might make it difficult for her to get drunk but she could if she drank enough. And Mandy had drunk a lot in the twenty or so minutes he and Melera had been away. *God—it's a wonder she hasn't passed out.*

He stood and held out his hand. "Give me the bottle, Mandy. You've had enough."

She twisted away from him, clutching it to her chest. "No. Mine."

"Give it to me."

Pouting, Mandy handed over the half-empty bottle.

Parker put the bottle on the bar and took her hand. "Come on. You need to sit down."

"Don' wanna siddown. Wanna drink." But she allowed him to lead her from behind the bar. In his peripheral vision, he saw her eyes widen. "Aagh!" she yelled and jumped into his arms. "It's her. Whass she doin' here?"

"Calm down, Mandy. Melera's not going to hurt you."

"She stuck a gun in my face."

"Well, Melera's very sorry about that. Aren't you, Melera?" He turned and gave her a meaningful stare.

Melera shook her head. Then she rolled her eyes. "Me sorry, Mahn-dee. But me you not attack, yes?"

Mandy didn't answer. She'd finally passed out.

Parker walked to the sofa and deposited her on its black leather cushions. "She'll wake up in a couple of hours or so. She'll be sober, then." He turned. A slow smile stretched his lips as he looked Melera up and down. "You always dress like that?"

She frowned. "Why?"

He sauntered over to her. "Because you look smokin' hot, babe," he whispered.

"Me not smoking now."

"Oh yes, you are." He slammed her against his chest and laid on a brutal kiss, heedless of the spikes digging into his skin. Releasing her, he stepped back and took her hand, then gave her a hard tug. He grinned. "C'mon. I know what we can do while Mandy's out. Last one upstairs is a rotten egg."

Melera was the rotten egg.

Three hours later, Parker and Melera returned to the great room. Mandy was still asleep on the couch. He walked over to her and dropped to his knees. Placing a hand on her shoulder, he gave her a rough shake. "Mandy. Wake up."

She moaned.

"Come on." He shook her again. "Wake up."

Mandy opened one brown eye. "Ugh."

He smiled. "How do you feel?"

"Like crap. My head's going to explode." She looked at him, bleary-eyed. "How can you stand that stuff?"

"I usually don't drink two and a half bottles at a time."

Mandy lifted her head, looked over his shoulder and then lay back down. "Oh, damn. I was hoping she was a hallucination."

"Melera's here because we have something to tell you. Can you sit up?"

"No."

"C'mon, I'll—"

"Park, if I sit up, I'll throw up, okay?"

Parker rolled his eyes. "Fine. I'll sit on the floor." He released her shoulder and sat. From the corner of his eye, he saw Mandy had rolled onto her side and was watching Melera.

Melera walked over to them and sank to the floor. Sitting on her knees, she opened her mouth to speak but Mandy spoke first. "Melera. What kind of zot are you?"

"Me not zot. Me be from Maqu. Nutser galasky, yes?"

Mandy frowned. "From where?"

"Mandy, Melera's an alien," Parker cut in. "An extraterrestrial."

Mandy narrowed her eyes. "What kind of idiot do you think I am? You hand me some bullshit on a plate and expect me to eat it? I'm your freya, Parker. Not your fool."

His lips tightened. "Look at her, Mandy. Have you ever seen a zot with eyes like hers?"

"Contact lenses."

"Okay, then. Melera, say something."

"Pawkher is right. I'm an alien," she said in Xia'saan. Her five-toned voice seemed to fill the room.

"Amazing what they can do with electronics these days, isn't it?" Mandy started to get up. "I'm not going to listen to this ridiculousness."

Parker's jaw set. "I'm not asking you to listen, Mandy."

Mandy stared at him for a second and then lay back down.

He turned to Melera. "Okay. Let's start from the beginning. What makes you think Beloc's here?"

She told him about the intruder on her ship and the tracker that was used to follow her. "Once get tsrough wormhole, Dirt only living planet near. Figger out not hard."

"If he's on Earth, do you think he came alone?"

"Beloc go nowhere alone."

"You think he knows where you are?"

"No."

"All right, I'll play," Mandy said. "Who is this Beloc and why is he here?"

Melera looked at her. "Bad man. Me in prison, he torture. Me get away. Now for me he look. Want me back."

"What did you do?"

She turned to Parker. "Word me know not."

He thought for a moment. "Treason. That's as good a word as any."

Mandy looked from one to the other. "Wait a minute," she said, her voice dripping with sarcasm. "Haven't I seen this movie before?"

Parker and Melera stared at her. "No," Parker said.

Mandy's lip curled. She struggled to sit up, then squeezed her eyes shut and placed a hand on her forehead. "Ow." She lay back down.

Parker turned back to Melera. "If Beloc was convinced you aren't here, would he take his troops or whatever and go home?"

"Prolly not."

"Why?"

She cocked her head and gave him an exasperated look. "Tsink."

He didn't say anything. Seconds later, his mental light bulb lit up. "Wait. You told me the whoever—"

"Tse Akkad."

He waved his hand. "Yeah. Anyway, even though they govern a good chunk of your galaxy, at bottom they're an exploration and mining corporation. For them, this solar system would be prime real estate—and ripe for the taking. And they'd use Earth as a base of operations." He raised his brows at her. "Right?"

She beamed and nodded as if he was a particularly bright child.

He gave her a smug look. "Never happen. We got nukes. We'll knock him out of the sky."

"You nukes not be powerful enough. You no idea how big ships are. Besides, tsey shielded."

No one said anything. Then he sighed. "Well, nukes or no, I haven't the slightest idea what to do next."

"I do," Mandy's voice said from above him. Parker turned. Mandy had stood up. "If you two want to play your little space fantasy, go ahead. But count me out. Somebody's got to take care of the pack while you're off role-playing, Parker." She marched past them to the stairs, then stopped and turned. "But don't play too long, Alpha. I don't know how long I can hold the pack together without my freyr." She gave them both a pointed look and started up the stairs.

"Mandy, get back here," he said in a commanding tone.

She didn't stop. "No, Park. I have to be at work in a few hours. I'm going home. Punish me later." Mandy reappeared five minutes later. Without looking at either of them, she opened the door and was gone.

Parker and Melera stared at each other without speaking for a long time. "How about a drink?" he broke the silence.

"Yes."

Rising from the floor, the two walked to the bar. Melera leaned on the counter in front while Parker went around back. He plucked two tumblers from the storage rack and placed them on the bar's marble top. Then he reached over and pulled the half-empty bottle of Jack toward him. He poured both tumblers full.

She took her glass and after clinking a toast with him, took a gulp. "Mahn-dee jealous."

"I know."

"What you do?"

"What can I do? I'm not giving you up, and she knows it."

Melera was silent for a moment. "Jealous make peoples do lots bad tsings, yes?"

"Like what?"

She pushed her empty glass toward him. "She turn on you? She turn pack on you?"

Parker filled it while shaking his head. "Never." He pushed the now-full glass back to her.

She picked it up and drained it. "You sure?"

He filled his own glass. "Sweetheart, she's more likely to send the pack after you. And it wouldn't take much convincing, either."

Melera sighed. "Is tangled, yes."

Parker stared at the countertop. He picked up his glass and poured the liquor down his throat. Its burn was welcome. "Yeah."

The two fell silent again. He let out a heavy breath. "And then there's Beloc. What are we going to do about him?"

Tightening her lips, Melera gave her head a shake but said nothing.

"God, all this shit is making my head spin. I can't think anymore." He put his head in his hands.

Quiet reigned in the great room for one or two minutes. "Tsere is one tsing we can do," Parker heard her deep voice.

He didn't look up. "What's that?"

"Go sleep."

Parker raised his head and grinned. "I have a better idea." He stepped out from behind the bar and held out his hand. She took it. Together, they walked across the great room. At the bottom of the stairs, he swept her off her feet and carried her to bed.

CHAPTER 17

The following morning at ten a.m., Kurt, sitting in his red velvet-lined office beneath his Last Chance nightclub, had just switched off his computer when the intercom buzzed. He pressed the answer button. "Yes?"

"Mandy Stewart to see you, Master," Julie, his human servant and executive assistant said.

"Show her in."

He rose from his massive mahogany desk just as the door opened. "Mandy—what a pleasant surprise." He looked at Julie. "Would you get us some tea, please?"

Julie nodded once and left the office.

Kurt studied Mandy as she walked towards him. Dressed in a severe navy blue suit, she looked every bit the chief of staff in the city's highest elected office. Immersed in the sea of city politics, she and Kurt had spent many a late night together, orchestrating the mayor's agenda and quietly clearing the way for Kurt's policies to become law. He'd come to know her well and almost considered her a friend.

Right now, she seemed troubled about something. He stepped out from behind his desk and walked over to a deep red sofa positioned against one wall. "I think we might be more comfortable over here." He held out his hand. "Please, have a seat."

"Thanks," Mandy said and sat. Kurt sat opposite her in a matching chair.

Julie returned bearing a silver tea service. She set it on the low table between them and started to pour. Kurt laid a hand on her arm. "No, my dear. I'll do that. You may go."

Inclining her head once, Julie left his office a second time.

Mandy chuckled. "I wish I could get my EA to do that."

Kurt smiled again. "That's the beauty of having human servants. Tea?"

"Yes, please."

He poured a cup and passed it. Then he sat back. "Now. What did you want to see me about, hmm?"

Mandy took a sip from her cup and set it on the table. "Melera's back in town. But I guess you already knew that."

He had not, but he wasn't going to admit it. "Yes, I did."

"How long has she been here?"

He frowned a bit, then hazarded a guess. "I believe she arrived sometime yesterday."

"What time? Has she and Parker been to see you? They both know your rule about introductions, no matter how many times someone's been here."

Kurt pursed his lips. "Mandy, why are you grilling me about Melera?"

She let out a little sigh. "I saw her last night. She broke into Parker's house."

He raised his brows. "Go on."

"Kurt, she thinks she's some kind of space alien. Worse, Parker does too."

"Oh, really. What did they say?"

"Some nonsense about her being in prison and now she's on the run from somebody named Beloc who wants to take her back and then how he'll probably take over the world. Stupid, huh? Like a bad movie."

"Indeed. I think Parker's been watching too much television. Melera too." He ran a perfectly manicured fingernail along his cheek. "Still, it's interesting. What else?"

"She thinks this guy might be somewhere on Earth."

"Why?"

"She says something happened during her trip here. Something about a tracker being planted on her ship. It was destroyed, but not before Beloc could follow her. And according to Melera, he's not alone."

"Who's with him?"

"Melera says his guards or something like that. I don't know." Mandy shook her head. "Why are we even discussing this? I want to know what you're going to do about it."

Kurt cocked his head. "Do about what?"

Mandy glared at him. "I want Melera gone, Kurt. The last time she was here, Parker fucked up the job of alpha wolf so bad the pack nearly turned on him. Tran and I were barely able to keep them from doing it. Now Melera's back, and I'm afraid it'll happen again. If it does, I don't know if Tran and I can keep the pack together this time. If we can't, they'll kill him for sure."

She sighed. "Park's a good wolf, Kurt. And he's a damned good alpha. But he seems to have this thing for bitches who aren't pack and it causes nothing but trouble. First Garrett and now Melera. Why can't he see that?"

Kurt gave her a knowing look. "Mandy, are you jealous of Melera?"

Mandy drew a sharp intake of breath and then frowned. "Don't be silly. But as freyr and freya, Parker and I have a duty to serve our pack, and Melera's presence is going to interfere with that. Again."

His smile didn't falter as he refreshed her cup. Her reaction had told all. She *was* jealous of Melera. His lips tightened. *That makes two of us.*

"Thanks." She brought the cup to her lips and eyed him over the rim. Then she lowered it. "Park told me about the debt the pack owes you. I should think you'd be just as interested in our well-being as I am, right?"

"That's true."

"So what are you going to do about Melera?"

"What would you want me to do?"

"Kick her out of your city. Have her put in a mental hospital. I don't care. All I know is I am not about to let my pack disintegrate because Park can't see past his dick." She looked at her watch, put her cup down on the table and stood. "I have to go. I've got a meeting in twenty minutes and it's across town."

Kurt walked her to the door and opened it. "Thank you for stopping by, Mandy. Let's keep in touch, shall we?"

She stared at him. "I'm counting on it."

He closed the door after her, walked to his desk and sat. Leaning forward, he tented his fingers before his nose. "Beloc, hmm?" he whispered. An idea began to take shape but there was just one catch. He had to find Beloc first. "And that," he muttered, "will be like looking for the proverbial needle in the haystack."

Kurt leaned back in his chair and gazed at the ceiling. *All right. This Beloc is a little green man but right now he's passing for human. He could be anybody. Melera undoubtedly has no idea what he looks like.* He blinked. "If I was an alien come to Earth looking for Melera, where would I start?" *The cities, of course. So many people.* Opening his desk drawer, he out a small remote, swiveled around in his chair and put his feet up on the credenza. He pressed the button. The wall behind him separated into two and disappeared behind the paneling on either side. Before him lay a ten-foot-wide map of the world.

"But which cities?" he whispered. If he was Beloc trying to find Melera, a few factors had to be considered. She was passing for human but at six feet, two inches, she was also tall for a human woman. She'd have to be somewhere where she wouldn't stand out too much. He pointed the remote at the map and pressed another button. A small, glowing white dot appeared, denoting Seattle since she was here. He aimed it at a different spot and a small star representing New York City appeared. He aimed it a third time and a star for London lit up. Then Paris. Chicago. Los Angeles.

By the time he finished, he'd decorated the map with twenty stars. He leaned back in his chair. Now that he decided where on Earth Beloc was most likely to be found, he had to figure out how to find him. *I'll definitely need some help. Who can I call?* He studied the map. The regents of every city except the Master of Brooklyn owed him a favor or three. He frowned. *I'd hate to be indebted to Charles. Can we do without Brooklyn?* Then he sighed. *No, I'll have to include him. Hopefully, he won't ask for too much in return.*

"Now that I've got the where, all I need is the how." He closed his eyes and let his mind wander. Presently, his thoughts centered on the scent of human blood wafting inside from under the door. He smiled. One of the powers that had returned to him was that he didn't need to feed every day. He hadn't fed since before Garrett had come over and they'd done their telepathic experiments. That was a week ago. Kurt didn't question his lack of need. It would last as long as it would last, and he was content with it.

His smile broadened. *Blood is the life. I can smell blood a mile away and I can tell if it's animal, human, or zot. If I know them, I can even tell who they are.* He took a deep sniff. *Robert and Mary Jane are in the hallway…I wonder if she knows she's pregnant…*

His eyes flew open and he sat straight up. *Stop. That's it. Melera's blood. Her blood chemistry would be different from everyone and everything on Earth. Her smell should be—well, alien.* He pursed his lips. The few times he'd been close enough to get a whiff of her, he'd been too distracted to remember her scent. He would have to figure out a way to get close to her again.

"That's easy," he whispered. He picked up the phone and punched a speed-dial button.

"Berenson," a voice on the other end of the line said.

"Parker—it's Kurt."

"I know. What do you want?"

"Must you be so rude? Anyway, I want to invite you and Melera to Harrow for dinner tomorrow night."

Parker was silent for a minute. "Mandy," he growled.

"Yes. But don't blame her. She's just concerned. And you were going to bring Melera to me sooner rather than later, hmm?"

He brushed aside the question. "Why do you want to take us out?"

"It's the least I can do after she saved you, Garrett, and me from that demon, don't you think?"

"I think she'd rather have a box of cigars."

"And so she shall." Kurt paused. "I could always order you to come to Harrow, but I'd really rather not."

There was a sigh on the other end of the line. "Oh, all right. What time?"

"Say, eight o'clock?"

"Fine. We'll be there." Parker hung up the phone.

Replacing the receiver in its cradle, Kurt sat back in his chair and smiled.

The next night at eight o'clock sharp, the maitre'd of Harrow showed Parker and Melera into one of the restaurant's private dining rooms. The dinner consisted of porterhouse steaks—nearly raw for Parker, rare for Melera—with steamed vegetables, shrimp scampi, and fresh dinner rolls. Kurt had a bowl of clear chicken soup. Unfortunately, the power to eat any human food he wished had not returned to him.

As soon as Melera walked through the door, he knew he was right. She smelled faintly of old silver with a whiff of cinnamon and some other scent he couldn't identify. "Welcome back to Seattle Melera," he said with a bow. "Please. Sit down."

They walked over to the medium-sized round table and sat. The two ate while Kurt made small talk. Neither was a scintillating conversationalist but that was all right with him. That wasn't why they were here.

After dessert, Parker fairly leapt from his seat, pulling Melera with him. "Well, thanks for dinner Kurt, but we'd better be going."

"Of course. But first…Melera, these are for you." He reached beneath his chair and brought out a cigar-sized, elegantly wrapped box with a white bow. "With my compliments, my dear." Then he stood and walked them to the door. "Thank you both for coming. Melera, it's wonderful to see you again." He picked up her hand and kissed it, discreetly taking a long sniff. A moment later, Melera pulled her hand away. "Good-bye, you two. It was a pleasure."

After they had left, he sat back at the table with the remains of their dinner. He wondered what Beloc smelled like. *Never mind—whatever he smells like, it won't be like anything anyone's ever smelled.* But now that he had some idea of how to find Beloc, he needed to figure out what to tell the other vampire regents when he asked them to go look for him. He stared at the ceiling. Ten minutes later, his face lit up. *Of course—play on the one fear that we all have—a zot pogrom. So I'll say there's a new kind of zot, a mutant, who is very dangerous and needs to be caught before he does something to spark one.*

Dissolving into mist, Kurt sped to his office and materialized in his chair. First, he'd call the Mistress of Chicago. Not only did the Mistress owe him a couple of favors but they were also friends. His fingers curled around the receiver and he began to lift the handset from its cradle. Then it occurred to him. It was so obvious he didn't understand why he hadn't seen it before. He let go of the phone and sat back. *It'd be ludicrous to think*

Beloc would attempt to look for Melera alone.

He spun his chair around and looked at all the cities he'd highlighted. His eyes widened. It would be foolish to try one city at a time. Melera could have come and gone by the time Beloc and his—*people?*—arrived. So there would be an alien contingent for each city. *And what of the other cities in the world?* Kurt thought his choices logically sound, but he really had no way of knowing which and how many cities Beloc had chosen to look. But that was almost beside the point. The real question was how many aliens would it take to comb a city the size New York or Los Angeles? Five thousand? Six thousand? More?

He stared at the map without seeing it. Mandy was wrong. To find Melera, Beloc couldn't have brought just "a few guards" with him. He'd have to bring something akin to an invasion force. Did Beloc plan to take Earth hostage until Melera was captured? Or, as Parker had speculated, was Beloc planning to take over the planet?

His lips tightened. Getting rid of Melera didn't seem so important anymore. "I can't tell them the truth," he whispered. "They'll think I've gone mad." He leaned back in his chair. His thoughts kept circling back to his original idea about mutant zots. It just seemed so silly, now. But what could he say to convince the other regents?

The telephone rang. He stared at the map for a few moments, blinking his way out of his reverie. Now in the present, he turned his chair to face the desk. He let the phone ring twice more and picked up the handset. "Kurt."

"I'm glad I found you in," a sultry female voice said on the other end.

"Ah, Ciara. My Mistress of Manhattan." He had been instrumental in her victory in the will contest for the borough, thereby securing her position as the top vampire. It had been a favor she could never repay and they both knew it. "What can I do for you, my dear?"

"I'll get right to the point. Kurt, has anything strange been happening in Seattle lately—say, over the past month or so?"

"Like what?"

Silence on the other end. "I don't know how to explain it."

"Why don't you tell me what's happened?"

"Several of my vampires have reported odd-smelling humans who can disappear."

Kurt's face went still. "What do you mean by 'odd'?"

"They don't smell human and can do things no human can do. One of my vampires insisted the man or woman he followed smelled like lead. Another of my vampires followed one who turned a corner into a blind alley. He got there just in time to see the human disappear. Not turn to mist, not shape-change. Disappear. And Kurt? He said he—or she—smelled like…sulphur."

Kurt pursed his lips. "What did they look like?"

"No one knows. They were wearing hoods. But they did look homeless."

"How many times has this happened?"

"Fifteen. All over Manhattan."

"Too many times for coincidence, then. Did any of your vampires try to make a meal?"

"No. And I've ordered them not to."

He tapped his finger on the desk. "Have you been keeping a record of these sightings?"

"Yes. I've got a map pinned on my wall. Place of sighting with different colors denoting the smell."

"Good. Keep it up. Have you called the other Masters and Mistresses in the city?"

"No."

"Don't. This might be confined to Manhattan. How's your relationship with the *weres?*"

"Not very good but they'll talk to me."

"Call them. Their nose for blood is almost as good as ours. If we can get them involved the faster we'll find a pattern if there is one."

"Thank you, Kurt. I-I'm glad I called you."

"As am I, Ciara. Keep in touch."

"I'll do that. Good-bye."

"Good-bye." Kurt hung up the phone and turned back to the map. "So the aliens have landed in Manhattan," he murmured. "How long before they spread to other parts of the city? Or the country?" He looked at the spot indicating Houston and Los Angeles. Should he alert the Master and Mistress of those cities? He shook his head. It was too early. *Best to wait a little while. Let's see what Ciara comes up with, first.*

Kurt picked up the remote and aimed it at the map. The door panels had just slid shut when there was a knock at the door. He placed the remote on the credenza and spun his chair around. "Come."

The door opened and Daniel, his colony's executor, stepped inside followed by a young, slender Asian man wearing worn but clean clothing. Kurt frowned. "Daniel, who is this?"

"This is Henry Wu. He's come looking for a job. He meets all of the...qualifications. Wu, Mr. Masters."

"Daniel, I don't have time..." Then he sighed. "Very well. I'll talk to him. Leave us, please."

Daniel handed Kurt a sheet of paper and withdrew from the office.

"Please, sit." He scanned the paper Daniel had given him while Henry made himself comfortable. "So...Henry Wu, is it? How did you find us?"

"I was sitting on a park bench and this lady came up to me and gave me a card. She said if I needed a job, I should go a certain address. So I did. I answered some questions and I was told to come here."

"What kind of job are you looking for?"

Wu's gaze was steady. "I'll do anything."

"Hmm. It says here you're from New York City. What brought you to Seattle?"

"I'm an actor. I was invited to join a small troupe but they folded. Now I have no money to get back to New York, or even to buy food."

"Have you tried the homeless shelters?"

Wu hesitated and looked down. "Yes. But...I-I can't go back there."

Kurt was silent for a few moments. "I understand. So what did you do in New York for work?"

Wu raised his head, leaned forward and grinned. "I was a waiter, mostly. Upscale restaurants. I also worked as a painter with a company that did interior renovations."

Hmm. Kurt reached over and pressed a button on the sleek intercom unit. "Daniel, would you send Sarah in here, please?" Sarah was Kurt's "human resources" officer.

Seconds later, there was a knock on the door. "Come." Sarah entered the office with a clipboard full of papers. "Sarah, what do we have open for a painter?"

Sarah flipped a few leaves and shook her head. "Nothing."

Wu's face fell.

Kurt noticed it. "What about wait staff?"

Flipping a few more leaves, Sarah consulted another sheet of paper. "Mmm…we have an opening at Harrow. Gary Medlow just gave a week's notice."

Kurt beamed. "Perfect. Henry, please go with Sarah and get fitted for a uniform. Your training starts now. Oh yes, and Sarah? Find him a place to sleep tonight." He pressed the intercom button again. "Daniel, come here, please."

Henry looked like he was about to cry. Kurt smiled. "Welcome aboard, Henry," he said genially and put out his hand.

Henry grabbed it and pumped hard. "Thank you, thank you, Mr. Masters. I won't disappoint you." He rose and left the room with Sarah just as Daniel came through the door. He sat in the chair Kurt's newest hire had vacated. "Well, what do you think? Are you going to make him into a servant?"

"Mmm. He is ideal. Orphan, homeless, far from what he's familiar with, desperate…" He paused. "We'll have to see. Wu does know what we are, doesn't he?"

"He must suspect, at least. After all, it is after dark. As far as I know, most employment interviews take place during the daytime, even for nightclubs and restaurants."

Kurt nodded. "All right. Let's see how he does and then we'll go from there."

"Sounds good." Daniel rose to leave. "I'm going to get someone to drink. See you later." Daniel rose from his chair and started across the office. He was just about to open the door when Kurt called out. Daniel turned.

Kurt stared at him. "Let me know if you see or smell anything… strange."

Daniel gave him a curious look. "Will do." Then he left the office.

Elbows on the desk, Kurt tented his fingers over his nose and thought about Henry Wu. He couldn't put his finger on it but there was something about the young man that bothered him. His responses—the crestfallen expression, the arm pumping—seemed overdone. *An actor, hmm? Well, actors tend towards the theatrical. Just look at Garrett.* Then something occurred to him. He frowned. There were many acting troupes in Seattle but he hadn't heard of any of them folding. *I'll ask Garrett about that. She's sure to know.*

His jaw tightened. *And if Wu is lying…he will be one permanently dead young man.*

CHAPTER 18

hree nights after their dinner at Harrow, Parker downed the rest of his shot of Jack and checked his watch. It was six-ten p.m. He looked over at Melera, who was curled up on the couch and thumbing through a picture book. "Sweetheart, the pack's coming at eight tonight for our new moon meeting. Do you mind disappearing for a couple of hours or so?"

"No." She didn't look at him.

"Good. I really appreciate—"

"Me not go."

Parker closed his eyes and then sighed. He'd had a hard day, and he wasn't looking for a fight. "Listen, I'm not asking you to stay out all night."

Melera looked up. "Me say me not go."

"Melera—"

"What part 'no' you not unnernstand? Me not go," she shouted.

"Come on, Melera," he said, trying to keep his temper. "Except for dinner with Kurt, you've been cooped up in this house for over a week. You won't go anywhere or do anything. The first time you were here, you were dying to get out. Now you're like some recluse."

Melera narrowed her golden eyes. "You say me pack. Me stay."

"Yes, I say you're pack but that doesn't mean you need to be here. They resent us, Melera. Being with you, they think I'm disrespecting them. And I am."

"Tsey know me here. Tsey smell me."

"True. But it's better if you're not here."

"Me stay."

That's it. "No you're not," he shouted. "You're getting out of this house if I have to throw you out!"

"You do, me not come back," she yelled.

"Are you threatening me?"

"Is promise!"

Parker threw up his hands. "What the hell's the matter with you? I ask you to go out for a while and you act like I've asked for the moon. Melera, I'm too tired for this. I said you're going out and you're going."

"Me say not." Her eyes spun fast. He knew her well enough to know that she was really pissed. She picked up a small but heavy crystal wolf and hurled it at him. Then she ran upstairs.

He caught the wolf and slammed it down on the bar. Then he ran after her. When he got to his bedroom, he flipped on the light and stopped short. Melera was pacing the bedroom, biting her thumbnail. But that wasn't what had startled him. He'd seen that look on her face only once before. She was frightened. He hurried over to her and caught her arm. "Sweetheart, what's wrong? Please tell me."

Melera said nothing, nor did she look up.

Then it dawned on him. Her unwillingness to go outside. Her more than was usual bitchiness. "Come on. Sit over here and tell me about it." He led her to the overstuffed chair by the bed and sat. Pulling Melera into his lap, he began stroking her hair. "Tell me."

"Beloc out tsere, Pawkher," she whispered. "Him and his stawlee-juns."

"You don't know that."

"But tsey might be."

Parker lifted her chin and stared into her whirling golden eyes. "God…what did they do to you?"

She told him. The lasers, the rapes, the beatings, the drugs, the mental tortures, and more. She told him about her many surgeries, mostly on her brain. "Me tsink tsat's why me have the see-zures, Pawkher. Beloc's 'bot sur-juns fooking in me head."

Listening to the details of the abuse she'd suffered was sickening. His jaw tightened. *Sonofabitch…if I ever find that asshole, I'm going to torch him.* After she'd finished her narrative, he pulled her close and kissed her ear. "No wonder you're afraid of Beloc."

Melera let out a light snort. "Beloc? No." She started trembling. "What he do if me he catch? Yes."

He pushed her to her feet and stood, then wrapped his arms around her waist. "I understand, sweetheart. Listen, you don't have to go. Just stay up here."

She shook her head. "No, you right. Me not stay. Me cause trooble. And like you say, Beloc and his stawlee-juns might no be here."

"Well, would you feel safer in Underground?"

"No. Me go ship. Me feel safer tsere."

Parker nodded. "Okay." He took off his watch and fastened it around her wrist. "You remember how to tell Earth time, don't you?"

"Yes."

He kissed her forehead. "Come back at ten and stay in the bedroom in case anyone's still here. I'll make this meeting as short as I can. And Melera?"

"What?"

"Today was my last programming job for the next two weeks. What say we go to your base in the South Pacific? Would you feel safe there?"

Her face lit up. "Yes."

"All right, then. We'll leave as soon as you return. I just have to make sure I'm back in time for the full moon."

She smiled. It was the first one he'd seen on her face in what seemed like forever.

He grabbed her wrist and looked at the time. "You'd better get going, sweetheart."

"Pawkher?" she said, her voice soft. "Me love you."

He gave her a gentle kiss on her lips. "Me too, baby."

She disengaged from his embrace and stepped a few feet away. "Me be back."

He grinned. "You'd better." He watched her eyes close. The bright flash from the universal fabric being torn blinded him. The Void's cold blast ruffled his hair. When he could see again, she was gone.

Staring at the spot where Melera had stood, a feeling of emptiness flooded through him. Then he left his bedroom and with slow, measured steps, walked downstairs and headed for his study. He sat in his old desk chair with the cracked leather seat and let out a tiny sigh. He was so lonely without her. But duty called and he couldn't shirk it.

Parker closed his eyes and rocked in his chair. A few seconds later he opened them and reaching over the desk, picked up a half-smoked joint and torched it. He took a few tokes and put it out. Looking up, he stared at the bookcase above his desk, then shook his head. The house was too quiet. Rising to his feet, he walked outside and lay on the patio chaise, letting the soft, cold rain envelop him. Now he could hear the sounds of the night, the rain hitting the patio stone and the occasional swish of car tires rolling down the street in front of his house. He stared at the eight-foot privacy fence and the hedges he'd planted that were almost as tall.

Sensing it was time to go inside, he glanced at his wrist and remembered he'd given his watch to Melera. He walked to the study window. Wiping the rain off with his sleeve, he saw by the clock that it was six thirty-five p.m. He entered his house, trudged to the front door and unlocked it. Then he went upstairs to change clothes.

Parker returned to the great room. Now clad in jeans and a sweatshirt, he crossed the great room to the bar, poured himself a shot of Jack and downed it. Pouring another, he went back into his study. He sat in his desk chair and swallowed his second drink. Picking up his joint, he smoked the last of it then stubbed it out in the ashtray. He put his elbows on the desk, hid his face in his hands and sighed.

Mandy would be here soon.

At precisely seven p.m., the front door opened and Mandy stepped inside. She closed her umbrella and dropped it into the stand next to the door. She turned to him. "My freyr."

"My freya," Parker said, sitting on the fourth stair on the staircase.

She took off her wet raincoat and hung it in the closet. Then she climbed the stairs and sat next to him. He turned and she licked his lips, the standard lupine gesture of greeting and submission. After she'd pulled away, he gazed into her brown eyes. "Wanna beer?"

"Thought you'd never ask."

He rose and walked into the kitchen, returning a minute later with two green bottles. "Here," he said, handing one to Mandy. Then he resumed his seat on the stairs. They toasted each other and drank.

A few seconds passed, then Mandy wrinkled her nose. "Is she here? I can smell her."

"No."

"Good."

Saying nothing, he took another swig of beer. Then he and Mandy began discussing the night's agenda. As usual, there was much to do. Parker hoped they could finish it all by ten.

At seven-fifteen p.m., Tasha arrived. A Fourth-ranked werewolf, her job was to prepare the snacks for the meeting. After taking off her coat, she greeted them in the lupine way and bustled off to the kitchen. If she had caught Melera's scent, she gave no sign.

By seven forty-five p.m, the rest of the pack came trickling into the house. Per pack protocol, Tran Ngyuen, the pack's beta and Parker's second in command, was the last to arrive. After taking off his coat and throwing it on top of the pile by the door, he greeted Parker and Mandy and took his seat on the third stair. Below him sat Rhonda, the pack's secretary, her laptop booted up and ready to go. It was now eight o'clock p.m.

Parker swept his gaze over the nineteen of the twenty-three wolves in his pack. Janet and Shirley, he'd excused from tonight's meeting since their cubs were too young to attend. A pang of sadness went through him. Last spring, his wolves had filled his great room. Now, after the revolution's slaughter, they didn't fill half that.

He also noticed the pack seemed restless. He was pretty sure it was because they'd caught Melera's scent. They were probably wondering if her presence would be a repeat of last summer, when he'd been so involved with her he'd neglected them. He thought about Melera on her ship, alone and scared. *Fuck them. I'm doing what I'm supposed to do.*

"Okay, let's get going," he said. "First order of business—let me introduce George Kolchak, visiting from Chicago." George stood, and the pack applauded. A minute later, Parker held up his hand for silence. His gaze swept the room again. "Speaking of out of town, who's going to be on the road over the next month?"

For the next two hours, he and Mandy slogged through the mundane administrative chores of running a wolf pack. It was time for a rotation, so they reassigned the pack duties of emergency contacts, cub sitters and drivers to the hunting grounds. They mediated the disputes between wolves. There had been no infraction of pack rules over the last month so there was no need to hand down punishments. It had occurred to him many times that from what he'd been told, pack life was far different than it had been a century ago when the pack had met once a month for the full moon's hunt.

They finally made it through the agenda. "All right, any new business?" Parker said. No one answered. "Okay, that's it, then. G'night and stay human." He watched his pack leave his house. He didn't want anyone lingering behind. When everyone had gone, he turned and walked upstairs to his bedroom.

He didn't have long to wait. Within three minutes, he saw the flash and watched as Melera entered the room. She ran into his arms and he kissed her, hard. "I missed you," he whispered into her hair.

"Mm-hmm." She squeezed him a bit tighter.

He finally stepped out of her embrace. "Come on. I can't wait to get out of here. Let me just pack a bag—"

"You need not wearings. Me have plenty."

Parker smiled. "You do? In my size?"

She nodded. "Rep-lic-ator. Make any wearings you want."

"Oh. Okay. Forgot about that. Well, at least let me get my shaving kit." He walked down the hall to the bath and threw his razor, a couple of cans of shaving cream and a few other items into a small bag. Then he returned to the bedroom. "Let's go."

He led her out of the bedroom and so was the first to see Tran standing at the bottom of the stairs. He whipped his head around. "Tran's here," he said in an urgent whisper. "Your eyes." He watched as Melera's czado disguised her alien eyes into the familiar dark amber, human-looking ones. They started down the stairs.

"She's ba-a-ack," Tran said.

"Tran. What are you still doing here?"

"Was she here the whole time?"

"No."

"Then how'd she get upstairs without me seeing her?"

Parker hesitated. "Tran, what's this about?"

Tran stared at him. "I want some answers, Park. I don't believe your story that Melera's some exchange student you knew in college. Who and what kind of zot is she? She's got a scent that makes me horny as hell.

Somebody with that kind of effect makes me nervous. Is that the hold she has on you? Because you're so pussy-whipped, you don't know whether you're coming or going. I mean, she leaves last summer and you're moping around, just going through the motions of being alpha wolf. Now she's back and all of a sudden you act like you really care about us."

Parker's eyes narrowed. "You got a problem with the way I run the pack?" he said in his wolf's growl.

"Don't change the subject. We're talking about Melera."

He sighed. "She's my lifemate, Tran," he said in his normal voice.

"Any fool can see that. But you know the rules. Nothing wrong with having a bit on the side but your freya is supposed to be your lifemate. And your freya is Mandy. So now I'm back to my question. Who is she?"

"You been talking to Mandy?"

"No. Should I?"

He took a breath to say something, but Melera beat him to it. "No try 'splain, Pawhker. Tran be you second. Is time for troots."

He frowned. "Sweetheart, are you sure about this? The more people who know——"

"Know what?" Tran said.

Parker took her hand and started down the stairs. When they reached the fourth stair, they sat. "Melera's an alien, Tran. As in from outer space."

Tran gave him a disgusted look. "You must think I'm some kind of moron." He turned and started for the door.

"Stop," Melera said in Xia'saan.

Tran stopped in mid-step and turned. His head swiveled left and right. "What was that?"

Parker said nothing. He watched Melera's human-looking eyes fade into her golden, slit-pupil ones. Then she spoke again. "It's true, Tran. I'm from another galaxy."

Tran spun around. His eyes widened. "Wha—say that again."

She did.

He stared, slack-jawed.

"She's got a spaceship, too," Parker said, his voice smug. "You wanna see it?"

Tran turned to him. "Hell, yeah."

Melera stretched out her hand. "You hold, and hold tight."

Parker watched her eyes close. There came the familiar flash, followed by the sensation of bone-chilling cold, and then the cold disappeared. He looked around. They'd materialized on the ship's bridge. He turned to Tran. "Now do you believe us?"

Tran said nothing. He looked around, his jaw hanging open again. "H-how'd we get here?" he finally said.

Melera smiled. "We skip tsrough Void."

"We skip through what?"

"Void. Nutsingness."

Tran walked around the bridge, touching everything and saying nothing. Then he turned. "This is unbelievable."

"Believe it," Parker said.

"Kyle," Melera said in Xia'saan.

"Yes, Shen'zae?"

"Show yourself."

A black humanoid with glowing red eyes appeared. Tran jumped. "What the hell?" His eyes bugged.

"Tsis Kyle," Melera said. "Me ship's..." she looked at Parker.

"Artificial intelligence."

"Yes." Then, with him tagging along, she took Tran on a tour of the corvette. She showed him how she could change the environment into anything she pleased. Then she showed him the large and small replicators and how they worked. They took the lifts below decks and she showed him where she kept her supplies and lastly, the drive deck.

After they'd returned to the main deck, Tran held up his hand. "Okay, I've had enough. System overload." He turned to Melera. "Would you take me back now?"

She nodded with a small, satisfied-looking smile.

Tran looked around again. "I am so not going to sleep tonight."

"Neither am I," Parker said with a wink.

Melera shot him a sideways look. "You ready, Tran?"

"Yeah."

She held out her hand and he took it.

"Wait," Parker said. "Tran, Melera and I are going to be away for about ten days or so. I'll be back in time for the full moon. Tell Mandy, will you?"

"Sure."

"Oh, and one more thing. I don't have to tell you not to tell anyone what you saw tonight."

"Don't worry. I don't like straightjackets."

Parker watched the two disappear. After they'd left, he returned to the bridge. Melera was back moments later. She stepped over to him and slid into his arms. "We ready?"

"Ready."

They parted. Melera sat in the command chair and Parker sat in the second's. She fired up the ship's four drives.

Then they took off.

CHAPTER 19

While Parker met with his wolves, Garrett, sitting before the mirror in her dressing room, dipped her cupped fingers into a white jar and then smeared a healthy dollop of cold cream on her face. Grabbing a tissue, she started wiping at the cream. The heavy stage makeup slid off her cheek. The play she'd starred in, *Jazzy*, had its last performance tonight, and tired as she was—playing the female lead had been a taxing role—she was looking forward to the cast party tonight.

A throbbing ache began behind her eyes. She stopped her wiping and jumping from her stool, ran to her dressing room door and locked it. Then she sat on the floor in front of it. Folding her legs into a half-lotus, she closed her eyes and dropped into a trance. It took only a second or two for her to reach the by-now-familiar woods. She chanted the spells that dressed her in silver and gave her strength. Sprinting through the trees, she arrived at the cave entrance and entered. A ball of witch-light appeared in her hand. She balanced it on her palm while she ran through the cave.

Reaching the cave's opposite wall, she tossed the ball toward the ceiling. In its glow, she could see her wolf's paws trying to move the rock holding it in its prison. She leapt. Mentally chanting *pondus*, she increased her weight by five times and landed hard on the rock. Her wolf's howl of pain reverberated through the cave and her paws disappeared from the rock's edge. "That's three times I've had to come down here to keep you in your place," Garrett panted. "When are you going to learn? I'm stronger than you are. Do you need another beating to make you understand?"

She heard a soft mewling and then a low growl. "Sor-ry."

Her heart skipped a beat. Her wolf was learning to talk. That meant her strength was growing. If she didn't learn that Garrett was in charge and soon, her beast might become too strong for her to contain. She shook her head. She couldn't think about that. Her wolf might hear. She pushed her fears aside and tightened her lips. "All right, then. Don't make me have to come down here again."

A hard pounding reverberated through the cave. Garrett looked up. She knew what it was. "Motherdamn," she whispered. She chanted the counterspells even as she ran through the cave. Bursting from the cave's entrance, she ran through the woods and in less than twenty seconds had reached the spot where she always materialized. A moment later, she popped out of her trance and was back in her dressing room. Now the pounding seemed deafening and the vibrations from the beaten door tickled her back.

"Garrett. Garrett! Are you all right?" a voice shouted.

She jumped to her feet, unlocked the door and opened it. "I'm fine, Sarah," she said with a smile. "I'm a little tired so I was just meditating a bit to get back some of my energy for the party tonight. Hope I didn't scare you."

Her understudy smiled back. "You did."

She returned to her makeup table. "Sorry. Come on in."

Sarah stepped through the doorway. "Does that meditation stuff really work?"

"Sure does. You should try it sometime."

"I'd only fall asleep."

Garrett chuckled. "It does take practice." She peered at Sarah's reflection in the mirror. "What's up?"

Sarah didn't answer right away. "Well, I, um…"

Her look turned questioning. "Spit it out, woman."

"What are you going to do with all these flowers?" Sarah blurted, her gaze roaming over the seven huge bouquets of flowers ranged about the dressing room.

Garrett shrugged. "Give them to whoever wants one, I guess. It'd be a shame to throw them away."

Sarah's face brightened. "Oo…can I have one?"

"Sure. Any one you want except that one." She pointed to the arrangement nearest the door. It had arrived that night, with birds-of-paradise and gladiolas. "That one's mine."

"Okay. This is the one I want." She gestured with her head at the arrangement with dark, purplish-red roses and baby's breath.

"Take it, then."

"Thanks, Garrett." Sarah bounded over to the large flower vase and lifted it. She staggered under its weight. "Much heavier than I thought."

"Why don't you get someone to help you?"

"Nah, I got this."

She watched Sarah wobble over to the door and ease through the opening. Then she heard the erratic click of Sarah's heels on the smooth hallway floor. "Hope she doesn't kill herself trying to carry that thing," she whispered. She'd just taken a second swipe at her face when Larry, her co-star, appeared in the doorway. "Sarah told me—"

Garrett smiled. "Anyone except that one." She pointed to the arrangement she'd indicated earlier to Sarah.

"Cool. I'll take this one." Larry picked up a basket of orchids and turned to leave. "You know, these flowers have been here all week and not one of them has started to wilt."

She nodded. "Amazing what florists can do these days to preserve them."

He fingered a card on the bouquet he held. "I wonder who this Basile Roche guy is. These weren't cheap."

"Probably some little old man with nothing better to do with his money than to go to the theater and send flowers to the female lead. Right now he's probably back in the nursing home, fast asleep."

Larry chuckled and left.

The scene repeated four more times. When all of the arrangements except the one she'd wanted had disappeared, Garrett turned her full attention to taking off her makeup. After she did that, she washed her face and neck, then braided her hair. She crossed the room to the clothes stand that held her street garb. Pulling a couple of items from the rack, she dressed in a pair of warm woolen stockings and a tunic sweater. Lastly, she retrieved her cloak from the stand, shrugged into it and grabbed her purse. She picked up the vase of flowers. Like Sarah, she staggered under its weight. Unlike Sarah, she had a ready means of alleviating her burden. Chanting a float spell, she felt the huge vase lighten until it was no heavier than an average load of laundry. She stepped out of her dressing room and joined the gaggle of actors and stage crew heading for the cast party at the Purple Penguin, a bar and restaurant a few doors down from the Stohlman Theater.

Outside, she walked to her car. It was cold, just the way she hated it. Unlocking the vehicle, she wrestled the flowers into the back seat. After securing her car, she turned to leave but stopped after hearing someone call her name.

"Garrett? Garrett Larkin?" a rich, masculine voice said.

She looked up. Under the parking lot lights, standing about six feet away, was one of the most beautiful men she'd ever seen. Of medium height and elegant in his obviously tailored coat and scarf, he had a smile that lit up the night like a Roman candle. She stared at him. His eyes bored into hers. Looking into them, she felt as if she were falling down a well.

"Miss Larkin? I'm Basile Roche." He held out his hand.

Garrett shook off the feeling and stepped forward. She took his hand and smiled. "The flower man."

He laughed. "Is that what you call me?"

"Well, anyone who sends huge bouquets of flowers every night for a week is bound to be called something."

His smile faltered a bit. "I've wanted to meet you since the first night I saw you in *Jazzy* a week ago. You were magnificent."

"Thank you." She peered at him. "You've been coming to the theater every night for a week?"

Basile nodded. "I just had to see you perform." Then his look grew tentative. "Would you like to have a cup of coffee or maybe a bite to eat with me?"

She thought about the cast party just getting started. She really wanted to go to the Penguin but if Basile had become a fan of hers over the past week, she didn't want to alienate him. And a cup of coffee sounded like a good compromise—that way she wouldn't have to linger. She smiled. "Coffee would be nice."

The Roman candle grin returned. "How about that little café over there?"

"Sure."

They began to walk. Neither spoke. "Are you from Seattle?" Garrett said to break the silence.

Basile smiled. "No, I'm from…elsewhere."

"What brings you here?"

"Business. I'm in import-export. I'm thinking about opening an office here and wanted to get a feel for the city."

A minute frown creased her forehead. Import-export could mean anything from drug smuggling to fine art. She gave him a covert glance while they walked, eyeing his expensive cashmere coat and silk scarf. "What sorts of things do you import?"

"Oh, a little of this, a little of that."

Definitely drugs. Now she had second thoughts about that cup of coffee. *Oh, come on,* a little voice in her mind said. *For all you know, he imports women's underwear.*

They reached the café. Basile held the door open for her. She walked inside, grateful for the warmth. The café was self-seating and he chose a table in the corner, away from the windows. After they'd made themselves comfortable, a waiter materialized and took their orders. While they waited, Basile began talking about his life. Garrett was fascinated. She was no stranger to the international set but Basile, it seemed, had lived all over the world. *He must be older than he looks.*

Their coffee arrived. He still hadn't run out of steam. Then she noticed something. Basile looked at her intently while he spoke as if trying to gauge her reaction to his stories. She wondered if that meant he was lying. *Doesn't matter. It's not like I'm going to see him again.* She continued to listen, enjoying herself.

"And then my family was killed in a zot pogrom," he said. "They simply got caught in the wrong place at the wrong time."

Her heart went out to him. "I'm so sorry. How old were you?"

"It happened a few years ago. I was living in London at the time." He fell silent. "Sometimes it's still hard to believe they're gone." He looked pensive for a moment and then gave her his dazzling smile. "Let's not talk about such a sad subject tonight. Why don't you tell me about yourself?"

Garrett shrugged. "There's not much to tell. I'm from Ireland, I studied acting at university and I came here about fifteen years ago when the Stohlman Theater invited me."

"Fifteen years? But you look so young."

She smiled. "Well, I left school when I was sixteen. And the

Stohlman invited me soon after that," she lied. The truth was that she was forty-four years old.

"Excuse me folks—we're closing," their waiter said.

She looked at her watch and raised her brows. She'd been so absorbed in Basile, she hadn't noticed the time. She'd better get over to the Penguin. They stood and he helped her into her cloak. Then he shrugged on his coat and wound his scarf around his neck. They left the café.

"I'll walk you to your car," Basile said.

"That's very kind of you, but it really isn't necessary. I'm going to the bar down the street for the cast party."

"Then I'll walk you there. It's late. I'd feel terrible if something happened to you on my account."

"Nothing..." She dipped her head. "Okay, sure." They walked along the deserted sidewalk in companionable silence.

"Ah...here we are," he said after a few minutes. "This is the one, right?"

Garrett looked up. "Yes." She wrapped her hand around the brass handle shaped like a penguin. "Basile, I had a nice time with you tonight. I hope—"

"I hope you'll go out with me again," he cut in.

She smiled. "Basile, I think—"

"How about tomorrow?"

Still smiling, she studied him for a moment. She had a strict policy about dating humans. To keep up appearances, she'd date them once but no more than that. She made sure of it by casting a spell beforehand that made her dates feel a vague discomfort around her. After their date had ended they might promise to call again but she knew they wouldn't. Basile had caught her by surprise but in the end, he would be no different.

She was readying her spell when a pang of regret went through her. She really did have a lovely time listening to Basile and his stories, and now it was over. But her policy allowed for no exceptions. Then she had an idea—one that would allow her to stick to her rule, yet continue to enjoy herself for the moment. Basile wanted to go out with her tomorrow? Her smile broadened. "How about tonight? Come in and join the party."

His expression was that of a little boy who'd just been handed what he wanted for Christmas. "A perfect idea." Removing her hand from the door handle, he grasped it and opened the door for her.

By now, the party was in full swing. Alice, the Penguin's proprietress, hurried up to them. "Hi, Garrett! We were wondering—" Then she saw Basile. "Sir, this is a private—"

"It's all right, Alice," Garrett said. "He's with me. Alice, this is Basile Roche. Basile, Alice. She owns the Penguin."

Alice and Basile shook hands. The Penguin wasn't large, and a few of the cast sitting closest to them turned their heads at the mention of Basile's name. Jimmy Lawless, the stage manager, stood up with a huge grin. Garrett could tell from where she stood that he was more than a little drunk. "Hey, everybody," he shouted, "it's the flower man!"

All talk stopped. Everyone in the Penguin turned and stared at them. Sue, Jimmy's wife, spoke first. "Jimmy, sit down." Jimmy obeyed, sliding drunkenly into his seat. "Forgive him," Sue said to Basile. "He's off his meds."

At that, everyone in the bar burst into laughter, including Jimmy. "Aw, Sue..." he said, and then said something else Garrett couldn't hear.

The laughter subsided and the partygoers surged toward the two of them. Basile, borne away by the crowd, left her standing at the door. Alice took Garrett's cloak. "Looks like you've lost your companion."

She smiled. "That's okay. I'm sure he'll find his way back."

Alice led her to a small table close to the leading edge of the bar. Garrett sat. "What'll you have?" she said.

"Red wine will do fine."

"You got it." Alice walked away, returning a few minutes later with her order. Then she went back to the bar.

Sipping her wine, Garrett watched the goings-on. Basile was a hit. By now, he'd charmed the entire group. Even Alice, a no-nonsense businesswoman, didn't seem to be immune. Then she noticed Kelly, one of the stagehands, sitting at the bar on the crowd's fringe. She was the only one who didn't seem to be amused by Basile.

"Kelly," she called. The other woman turned. "Come sit with me." Kelly grabbed her drink and purse, then walked to the table. She pulled up a chair and sat. Her eyes were glassy. Garrett took another sip of her wine and eyed her, wondering why Bryan, Kelly's fiancé, wasn't here tonight. "Where's Bryan? Something wrong between you two?"

Kelly's eyes became even shinier. That was when she realized the look in her eyes wasn't drunkenness, but tears.

"Bryan disappeared."

"What?" she said, horrified.

Kelly nodded. "He's gone, Garrett."

"What happened?"

The other woman bowed her head. "It was awful. Bryan and I were supposed to go out last Wednesday night. I called and called but he never answered. I called his office the next morning and they said they hadn't seen him, either. Then the special police came to my apartment and took me downtown."

"That was Thursday, the day you called to say something had come up and you wouldn't be in."

"Right. They gave me a GST and when it came back human, the police grilled me for hours about whether I knew Bryan was zot, promising a plea deal with the Special D.A. if I'd just admit the truth." Kelly looked up. "Well, I *was* telling the truth. I didn't know. Finally, they gave me a lie detector test—you know, the ones that are supposed to be super-duper accurate?—and that proved it. After that, I asked what kind of zot he was. They said he was a werewolf. I told them he didn't change with the moon or anything like that and they…they said the GST indicated he had more than enough genetic material to classify him as a zot. I asked who sniffed him but of course they wouldn't tell me." She fell silent a moment. "Bryan was scrum, Garrett. Not even a real werewolf." A single tear trickled down Kelly's cheek.

Garrett handed her a napkin. Neither woman said anything for a long while. "You know," Kelly broke the silence, "I was raised to believe all zots were evil. And last year's revolution seemed to bear that out. But Bryan…Bryan was the kindest, gentlest man I've ever known. I've spent several nights wrestling with myself since he disappeared but my upbringing be damned—I loved him, Garrett. Even if I'd known Bryan was scrum, I'd have married him. I'd have married him even if he was a full werewolf."

"But you'd go to prison if anyone found out."

Kelly shrugged. "What's ten years in prison compared to the rest of my life without Bryan?" She bowed her head again and stared at the table. Then she looked up and sighed. "I want to go home. All this"—she waved her hand—"camaraderie is getting to me." She stood. "Thanks for listening, Garrett. I...I needed to talk to someone." Leaving her glass on the table, she watched Kelly go to the coat rack, grab her coat and walk out the door. No one seemed to notice her leave.

Garrett tightened her lips and stared into her near-empty wine glass. *Motherdamned sniffers.* Sniffers were human men and women who had the uncanny ability to distinguish zots from humans with pinpoint accuracy. No one knew how they did it. No one knew who they were— not even, in all likelihood, the special police. All anyone knew for sure was that they were rare.

But not rare enough. She drained her wine. She'd long suspected that sniffers—whoever they were—were also phenomenal psychics. How else would they be able to tell the police the identity of the zot they'd sniffed, much less where they lived?

"I'm sorry I've neglected you," Basile's voice sounded, almost in her ear. Garrett jumped a little and turned. Basile stood to her side, smiling. "You looked like you were deep in thought. I hope you were thinking about me." She smiled back. "Actually, I was thinking I should go home. I'm tired, and it's catching up with me."

"Then by all means, you should. Here—I'll get your cloak." He walked to the coat rack and returned with Garrett's cloak and his own coat. She stood and he helped her put it on. He slipped on his coat and buttoned it up. His smile broadened. "Shall we?" He raised his arm. She took it and they headed for the door.

"'Bye, Garrett," someone called out. She turned. It was Stan, the lighting engineer. She waved. "Goodnight, everybody," she called back. "I'll see you later."

Outside, it was just as cold as it had been earlier. She turned. "Well Basile, I've had a good time tonight and I know you have, too. It's always a pleasure to meet a new fan and I certainly enjoyed meeting you." Smiling, she mentally cast her spell over him.

Basile put a hand on her arm. "Oh, but this won't be the last time, will it? I must make amends for ignoring you tonight."

Garrett stared at him in shock. Her spell hadn't worked.

Basile peered at her. "Garrett? Is something wrong?"

She recovered herself. "No, no…I'm all right. Basile, I really need—"

"Is Sunday all right with you? How about brunch?" he talked over her and gave her that Roman candle grin.

"Brunch is fine." Flustered, right now she would say anything to get away from him. She fished in her purse for a small, silver-colored case, and drew it out. Opening it, she extracted a card. "Here's my cell number. Why don't you give me a call Saturday to make sure nothing's come up?"

Basile took the card eagerly. "This is one meal I look forward to. And now, I'll walk you to your car."

Garrett started to protest but gave up when she saw the resolution in his eyes. He was gallant; she had to grant him that. They walked across the street to the mostly empty staff parking lot. She located her car and unlocked the vehicle, got in and started the engine. She stuck her head out the window. "Goodnight, Basile. I'll see you on Sunday." She pulled out of the parking lot. In her rearview mirror, she saw Basile wave to her.

She didn't wave back.

Driving through the streets, she thought about what had happened. She bit her lip. Why hadn't her spell worked? It wasn't a spell for a novice but for someone like her, it should have been child's play. And she hadn't had any trouble using her magick before now. What had changed? Had the tryst taken more of her talent than Feodor had thought? Frightened, her mind churned with various possibilities and none of them good. Then something he'd said came back to her. "Your magick may be erratic, cherie. Sometimes it will work just fine and at others, not so much. When it doesn't, you mustn't fret. You must simply try again." Comforted by the memory of her mentor's words, Garrett's small hands loosened their death grip on the steering wheel. "Okay, Feo," she whispered in the dark confines of the car. "I'll try again."

Coming out of her fog, she was surprised to see she was almost home. She drove the last couple of blocks and parked in her usual space in front of her cozy little house. She got out of the car, hauled the flowers out from the back seat and then secured the vehicle. Walking up the front steps, a wave of tiredness crashed over her. Between the play, Basile, and worrying about her magick talent, she'd had enough of the evening and just wanted to be in bed.

Reaching her front door, she set the vase of flowers on the porch and then fished in her purse for her keys. She was about to put the key into the lock when she decided to try something. Concentrating a moment, she muttered an unlocking spell and was rewarded by the sound of the tumblers turning. It was an easy spell but it made her feel better. She thought about Basile and what had happened—or hadn't happened— earlier and gave her head a little shake. As for him, well, she'd just have to wait until Sunday.

Picking up the flowers, she turned the handle, pushed the door open and walked inside.

CHAPTER 20

Garrett and Basile's Sunday date didn't start out well.

Saturday had been a tough day for her. She'd spent most of it at Balthus Temple working with seven other witches to refresh the Pax Omnia, a peace spell that they'd been maintaining over the city since the revolution to help keep human hostility toward zots at a low ebb.

It had been her turn to serve as the spell's focal point. All of that magick concentrated in her body had left her worn out. She had many errands to run after the spell had been cast and on one, while she'd been at the makeup counter, Basile had called about Sunday. The clerk had been asking her questions so she'd said yes to get him off the phone. By the time she'd returned home, it was late. On top of that, despite drinking two cups of chamomile tea, she hadn't slept well. So today, tired and cranky, she was in no mood to see anyone, much less go out on a date.

Watching out of her living room window, Garrett saw a gleaming black stretch limousine pull up in front of her house. "Oh, no," she whispered. A zot's survival in human society depended in large part on remaining inconspicuous and this car was about as inconspicuous as an elephant on roller skates. She watched a chauffeur in full livery emerge from the car, walk up the steps and ring her doorbell.

If Basile's trying to impress me, it's not working.

She opened the door and started. The chauffeur obviously had been badly injured sometime in the past. His face was lopsided, with one gray eye lower than the other one. His skin looked like a mass of burn scars and his mouth wasn't much more than a hole in his face. He barely looked human.

"Miss Larkin," he said. His words sounded slurred. "Mr. Roche is here for you. Please come with me."

"Y-yes." The chauffeur's impassive gray stare made her nervous. "Just let me get my coat." She ran to the closet and choosing her brown alpaca wool cape, threw it on. Then, plucking her purse off the sofa, she walked to the front door. "Ready."

Without a word, the chauffeur turned and headed down the stairs. Garrett shut the front door and followed. Reaching the car, the chauffeur opened the car door for her and she slid inside the vehicle's plush interior.

Basile took her hand and kissed it. "Garrett. I'm so glad you could come today."

"No problem. So where are we going?"

The car pulled away from the curb. If it hadn't been for the scenery flowing by outside the window, Garrett would swear they weren't moving at all.

"Well," Basile said, "first I thought we'd have brunch at the Rose and then we'd visit an art museum. I haven't been to any of them since my arrival and I'm anxious to go. What do you think?"

"Fine with me."

Then Basile started prattling about his interesting life again. She listened for a moment. His chatter had been fascinating the night of the cast party but right now it irritated her. *Bad enough he picks me up in a limo but brunch at the Rose? One of the most expensive restaurants in town with the most mediocre food. And does he ever stop talking? Oh, Mother—why did I agree to go out with him?* Suppressing a sigh, she did the only thing she could do in a situation like this—her ears tuned him out, while her mouth and throat made polite noises when it was called for.

As always these days, her thoughts turned to Kurt, Parker, and Feodor. Feodor had called the other night to give her an update. "Nothing yet, cherie. But I am still digging. How are the three of you making out?"

Her hear had sunk. "We're hanging on, Feo." She didn't tell him about her last episode with her wolf, deciding it was better not to put him under any more pressure than he was under already.

"Garrett," she heard Basile snap. She jumped. She'd been so deep in her thoughts she didn't realize they'd reached their first destination. She turned. "Oh. I'm sorry. I was thinking about our next production at the theater." Basile, she thought, looked a little miffed. *Too bad. Maybe this'll let you know you're Mr. Boring.*

The chauffeur came around to open the door for her. She noticed they were getting looks from some of the people on the street. It made her cross. *Haven't you ever seen someone get out of a limo before?* she wanted to say. But she didn't.

She heard Basile giving instructions to the chauffeur and then he was by her side escorting her into the restaurant. The maitre'd seated them and with a flourish, presented them with menus. Garrett tried not to roll her eyes. They each studied a menu for a few moments, then looked up. A waiter walked over to them, took their orders and left. Then they were alone again.

Basile gazed into her eyes. "Enough about me, Garrett. How do you feel about zots?"

Her brows twitched in surprise. This was the last question she would have expected out of Basile. *Remember, he thinks you're human.* "They should be shot on sight," she said, spewing the party line. "The only good zot is a dead zot."

"Why?"

"They're unnatural and they shouldn't be allowed to live. Thank God for the genetic screening test. Otherwise, we'd never know who they are." Garrett felt sick after her invective but it had been necessary. More than ever now, she just wanted to go home and hide under her blankets.

She'd been just about to tell Basile she had a headache when their food arrived. She decided to give him a chance to eat before asking him to take her home. While she waited, Garrett toyed with her spinach omelet. She didn't feel like eating.

Basile took four bites of his eggs benedict and put down his fork. "This is just awful. And they charge how much for this?" He leaned forward. "I notice you haven't eaten your omelet. Did you know the food was this bad?"

She nodded.

"Why didn't you say something?"

"I thought you were trying to impress me."

Basile threw his head back and laughed. "Well, yes, I was," he said after his laughter subsided. "A business associate of mine suggested this place." Then he frowned. "He didn't say anything about the food, though.

I really don't know how they stay in business, especially with these prices."

Garrett saw her opportunity. "Speaking of trying to impress me, that limo out there doesn't do it for me, either."

Basile looked embarrassed. "It's not meant to impress you. I don't drive very well. I've never been in an accident but I think I've caused a few. So for my own and other drivers' safety, I hire a limo and driver wherever I go. I usually hire a simple sedan but this was the only car the service had left."

Garrett smiled, her first genuine one of the day. "Listen, Basile. There's a little bistro around the corner that serves excellent food. Let's go there and have brunch and then we'll go to the museum. Okay?"

He smiled back. "Sounds perfect." His smile turned into a grimace. "First, though, I want to speak to the maitre'd about this horrible food. I'm not paying a dime for it."

She waited while Basile conferred with the maitre'd. In a few minutes, the two were walking toward her. As they came closer, she thought the maitre'd looked terrified. She didn't know what Basile had said to the poor man but he practically shooed them out of the restaurant.

Brunch at the bistro was much more relaxed. Basile no longer talked about himself, and seemed more interested in her, asking what it was like to be an actor and how productions are chosen for a particular season. After they'd finished, he asked which museum she'd like to visit.

"Let's go to the Mitter. There's always a new exhibit there and it's only a couple of blocks away."

"Okay, let me call James and tell him where to meet us."

"James is the chauffeur?"

"Yes, why?"

"Oh, nothing. Just nice to be able to call him by his name instead of 'hey, you.'"

While Basile called James on his cell, Garrett took a few discreet steps away. "All right," he said. "James will meet us at the museum when we're finished. Come on. I want to get out of this cold."

She laughed. "Well, that's something we have in common. I hate cold weather, too." They hurried along the streets to the Mitter. Basile paid the entrance fee while she waited. Then the two set about wandering through the museum.

Garrett was pleasantly surprised that he knew so much about art. "Well, art has always been one of my interests." Basile looked around and then pointed to a nineteenth-century painting of a red-haired girl tending sheep. "Take this one." He leaned in close. "It's a forgery," he whispered, "and an excellent one."

"How can you tell?" she whispered back.

"I imported the original for a private collector in England some years ago."

"Do you think the museum knows they have a fake?"

He chuckled. "I've no idea. But then, it's not my problem, is it?"

All too soon, the museum was closing and they had to leave. Basile called James and by the time they got to the door, the black car was waiting for them, James holding the door open. Garrett climbed in first, then Basile. A minute later, they were headed for her house. Neither spoke during the ride uptown.

When they arrived, she realized she didn't want their date to end. She'd cast an identification spell to learn whether he was zot or human while they were in the museum but it hadn't worked. It disturbed her but she'd shaken it off, figuring her magick was being erratic again. Still, she'd never felt so relaxed when out on a date. Usually she was on hyper-alert, monitoring her every move so as not to do or say something to give her magehood away. Today, she took some care not to reveal her true nature but she didn't feel like she was under siege while doing it. But that didn't mean she would date him again. Some zots couldn't be trusted any more than humans—all it took was an anonymous phone call.

She turned to find Basile giving her an unreadable look. "Would you care to go out with me again?"

Garrett smiled. "I'd love to," her mouth blurted before her brain could stop it. Basile's return smile seemed to light the car's interior. "Well, I've business out of town for a couple of days, so why don't I call you when I get back?"

"Fine." She exited the car while James held the door for her. "Thanks, James," she said but the chauffeur said nothing. He didn't even acknowledge she'd spoken. She gave a minute shrug. *Maybe that's his training.* She walked up the stairs to her little house and fitted the key into the lock. After opening the door, she turned and waved. The black car glided away from the curb.

Stepping inside, Garrett closed the front door and walking to the closet, hung up her cape. Then she paused. What was she doing? She shouldn't be dating anyone. Not while she, Parker, and Kurt were still connected like they were. Not while she was still part werewolf. But for those few hours she was with Basile, all of the tension that had kept her tied in knots over the past two months had disappeared. Feeling at ease had almost felt foreign to her.

Then she yawned. Though it was only late afternoon, she felt more than tired—she felt whipped. She closed the closet door and trudged upstairs to her bedroom. The spreader bar was still in the corner where she'd left it, and the handcuffs were still attached to the bedposts where she'd left them after one of her and Kurt's scenes the other day. Her box of toys sat in the closet doorway. She shook her head. She'd clean them later. Right now, all she wanted to do was sleep.

Garrett disrobed and pulled a warm nightgown over her head. Then she crawled underneath the blankets and closed her eyes. She opened them a few seconds later. She couldn't stop thinking about Basile. *Maybe he'll forget about me.*

But she doubted it.

CHAPTER 21

The following afternoon, in one of Harrow's private dining rooms, Kurt sat at a linen-draped table with an enormously fat man, Mr. David Alter. The remains of a sumptuous lunch littered the space around Alter's chair.

The fat man shook his head. "I don't see how you can get along with just a bowl of soup. I'd be starving by dinnertime."

Kurt smiled. *You'll be starving within the next hour,* he wanted to say but kept his mouth shut. He didn't like Alter but he'd just closed a deal for two hundred million dollars to build an office tower for the man and he wasn't about to offend him. "Well, Mr. Alter—"

"Dave."

He dipped his head. "Well, Dave, I usually have something a bit more…robust in the evening."

"Urmph. I don't understand anyone who doesn't like to eat."

Kurt's smile tightened. *I'll bet you don't.* Then he frowned a bit. "I know it's a tad early, but would you care for some cognac to celebrate our mutual good fortune?"

Alter beamed. "I certainly would."

Kurt signaled Henry Wu, who was waiting on them. "Henry, we'd like some cognac, please."

"Anything special, sir?"

He had just opened his mouth to suggest a vintage but Alter beat him to it. "Just bring out the finest you've got." He turned to Kurt and grinned. "Nothing but the best for your clients, eh, Kurt?"

He gritted his teeth. "That's right, Dave." The man had already drunk two bottles of Harrow's top-rated wine, which went for four hundred dollars per bottle.

Henry returned two snifters. Placing one before each man, he poured the cognac with an expert touch. Then he withdrew and left the room, bottle in hand.

The fat man raised his glass. "Let me propose a toast. To the Alter Corporation and its new digs." They clinked glasses and drank.

A moment later, Alter coughed into his drink. "What the hell is going on?" he sputtered, sounding outraged and frightened at the same time.

Kurt looked at him with alarm. "What are you talking about?"

"That," Alter said in a loud voice. "Your reflection—it's gone."

Damn. This was the only one of the "little magicks" he hadn't quite mastered. Unlike the other spells Garrett had taught him he couldn't seem to make this one last more than four hours or so, and if he didn't renew it regularly his image would fade out. He'd spent most of the morning with Alter in his downtown office where there were no mirrors and so didn't think about it. He muttered the spell while turning in his chair. By the time he'd turned completely around, his reflection was visible.

He turned back in his chair and peered at the fat man. "Are you all right? Maybe what you saw was a trick of the light. It's dim in here. And that's an old mirror. It's probably flawed."

Alter's face knotted and turned red, almost purple. "I know what I saw," he shouted. "Your reflection disappeared and then it came back. What the hell are you? Some kind of zot? You must be a vampire. I'm calling the police." He snatched his cell phone from his breast pocket.

Kurt sat back in his chair and gave the other man an incredulous look. "Dave, calm down. Think about it. I can't be a vampire. It's the middle of a beautiful sunny day."

Alter's angry expression melted into uncertainty. "I've heard tell of vampires who can walk in daylight."

Kurt let out a heavy sigh. "Well, how about this? We just sat here and had lunch. Have you ever heard tell of vampires being able to eat human food?"

The fat man hesitated. "No."

Kurt smiled. "So you see, I can't be a vampire, hmm? Besides, if I was a vampire, you'd be dead right now, don't you think?"

Now Alter sighed. His color returned to normal. He looked at the mirror, then back at Kurt. "I guess I would." He shook his head. "Sorry for the misunderstanding." The fat man returned the cell phone to his breast pocket.

"Not a problem, Dave. I wouldn't deal with a zot, either. Disgusting creatures. At any rate, I'll talk to the management and have them replace that mirror. Wouldn't want this to happen to anyone else. They might not be as reasonable as you are."

They finished their drinks while talking about construction schedules. The two men rose from the table just as Henry walked through the door. "Your limousine is downstairs, Mr. Masters."

"Very well. Please take Mr. Alter wherever it is he wants to go."

Alter frowned. "You're not coming?"

Kurt smiled. "No, I think I'll walk back to my office. Catch a little sun, hmm? Besides, I've decided I'd like a word with management before I leave here. The faster they know about that mirror, the faster they can get it replaced."

Alter nodded. "I'll see you in a few weeks with those architectural drawings."

Kurt's smile broadened. "Of course." Henry and Alter left the dining room. He walked over to the gargantuan, ornate mirror that had hung in his office beneath Chance before he lost his powers. Staring at his reflection, he narrowed his eyes and rapped a knuckle on the glass. "Traitor," he muttered. He sighed. It wasn't the mirror's fault. Then he thought about Jack Hewitt, whose hotel one of his other companies was renovating. This was the second time his powers had deserted him while lunching with a human. *Perhaps I should take a long vacation before I end up permanently dead.*

In the mirror's reflective surface, he saw the door behind him open. Henry stepped inside. "Is he gone?" Kurt said.

"Yes, Master."

"Thank you, Henry. That will be all."

Henry inclined his head and left.

Kurt turned his attention back to his reflection. *Did Henry hear what happened? I hope not.* The last thing he needed was for his human servants to know something was wrong with their master. Though he'd laid a psychic block on them so that they couldn't speak to anyone about his special powers, even among themselves, he didn't know whether that block had held up after he'd lost them.

"There's got to be a way out of this disaster," he whispered.

He sighed again. *I need to get out of here. Be alone for a while.* Dissolving into mist, he flew to his penthouse.

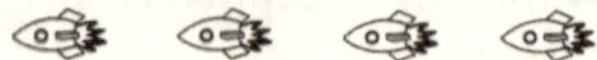

Inside his penthouse, Kurt lay stretched on the sofa, his hands behind his head. He stared at the ceiling, wondering if Feodor had found a cure for the three of them. *Well, we haven't heard from him, so I guess he's still working on it. He'll let us know as soon as he finds something.*

He closed his eyes, wishing he could erase Alter's memory of what he saw. But that too was one of the powers he'd lost. Worse, the ability to erase memories was just a run-of-the-mill regent's power. *I wonder if there's a spell for that. Maybe Garrett could teach it to me.*

His cell phone rang. "Damn," he muttered. He'd forgotten to turn it off. Pulling the phone from his breast pocket, he looked at the caller ID. It was Mandy. He pressed the talk button. "Hello, Mandy. How nice to hear from you. What can I—"

"Thanks for kicking Melera out of your city." Her voice dripped with scorn.

Kurt blinked. *Oh, no.* "I, uh—"

"Problem is, Parker went with her."

His eyes widened. "What?"

"Any idea where they went, Kurt?"

He placed his arm on his forehead. "No. I've no idea."

"Well, if you hear from your *servant*, tell him to call me so I can string him up by his balls."

"Mandy, I—"

She hung up. Kurt took the phone from his ear and stared at it. No one, but no one, had ever hung up on him before. His lips tightened. He would not tolerate such disrespect. Not from Mandy nor from any other zot in his city. She would pay for that. His thoughts flashed on his present, weakened state. *Someday, anyway.*

Still, he'd lied about not knowing where Parker and Melera were. He knew perfectly well they were on her base in the South Pacific. He'd heard them talking about it last summer after the two had returned from one of the uninhabited San Juan Islands, where she'd hidden her ship. She'd promised Parker she'd take him there someday. "And there's absolutely no way to get in touch with them," he muttered. "Out there, they might as well be on the moon." He turned off his phone, threw it on the low table beside him and grimaced. Then he had a thought. *Maybe I could find Melera's base.* He stared at the ceiling, pondering.

Kurt rolled his eyes. "No. That's just idiotic. How many deserted islands are there in the South Pacific? Even if I could find it, how would I get in? Knock on the front door?" He shook his head. He needed Melera in order for his plan to get rid of the aliens to work but it would have to wait until she and Parker returned. He just hoped they wouldn't be gone too long.

He lay on the sofa, his thoughts drifting until they settled on Henry Wu. He'd turned out to be a fine waiter, one of the best on Harrow's staff. But even though Kurt had made him into his servant, he still didn't trust him. The young man had probably lied about his acting troupe folding. Garrett had told him no company had come to Seattle that she knew of but cautioned that if the troupe was small enough, she might not know about it, especially if they folded before they had a chance to book any performances.

Kurt decided to see if he could find out what Henry was up to now. Closing his eyes, he pictured the young man in his mind. This particular power of his was unpredictable. Most times it didn't work but every so often he could tune in to one of his servants. This time he felt a movement in the ether. He concentrated harder. Henry's fuzzy image appeared in his mind's eye and slowly cleared. The young man was talking on the phone to someone in one of Harrow's private dining rooms. He frowned. What was Henry doing calling someone while he was on duty? If he was on break, why wasn't he calling from the phone in the break room? More than that, if he didn't know anyone in Seattle, who would he be calling? Then Henry's voice came through but it was hard to understand, sounding like a radio transmission full of static. He waited. It too slowly became clear.

Henry was speaking Chinese. Kurt was fluent in Mandarin and Cantonese but this was a dialect he didn't know. He listened some more.

He was sure he'd heard the dialect before but he couldn't place it. But whether he could understand or not, it still left open the question of who Henry was calling. Kurt had never forbidden his human servants who lived with the colony—like Henry—use of the telephones. But not all telephones were for personal use. For a brief moment, he thought about misting over to Harrow and confronting him but then thought better of it. *He's still pretty new. He might not understand all the rules, yet.* Regardless, he shouldn't have been using that particular telephone.

He watched Henry hang up and leave the room. Changing his mind, he decided to speak to Henry about using the phones in Harrow's private dining rooms. *Put a little fear in him, let him know I was watching.* He would do that after Henry's shift ended. He looked at his watch. *Which will be at four and it's just after two oh-five now. Tonight I'll take a look at the daily call log and see where he called.* He thought for a few moments. *Meanwhile, I should get going on drafting a construction schedule for Alter's new building.*

Rising from the couch, Kurt took one last look around his penthouse. Dissolving into mist, he flew to his downtown office.

Late that night, in his velvet-lined office underneath Chance, Kurt finished the last of the paperwork that was the lot of the successful businessman. He sat back in his chair and thought about Henry Wu. He'd confronted him after his shift was over about using the telephones in Harrow's private dining rooms. "The phones in the break room are for staff use," he'd said. "Not the dining rooms."

Henry's eyes had widened as if in shock. Then his expression had turned stricken. He'd clapped his hands to his ears and shook his head. "I'm so sorry, Master. I was on break, and...I didn't know. I won't do it again. I'm really sorry." He'd let his hands drop to his sides, a pleading look on his face.

Kurt had smiled. "Quite all right, Henry. You're still on a learning curve and there's a lot to learn about working for me. You're doing fine."

Henry had looked as if he was about to cry and fall on his knees in gratitude. "Thank you, Master. Thank you."

"Very well. You may go now."

Henry had turned and fairly run out of Harrow's management office.

Back in the present, Kurt pursed his lips, thinking on that conversation. He shook his head. *Such theatrics. Is he really that demonstrative? Or is he acting? If he's acting, he should leave it for the stage.* Giving his head another shake, he turned his attention to the computer. "Now to look up that call," he whispered. Pulling the keyboard to him, he opened the menu and selected the appropriate file. Rows and rows of calls made that day from all of his offices appeared on the monitor. *Let's see…it was about two o'clock when I tuned into him.* Clicking on a few keys, he jumped down the list to the calls that had been made in the early afternoon. He peered at the screen while slowly scrolling down the rows. It wasn't long before he found it. His eyes widened. Then his brow darkened and his eyes narrowed. Anger surged through him.

Henry Wu had placed a call to Shanghai.

"Li An," he muttered. "You bitch." Curling his hand into a fist, Kurt pounded the desk a few times. Then he leapt to his feet. He strode across his office but stopped when he reached the door. *Wait. There might be a better way.* Returning to his desk, he sat in his leather executive's chair. He leaned back, closed his eyes and put in a telepathic call to Daniel, his executor.

In moments there came a knock at the door. Kurt opened his eyes. "Come."

Daniel opened the door and entered. "You rang?"

"Yes." He pointed to a chair. "Sit down. We've urgent business to discuss."

Daniel sat. "Like what?"

"Henry Wu is Li An's spy."

Daniel frowned. "What makes you say that?"

"Come here." Daniel walked around the desk and stood behind him. "Look. This is the call log for today. At one fifty-seven, Henry called someone in Shanghai."

"That doesn't mean anything. Maybe he was calling his—"

Kurt looked up. "Didn't you say he was an orphan?"

"Yes, but that doesn't mean he doesn't have living relatives. Aunts, uncles, cousins…maybe even brothers and sisters."

He said nothing at first. "Maybe. But I still think it's quite a coincidence."

Neither vampire said anything for a minute or two. Daniel returned to his seat and cocked his head. "May I ask a question?"

"Of course."

The other vampire stared at him. "Why would Li An send someone to spy on us?"

Kurt gave a minute start. He'd been so angry, he didn't even think about what he was doing by calling Daniel. Well, it was too late now. He could lie with the best of them but he wouldn't lie to Daniel. Daniel was more than just his executor—he was his closest friend.

"It's very complicated," Kurt said slowly. "I won't bore you with the details unless you really want to know. The bottom line though is that I've lost most of my regent's powers. But I've also acquired mage-level magick powers. I've been getting along by using the spells Garrett taught me."

Daniel still stared. "So what does Li An have to do with it?"

"Li An suspects I've been sorely weakened. If I know her, she will find a champion to wrest my domain from me. Or maybe she'll even challenge me herself."

"Why would she do that?"

"She hates me. She had to put down a rebellion in her colony soon after she became Mistress and I wouldn't help her. She's never forgiven me." He leaned back in his chair. "And so, that's why I think Henry Wu is Li An's spy. To see how weak I really am."

"And you think Henry had something to report?"

Kurt nodded and told him what had transpired that afternoon with his client during lunch. "I think Henry was listening at the door. Of course, it wouldn't have been difficult. Alter was yelling loud enough to wake the dead."

Daniel said nothing for a long while. "Kurt, why didn't you tell me this earlier?"

"The truth? I was frightened. I *am* frightened. I figured the fewer people who knew—only Parker, Garrett, and a mage named Feodor know—the better off I'd be."

"So what are you doing about it now?"

"Feodor's working on a spell that can get us back to normal."

"Us?"

Kurt sighed. "Yes. It involves the three of us. Parker's got much of my power and Garrett has some too, though she has mostly Parker's powers—she's part werewolf."

"Which means Parker's part vampire."

"Yes."

Daniel let out a breath. "This is seriously messed up." He shook his head. "Okay, Kurt. I'll cover for you as best I can. Meanwhile"—he gave Kurt a meaningful look—"what do we do about Henry Wu?"

"Spy on the spy, of course. I want him to have as many friends in this colony, vampire and human, as he can. I want to know every move he makes. And I'm taking him out of Harrow and putting him to work in Chance. I want to give him every opportunity to spy on me."

"Are you sure that's wise?"

"I'm sure it isn't. But I want him to keep reporting to Li An for now. Let her think her plan is working."

"You're not going to—"

"Allow Henry to see my weaknesses? Only a few. I'll fake others. Just enough to lay the bait. And then…"

Daniel cocked his head. "What?"

Kurt smiled. It wasn't pleasant. "I'll invite Li An here. And then I'll kill him. Right before her very eyes."

"You kill her servant, she could declare war on us."

He shook his head. "She's already invaded my domain by sending him to us. I'm perfectly within my rights. If anything, I should be declaring war on her."

"Are you going to do that?"

Kurt snorted. "I don't have time for such pettiness."

Neither vampire said anything for a long while. "Kurt," Daniel broke the silence, "is there anything else I ought to know?"

He opened his mouth to say "no" then closed it. Should he tell him about the aliens? As his second, he had a right to know about anything that might affect the colony. He thought for a minute and made up his mind. "Daniel, I know you're going to think my weakness has addled my brain, but we have space aliens in our midst."

Daniel's face was impassive. "Go on."

Kurt told him the whole story, as much as he knew of it. "So before you ask the answer is no, I don't think Beloc will leave if we give Melera up to him. An entire planet ripe for the taking? I certainly wouldn't. He could set himself up as some sort of emperor and we'd be his slaves."

Daniel's face remained impassive. "But you don't know how an alien's mind works."

"But I know how business works. I suspect that whatever else he might be, at bottom this Beloc is a businessman. And he holds all the cards, so to speak." He tightened his lips. "We've got to figure out a way to get him to leave. Preferably before he announces his presence to the world." He peered at the other vampire. "Do you believe me?"

Daniel didn't answer at first. Then he smiled a little. "My head tells me you've lost your mind. But my gut tells me otherwise." He paused. "I believe you. What now?"

"I have to gather the Masters and Mistresses of all the cities where I think Beloc might be looking for Melera. That'll be twenty of us." He told Daniel which cities he'd targeted.

Daniel frowned a little. "Why those cities? There are so many to choose from. Why not, say, Lima, Peru?"

"You've seen Melera. She's over six feet. The average height for a man in Peru is about five feet five inches and the women are even shorter. She'd stick out like the proverbial sore thumb. Then there's her skin color. She'd have trouble in a place like Moscow. That night in her apartment—you remember?—I learned she's a shifter, so yes, maybe she could blend in that way, but the fact that she's constantly in her natural form tells me she can't hold on to a different one for long. Not more than a few hours, I would think."

"All right, I'll buy that. But those are all big cities. What makes you think this Beloc's going to be looking for her in a mid-sized city like Seattle? I know the metro area numbers in the millions but surely he's not going to comb the suburbs and the rest of the cities, too."

"Never know."

Daniel looked at the ceiling and then back at Kurt. "Okay—say Melera is willing to out herself. Where will you stage it?"

"In my dungeon. We won't be disturbed there."

Daniel nodded. "How can I help?"

"Nothing at the moment. I have to talk to Melera first."

"What will you tell the regents?"

"That their cities may have been invaded by a new kind of zot—one that could spark a pogrom. Which really isn't that far from the truth."

Neither vampire said anything for a minute or two. Then Daniel rose from his chair. "When you're ready, let me know what I can do." He started for the door.

"Daniel."

He turned.

Kurt smiled. "Thank you, Daniel. For everything."

Daniel smiled back. "When you rebirthed me, I thought I'd get tired of being a vampire after about a hundred years or so. I mean, after you've seen it all it gets boring. But if there's anything I can say about life with you, it has never been that. Keep up the good work." He laughed.

Kurt laughed, too. "I'm certainly doing my best."

Still laughing, Daniel left the office.

Kurt's laughter subsided into another smile. For the first time in what seemed like ages, he felt some measure of peace.

He wondered how long it would last.

CHAPTER 22

Inside Melera's huge cavern base, Parker lay on her bed half asleep, luxuriating in his vacation from the world. These last eight days or so with Melera had been like heaven. No phones, no clients, no pack, just the two of them.

He smiled as he listened to her play her whatchamacallit and sing along with it. At first, it sounded more like noise—screeches, howls, and growls—than music. But the more he listened, the easier it was to make out themes and motifs and at times, he could even follow its syncopated rhythms. He'd gotten to the point where he actually kind of liked the piece.

His smile faltered. She wasn't playing her instrument for his benefit, he knew. It was the code she was trying to break, that would alert her battle fleet for delivery to the Vst.

The first day after they arrived, Melera had reacquainted him with her equipment. While she showed him how the small and large replicators worked, he'd heard a loud chirping from the other side of her living quarters. He swiveled his head and looked at a cluster of machines she'd told him served as her communications center. One of the colored bands on a tall, free-standing column was pulsating. He followed her over to it.

She'd looked at the colorful column. "Is message from Vst." Parker thought she didn't sound too happy to hear from them. Placing her hand on a lit, fluorescent-colored panel, he watched it turn orange as her hand sank below its surface. A message appeared over another darkened panel and seemed to float in mid-air. "Sheet. Akkad take back Kyren star system." Her lips had tightened. "Me need to work." She'd lifted her hand from the lit panel and turned away.

"Hey, wait." Parker had grabbed her arm. "I thought you hated these guys as much as you hate Beloc and his kind. Why are you working so hard for them?"

Melera had looked at him. "Is complicated."

"Try me."

She'd sighed. "Me do because me must, Pawkher. Me give ka on promise to me fawtser Tarq—"

"You gave what?"

She'd shaken her head. "Easier to show you." She took a few steps backward. "Me no more help Vst."

To Parker's horror, Melera had screamed and fallen to her knees. He rushed over to her.

"Touch me not," she'd panted, her arm lifted as if to stop him. "Me be ohh-kay."

A few minutes later, he'd helped her to stand. "What the hell just happened to you?"

"Tse ka. Me swear by me ka to give fleet to Vst. If me not do, ka drive me cray-zee."

Parker thought about it. "So this, whatever you call it, is like a piece of your soul, then?"

Melera had frowned. "Soul? What is soul?"

"Never mind. It's complicated. But I think I understand now." He'd nodded at her instrument. "Go on. Get to work."

She'd smiled a little. "Sound you do like me czado."

"Maybe, but I bet it can't do this." He'd swept her into his arms and kissed her hard. Then he'd ended it and had given her ass a little slap. "I'll be in the kitchen with Dinah if you need me."

"Huh?"

"Old Earth saying, sweetheart. I'll explain it to you one day."

Now, about to fall asleep, Parker roused himself when he realized the music had stopped. Raising himself on one elbow, he watched as Melera rose from her bench and walked to the smaller replicator. She turned to him. "Me need drink. You want?"

"Sure. Whatever you're having." Before she turned around, he thought he saw a small smile appear on her face—the one that told him she was up to something. *Just your imagination, dude,* his wolf growled.

Oh, I don't know. We both know how much she likes to pull a fast one.

The replicator dinged. Parker got out of bed and joined her at the table. He pulled a chair out for her before sitting down himself. Melera shoved an open black bottle toward him. He picked it up. It was ice cold. "Cheers," he said and raised it in a toast. They clinked bottles. He took a deep draught.

Parker thought the top of his head would come off. Choking, he spewed liquid from his mouth, then went into a coughing fit. When it had subsided somewhat, he looked at her, horrified. "What the hell is this stuff?" he said between hacks.

Melera laughed so hard, she nearly fell off her chair. "Skt," she said when she could talk again. She thumped her chest. "Is strong drink for strong peoples, yes?"

"You could have at least warned me."

She grinned. "No fun."

"Hmph." He lifted the bottle and took a tentative sip. Then he took a bigger one. So far, so good. Then he took a hefty swig and swallowed. "Hey, this stuff's pretty good once you get used to it."

They finished their Skts in silence. Melera took the bottles and dropped them into the recycler. "Want nutser?"

"If you're having one."

She turned to the replicator and fiddled with it. The machine dinged about ten seconds later. Taking them out, she returned to the table.

While Melera had been busy at the replicator, a warm glow had spread throughout his body. *Uhrmm, that feels good,* his wolf growled. *Better than Jack.*

Sure does. Maybe we can bring some home when we leave.

"Here," she said, interrupting his thoughts.

They clinked bottles again and drank. Parker felt the warm glow turn into a slow burn. "This is great, Melera. I could drink it all night."

She smiled. "We will, may-be."

It was not to be. By his fifth bottle, he knew he'd had enough. His head felt so heavy he thought it would fall off his neck. The room swam. Melera had been jabbering away at him in Xia'saan and he swore he understood every word.

He turned to her. His eyes burned. "Melera," he slurred. She kept talking. "Melera," he said a little louder. Still no response. "Melera," he shouted. Silenced, she raised her brows and gave him a quizzical look. "I gotta go to bed, sweetheart. I'm—"

"Droonk," she finished for him.

Parker closed his eyes and nodded. Then he opened one and squinted at her. "Aren't you?"

She giggled. "Yes." She stood, swaying a little. At least, he thought she was swaying. It was hard to tell when the rest of the cave was spinning, too. He watched her walk over to him and felt her arms slip under his armpits. She pulled him upright but lost her balance. The two of them crashed into the table and then fell to the floor, with Parker on top.

He rolled off of her. "Oh, shit—are you okay, sweetheart?"

She giggled again. "Oops." Then she laughed, her five voices trilling like flutes.

It was infectious. Parker stared at her for a moment and then started laughing, too. "C-c'mon, baby. I think it's time we both went to bed." Legs feeling like rubber, he rose from the floor. He took her hand and pulled her to her feet, almost falling again in the process. "Okay. I think we can make it now." Holding on to one another, they stumbled over to the bed and fell onto its cushion, laughing uproariously.

When their laughter subsided, he stared into her golden, whirling eyes. He stroked her large, tantalizing breasts through the soft material of her robe. "Off with your clothes," he whispered, tugging at the thin material. He threw it to the side. Then he did the same with his jeans. Lying down, he pulled her on top of him. Her scent was an airborne aphrodisiac, driving him and his wolf crazy with lust. Kissing her neck, he wondered if he was too drunk to perform. Then, rolling over, he kissed his way down her lush body until he reached her crotch. She was already wet. He licked her juices and then sucked on her large, inch-long clit, which was sticking up at him like a tongue.

To his surprise, he was hard. He kissed his way back up her body until he'd positioned himself just right. He slid into her. It hurt. Melera's vagina didn't have teeth like he'd thought the first time he'd fucked her but it was ribbed. The stiff ridges scraped him, abrading his skin. His self-healing ability could barely keep up. But he'd long since learned to find pleasure in the pain and he pumped her hard.

Nibbling on her neck, the hunger hit him. His teeth morphed

into his wolf's fangs. He bit her. She didn't flinch. He knew she was used to his wolf's love bites, and even enjoyed them. Her blood flowed copiously and he drank deep, savoring every drop, so lost in the heady fog of blood lust, he didn't feel her weak pushing against his chest or hear her whispered protestations. It wasn't until she stopped moving that he realized something was wrong. He quickly sat up and peered at her.

Melera was unconscious. "Oh, fuck," Parker yelled, scrambling for something to keep her warm. He found the blanket on the floor at the foot of the bed, snatched it up and swathed her in it. Then he wrapped his body around hers for extra warmth. "Please, please, please," he whispered over and over. "Please don't let me have hurt her."

An eternity later, Melera woke up. "Pawkher? What you do me?" She tried to move but between the blanket and him, it was just about impossible.

"I'm sorry, sweetheart. I just got carried away and…"

"You never do tsis before."

"I…I know. Listen, there's something I have to tell you. I'm part vampire. I'm sorry I didn't tell you before, but I thought…I mean, I know you don't like vampires."

She stared at him. "Me know not enough vam-pires to not like. Me not like Khurt."

"Are you mad?"

"Mad? Me you damn near kill." She thrashed some more. "Get tsis tsing off me."

Parker unswathed her in silence. *Oh, dear God, please don't let her hate me for this.*

Finally, she was free. She stared at him, her eyes spinning fast. He knew she was pissed. "Did you tsink tsis mean me stop loving you 'cause you tsink me not like vampires?"

He nodded.

Melera sucked her teeth. "You worse tsan silly, silly. You stoopid. Me care not what you is, Pawhker. Me love you. Whatever you is."

Parker nearly cried in relief. "I'm sorry…it won't happen again."

"It not happen again damn right. You get cupful me blood every day. You tsink tsat enough? Me can always make two."

"But sweetheart, you know what your blood does to me. I lose control. I just have to fuck you."

She smiled. "What wrong wits tsat?"

He smiled back and touched her cheek. "I've heard that before." He paused. "I took a lot of blood. Is there anything I can get you?"

"No." Melera closed her eyes. In ten seconds, her color was back and the wound he'd made on her neck had healed. "Me need sleep, now. You coming?"

"Yeah." He lay down and spooned her.

"No biting."

"No biting."

But Parker couldn't sleep. He stroked Melera's hair and listened as her breathing became deeper. When he was sure she was deeply asleep, he gently disentangled himself from her. Then he got out of bed, walked to the table and sat. He crossed his arms and lay his head down. "God, this is bullshit. We've got to find a way to get out of this mess," he whispered.

He stayed that way until Melera screamed.

"Yaah!" he yelled, jumping out of his seat and falling on his butt. "Melera, what the hell—" he started, but got no further. She thrashed about on the bed, her movements jerky and obviously out of control. He saw her muscles rippling under her skin. "Oh, no," he cried, realizing she was in the throes of a seizure. She screamed again and threw herself off the bed, landing on the cave's smooth floor with a hard thump. Then she started clawing at herself, her nails plowing deep furrows into her flesh.

Parker reached her in two bounds and tried to grab her arms. She smacked his face, leaving long, bloody scratches. He wrestled with her but it was impossible to gain control over her flailing limbs. Every time he thought he'd gotten her blood-slicked body under control, she'd slip out of his grasp and the fight would begin anew.

Let me try.

"Be my guest…hoo!" he gasped. She'd just kneed him in his groin. He morphed without feeling it, the pain of the change eclipsed by his worry and fear.

His wolf went to work. Melera's tortured spasms were no match for his eight-foot *were*. In seconds, he was on top of her, pinning her to the floor with one wrist in each giant, taloned paw. Melera continued bucking but his wolf always forced her back down.

It was over a few minutes later. She went limp under his wolf's pelted body. When he was sure she was unconscious, he slowly got to his feet then picked her up and deposited her on the bed. He got down on his knees and gave her nose a little lick. "You can have your body back now," he snarled. "I feel like killing something."

I hear you. Parker braced for the change. "Mmph!" he grunted while his bones and sinews reverted to human form. Parker-the-human stared at his lover's blood-spattered face. *She said they usually come after one of her nightmares, but… Did I cause that by draining her?* He pinched the bridge of his nose with a thumb and forefinger. *I should have stayed in bed.*

And what good would that have done? She probably would've busted your jaw.

Parker said nothing. He climbed into bed and held Melera close to him. He'd just started to fall asleep when he felt Melera stirring next to him. "Sweetheart?" he whispered. "Are you all right? Sweetheart?"

She looked up at him and frowned. "Klon ta bier?" she whispered in the language he'd heard her speak when he'd brought her home that first time. Then her eyes widened. She started pushing at him. Parker let go of her and she rolled off the bed. "Klon ta bier?" she shouted. She glanced at the holster hanging on the bed hook and grabbed her pistol. "Klon ta bier?"

He stared at the gun aimed at his chest. He'd no idea what she'd just said but he was sure she'd shoot him if he gave the wrong answer. He hazarded a guess. "It's me, Parker," he shouted back. "Parker. Come on, put the gun down. Melera, you have to remember!"

She blinked a couple of times. "Pawkher?" She squeezed her eyes shut and dropped the gun. Then she fell on her knees beside the bed and began a chant in Xia'saan. Hands clasped and her arms stretched before her, she looked as if she was praying.

Finishing her litany, she looked up. There were tears on her face, washing away the dried blood. "Me sorry, Pawkher," she whispered. "Me remembuh now." She crawled back into bed and into his arms. Clinging to him, she started to shake. Parker thought it was another seizure but then she spoke.

"Me must take you back. Tsis not work."

He frowned. "What do you mean?"

She lifted her head. "Pawkher, me almost kill you."

"And?"

"Pawkher, is too dangered to be wits me. May-be next time me kill before me remembuh."

Parker's eyes narrowed. "Uh-uh. No. I'm not leaving. If you end up shooting me, well…then you do. But I stay here."

Melera peered at him, uncertainty etched across her face. "You sure?"

"I'm sure." Stroking her hair, he thought of something. "But Melera, there is one thing you can do for me. Two things, really."

"Yes? What?"

"Teach me that language of yours. The one you were speaking when you were going to shoot me. And then you can teach me whatever it was you said when you were kneeling by the bed. It seemed to bring you out of it."

She nodded. "Is good idea. Ka always bring remembuh back, but sometimes take a while." She fell silent a moment. "But Xia'saan you no can talk."

"Doesn't matter. If I can speak that other language, maybe just saying it will help."

She cocked her head. "Start now?"

"No, sweetheart. You need to rest. From what you've told me, you won't have any more seizures. At least not for the time being." He gently pushed her head back down on his chest. "Just sleep. I'm here."

Like he had earlier, he listened to her breathing until it became slow and deep. He relaxed. Then he, too, went to sleep.

CHAPTER 23

The next morning—or night, it was hard to tell inside the fortress—Melera led Parker to her corvette. They climbed aboard and headed for the bridge. Reaching it, she pointed to the command chair. He sat. Making himself comfortable, he watched her stride about, opening little cabinets, pulling open drawers, and closing them again as if looking for something. "Can I help with anything?"

"No…ah. Here is." She withdrew her arm from a cabinet and lifted it. In her hand, she held a silver-colored circlet.

He peered at it. "What's that?"

She walked over to him and after fiddling with it, fitted the circlet on his head just over his brow. "Tsis teach you Toro." She paused. "And Xia'saan." She lifted the circlet and fiddled with it some more. Then she fitted it over his head again. "You prolly have head hurt when done. Not last, tsough." She stepped back and sat in the second's chair.

Parker waited, but nothing happened. "So when—"

Even as he spoke, his sight shifted. For a second, all color and depth bled from his field of vision. He saw Melera in black and white and in two dimensions, much like a printed comic strip. Without warning, she disappeared and myriad colors erupted around him, some of which he'd never seen before. They swirled before him, seeming to slide one way and then the other. It was like being in a psychedelic chamber. In a few seconds, the colors began spinning. His brain was spinning, too. Dizzy, he squeezed his eyes shut and swallowed hard, trying not to puke.

Then he felt something tugging on his brain from the inside. Whatever it was pulled harder and harder as if his brain was being sucked in on itself. The pain was excruciating. He was just about to scream when the agony stopped. His brain seemed to pop back into its proper dimensions inside his skull. After about thirty seconds, he cautiously opened his eyes.

Melera still sat in the second's chair, watching him. "How do you feel?"

Parker closed them and pinched the bridge of his nose between a thumb and forefinger. "Like I just got hit by a truck." Then his eyes flew open. He'd understood her perfectly—no translating involved. His head snapped up. "Wait a minute. You…we're…"

She laughed. "Speaking Toro."

"Say something in Xia'saan."

"Something in Xia'saan," she sang her musical tongue. Her five voices reverberated around the small bridge.

He grinned. "Smartass."

"That's me," she sang.

Parker rotated the circlet in his fingers. "I wonder if we can program this thing for English."

"Why?"

"So you can learn to speak the language."

Melera frowned. "Me talk good Ink-lees, yes."

He eyed her. "No, sweetheart. You don't."

She twisted her lips but said nothing.

Then he had an idea. "Hey, here's something we can do. Whenever it's just you and me, why don't we speak Toro? Give me some practice. What do you think?"

"Me tsink you not want me talk Ink-lees."

"Well, yeah."

Melera shot him a look. Then she sighed. "Ohh-kay."

Parker stood. "Now that that's done, let's get something to eat. I'm hungry," he said in Toro.

She shook her head. "Later. Now I'm going to teach you to drive my ship."

His jaw dropped. Then he grinned with delight, his hunger forgotten. "Really? You're going to teach me to fly this thing?"

"No. Drive. We say 'drive ship,' not fly." She shrugged. "Anyway, if something happens to me, you have to know how."

"What could happen to you?"

"Anything. I could get sick, maybe die…or something might happen to Kyle."

For a second, the thought of Melera dead flashed through his mind. He shoved it away. "Okay, what do I do first?"

"Sit." She indicated the command chair.

He sat. "Now what?"

"Put your hands in there." She pointed to a large rectangular opening just below the command console's lip.

He did so and looked up just in time to see her walk around him and stand next to the console to his left. She leaned against the bulkhead. "Kyle, get to know him."

Parker looked down. The gap began to glow orange, brighter and brighter. When the light reached the point where the port looked like a mini blast furnace, it began to pulse, faster and faster until it looked like a strobe light. Then it slowed until it matched the rhythm of his heartbeat. A tingling sensation started in his hands. The feeling was uncomfortable but it didn't hurt. Twenty seconds later, the glow faded and the tingling in his hands stopped. He raised his head. "What was that about?"

"Kyle knows you, now. When you tell it, the ship will obey."

"Oh. Okay."

Melera next instructed him on the corvette's various readouts. He managed to follow along as she pointed out each symbol on the heads-up display but it was difficult. There were so many of them. Understanding the manual controls was tough, too. They were touch-activated but one had to know the exact sequence of finger beats in order to make them work. When they'd finished, he frowned and turned in his seat. "Why's it so hard?"

"So no one steals my ship. Kyle won't respond and if you don't know the manual code, the ship goes nowhere." She patted his thigh. "Don't worry. Kyle will help you. It'll teach you in no time."

Parker wasn't so sure about that but he didn't pursue the matter. His stomach rumbled. "Can we eat now? I'm hungry."

Melera smiled. "Ohh-kay. But after we eat, we're going for a happy ride. You drive."

His eyes lit up. "You're gonna take me for a joy ride?"

"No. You're taking me for a—what did you say?—joy ride. There are more things to show you but I can only do that if you're driving."

A huge grin split his face. "Ohhh, cooool."

After eating, they reboarded the corvette. Parker sat in the command chair and Melera sat in the second's chair. She turned. "Ready?"

"Ready."

"Tell Kyle to take us out. Stealth shields on."

He did so and the corvette's drives began to hum. The whine from the pylons retracting into the ship grated in his ears. He felt movement and the view outside the ship shifted and kept shifting until he could see the rock wall. Then the wall disappeared. Looking out, he saw it was dark. The ship's drives revved until the hum became a roar. A moment later, they shot through the opening and into the night.

Once in deep space, Melera taught him the second way to drive the corvette. "Put your hands into the port again."

"Okay."

"Tell Kyle to give you the ship."

"Kyle, give me the ship."

The port began to glow orange again but this time the light wasn't so bright. For a second, the tingling feeling flashed through his hands. He peered at her. "What happened?"

She nodded once. "Now you have control. Turn right."

"How do I do that?"

"Just think."

Parker thought about turning to starboard, and the corvette obeyed. Then, per her instruction, he turned it to port. He practiced turning to starboard and port for a while, then he thought at the corvette to fly *straight*. He thought *up* and the ship rose. *Down*. The vessel's nose dipped.

"So how does this thing work, anyway?" he said.

"It's a biointerface port. We call this nervejacking. You're nervejacked into the ship."

He frowned. "Nervejacked? What does that mean?"

"It means you're hooked into the ship through your nervous system. It's like you and the ship are one."

"What about Kyle?"

"Kyle's here, too. But being nervejacked frees up Kyle to do other things."

After he'd gotten the hang of flying the ship as fast as he could think, Melera turned. "Where do you want to go?"

Parker grinned. "I've always wanted to see Saturn up close."

"Sa-turn?"

"The planet with the big rings."

"Then we'll go there." She ordered Kyle to give him the planet's coordinates and he thought them into the corvette's memory. Once he'd done that, she told him to think about putting the ship into hyperdrive. He did so. Nothing seemed to happen. Then, without warning, the stars winked out and they were surrounded by blackness.

"You can let go of the ship, now," she said. "It'll take a couple of hours."

He thought about relinquishing control over the corvette. The tingling sensation flashed through his hands again and the port went dark. "Now what?"

"Nothing. We wait. Come on. I'll show you how to work the ship's enviro."

"Enviro?"

"Environment." She stood.

Parker rose from the command seat. Together, they left the small bridge and descended below deck. Now they were in a large room almost the width of the corvette. He'd seen it when he'd first boarded the ship last summer and thought it bleak. The walls, ceiling, and floor were a shimmery gray. There was no furniture. He couldn't imagine taking a long space flight in such surroundings.

He followed her to a small panel set into the wall. Melera opened it. Inside was what looked like a square black hole with two stacked indentations to the right. She pointed to the one on top. "Tap it."

Obeying, in a moment a holographic mountain scene appeared. He gasped. It was beautiful.

"This shows you what you want," her voice sounded beside him. "Tap it again, it'll show you something else."

He tapped the indentation a second time and a cityscape appeared. To him, it looked utterly strange with its soaring, bulbous pink spires of varying heights. "I want to go there."

"Tap the other one."

Parker tapped the indentation below the first one and then they were in the city at street level. He swiveled his head left and right. Aliens of every shape and size plied the sidewalks. One looked like a fire hydrant. Another looked like a fish head with six short legs. Conversations, some in Toro, most undecipherable, floated around him. Flitters roamed above them, making putt-putting noises. His keen olfactory sense detected myriad smells and none of them familiar. He looked down, feeling the hardness of the—*concrete?*—beneath his feet. He knew it was just a holosensory projection but it seemed so real.

"Want to go for a walk?"

"Sure."

Melera took his hand and they started walking. "This is Struma. It's on Meril, in the Beyron star system." As they walked, she kept up a running commentary about the city. He peered into what he assumed were shop windows. Examining the merchandise, he recognized nothing.

A chime sounded. "We're here," Melera said. She gave a command and the holosensory projection disappeared. They walked to the lift and rode up to the bridge level together. Once on the bridge, they took their respective seats and Parker placed his hands in the biointerface port again. The sensors detected his presence and then he was nervejacked into the ship.

"Bring us out of hyperspace."

He thought about being in three-dimensional space and a split second later Saturn loomed before them on the viscreens. "Wow. It's even more impressive than the pictures. Prettier, too."

"Put the viscreens on bubble."

Parker thought about it and then they seemed to be floating. He looked down. Even the deck had disappeared.

She turned. "What now?"

"I want to see what's below those clouds on the surface." He gave a mental command and they were flying through the rings.

"Watch for rocks."

He nodded. From what he remembered, the rings were made of dust, rocks, and ice, some pieces as big as houses. He decided to avoid the rings and soared above them. Soon they'd left the rings behind and were orbiting the planet. He dove the corvette toward the surface and then they were below the gas clouds. The winds, which he suspected were stronger than anything on Earth, buffeted them. But there was really nothing to see because it was dark beneath the clouds and the ship's lights illuminated little. It didn't matter. He was doing something no one—no one from Earth, anyway—had ever done before. He was the first man to visit Saturn. *Too bad I can't tell anybody.*

After he'd seen enough, he directed the ship to leave the planet. They flew under the rings this time and then they were on their way back to Earth. After putting the ship into hyperdrive, they went below deck. Parker chose a different environment this time—the mountains he'd seen when Melera had first shown him the controls. The peaks, a delicate shade of blue with light pink snowcaps, appeared around them. There was no one about. They lay in the coral-colored grass, neither of them saying much. He took her hand and closed his eyes. "This must be what heaven is like."

"Heav-en? What's that?"

He explained it to her.

"Oh. Other people in Maqu think the same kind of thing." She paused. "You believe?"

He didn't answer at first. "I really don't know. I mean, if there is a God, He sure as hell hasn't done me any favors."

The chime sounded. They left the environment and returned to the bridge. Melera instructed him to nervejack into the ship. He navigated his way around the satellites and other debris orbiting Earth and then they were over the Pacific Ocean, heading for her base. Once there, she instructed him to let Kyle take over. "We'll practice going in and out later."

Kyle landed the spacecraft in the enormous cave and then the two left the corvette. Parker took her hand. "That was serious fun. Can we do it again sometime?"

She smiled. "Why not?" Then she sighed. "But now I have to work."

"Okay. I'm going to get something to eat."

"You eat all the time."

"Have to keep my strength up." He grinned.

She shook her head and headed for her instrument. He headed for the small kitchen. Punching a code into the replicator, it produced a large, meat-laden sandwich for him. Then he punched in the code for a bottle of Skt. He ate and drank while Melera played. Finishing his meal, he rose from the table and threw his plate and the bottle into the recycler. Then he sat and leaned back in the chair.

He closed his eyes and listened to Melera's playing, thinking about what he'd told her about religion. Did he believe? If there was a benevolent, all-seeing, all-knowing God and all beings were His children, why would He allow humans to slaughter zots wholesale? Even in Seattle, where humans were considered to be mellow by most world standards, it seemed not a month went by that the underground grapevine delivered the news that at least one of their own had disappeared. How could He let it happen? More importantly, why would He let it happen?

A memory blossomed in his mind's eye. His mother stood at the kitchen sink, loading the dishwasher. "God works in mysterious ways," she'd said. *Yeah—it's a damned mystery, all right. My own fucking father wants me dead because I'm a werewolf and he's supposed to be a God-fearing man.*

Another memory surfaced. This time it was of his father, the county judge, wielding a shotgun loaded with silver-coated pellets pointed at his stomach. His mother was screaming, begging her husband not to shoot her baby.

Parker, staring at Judge Berenson, had never been so scared in his life. Would his father really kill him?

"Shut up, Clara," the Judge had roared, spittle flying from his mouth. "It's not your baby anymore. It's not even human. It's a...*thing*, not fit to be walking the earth!"

The room had gone silent, except for the low keening issuing from his mother's throat.

"But I tell you what," the Judge had said, his voice tight with anger and disgust. "For Clara's sake, I won't kill you. But if I see or hear tell of you in my county ever again, I'll make sure you don't leave here alive. Understood?"

Too petrified to speak, he'd simply nodded.

"Get out."

Parker had turned and fled from the large, Colonial-style house where he'd grown up. Running to his car, he'd prayed his father wouldn't change his mind. He'd reached the vehicle unscathed and dove into the driver's seat. Fumbling the keys into the ignition, he'd started the engine and peeled rubber out of the driveway.

The images faded away. He stared at the cave ceiling. He'd escaped death by a wolf's hair that night. Was that one of God's miracles? And then there was Melera. That she, an alien of all things, had come into his life totally unexpected and that he'd fallen so deeply in love with her—was that a miracle, too?

He shook his head. He couldn't think about this anymore. His brain was starting to hurt. He'd leave the arguments on whether there was or was not a God up to the theologians and the philosophers. As for him, he was just a poor werewolf trying his best to survive in a world that wanted him dead.

Rising from the table, he threw his empty bottle in the recycler and programmed the replicator for another bottle of Skt. While the machine worked, he leaned against it, listening to Melera's playing and singing.

Parker smiled. Today had been a great day. Learning alien languages, rocketing about in a real, live alien spaceship, visiting Saturn…all with his lifemate by his side.

He didn't think about whether there would be a tomorrow.

He never did.

CHAPTER 24

The ten days passed and then it was time for Parker to return to Seattle for the full moon's hunt. Melera would rather have stayed a few more days but she understood he had his pack to think about.

The phone rang in Parker's bedroom just as the two emerged from the Void. "Damned clients won't leave me alone," he muttered. He walked over to the handset on the nightstand and picked it up. "Berenson."

Melera watched his eyes roll. "Oh, it's you. What do you want?" Turning to her, he placed a hand over the receiver and mouthed "Kurt." Now it was her turn to roll her eyes. He motioned for her to come closer so she could hear the conversation.

"—to talk to you and Melera," Kurt said. "It's very important."

"What about?"

"I'd rather not discuss it over the phone. But I really need to talk with the two of you."

"No."

There was a pause. "Then I order you to come and talk with me."

"No."

"Parker—"

"What're you gonna do? Punish me? Like to see you try."

She grabbed the receiver out of his hand. "Khurt. We come. Tell Pawkher where you be." She handed it back to him.

He gaped at her. Then he turned his head and frowned. "What? Okay, where's that? When? Okay, got it. See you tomorrow." He paused. "What?" There was another pause. "Mandy's looking for me? Why?" He fell silent, then let out an explosive breath. "Fine. I'll call her later tonight."

Parker dropped the receiver back in its cradle. "Can't even go on a goddamned vacation without somebody bitching about it." He turned. "And you—since when do you even want to hear Kurt's name, much less go see him?"

Melera shrugged. "He only wants to talk, Pawkher. No harm in listening, right?"

"Depends on what he wants to talk about."

The night of December twenty-third, Melera and Parker stepped off the elevator cab and into Kurt's penthouse. He stopped his pacing and turned. "Ah. There you are. Welcome. Come sit by the fire."

They followed him deeper inside. Kurt led them to the conversation pit in front of the massive fireplace. The two settled themselves on the sectional couch.

Kurt looked over at Parker. "Parker, do you need a glass of bloodwine?"

The wolf shook his head. "Melera is giving me all I need."

"Lucky you." Kurt sat across from them. Settling back into the cushions, he turned to Melera. "My dear, I know about Beloc. I know he's looking for you."

"How you know tsat?"

"That's neither here nor there. What's important is how he's going to go about finding you. I can think of only one way." Kurt took a sip of wine, set his glass on the low table, and leaned forward. "He has sent his people down here to comb the Earth for you."

She nodded.

Kurt stared. "In order to do that, he must have sent thousands. Maybe tens of thousands."

"Yes."

"And I also know that he just might want to stay here permanently. So tell me—what would Beloc want with Earth? In technical terms, we're light-years behind. What's in it for him?"

She turned to Parker. "You 'splain."

Parker told him about the mining and exploration purposes of the Akkad. "This solar system—and beyond—is wide open. Earth would make an excellent base of operations."

Melera looked at him and nodded again.

He stared into his wineglass. Then he looked up. "Melera, what kind and how many ships do you think Beloc has brought with him?"

"Pri-son ship, yes. Beloc travel with big fleet so he not get attack by Vst."

"How many of those ships would it take to subdue Earth?"

"Eight, may-be nine? Not many. Tsis planet no can fight even small fleet of Akkadian warships."

"I see."

The room went quiet. "I wonder where Beloc's people are now," Parker said.

Kurt turned. "I know they're in New York—Manhattan to be precise." He told them about the call he'd received from Mistress Ciara.

The wolf raised his brow. "So that's how we find them? We sniff them out?"

He nodded. "If what Mistress's vampires said was true—and there's no reason to doubt them—it should be pretty easy."

"Then what?"

"We kill them, of course."

"How? Rip their hearts out? What if they're hearts aren't in the same place as ours?" Parker fell silent. "Well, I suppose we *weres* could just tear them apart. If we do that, we're bound to hit something vital."

Kurt smiled. "That's one way of doing it."

"What's the other way?"

"I'm betting that Beloc's force is as human-like as possible. Their lungs may be where their stomachs should be but they are almost bound to breathe through the mouth and nose. We cut off the airways—"

"Strangle them, you mean."

He nodded and smiled again.

Parker rubbed his chin. "Could work."

Melera leaned forward. "One difficulty me see."

"What's that?" Parker and Kurt said at the same time.

"Personal stealts shields. Tsey see you coming, tsey disappear and excape, yes?"

Kurt cocked his head. "That's not a problem for vampires. We just mist and sneak up behind them."

"Yes, but what about tse *weres?* They no turn to mist."

Parker turned to her. "Surely we can sneak up behind them. We're pretty stealthy, you know."

Melera shook her head. "Some have best hearing, Pawkher. Tsey can hear flap your pretty bugs' wings." She waved her hands in a fluttering motion.

Kurt frowned. "What?"

Parker smiled. "I think she means butterflies, Kurt. Some of them can hear a butterfly's wings flap."

She nodded. "Like me."

Kurt stared at her. "You can hear a butterfly's wings?"

She nodded again.

Without warning, Kurt dissolved into mist and reappeared a few seconds later. "Did you hear that?"

"Yes. It make sound like ssst."

"Fantastic, huh?" Parker said with a big smile.

Kurt sighed. "Actually, it's not."

Parker's smile slowly faded. "Oh. They'll hear you." He paused. "Some of them, anyway."

"And we don't know which ones."

"And tsen tsey tell tse otsers, yes?" Melera spoke up. "Be lots more careful, tsen. To kill be even harder."

Kurt tapped his cheek with an index finger. "Maybe not."

Parker cocked his head. "How so?"

"We'll be in mist form, remember? We can always kill…oh."

"Oh, what?"

"It just occurred to me. We can't just kill them on the street. We have to hypnotize them into coming with us into an alley or something. To do that, we have to be in human form."

"So?"

"Brains, Parker. Alien brains. They didn't evolve on Earth so their brains are sure to be wired differently than humans. Our brand of hypnosis might not work on them."

"How do you know?"

"Well, let's test it, hmm?" He turned to Melera and stared at her. His preternatural ability to hypnotize was one of the vampiric powers he hadn't lost and he turned it on full force. At this level, he could hypnotize a ballroom full of humans with no trouble. From the corner of his eye, he noticed Parker's eyes glaze over. As if in a dream, the wolf rose from the couch, marched over to where Kurt sat staring at Melera and stood beside his chair.

She blinked at him with a small, puzzled frown. "Why you stare at me like tsat? Why Pawkher get up?"

Pursing his lips, Kurt shut off his power but said nothing. He gazed up at Parker. The wolf's bright green eyes were vacant. A moment later, his eyelids fluttered and he gave his head a hard shake. He swiveled his head, looked at the sofa and then down at him. His eyes narrowed. "You hypnotized me, you bastard," he growled through his teeth. He spun on his heel, stalked to the couch and plopped onto its cushions.

Kurt gave a single nod. "Yes. But I was trying to hypnotize Melera. You just happened to be in range."

"So did you hypnotize her?"

He turned to Melera. "Well? Did I?"

"Did you what?"

"Hypnotize you."

She shook her head. "Me not unnerstand."

Parker placed a hand on her thigh. "You saw what happened to me, sweetheart. It was like being in a dream. I couldn't stop myself even if I'd wanted to."

"Oh. It not work."

Kurt sighed. "That's what I was afraid of."

No one spoke for a long while. "So there's nothing we can do, then," Parker broke the silence.

Kurt tightened his lips. "I'm not giving up. All those aliens running around here? I'm sure they're not all from the same world"—he looked at Melera for confirmation, who nodded—"so there have got to be some who aren't immune to a vampire's hypnotic power." He paused. "But if there's anything we have to do, it's to convince the other zots we have aliens in our midst."

Parker shook his head. "They'll think we're insane."

"Not if we can prove it." He turned to Melera. "My dear, would you be willing to out yourself?"

"Kurt," Parker growled.

Kurt shot him an annoyed look. "Wolf, I didn't say we'd do it. But I have to ask." He turned back to Melera. "Would you?"

She peered at him. "Out?"

"Reveal what you are."

Her look turned incredulous. Then she burst out laughing.

Spellbound, he stared at Melera wide-eyed. He'd never heard her laugh before. Were there really five different voices coming from her throat?

Melera's laughter abruptly died. "No. You cray-zee? Me somebody give to Beloc for sure."

Kurt stared at her a moment longer and then blinked a few times, bringing him out of his trance. He sighed again. "I thought you'd say that. Then we have no choice but to take the alternative route."

Parker frowned. "What's that?"

"We have to capture one. Alive."

"How?"

"They're looking for Melera, aren't they? She'll be the bait."

She sat up and narrowed her eyes. "You make joke, yes?"

Parker patted her thigh. "Of course he is, sweetheart." He turned and raised his brow. "Aren't you?"

"I'm not."

Melera and Parker's jaws dropped at the same time, identical expressions of shock on both faces. Parker recovered first. "Are you nuts?" he said, his voice tight with anger.

"Not at all." Kurt paused. "Think about it. It's the surest way." He looked at Melera, who glared back. To him, it seemed her eyes spun faster than they usually did.

She let out a small hiss. "Why you not find one you hyp-no-tize and tsen kill? Bring you dead one and tsey see."

"It'll be more effective if our captive is alive. We're not talking about a bunch of gullible humans, my dear. These are the Masters and Mistresses of their colonies. They've been around a long time and it'll take a lot more than a dead body to prove there are live aliens roaming around Seattle and goodness knows where else."

Parker shook his head. "I say we should wait for your vampires to catch one of these aliens and bring it back alive. One of them is bound to get lucky."

"And if Beloc makes a move while we're waiting for luck to strike? Earth would be in chaos. Is that what you want?"

"No, but—"

Melera sighed. "Ohh-kay. Me be bait."

Parker turned and gazed at her, an earnest look in his eyes. "Sweetheart, are you sure?"

She nodded. "Khurt right. May not be only way but is best way." She squinted at him. "Where we take prisner? Pawkher's house?"

Kurt smiled. "No. I have the perfect place." He stood and held out his hands. "Come on. We're going to the club."

Parker eyed him. "No, we'll drive over and meet you there."

"Don't be such a big baby. It's the fastest way. Besides, you can mist so what are you afraid of?"

He watched Melera poke the wolf's thigh. "You 'fraid of mist? Why?"

"I'm not afraid. I just don't like it, that's all."

She twisted her lips. "Sometimes we do tsings we like not. Like me be bait." Rising from the couch, she stepped over to where he stood and grabbed his hand. "Come, Pawkher."

Parker got up. With a small sigh, he walked over and took Kurt's other hand. He sighed again. "Okay. I'm ready."

Kurt dissolved them into mist and they flew over Seattle. *So Melera—what do you think? Not a bad way to travel, hmm?*

Me remembuh night you turn mist. Me make fire.

If Kurt had been in human form, he would have winced. Melera had trounced him that night in her temporary base in Underground. It was not a night he cared to remember.

A few minutes later, they reached the nightclub. He flew them around to the back. Still in mist form, they slipped under a door marked for deliveries. Then they resumed their natural shapes. Lights flickered on. On the left, a second door beckoned. He unlocked it and they stepped through. More lights flickered on. The three walked down a flight of stairs. At the bottom, they walked through another door.

It was pitch black inside. Even Kurt couldn't see, despite his vampiric vision. He felt along the wall, found the switch and flipped it. The space flooded with dim light. They stood before another staircase. "This way." He started down these steps, Parker and Melera following. At the bottom of the stairs was yet another door. He opened it. Pitch darkness lay behind it too, but he could see well enough by the light in the stairwell to find the switch. He flipped it. The three stepped over the threshold. Now they were in a brick-lined hallway. They started walking.

"Where are we going, anyway?" he heard Parker's voice behind him. "You'll see."

Kurt led them along the corridor and stopped at a metal door transected by a bar with a numeric fingerpad on the door's right side. Resting his left hand on the bar, he entered a code. A faint click sounded. He gave the bar a push and the door swung open. Bright lights flickered on after he'd stepped inside. He walked to the room's middle and stopped. "This is where we bring the alien."

He watched Parker turn in a slow circle, obviously taking in the room's contents. A giant cast iron bed with four ornately decorated posts lay perpendicular to one wall, its head lying flush against the brick. Chains had been welded to the posts, which ended in leather cuffs lined with woolly sheepskin. More chains with cuffs hung from the ceiling. One set of chains anchored a suspended iron bar. A leather-clad horse, with chains attached to the floor on each side, was positioned not far from the bed. Dominating the room was a huge, X-shaped cross with padded iron cuffs on each leg.

"A Saint Andrew's cross," Parker said, his voice full of wonder. "I've never seen one but I've heard of them." He looked at him over his shoulder. "What is this place, anyway?"

Kurt smiled. "My dungeon. I sometimes bring those of this persuasion down here." He paused. "Only zots, though. No humans."

"Did you bring Garrett down here?"

He smiled again. "Of course." Then he shrugged. "Anyway, this is where I thought we'd bring our alien. That way we won't be disturbed."

Kurt noticed Melera looking about the room, blinking as if she were memorizing it. "So what do you think, my dear?"

She turned. "Me be in place like tsis before. Look like one of Beloc's bad places. But his badder."

He frowned. "Bad places?"

"Torture chamber," Parker said.

His eyes widened and his frown deepened. Melera, tortured? For what? Yet, she didn't seem disturbed by what was in the room. *No PTSD. Amazing woman, this.* His respect for her, not much to begin with, went up a couple of notches.

"Seen enough, sweetheart?" Parker interrupted his thoughts.

Melera nodded. "Me know where go."

Kurt's frown disappeared, replaced by a puzzled look. "What do you mean?"

Parker smiled. "Melera has an interesting way to get from one place to another." He swiveled his head and looked at her. "Why don't you show him?"

"Ohh-kay."

He watched her eyes close. There was a flash of blinding light, immediately followed by a bitterly cold blast of wind. When he could see again, Melera was gone. His jaw dropped. "Where did she go?"

Parker shrugged. "Dunno. I'm sure she'll tell us when she gets back."

A moment later, the light flashed again and Melera stood in the same place she'd been standing when she'd left. "Where'd you go this time?" Parker said.

She smiled. "Khurt's."

Kurt goggled at her. "How on earth did you do that?"

Melera opened her mouth but Parker beat her to it. "She skipped through the Void. It's the space between here and there."

She nodded. "Is how I get prisner to here."

The dungeon was silent for a few minutes. "So when do you want to do this? Show the others, I mean?" Parker said.

Kurt turned to him. "As soon as we can after we capture one of Beloc's…people."

"Okay. Now can we go back, please? This place gives me the creeps."

He smiled and winked. "Why, Parker—I thought you might want to stay awhile. I could give you a demonstration."

Twisting his lips, Parker glared but said nothing.

From the corner of his eye, he saw Melera's small smile. "Pawkher right. Me know where tsis be, we go back now, yes?"

Kurt dipped his head. "Of course." He held out his hands.

Melera grinned. "No. We go my way. Much faster."

He shook his head. "Oh, I don't think that's—"

Parker smirked. "What, Kurt? You scared?"

"Of course not. It's just that—"

"Tsen we go, yes?" Melera held out her hands.

Kurt sighed. "Fine." He took one and Parker took the other. There came that blinding flash but no wind this time. A near-instant later, the three were back in his penthouse. He blinked to clear the spots before his eyes. After his sight had cleared, he looked around. "That was incredible."

"Isn't it?" Parker said. "I wish I could do that. Imagine how much money I'd save on gas."

He chuckled. "Come, sit. We have some planning to do."

"Uh, Kurt? Before we start, you got anything to eat in this place? I'm starving."

"Of course. The way you *weres* eat, I knew better than to leave the refrigerator bare. Go look. Take anything you want."

Parker grinned. "Thanks."

With a small smile, he watched Parker stride into the kitchen. He looked at Melera. "What about you, my dear? Are you hungry?"

"Me ohh-kay." She walked to the sectional and sat. Kurt took a seat across from her. Neither said anything.

Hew heard the refrigerator door close and then Parker strode into the room carrying a bowl almost overflowing with raw beef cubes. He plopped on the sectional next to Melera. Scooping up a handful, he stuffed them into his mouth and chewed. A contented smile appeared on his face. "Mmm, nice and juicy."

Kurt felt a pang of envy. He considered himself a gourmand and missed eating human food. He shook it off. "Well, now. We need to consider our next move."

"How do we know the aliens are in Seattle?" Parker said around his mouthful. He swallowed and grabbed more cubes from the bowl.

"We don't. The only thing we can do is send Melera out, have her walk around and see what happens. If they're here, they'll find her."

Parker grabbed another handful of cubes. "I assume we're going to do this at night?" He stuffed them into his mouth.

Kurt nodded. "The later the better. Too many people about in the evening. I think two or three in the morning after the clubs close would be best."

"Okay, now we know when. Where?"

"We can rule out the neighborhoods. A homeless person would stand out. We should concentrate on Pioneer Square, uptown, and downtown."

Melera looked from one man to the other. "When we start?"

He looked at her. "When do you want to start? Keeping in mind we should do this as soon as possible."

She shrugged. "Tomorrow ohh-kay."

Kurt nodded once. "Very good. Meet me—"

"I'm going with her," Parker cut in.

"You can't. Melera has to be alone."

"I didn't say I'd be in human form. I'm going to mist. Just in case something goes wrong."

Melera smiled. "Nutsing go wrong, Pawhker."

He put the now-empty bowl on the low table. His jaw set. "I'm going."

Still smiling, she patted his shoulder but said nothing.

Kurt pursed his lips. "I suppose that's settled, then. Meet me at Chance at two a.m."

Parker stood. "Will do." He took Melera's hand and she stood, too. "Come on, sweetheart. We'll need a good night's sleep if we're going to do this." His brow creased. "We should probably nap tomorrow at some point, too." Giving her a little tug, he headed for the penthouse's private elevator, with her in tow.

Kurt followed. Reaching the elevator, he unlocked it and the doors whisked open. Parker and Melera stepped inside the cab. "See you tomorrow, Kurt," Parker said. "And thanks for the snack."

"You're welcome. Until tomorrow, then." He pressed the button on the wall next to the elevator and the doors closed. He stared at the brushed steel for a moment, then turned and walked deeper into the big room. Resuming his seat in the chair, he picked up his wine glass and sat back. He took a sip. *Is Beloc going to make a move on Earth before or after he finds Melera? If I were he, I'd make a move before, with my insincere promise to leave after she'd been found. That way, the whole of Earth would be looking for her, and he'd find her that much faster. We zots would sniff her out. Not to mention the sniffers. If they can figure out who we are, I'm sure they can figure out who's an alien.* His thoughts turned to Melera. *A shifter…if she shifted into human form, I wonder if her scent would change, too? Then no one would ever find her. And Beloc would never leave.* He snorted. *Not that he'd plan to, anyway.*

Then he thought about his bid to get the twenty vampire regents from the world's largest cities where Beloc might be looking for Melera together in one room. It would be dangerous. Regents weren't exactly one big happy family—especially these twenty. Charles, the Master of Brooklyn, hated Corwin, the Master of Houston, for no reason Kurt could fathom. Raina, the Mistress of Los Angeles, had a long-standing grudge against Gerard, the Master of London, for staking her sister two hundred years ago. And most of the rest just plain didn't like each other. He could almost see more than a few of them getting into an altercation of some sort. Given their powers, it wouldn't take much to bring down the entire building. And he, in his weakened state, would be powerless to stop them.

Kurt shook his head. He couldn't think about this now. He *had* to get them in a room together, come what may. Otherwise, they were all doomed. He shook his head again and set his wineglass back on the table. Standing, he took one last look around his penthouse, then misted and headed for Last Chance.

CHAPTER 25

Late on New Year's night, Basile's limousine pulled up to Garrett's little house.

Her lips tightened. *Tonight's the night.* She tried not to be nervous but it wasn't working. Despite all the time they'd spent together over the last three weeks or so she'd never invited him inside. For their own protection, zots are reticent when it comes to meeting new people.

She drew a shallow breath and turned. "Basile, would you like to come in for a glass of wine?"

His face lit up. "I'd love one."

James got out to open the door for her. By now she'd gotten used to his looks but still had to resist the temptation to smile and thank him. "James is well paid for what he does," Basile had said. "Think of him as a robot. He neither wants nor needs your thanks for doing his job." His attitude towards James was the only thing about Basile that bothered her. *But everything else about him is perfect.*

Walking up the stairs leading to the porch, she heard Basile's voice, obviously giving instructions to the chauffeur. She couldn't quite hear what he said but she thought she caught the word "wait." Fishing for her keys, she heard his footsteps behind her. She had just put the key in the door when he gave her shoulder a light squeeze. "Thank you for inviting me in. I know you're a very private person and this must be a big step for you."

By now, she had the door open. "What makes you say that?" She stepped inside and made room for Basile to enter.

"The way you never talk about yourself. I gave up prying a long time ago."

She thought about this while slipping out of her cloak. "Yes...now that I think about it, you have."

"Does this mean I'll get to hear some of your secrets tonight?"

Garrett took his coat and smiled. "No."

Basile smiled too, but it soon died. "Doesn't matter," he said, his voice soft. "As long as I'm with you."

Her eyes widened a fraction. She knew he meant it but the surprising thing was that she felt the same way. "Here," she said, trying not to stammer. "Let me put the coats away and I'll get us the wine."

In the kitchen, she opened the doors to the cabinet that held her best Irish crystal. On the second shelf, the stemware was almost out of reach. But through long practice, she knew she could retrieve them without dropping anything. She took the first glass off the shelf and set it on the counter. Then she reached for the second one.

"Garrett," she heard Basile's voice close behind her. Startled, she dropped the second glass. But her zot reflexes were quick. *Inpeditus.* The glass floated in mid-air, inches from the kitchen's ceramic tile floor. Her skin paled upon realizing what she'd done. She bent forward and picked up the glass, feeling Basile's stare boring into her head. Her mind raced. *What do I do now? Act like nothing happened? Maybe he didn't see it?*

Straightening, she placed the glass on the counter, then turned. One look at Basile's face told her he'd seen what happened. "I...I..." Her shoulders sagged. "If you want to call the police, go ahead," she said, her voice low and heavy. "Just give me thirty minutes head start. That's all I ask."

"How did you do that?" he said as if he hadn't heard her.

"I—"

"You're a zot," he said in a soft voice. "But you spoke so harshly of them."

She swallowed. "We have to be careful. That's the way humans feel about us. So to fit in, we have to be bigoted, too."

"It must be a horrible way to live."

"It hurts. And it's tiring being on your guard all the time, especially with your human so-called friends. But you get used to it, eventually. Sort of."

Garrett turned back to the counter. "So you won't call the police?"

Basile's footsteps echoed behind her and then a strong pair of arms wrapped around her waist. "I have a better idea. How about that wine?"

he whispered into her hair. She nearly cried out with relief and turned in his arms. "Thank you, Basile," she whispered back.

Before she knew it, his lips were on hers, kissing her long and deep. After pulling away, he stared into her eyes. "I've been wanting to do that for the longest time."

She nodded. "Me too, but I was just—"

"Afraid of getting involved," he finished for her.

She nodded again but said nothing.

He rubbed her shoulders. "Tell me where the wine is and I'll pour."

Garrett pointed at a bottle of red sauvignon on the counter. A corkscrew lay next to it. "Over there."

Basile stepped forward. Picking up the bottle, he opened it with a few deft moves. Then he returned to where she stood and filled their glasses.

"A toast. To Garrett, and to all the other zots in Seattle." He raised his glass and she did, too. After re-corking the bottle, he took her hand and together they walked into the living room.

She placed her glass of wine on the low table in front of the couch and sat. Basile set his glass nearby and sat next to her. "Now will you tell me about yourself?"

Garrett sighed. "There really isn't much to tell, Basile. My family died in a pogrom like yours did and you pretty much know the rest. I just left out the part about being a mage."

He chuckled. "No, Garrett. There is much more you're not telling me. Well, that's all right. I suppose you'll tell me when you're ready."

She thought about Parker and Kurt. *No. Never.*

They finished their wine in silence. Then Basile dragged her onto his lap. He kissed her again, long and deep. "I think I'm a little tired after our evening. How about a nap?"

Garrett felt his hardness against her hip. "A nap, huh? You must be getting old, Basile."

"That's me—an old man. Come on. I'm getting very sleepy."

Her lips curled into a small smile. "Liar."

He chuckled again but said nothing. Pushing her off his lap, he stood and offered her his hand.

She took it. Basile pulled her to her feet. Their hands still clasped, she led him upstairs. Her lips stretched into a grin of anticipation. She hadn't planned on this happening but now that it was, she was not about to stop it.

Garrett stepped inside her bedroom and stopped short. She hadn't put away the toys she and Kurt had used during their last scene yesterday. The padded manacles were still attached to the bedposts and a chain, also with manacles, still hung from the large hook screwed into the ceiling about four feet from the bed. Floggers and paddles lay haphazardly on the chair. A tube of lubricant and a vibrator lay on the small table nearby. The spreader bar lay on the floor.

She turned. "Um, Basile? Maybe we should do this another time."

He wrapped his arms about her. "This is what I meant by secrets, Garrett. And I know you have plenty more." Then he grinned. "And I think now is the perfect time."

"You mean you—"

"Oh, yes."

"Okay. Let's negotiate. I'm usually the submissive—"

Basile smiled. "That's usually the submissive, Sir."

Garrett let her expression turn neutral. "Yes, Sir."

"Very good." He traced her jaw with his index finger. "Masochist?"

"Yes, Sir."

"Humiliation?"

"Yes, Sir."

"Forced orgasms?"

"Yes, Sir."

"Obedient?"

"Sometimes, Sir."

"Marks?"

"No, Sir."

"Water sports?"

"No, Sir."

"Use magick?"

"Only when given permission, Sir."

"Safeword?"

"Pineapple, Sir."

He paused and looked at her intently. "Trust me?"

Garrett didn't answer at first. Staring into his dark eyes, her heart beat a little faster. "Yes, Sir."

Basile smiled again. "Good." He leaned over until his face was just inches from hers. "I think we're ready to begin," he said in a soft voice. "Do you agree?"

"Yes, Sir," she whispered.

"Then come with me." He took her hand and led her deeper into the bedroom, halting her by the edge of the bed. "Stand here."

She took a small step forward but said nothing.

He gave her cheek a light slap. "Oh, ho. You *are* a disobedient little bitch, aren't you?"

"Yes, Sir."

Basile picked the floggers, paddles, and other items off the chair and put them on the table. Then he turned and sat. "Now. I want you to take off your clothes. Slowly."

"Yes, Sir." Garrett started with her dress. It was a tank-style, with no zippers or buttons. She leisurely pulled it over her head and dropped it to the floor. Then she took off her bra.

"Stop," he said after she'd done so. "Turn around. Let me see all of you."

This time she obeyed. Now wearing only a garter belt, stockings, and a thong, she turned in a slow circle. Having him stare at her like this was exciting. Her panties were damp already.

"All right, keep going."

Starting with her left leg, Garrett unhooked the garters one by one, rolled the stocking to her feet, and slipped it off. Then she did the same to her right leg. She undid the belt and let it fall to the floor. Finally, she slowly lowered her thong and dropped it to the floor, too. By now her crotch was soaked.

Basile stood. "Come here."

She stepped over to him. "Now take off my clothes." She started to reach up to unbutton his shirt when he grabbed her hand. He smiled. "With your teeth."

Her eyes widened. She'd never done this before. "Why can't I use my hands, Sir?"

He grabbed a hank of her hair and yanked hard, jerking her head back and exposing her throat. She stared into his face.

His expression was stern. "Because I said so. Do you have a problem with that?"

"No, Sir."

"Then do it." He let go of her hair.

"Yes, Sir." Then she saw a hitch. Basile was tall enough so that she couldn't reach the top buttons on his shirt. "Um…Sir, I'm too short to reach the top buttons."

He gave a slow nod, his look thoughtful. Then he smiled. "We can fix that. Stand on the bed."

She walked over to it, climbed onto the mattress and stood. Turning, she saw Basile standing before her. He took a step forward. Now she looked down on him. He smiled. "Begin."

Garrett crouched and started at the top button. She worked at it with her tongue until she'd positioned it just right, then pulled at the shirt with her teeth. The material parted. She did the same with all the buttons she could reach in her stooped position. Then she got on her knees and undid the rest, down to the waistband of his trousers. Sitting back, she stared at his belt with a tiny frown. A moment later, she leaned forward, grabbed the belt's leather strip between her teeth and pulled it through the loop. Now she had to undo the buckle. She pulled the leather strip backward, hoping the prong would fall out from the hole. It didn't. She tried again, pulling harder this time.

He gave her head a gentle cuff. "Careful."

"Yes, Sir. Sorry, Sir." She kept working at the belt buckle. Minutes seemed to pass. After what seemed like forever, the prong slipped out of the hole. She pulled the belt through his trousers' fabric loops and dropped it to the floor.

She loosed the button on his trousers. Tonguing the pull tab until it lay between her lips, she clamped her jaws shut and slid the zipper down. Basile's trousers now hung loose on his body. She grabbed a small bit of material in her teeth and tugged. With a sound like a whisper, his trousers pooled around his feet. She undid the rest of the shirt's buttons. Rising from her kneeling position, she slipped the shirt off his shoulders. Then she got back on her knees again, caught the lower edge of his shorts in her teeth and pulled. They came down almost as easily as his trousers. His dick, hard and long, swung in her face. He slapped her with it.

All that was left now was his socks. She started to get off the bed but Basile stopped her. "You're too slow." He pulled off his socks himself and dropped them to the floor.

"I'm sorry, Sir." She bent her head and stared at the comforter, listening to the sound of the light whooshing the sock material made as he slipped them off. She raised her head. He stood before her, his cock bobbing gently in her face. "Suck me," he said in a commanding tone.

Garrett looked up at him from beneath her lashes. "I—"

Before she could utter another word, Basile shoved his member into her mouth. "I said suck me, whore." He gave her a firm swat on the top of her head with his fingers. "And I didn't give you permission to talk."

With a shiver of pleasure, Garrett began sucking his dick. Little by little, he pushed deeper into her mouth. Now he was almost at the back of her throat. She leaned forward. She'd long since learned to control her gag reflex and wanted to take in all of him.

He rubbed her scalp. "All right?"

She bobbed her head once.

Basile pushed the rest of his cock into her mouth. Nose to crotch now, she worked her throat around him, squeezing and relaxing, again and again. He grabbed the back of her head and pulled her into him, grinding his hips against her face. His balls, dripping with her saliva, smacked her chin. A few minutes later, he let out a little groan and came. She felt his cock pulse as hot cum shot down her throat.

After he'd spent himself, he held her in position for about a minute, then slowly pulled out of her throat and mouth. The tiniest of frowns creased Garrett's brow. Basile tasted odd but not unpleasant. As a healer, she knew the taste of bodily fluids, to some extent, reflected one's diet. For a fleeting moment, she wondered about the foods he ate.

She stared at his crotch, watching the last of his cum dripping from the tip of his cock. To her surprise, he wasn't completely flaccid. She looked up. He smiled. Then he thrust his hips forward and started grinding against her face again. After a moment, she realized it was to dry himself off. A spasm went through her cunt. Being used as a towel was wonderfully humiliating.

Finished, Basile turned and walked over to the hook in the ceiling. "Come here," he said over his shoulder. She climbed off the bed. Reaching him, she raised her arms above her head and he manacled her hands. Now she stood nearly on her toes. She felt the chain jerk a couple of times.

The next thing she knew, a leather flogger whacked her across her back. "You're a horny little slut, aren't you? Tell me what you are."

Garrett closed her eyes and smiled. "Yes, Sir. I'm a horny little slut, Sir."

"Open your eyes, whore." She did so. Basile stood before her. Smiling, he swatted her breasts. She gasped. It didn't hurt, but the feel of the leather against her tender skin heightened her excitement.

"Do you like this?" he said.

"Y-yes, Sir. I like it, Sir."

He swatted her a few more times and then obviously spied something behind her. "Oh, ho. Look what I see." He stepped away. A moment later, she heard the sound of metal sliding on the wood table. On his return, Garrett saw he held a pair of clamps. Still smiling, he fastened them to her nipples. Her breath caught at the small bursts of pain radiating through her breasts. He picked up the flogger and slapped her again, harder this time. Circling behind her, he whacked her on her back again. His blows hurt. Her juices ran down her legs.

Basile stopped whipping her. "I want to see sparks fly."

"Yes, Sir." *Ignis corius colo,* she mentally chanted. "Ready, Sir."

He lashed her. She knew that small bursts of colored light rose off her skin whenever the leather made contact with her flesh.

"Pretty."

"Thank you, Sir." In the next instant, the flogger's tails whacked her hard across her back. The burn and sting from the leather strips made her shiver with pleasure.

"Did I tell you to speak, cunt?"

"No, Sir. I'm sorry, Sir."

Basile gave her a few more swats and threw the flogger across the room. "I'm bored with this. Where's that paddle again?"

"On the table, Sir," she panted.

He retrieved the paddle and gently smacked her ass with it, over and over, each time with increasing force. Garrett's cheeks grew warm and warmer still. Then he spanked her hard. Her skin quivered. His blows became more intense. Now it was getting to be too much—her cheeks were on fire. Biting her lip, she was ready to cry out her safe word when he stopped paddling her. His blessedly cool hand caressed her, soothing her fevered skin.

Basile stopped his caressing, enveloped her in his arms and kissed her ear. "Spread your legs, whore," he whispered.

"Yes, Sir."

He cuffed each of her ankles to one end of the spreader bar. Now she was completely open to him. He slipped two fingers into her dripping pussy, making her squirm. "Oh, you like that, then." He curled his fingers and wiggled them about until she was ready to cum. When he obviously felt her muscles tightening, Basile pulled out of her. "You cum when I tell you to cum, you dirty girl."

"Yes, Sir," she panted.

"Yes, Sir, what?"

"I won't cum until I am told, Sir."

"That's good. You understand." Then he probed her lips with his sopping fingers. "Suck them," he commanded. Garrett sucked them clean, tasting her juices. Then, circling behind her, Basile grabbed her hips, slid into her opening and pounded her hard. She squeezed her eyes shut. Just when she was about to cum, he stopped and gave her ass a hard smack.

"Sorry, Sir. I didn't mean to—"

"Don't give me any excuses, bitch." About fifteen seconds later, he inserted a finger covered by a cool, slippery substance into her bunghole and probed deep. A few more seconds passed. With a hard thrust, he shoved his cock into her ass. She nearly screamed. Basile started rubbing her clit, making little whorls, lubricating her with her juices. Then he pushed the vibrator into her pussy. Between the humming vibrator and his cock, her body started to spasm, taking her higher and higher towards orgasm. He gave a little grunt and his cock throbbed inside her.

Seconds before she reached her peak, Basile pulled out of her. "Let me see you cum."

Garrett opened her eyes. He was facing her. The vibrator still shivered inside her and then he started playing with her clit again. The sensation pushed her over the top. Opening her mouth, little cries of pure animal pleasure escaped her throat while waves and waves of her climax coursed through her body. The pressure on her nipples from the clamps disappeared. The pain was deliciously unbearable. She screamed. A few seconds later, she went limp.

The next thing she knew, Basile had lifted her head by the chin. She regarded him through bleary eyes. Leaning forward, he gave her a deep kiss. "That was fun," he said after pulling away. "We should do this again, sometime." He smiled. "Let's get you down from there."

After releasing her from the spreader bar and the cuffs, Garrett collapsed into his arms. Picking her up, he carried her to the bed and tucked her in. Then he started getting dressed.

"You're not staying?" she said, her voice heavy with satiation.

He bent down and gave her forehead a light kiss. "No. I have a meeting in the morning. An early one."

"Okay."

"You want me to lock the door?"

"It's self-locking. Just pull it shut."

Basile finished dressing and headed for the bedroom door. "Good night, Garrett. I'll call you tomorrow."

"Please, Sir."

Then he was gone.

She fell asleep, much faster than she usually did. For her, sex was a better sleeping aid than her best potions. So deep was her slumber, she didn't sense her body awaken and rise from the bed. She opened the window. It was cold, but she didn't feel it.

Covered with dense fur now, Garrett-the-wolf leapt from the window and into the night.

CHAPTER 26

By the time the wolf got downtown, she still hadn't found what she was looking for. Keeping to the shadows, she headed across town to Pioneer Square. Reaching the historic area, she saw that there were humans about but not many. That suited her purposes perfectly.

The wolf chose her prey with care. It was a male, walking along a side street. There was no one else around. She slipped into an alley. When the male was abreast, she leapt out of the shadows, claws out. "Hey," the man yelled and fell to the ground. She tore out his throat. Gouts of blood splashed the alley walls. Dragging the man deeper inside, she ripped open his chest, tore out his heart and started to feed.

Engrossed in her meal, the wolf didn't hear the sounds of running feet. When she did, she dropped the morsel of heart she'd been chewing and began looking for a way out. The alley walls were unbroken by a door or window. She looked up. The wall behind her, about twenty feet high, was easily scalable. She jumped and landed on top. A shout went up behind her. Pools of light flashed on the wall. "There it is," someone yelled.

She turned her head, only to be caught full in the face by a bright light. A near-deafening *crack!* echoed in the alley. She let out a roar and disappeared over the wall. Keeping to the shadows again, she ran through the alleys and dark side streets, eventually leaving the Square far behind. Instinct said she should return to her other's den.

Garrett woke up a block or so from her house. Her wolf instantly retreated. Disoriented, she looked around her, wondering why she was outside and naked. Then she looked down and saw the blood. With a little cry, she started running for Parker's house. It was the only place she could go.

Her speed bolstered by her fear and her magick, Garrett arrived at Parker's house only a few minutes after she'd left her own, even though it was over a mile away. She spelled the lock on the back gate and slipped inside, somehow remembering to lock it behind her. Then she ran across the yard to his back door and began pounding on it.

Parker opened the door seconds later. "Garrett." He pulled her inside, shut the door and turned off the patio light. "What'd you kill this time?"

"A…A human," she said in a small voice.

"Oh, that's just fucking great." He peered at her. "Anybody see you?"

She nodded. "Several people. They shone lights, and someone took a shot at me."

He squeezed his eyes shut, then opened them. "That's even better. If we're lucky, it wasn't a cop. Just some dude with a gun." He shook his head. "I hope to God this doesn't spark a pogrom." Then he sighed. "Go upstairs and clean yourself up. We'll try this again."

Garrett ran upstairs to the bath and turned on the shower. Stepping inside, she scoured every bit of blood off her body, paying special attention to her fingernails. Now clean, she turned the water off and stepped out of the tub.

On returning to the great room, she saw Parker waiting for her with the chain. She lay on the floor. While he tied her with it, she couldn't help but think this was the second time tonight she'd been chained.

"Okay, call your wolf."

She put herself into a deep trance. After reaching the wood, she cast the two spells—one for armor and the other for strength. Ready now, she went to the cave. Her wolf must have heard her coming because she leapt out at her before she had even stepped inside. Garrett instinctively raised her arm to protect her face. One of her wolf's paws smacked against the silver brace. She howled and fled into the deeper recesses of the cave.

Garrett followed. Conjuring a ball of witch light, she saw her wolf crouched against the far wall, holding her hurt paw. She marched to the back of the cave. Her wolf stood and growled at her, which swelled into a roar. She leapt at her again. Garrett caught the wolf in both hands and hurled her against the wall. While her wolf lay in a daze, Garrett ran up and gave her a swift kick in the ribs. She heard something crack. Her beast screamed in pain. Garrett balled her fist and hit her square on the jaw. Her wolf's head snapped sideways. Recovering, she tried to grab Garrett's upper arm but Garrett jumped back just far enough so that her wolf caught the brace instead. She roared again.

Once again Garrett thrashed her wolf within an inch of her life. A half-hour later, she cowered against the back wall, staring at Garrett in fear. She picked her up. Her beast whimpered. Carrying her to the hole, Garrett dropped her at its edge, then kicked her inside the pit. "This is fourth time I've had to come down here. Let me say it again. You'll obey me. You'll come only when called and when I say go back, you'll do it." She paused. "And understand this. I'm not afraid to die. If you try this one more time, I will kill you. I will kill us both. You got that?"

"Yes," her wolf mewled.

"Good." Garrett pushed the lid back over the pit.

Then she left the cave. Soon she was back in the place where she'd arrived and floated out of her trance. She opened her eyes to see Parker staring at her. "I hope you kicked her ass good this time."

"I think so." She told him what had transpired.

"Whew. Your wolf might never come out again."

"Okay by me."

He smiled for the first time that night. "Why don't you go upstairs and get some sleep? I'll take you home in the morning."

She grinned. "You mean later this morning."

"Oh. Right. But would you like a drink first? Might help you sleep after all that fighting."

"I'd love one."

He stood. Walking to the bar, he poured them both a tumbler full of whiskey and handed her one. "Cheers," he said and drank deeply.

She took a deep draught and almost coughed. But she was game. If Parker could do it, so could she.

"Pawkher?" she heard a familiar deep voice.

"She's back?" Garrett said in an urgent whisper.

"No need to whisper," he said in a normal voice. "She can hear every word."

Garrett sensed Melera behind her and turned. "Hi, Melera," she said, hoping she didn't sound nervous. She'd seen for herself what the other woman could do with her alien powers and it was awesome. In truth, she was scared of her.

A sly-looking smile stretched Melera's lips as if she knew Garrett was afraid. "Hel-lo, Gharrett. Pawhker tell me you woof, yes?"

A flash of anger banished her nervousness. She turned and glared at Parker. Who was he to be spreading her business around? "Yes," she said through her teeth.

He shrugged. "Well, considering I'm a vampire and drained her into unconsciousness, I thought she deserved an explanation about what was going on with the three of us."

Garrett tightened her lips. She was still annoyed that he'd told Melera but it made sense. She nodded. "So what now?"

"I think you should lay low for a while," Parker said. "You said a bunch of people saw you, so—"

"Park," she interrupted. "I've got rehearsal. I can't lay low."

His eyes narrowed. "Garrett, let me repeat. People saw you. Aren't you afraid someone will recognize you?"

"It was dark. Besides, my wolf is hairy with big teeth."

"Didn't you say people shone lights on you?"

"Yes, but it was only for a second."

He shook his head. "I can't believe you're being so pig-headed about this. Garrett, you go out there and you could be putting all of us in danger. Don't you understand that?"

She blew an explosive breath. "Park, nothing's going to happen to me. Or to anybody else. Remember that peace spell the coven cast last April? Well, we recast it and we've been maintaining it. It'll keep the humans quiet."

"Pawkher's right," Melera said. "You should—"

"I'm not doing it, okay? I can't. Besides, Basile—"

"Basile?" Parker said.

Garrett felt her face redden. "Basile Roche. He's my…my new friend."

"What kind of zot is he?"

She felt her face redden further. "I don't know."

Parker's eyes widened. "What do you mean, you don't know? Garrett, what the hell's the matter with you? You know—"

"I mean, my spells didn't work on him. My powers are erratic, remember? Still, I'm pretty sure he's not human."

"Does he know you're a mage?"

"Yes."

He threw up his hands. "Garrett, of all the idiotic things you could do, this has got to be the worst. How do you know the guy isn't a lorelei?"

Her eyes flashed. "He's not a lorelei. He's extremely trustworthy. Believe me, I know."

"So you had sex with him, right? With your little toys?"

"Yes."

"So that makes him trustworthy."

"Yes."

Parker clapped his hands over his face but said nothing.

"Gharrett, you meet this Basile when?" Melera said.

"What's that got to do with anything?"

"You answer me question, yes?"

She sighed. "About three weeks ago, after my last play's run."

Melera raised her brow and nodded once.

"What?" Garrett said, her voice loud in the confines of the great room.

Parker had lowered his hands and now looked concerned. "What are you thinking, sweetheart?"

Melera let out a slow breath. "Nutsing." Then she smiled. "Me tired, Pawkher. Me go bed now."

He smiled back. "Okay, sweetheart. I'll be up in a few minutes."

Garrett watched Melera climb the stairs. Then she turned. "Look, I'm sorry if I—"

"What I want to know is what you're going to do now."

"Park, it's cold outside. You know how much I hate winter. I'll just make sure I'm bundled up good when I'm on the street. Besides, I can always cast a non-recognition spell or a forgetfulness spell, or even an obscuring spell. No one will see me, Parker—much less recognize me. Okay?"

"You just said your powers are erratic."

"Then I'll just keep casting until it takes."

Parker sighed. "Once again you've got it all figured out, Garrett.

This time, I hope you're right." He sighed a second time. "I'm going to bed. I've got a job today and it promises to be a bear. We'll be leaving pretty early. You know where everything is. The guest room is all yours." He yawned. Then his look turned serious. "I want to see you tomorrow night after rehearsal. Understood?'"

She bristled. "Park, I'm not one of your pack."

He leaned forward until his face was inches from hers. "You got a wolf, dontcha?"

She said nothing.

"Then you're one of my pack."

With that, he straightened and drained the rest of his drink. Walking out from behind the bar, she watched him cross the great room and then run up the stairs.

Garrett took another sip of whiskey and thought about the Stohlman Theater's upcoming production. It was a musical. *Thank the Mother Park didn't ask about it.* Her eyebrow twitched. *Not that he'd be interested.* The one time she'd dragged him to one of her plays, he'd told her afterward he'd been bored out of his mind and refused to go again.

Though she often played the lead in the Stohlman's productions, in this one she wouldn't, even though she was one of the best actors in the company. She'd be in the background this time, part of the chorus. Garrett could sing but her singing voice was little better than average. She could have spelled her voice to be stellar but acting was her passion, and she wanted it to be her, just her, up on stage. She'd clawed her way to the top without magick and if she wasn't much of a singer, so be it.

But the costumes worried her. The designer was trying something different. Instead of using body makeup, he wanted the actors to actually look like the characters they portrayed. He'd shown her the drawings a few months ago and they were wonderful. She'd had several fittings already and with each one, she looked more and more like the character she'd been assigned.

And tonight she'd been seen in all her hairy glory. A knot of fear formed in her stomach. Maybe none of the humans who saw her tonight were theatergoers. She prayed for it to be true.

For the Stohlman was closing the theater season with the musical *Cats.*

CHAPTER 27

Melera, dressed in black jeans, a heavy black sweater, black woolen jacket, and engineer's boots, tramped through Pioneer Square. She'd done this so many times since Parker's and her meeting with Kurt she now knew the historic district by heart.

It was four-thirty a.m., a week after the day hu-mans called New Year's and it was raining hard. There was no one about. Cold and tired, she'd been wandering for hours in the wet weather. Shivering, she turned up the collar of her jacket—not that it did much good. She was soaked through and her sopping clothes, especially her jacket, felt like weights. She sighed.

Melera knew Parker, in mist form, floated somewhere above. Envy filled her. She also knew the rain was having no effect on him. He'd materialized on a corner about two hours ago. His startling green eyes full of concern, he'd asked if she wanted to go home. His clothes, she'd noticed, had been dry.

Melera had shaken her head. "I'm ohh-kay, Pawhker," she said in Toro. "The longer I walk, the faster they'll find me."

But that was two hours ago. Now all she wanted to do was go back to his house and get warm. *This is insane. Damn Khurt and his stupid idea. Beloc's starlegions aren't here. They're probably everywhere* but *here.* She plodded along, her mood growing fouler by the second. By the time she reached the corner, she decided she'd had enough for one night. She lifted her head, scanning above her for any sign of Parker but didn't see him. Of course, it was nearly impossible to see anything through the driving rain.

Melera turned the corner. She'd gone ten steps when the hairs on the back of her neck stood up. She could barely make it out because of the rain but she heard footsteps behind her. She was being followed—maybe by a legionnaire, or maybe not. But then, who else would be out on a night like this? To test her theory, she quickened her pace. So did the person behind her. That convinced her. She was definitely being followed and she was sure it was a legionnaire. Breaking into a trot, she started looking for an alley she could duck into. She didn't see any.

The footsteps were getting closer. She started running. So did her pursuer. But she was faster. The legionnaire was falling behind. She rounded another corner, still looking for an alley. There—up ahead and across the street. She dashed toward it, her boots sending up sprays of water with each long stride. Entering the dark space, she ran to its far end. Panting, Melera looked around and could see there was no way out. From the streetlight's ambient glow, she made out the shadowy outline of a large door. She wondered if it was one of the entrances to Underground.

The sound of running feet, growing closer, yanked her attention back into the moment. She whipped her head toward the sound. Her pursuer appeared at the alley's entrance and stopped. Then the other alien started walking toward her with slow, deliberate steps, head swiveling left and right. She almost let out a sigh of relief. The scanning implant in the legionnaire's brain was standard issue—it could give the general area where she was located but it couldn't pinpoint her.

Almost at the alley's back end, Melera calmed her heavy breathing and pressed her back against the wall, hoping she blended in with the darkness. For the first time since coming out tonight, she was glad it was raining. Between that and the hooded jacket her pursuer wore, it cut down on visibility.

She watched the legionnaire come closer and closer still. Then it was abreast of her. It took two more steps. She made her move. Leaping from her hiding place, Melera grabbed the legionnaire's hood with one hand, yanked it down and reaching inside with her strong fingers, clutched the material where the hood met the jacket's back panel. She placed her other hand at the small of its back and gave an especially hard shove. The legionnaire's face rammed into the wall. While it was in a daze, she spun it around, ripped open its jacket and tore off the thin, blinking tube around its neck. The lights went dark. Then she punched it in the face as hard as she could. Expecting to hear bones crack, she was surprised when all she heard was a loud splorp. Then she delivered a debilitating blow to its midsection. The legionnaire let out a grunt and crumpled to the ground.

She squatted and lifted the legionnaire's head by its chin. Its nose was mashed but there was no blood, which told her the nose had been fake. But it was unconscious, which was what she needed.

Sensing movement, she looked up. Parker had materialized beside her. "You got him. Or her. Or it. Good. Let's get back to Kurt's dungeon." She nodded and picked up the broken neck collar. Hefting the legionnaire, she held it tight under one arm. Parker took the other. Melera closed her eyes and pictured the dungeon in her mind. Her czado opened the portal and she skipped them.

Inside Kurt's dungeon, Melera let her burden fall to the floor. The thin sheet of ice encasing the legionnaire shattered. She was encased in ice as well. She knocked it from her face and hands but didn't bother with her clothes or hair. It would melt soon enough. She bent down and started stripping the legionnaire. While doing so, she eyed Parker and Kurt. "Me you help. We want it not to wake up first."

Working together, the three had the alien's clothes stripped in no time. She stared at the nude body. "Is male."

Parker squinted. "How can you tell?"

She gave him a look. "Never mind. Me you help lift." Each of them taking an arm, the two picked up the unconscious legionnaire from the floor and held his body upright while Kurt fastened his wrists to the top arms of the St. Andrew's Cross. Then he bent down and secured the legionnaire's ankles. "All done." He stood and took a few steps back.

They gazed at their prisoner. Well-muscled, his skin was the palest shade of purple. Short appendages, about four inches long, made a fringe from his armpits almost to the middle of his chest. Three deep dimples, looking like belly buttons stacked on top of each other, were located on his chest in the area between the fringe's edges. An ugly, bluish-purple bruise was forming on his midsection. Where his genitals should have been was a smooth expanse of skin. Though he had five fingers, he had only four toes. His head was small for his size.

"When do you think he'll wake up?" Parker said.

Melera shook her head. "No idea. Me hit him very hard." She took a breath and sneezed, six times in a row. Then she began to cough.

"Melera, my dear, are you catching a cold?" Kurt said.

Parker pulled a cigar out of his breast pocket. "No. She's allergic to Earth."

Kurt frowned. "A cigar?"

"Alleviates the symptoms. For her, it acts like an antihistamine."

"Ah. Now I understand why she always wants cigars."

Melera watched through watering eyes as Parker walked toward her. "Here, sweetheart." He torched the business end of the slim brown cylinder and handed it to her.

She took it. "Tsank you, Pawkher." She inhaled several times, feeling the tow-bac-co buzz clouding her brain. It felt good. Not as good as weed but good enough. By the time her mind had stopped humming, her symptoms were gone. She wiped her eyes clear, took another drag and sighed in appreciation and relief.

She saw Parker walk to the spot where they'd materialized and pick up the collar. He turned it over and back again, inspecting it. "Melera, what's this?"

"Is for call prison ship, personal stealts shield, and self-kill."

"How does—"

A groan made them turn. Their prisoner was waking. Melera regarded him. He lifted his head, shook it a few times and then opened his eyes. They were olive green and human-looking. She raised her brow. *Surgical alteration. Byringa eyes are slit-pupil and red.* She looked him over some more. *His skin's been bleached, too. And one of those fingers is fake. Probably the smallest one.*

She walked over to him. "What's your number?" she said in Toro. She heard Parker speaking in a low voice, obviously translating for Kurt's benefit.

The Byringa didn't answer. He stared at her with a blank gaze.

Melera stared back. Then she took a few steps forward. Now she stood directly in front of the pale purple alien. She took a drag from the cigar. "Number, please."

The Byringa remained silent.

She nodded a couple of times. "All right." She grabbed one of the appendages on his chest and pulled it up. Holding it by its tip, she placed the burning end of the cigar near its base. Smoke curled up.

The alien screamed.

A noxious odor filled the dungeon. The legionnaire screamed again and again but Melera didn't let up. Finally, the member separated from the alien's chest. She stepped back a few paces, took a drag on the cigar and blew out a stream of smoke. After the legionnaire had stopped his screaming, she held the appendage up to his face. "Number, please." From the corner of her eye, she saw Parker's look of horror. Kurt looked surprised. Then she heard them talking in very low voices. She ignored them.

The Byringa's head dropped to its chest. It mumbled something she didn't quite catch. Melera dropped the appendage she was holding to the floor, reached over and picked up another one. "Louder."

The alien's head snapped up. "JL8762."

She smiled. "Well, JL8762—welcome to Dirt. How many of you are in this city?"

"I don't know."

"You sure?"

The legionnaire didn't answer.

With the speed of a laser shot, Melera reached up and snatched off the other alien's smashed nose. He howled as light blue blood poured down his face into his mouth, flowed along his chin and dripped to the concrete floor. After the legionnaire's bawls had subsided to whimpers, she held the misshapen appendage up to his face. "You didn't need this, anyway." She let go of it. The fake nose hit the floor with a soft plop.

She stepped back and regarded the legionnaire. Where the nose had been was a small, round bump with an even smaller hole in the middle. "Now you look more like a Byringa." Smiling, she cocked her head. "Are you ready now to tell me how many of you are in this city?"

"I don't know."

"I think you do." Taking a drag on her cigar, Melera stepped forward and smacked JL8762 hard across his face, twice. His head whipped back and forth from her blows. Fresh blood dribbled from his mouth. "I'll ask again. How many?"

The legionnaire remained silent.

She sighed. "Why are you making this so difficult?" Reaching up, she ripped off the smallest finger from JL8762's left hand. She heard a small pop. The legionnaire gasped and then shrieked. Blood poured from the hole where the finger had been. Inspecting the finger, she could see bone and gristle. Her brows shot up. "Oh. That was your real finger. I thought it was fake." Then she shrugged. "Oops."

Melera fitted her cigar into her mouth and started playing with the legionnaire's torn finger, juggling it. "Still won't tell me how many of you are here?"

The other alien hung his head. "Two hundred. As far as I know. Mag Beloc may have sent more."

She smiled around her cigar and let the finger fall to the floor. "See? That wasn't so hard, now was it?" Her smile died. "Is Beloc here?"

The legionnaire didn't answer.

She sighed a second time. "Are we going to have to do this again?" Taking the cigar out of her mouth, she stepped forward.

JL8762's head snapped up, his face knotted with horror. "No," he cried. "No more. Please!"

"Then tell me if he's in this city."

"Mag Beloc came down with our unit. I don't know if he's still here."

The blood drained from Melera's face. *Beloc's here... BelocishereBelocishereBelocishere!* She shook her head hard. Back in the moment now, she closed her eyes, took a deep breath and then opened them. "Do you know what he looks like?"

"No."

Stepping even closer, she raised her cigar. "You sure?"

The horrified look returned to the other alien's face. "I don't. I swear I don't."

Melera said nothing for a minute or two. "All right." She stared at the legionnaire but said nothing more.

JL8762 stared back. "Are you going to kill me now?"

She shook her head. "Later. We're going to keep you around for a while. But when I do kill you, I promise it will be quick."

He eyed her. "How do I know you'll keep your promise?"

She grinned. "You don't." Looking down, she saw the stub of her cigar was almost out. She swiveled her head but didn't see any ashtrays. She flicked a glance at the legionnaire. A small smile curved her lips but it soon died. Continuing to inflict pain by putting the cigar out on JL8762's body after the information had been obtained was something Beloc's people would do. She wouldn't stoop to their level. She dropped the cigar stub to the floor and ground it out with her boot.

Turning, Melera walked over to where Parker and Kurt stood. Parker, she noticed, looked a little pale. "Khurt, how soon you have otser vamp-ires here?"

"I'll start making calls tonight. I hope within the week."

She nodded and then looked over her shoulder at JL8762. His head hung, chin on chest. She turned back to Kurt. "Tsese lights go up and down, yes? Or are tsey steady?"

"They have a dimmer switch. Why?"

"Me want you turn lights way low." She jerked her head in the direction of the legionnaire. "Me know he not see well. It almost dark in here, it be dark to him." She gestured around the room. "Make noises wits chains—"

Kurt smiled. "Don't worry, my dear. I'm well-versed in this sort of thing."

"Good." She turned to Parker. "Me ready go you house now, Pawkher. You ready?"

Still pale, he nodded but said nothing.

Melera took his arm, skipped them, and then they were in his great room. Parker headed straight for the free-standing bar. She followed. Walking behind the bar, he pulled out a bottle of Jack and grabbed two shot glasses from the storage rack. He poured both glasses full and handed one to her. She raised her glass in a toast but he only upended his glass and poured the liquor down his throat. Then he poured another and did the same with that one.

He poured a third glass. Melera hadn't even taken a sip of hers. She frowned. "Pawkher, what's wrong?" she said in Toro.

Parker shook his head. "I need a joint." Stepping out from behind the bar, he walked into his study and was back a few minutes later with a joint the size of a commercial cigarette. Back behind the bar, he torched it. He took several drags and offered it to her.

She took it. Inhaling long and deep, she exhaled and took another toke. Then she handed it back. "Pawkher. I'll ask again. What's wrong?"

Parker, still obviously upset, stared at her. "You tortured him, Melera."

She blinked. "Yes."

"Did you have to do that?"

"He didn't answer my questions."

"Couldn't you have just kept hitting him? Did you have to be so… barbaric? And what's the point of keeping him in the dark and scaring him half to death? You got the information you wanted."

Melera's jaw dropped a little. "What do you think this is, Pawkher? This is not a game. This is war."

"But—"

"But nothing. This is how it is when you fight a war. Everybody knows it, everybody expects it." She pointed at him. "Your problem is you've never fought a war before."

"Now wait a minute. I have so. We had an interpack war—"

"Did you take prisoners? Or kill them?"

"We killed them."

Her eyes narrowed. "If you took prisoners, what do you think you'd do with them?"

He lowered his gaze to the countertop. "I…I don't know." He seemed to stare at it for a minute, then looked up. "I just…I just never saw this side of you before. And—"

"And you don't like it."

Parker hesitated. "No."

Melera's temper flared. "Get used to it," she said through her teeth. She downed her drink, slammed the glass on the countertop and stalked toward the stairs. She was angry enough that she didn't feel the usual effects of weed on her libido.

"Melera, wait!"

She didn't. Reaching the stairs, she took them two at a time. Melera stomped into the bedroom and headed toward the bed, stripping off her wet clothes along the way. She climbed in, pulled the blankets up and turned to face the wall. She stared at it. *How dare he judge me? He's got no idea what it's like out there.*

She heard Parker's footsteps on the stairs and then in the hallway. She closed her eyes and listened as he entered the bedroom. "Sweetheart?" he said, his voice sounding tentative. His footsteps came closer to the bed.

Melera didn't move or open her eyes. She sensed him kneel before her. "Honey, I'm sorry. I…I've never seen anything like that. Not in real life, anyway. It…unnerved me, that's all." He paused. "Melera, open your eyes. Please look at me."

She slowly opened her eyes. He looked anxious. "I love you, Melera. I can get used to it. I will get used to it. Just don't think I love you any less because of it. Okay? Please?"

Melera rose up onto one elbow. Her anger dissipated by his words, she reached out and cradled the side of his head in her hand. He turned his face into her palm and kissed it. "I love you, Pawkher. I'll do anything for you. You want me to stop? I will."

"No, sweetheart. I don't want you to stop. It's part of who you are. And I love every part of you." Sliding his fingers around her wrist, he leaned forward and gave her a tender kiss. After a minute, he pulled away. "So tell me—what did you burn?"

Melera frowned a little. "His…what do you say? Balls?" She shrugged. "One of them, anyway."

She heard Parker's sharp intake of breath and watched his eyes cross. "Oww." Uncrossing his eyes, he smiled at her, then stood and stripped off his clothes. "Move over, baby." She scooted over to give him room, and he slipped under the blankets. Wrapping his long, hairy arms about her, he held her close. "My beautiful alien warrior queen," he said in a low voice. "Mean as a rattlesnake." He chuckled.

"What's a rat-tell snake?"

Parker chuckled again. "You." He kissed her hair.

Neither one said anything for a long while. "Beloc is in See-at-tell," Melera whispered. She trembled a little.

He held her tighter. "Maybe. You heard what JL8762 said. He might not be here anymore."

"Doesn't matter. He'll come back. Especially if any more of his starlegions spot me."

Parker said nothing for a few moments. "Maybe you should just stay here. Stay inside, I mean. Beloc's starlegions aren't likely to come this way. Dressed the way they are, they'd be spotted right off the bat. And that's not what they want." He shifted so that he looked into her face. "Or would you feel safer at your base?"

"Base would be safest. But I don't want to leave you."

"I could always come with you."

"But what about your pack? They need you. And what about your business?"

Parker sighed. "True." He seemed to think a moment. "What about Underground? Can you hide there?"

Melera shook her head. "They'd find me. Their scanners go five hundred feet everywhere from their bodies. Underground isn't that deep."

"Yeah, but first they have to find their way in. And there's a different trick to opening each door."

"They'd find a way, Pawkher. They've been ordered to bring me back. They won't stop until they do." Lowering her eyes, she fell silent for a few moments. Then she looked up. "I have an idea."

"What?"

"I'll stay here like you say. When I go somewhere, I'll skip. They can't track me through the Void."

Parker's expression turned thoughtful. "Don't see why that wouldn't work." He smiled. "Now that we've got that settled, we should get some sleep."

"I'm not sleepy."

He grinned. "I can make you sleepy."

"How?"

"Like this."

And he did.

CHAPTER 26

ive days after the alien's capture, Li An leaned forward in her chair, rested her elbows on the desk in her Shanghai office and clasped her hands. She stared without seeing the ancient silk tapestries in their environmentally controlled cases, some of which had been in her family for over nine hundred years and at the porcelain vases and other antiquities that were even older. "Mei, I think we might have a problem."

Mei looked up from her computer. "What's that, Mistress?"

"I received a phone call from Zhang, or Henry Wu as he's calling himself. He had some more tidbits to share about Kurt. Apparently, the Master has a need for blood. Zhang saw him sneaking out of his blood bank with two pints of it. Zhang followed him to a room deep in the recesses of his nightclub. He waited until Kurt came out and hid behind some boxes so he wouldn't be seen. Kurt walked by without a second glance."

"Why is that a problem? It means he's lost his nose for blood. If that's so, he's very weak, then—maybe weaker than you thought."

"I didn't tell you this part. The second phone call Zhang made to me after arriving in Seattle? He was in one of the dining rooms at Kurt's restaurant. Kurt saw him and confronted him about it. But Zhang was alone at the time."

"You mean—"

Li An nodded. "Right. Kurt tuned in on my servant. No vampire I know of has the ability to watch another's servant. Which means Kurt's stronger than anybody would have thought."

"So you think he's on to Zhang and might be faking it?"

"It's possible. And Zhang also told me he's being watched. Many of Kurt's human servants have made 'friends' with him and some of the vampires, too." She placed her hands on the desk and leaned forward in her chair. "Now you tell me—since when are vampires friendly with human servants? Kurt must have told his colony to take Zhang to their collective bosom, so to speak."

Mei said nothing.

Li An tightened her lips. "But I know what I saw—Parker, Kurt's servant, was the reason I couldn't lay a stasis on him. Not Kurt. The bloodwine Kurt was drinking when I visited with him. Then there's the mirror incident Zhang told me about with Kurt's client." She threw her hands into the air. "I don't know what's real and what's not."

"Should we get him out of there?"

Li An tapped a long manicured nail on her desk top. "No…I don't think so. Not yet, anyway. Let's see what else he comes up with and maybe we can sort it out." She pursed her lips. "And there's one more thing. Abaeze, the Master of Lagos in Nigeria, called and told me Kurt's been contacting regents in certain cities for a meeting in Seattle. It's supposed to take place two days from now. Abaeze said he wasn't invited."

"What's the meeting about?"

"He said Master Corwin from Houston—that's in America—told him Kurt said there was a new race of mutant zots that may be in his city. A race that doesn't play by the rules—which might spark a pogrom."

"Did Master Corwin know which regents Kurt's contacting?"

"Corwin said judging from the other regents who've been in touch with him about the meeting, the cities are mostly in America and Europe." Li An tapped her nail on the desk again. "I don't like it. If what Corwin says is true, Kurt should be contacting all of us."

"Maybe he'll give you a call tonight or tomorrow."

Li An grimaced. "Maybe, but I'm not betting on it." She shook her head. "Kurt's planning something. Something big. I want to know what it is. If there are mutant zots around, he's leaving the rest of us to hang in the wind." She shook her head again.

Neither one said anything for a while. "Do you think Zhang could listen in on the meeting?" Mei said.

"I doubt it. Kurt will probably hold it someplace where his human servants aren't allowed to go. That way he can be sure they won't be disturbed."

"Then what can we do?"

Li An glared at her executor. "Nothing. Absolutely nothing."

While Li An fretted in her Shanghai office, Mag Beloc, alone inside his prison ship's spacious situation room, paced around the holographic map of Earth in the room's center. Twenty-five unevenly spaced white dots, glowing like stars, decorated the planet. These were the cities he'd targeted in which he thought Melera might be hiding. Though his starlegions had yet to find her, he considered this part of the mission a success. Dressed as the homeless, his legionnaires had been able to wander the streets without garnering much attention from the natives. The only giveaway would be the collars they wore, a device for communications, activating their personal stealth shields, and their means of suicide, if necessary. For those in the colder northern climes, their neck collars were amply covered by the hooded coats they wore. Legionnaires in the warmer, southern regions, more human-looking than those in the north, wore waist belts covered by loose-fitting shirts.

The collars' communications modules were set to signal the ship once a Maqu standard day, every twenty-eight hours. The signal didn't pinpoint a legionnaire's location. It was only meant to alert the personnel monitoring the mission that all was well. If a legionnaire had to commit suicide, the collar sent a different signal. His executive officer had reported to him that of the thirty-one thousand starlegions he'd sent to Earth, four thousand, twenty-two had sent the suicide signal. His brow twitched. *Four thousand, twenty-two isn't bad. I expected a lot more. But then, the mission isn't over yet.*

It was the four thousand, twenty-third legionnaire that disturbed him. JL8762 hadn't been heard from for five standard Earth days. If JL8762 had been captured by the Terrans, they would know immediately the legionnaire was of alien origin. His lips tightened. *The last thing I want right now is for the Terrans to know we're here.* When he'd followed Melera into this galaxy, he hadn't expected to find a planet like Earth. It was a perfect place to establish a base of operations to explore and exploit this piece of the universe. The problem was he didn't have an invasion force with him. *I've only enough ships to protect me from an attack by the Vst.*

His eyebrows rose. *Wait. Maybe I could leave some of the fleet here. This planet is defenseless. One battleship and maybe eight, nine destroyers? Wipe out their communications, annihilate a couple of cities…that should be enough to scare the Terrans into surrendering. I'll be vulnerable in Maqu, but I can always stay off the charted routes. And the Vst can't track me in hyperspace. An ambush would be impossible.* He thought about it some more. Could he afford to leave even a part of his fleet behind? He needed every ship he had to fight the Vst.

That was where Melera's Xia'saan battle fleet came in. He would use it to put down the rebellion once and for all. Despite his shipyards operating twenty-eight hours a standard day, the Akkadian martial forces were stretched thin. To compensate, he'd had to call in all of the military vessels that accompanied the research ships to fight the war. Since he couldn't send out armed escorts, galactic exploration in Maqu had come to a grinding halt. He grimaced. *Without Melera's battle fleet, neither I nor the Vst can win this war. It will just go on and on and on until the last star burns itself out.* Beloc shook his head. He'd decide the fate of this planet later. Right now he had to find Melera, and the sooner the better.

Walking through the holographic display, he crossed the situation room to the far side of the circular table and passed his hand over a small, dark square on its surface. A calendar appeared, floating in mid-air. He studied it and decided he'd been away long enough.

It was time to return to Earth.

Two days after Beloc's return to Earth, Kurt stood in his dungeon next to the St. Andrew's cross, now covered with a sheet. It had been a week since Melera had captured the alien called JL8762, and tonight was the grand unveiling.

His gaze swept over the assembled vampires. These twenty were some of the oldest and most formidable regents in the world. Their collective power vibrated the air. So did their hostility. Kurt had asked they put aside their differences for this exercise, and all promised they would. But then, most regents weren't known for keeping promises.

Hands clasped behind his back, Kurt rocked once on his feet. "Thank you for coming. We face a situation that we have never encountered before—one that could be dire for all of us. But before we begin, how many of you have had reports of odd-smelling zots roaming your streets?"

All of the regents raised their hands. "In fact, I smell something odd right now," Jermaine, the Mistress of Chicago said.

Kurt nodded. "I told you that these zots were mutants. The truth, however, is far worse than that. They're not mutants. They're space aliens."

"You brought us here for this?" Charles, the Master of Brooklyn said. He did not sound pleased. "Do you think we're fools?" He glared at Kurt. "I'm leaving. This is ridiculous." There were murmurs of agreement.

Kurt glared back. "I can prove it."

"Do it."

He snatched at the sheet covering the St. Andrews cross and was rewarded by the collective gasp of the assemblage. "This is an alien my vampires captured. As you can see, he—we assume it's a he—looks somewhat human."

Charles curled his lip. "That purple color. It's just body makeup."

"It isn't. Watch." Kurt waved an index finger at JL8762. He'd practiced this particular power on the legionnaire earlier and had been relieved to find it hadn't deserted him. Having to do this with a knife would have sent a clear signal to the others that his powers had waned.

A deep gash opened on the alien's upper left arm. JL8762 yelped and turned to stare at him with seeming hatred. Light blue blood spurted from the wound, dripped down his arm and then to the floor.

He turned to his guests. "Now I ask you. Have you ever seen or heard of a zot with blood like this?"

A chorus of "noes" greeted his ears. Others shook their heads.

"All right," Charles said. "I believe you when you say this is an alien. The obvious question is why are they here? What do they want?"

Kurt shrugged. "All I can tell you is what I think. I believe it's a precursor to a full-scale invasion. I'm just guessing but I think the number of aliens here now is too small to be anything else but some kind of advance scouting contingent."

"Why is that?" Gerard, the Master of London said.

He turned. "Because no government that I know of has been contacted."

"Do you think ours are the only cities where they've landed?" Charles said.

"Again, I don't know, Charles. I asked you and the others here because I thought they might decide to reconnoiter the most populous cities first."

"Then why isn't Nobuo, the Master of Tokyo, here? His is one of the biggest cities in the world."

Kurt pursed his lips. He had to be careful not to give away how much he knew. "I based my decisions on the alien we captured. I don't know what the rest of them look like. But this fellow—look at him. His height, his build—he'd stick out in Tokyo like a scarecrow. Don't you agree?"

Charles nodded. "I see what you mean."

Pieter, the Master of Johannesburg, jerked his head in JL8762's direction. "So what are we going to do about them?"

Kurt gave him a small smile. "Kill them, of course. In any and every way we can. I suggest you alert all the zots in your cities. Be on the lookout. We have to make this planet seem like too much trouble for the effort." He looked around at the other regents. "That's all I can say for now. Does anyone have any further questions? Suggestions?"

The room was silent.

He looked around at the assembled vampires. "Then I wish you happy hunting and good luck."

The room grew misty with dematerializing regents. When the mist cleared, there was one left. Mistress Ciara of Manhattan stepped up to him. "I just wanted to thank you for believing me when I first called you. I owe you yet another favor."

He smiled. "Nonsense, Ciara. The danger to all of us is too great to be worried about who owes whom a favor."

Ciara smiled back, took a step forward and kissed his cheek. "Thank you. I'll be going now. I'll talk to you soon." She misted and slipped under the closed door.

Kurt waited a few minutes. "All right. You can come out now."

Parker and Melera materialized behind the St. Andrew's cross and stepped around it. Parker raised his brow. "You turned down a favor? I don't believe it."

"Ciara owes me a debt she can never repay. Why demand more?"

"Good point."

Melera stood before the cross. Kurt saw she was dressed in a form-fitting black suit, partially unzipped, with a wide, golden neck collar underneath. A holster was strapped to her thigh, with the butt of a gun sticking out of it.

She and JL8762 stared at each other. With a movement he almost didn't see, she whipped the pistol out of its holster and shot the other alien between the eyes. JL8762's head dropped to his chest. A foul odor filled the room.

Kurt waved his hand before his face. "What on earth?"

Parker looked nauseous. "It's a plasma pistol. The shot fried his brains. Literally."

He noticed Melera didn't seem bothered by the smell. She zipped up her suit. "Te'po." A golden halo enveloped her. Then she looked from one man to the other. "Him we take down now, yes?"

Melera stepped up to the cross. Kurt unlocked the right arm cuff, then walked around her and unlocked the left. JL8762's upper half fell forward. She caught him. Then he unlocked the alien's ankles. Free now, she hefted JL8762's body over her shoulder. "Me be right back." He watched her close her eyes. There came the now-familiar flash of light and gust of wind. She disappeared and returned a few seconds later without the body.

Kurt frowned. "Where'd you go this time? Where'd you put him?"

Melera unzipped her suit partway. "Sen'po." Her halo disappeared. Then she looked up. "Me go nowhere. Drop him in Void. Nobody ever find."

He looked her up and down. "Do you do that often?"

"What?"

"Drop people into the Void."

Melera gave him a toothy grin. "Before me be Shen'zae, me be assassin for me fawtser. Is where me rid bodies."

His eyes widened.

Parker laughed. "Now you know, Kurt. Never get on her bad side." He chuckled a few more times. "Well, now that's over, Melera and I will be leaving."

Kurt held up his hand. "Wait." He paused. "Melera, you're really the only one we know of who can definitely get close to these legionnaires. Would you be willing to act as bait again to kill another?"

"No. Too risky," the two said as one.

He shrugged. "Just thought I'd ask." He fell silent a moment and looked at Parker. "Have you heard from Garrett lately?"

"Yeah, since she's one of my wolves, now. Why?"

"I was wondering if she'd heard from Feodor."

"I think she'd tell us if she did." He cocked his head. "How are you doing?"

"Better than I thought I would. Garrett's magick spells have been a blessing."

Parker nodded. "Good. We'll see you later." He took Melera's hand.

"Of course." Kurt watched Melera close her eyes again and the two disappeared.

He looked around his dungeon and sighed. Now there was just one thing left to do. They had to figure out their next step to catch Beloc before he caught Melera. Problem was, no one knew what he looked like. Then he chuckled. "Me, trying to protect Melera. I never would have thought."

With that, he dissolved into mist and headed for his office.

CHAPTER 30

Almost two weeks after Kurt's meeting with the regents, Garrett sat at the table in her kitchen drinking a morning cup of tea and thinking about aliens.

Kurt had told her about the strangers in their midst right after the regents' meeting while she was at his penthouse teaching him new spells and that they were trying to capture Melera. She was angry at first because he'd kept her in the dark for so long but relented after he'd explained that before they'd captured one of the legionnaires, there was really nothing to tell because no one was sure of anything. By now, all of Seattle's zots knew about the aliens and were keeping vigilant. One had been caught and killed. Another, she understood, had disintegrated into dust after being cornered by a small leap of wereleopards.

The witches were doing their part. They tried to use identification spells but soon discovered they didn't work on aliens. So when they came across a homeless person on whom the magick didn't work, they knew what they were dealing with and alerted the others, giving a magickally accurate description.

She took another sip of tea and picked up the morning paper. The kitchen extension telephone rang. Hoping it was Basile, she snatched the receiver out of its cradle. "Hello?"

"Cherie, it's Feo," the voice on the other end of the line said.

Garrett's heart leapt. "Feo! How are you?"

"More important, how are you?"

She gave a little shrug. "I'm as well as can be expected, I guess." She hesitated a moment and again decided not to tell him about her wolf, or that Parker was a vampire.

"How is your magick?"

"Like you said, it's a bit erratic but it's working well enough. I mean, nobody suspects anything's wrong."

"Bon." There was a short pause. "I have created another spell. How soon can you, Kurt, and Parker come here?"

"Well, let's see…today's Friday, January twenty-ninth and I've got a performance tonight—it's the last one, thank the Mother—but after that I'm free until the theater season opens in the spring."

"Good. Please tell Parker and Kurt. I'd like to do this as soon as possible and the sooner the better."

"I'll do that. I'll give you a call after we've worked something out."

"Very good. I will speak with you later, then. Au revoir."

"Au revoir."

Garrett and Feo hung up on each other. Then she called Parker. The phone rang several times before he answered.

"Berenson." He sounded sleepy.

"Park, I'm sorry to wake you but I just heard from Feo. He's got another spell worked out and wants us there pronto. How soon can you make it?"

"Let me get my calendar." He sounded wide awake, now. There was a long pause and then he came back on the line. "I've got a quick job on the first but after that I'm clear for ten days. So I can go on the second."

"Great. I'll tell Kurt. I'm sure he'll be able to go, then."

"Let me know. Oh—and I'm bringing Melera."

"Are you sure that's—"

"I won't leave her here alone, Garrett."

"Can't she go to—" Then she sighed. She knew Parker well enough to know that once he'd made up his mind, there was no point in trying to change it. "Okay. I'll tell Feo. 'Bye."

"See you."

Garrett called Kurt immediately after hanging up with Parker. She told him about Feodor's call and that she and Parker could go to France on the February second. He was free, so Garrett called Parker back to let him know they'd set the date. Finally, she called Feodor. "Hi, Feo. We're coming on the second." She paused. "And Parker's bringing Melera if that's okay."

"His space alien love?" Feo sounded surprised. "I thought—"

"No, Feo. She's real."

There was a long silence. "I would like to meet this Melera."

"Well, you're going to get your chance. We'll see you on the second. Au revoir."

"See you then. Au revoir."

She placed the receiver back in its cradle. Clasping her hands, she bowed her head. *Mother, please, I beg of you—let this work.*

That night, after the final performance of *Cats*, Garrett sat in her robe at her dressing room table and peeled the last piece of fur-covered latex from her cheek. She dropped it into the box and peered into the mirror. There—she looked like herself again. Dipping her fingers into a jar of cold cream, she spread it across her face. She did this several times until her face was covered in a thick layer. She waited a few minutes then picked up a soft cloth.

She had started wiping her brow when someone knocked on the door. "Come in," she called. The door didn't open. "Come in," she called in a louder voice. The door still didn't open. Frowning in annoyance, she rose from her chair, crossed the small dressing room and opened the door. Two men, one in a gray suit and another in uniform, and a uniformed woman stood just behind the threshold. All three were big and burly.

"Miss Larkin, I'm Special Agent Wilcox," the man in the suit said. He pulled out a small leather case and flipped it open. Affixed to its upper half was a metal badge with the words "Special Police" embossed across the top. The bottom held an identification card with his picture on it under plastic. He held it up to her face. She stared at the picture and then up at the man holding it. It was definitely the same person.

She paled beneath her cold cream. *Oh, Mother—someone who saw me came to the theater tonight!* For a split second, terror and instinct overrode her common sense. *Should I call my wolf? Cast an obscuring spell and get out of here?* Then her common sense returned. If she morphed into her wolf or cast a spell, they'd know she was zot and would hunt her down until she was caught.

"Can I help you?" she said, amazed her voice sounded so calm.

Wilcox glared at her. "You are under arrest on suspicion of being an exotic. Please come with us, Miss Larkin."

Garrett smiled beneath her layer of cold cream. "I think there's been some mistake."

"Please come with us, Miss Larkin."

She looked down and then at Wilcox. "Can I get dressed? It's freezing out there."

"No."

Her jaw dropped. "Can I at least get my coat and purse?"

Wilcox stared a moment longer, then nodded once. She turned and walked to the rack, took her sleeved cloak off the hanger and shrugged into it. Then she picked up her purse. Her hands started to shake. *Stay calm. There's a way out of this.* Glancing in mirror, she saw the policewoman standing behind her. The woman stood with her arms hanging stiffly at her sides, watching Garrett's reflection with no expression. Her gray eyes looked like pieces of flint.

Garrett swallowed hard. "I'm ready."

The policewoman stepped away from the doorway into the dressing room and motioned for Garrett to go out first. She did so, and the policewoman followed, leaving the door open. The officer took her purse. She frowned in surprise. "What are you—"

Before she could protest further, the policeman roughly spun her around, jerked her arms behind her back and handcuffed her. She swiveled her head and gaped at Wilcox. "Why are you doing—"

Wilcox's stare didn't waver. "Please be quiet, Miss Larkin. This is just a precaution."

"Against—"

Just then, Basile came striding along the corridor. "What's this?" he said, his voice loud. "Who are you?" He reached them and glared at Wilcox and the uniformed officers in turn. "Why is she handcuffed?"

Garrett shook her head. "It's all right, Basile. These are the special police. Someone has mistaken me for a zot and I have to go downtown and for a genetic screening test."

"Who are you, sir?" Wilcox said.

He turned. "Basile Roche. I'm a friend of Miss Larkin's." He turned back to Garrett and narrowed his eyes. "I'm coming with you."

She gave him a pleading look. "No, Basile. Really, it's all right. There's been a mistake, that's all. Just meet me at my house. I'll be along." She paused. "Please."

Basile stared at her for a moment longer then nodded. Giving the law one last look, he turned and strode along the hallway the way he'd come.

The policewoman took one of Garrett's arms and the policeman the other. With Wilcox in the lead, they marched along the corridor leading to the theater's back entrance. Everyone must have heard her and Basile's exchange because now the cast members were peeking out their partially-opened doors. Holding her head high, she didn't look at them.

They reached the door. Wilcox opened it and they stepped outside. A cold wind blew and Garrett shivered inside her cloak. How much of it was from the wind and how much from fear, she couldn't tell. The four marched toward a late-model, dark-colored sedan. Reaching it, the uniformed officers released her arms. The policewoman opened the car's passenger side rear door and helped her inside, guiding her head so she wouldn't hit it on the metal roof. While she climbed into the car, the other policeman had walked around to the driver's side and opened the rear door. The two burly officers slid into the car beside her. Sandwiched between them, she felt very small.

Wilcox started the engine and they left the theater. He drove along the darkened streets, headed for downtown. Except for the sound of the car's engine, the interior was silent. She kept her gaze straight ahead, noticing how few people seemed to be out tonight even though it was a Friday and not that late.

Presently, they reached a small, squat building with no identification on it. Just under the roofline was a row of rectangular, reinforced windows. To her, it looked like a prison. Wilcox turned the corner and drove around to the building's rear. He pulled up to an iron fence at least twenty feet high, topped with concertina wire. Stopping the car at the fence's gate, he reached up and tugged at the visor. It swung down, revealing a card in a holder attached to its rear. Extracting the card, he rolled down the driver's side window and inserted it into a slot in a rectangular box. The machine spat the card out a few seconds later. He took it and the iron gates parted. Wilcox drove through them, found a space in the first row of cars and parked.

The four exited the vehicle. The two uniformed officers each took one of Garrett's arms and the three escorted her to the door of the building. Like the gates, it too appeared to be made of iron. Wilcox pressed his thumb on what looked like a black inkpad attached to the building on the door's right side. The door clicked a moment later. He pushed it open, holding it for the other three to enter.

The door swung shut with a clang that sounded like a death sentence. They traversed a middling-length hallway and eventually came to a room marked "GST." The male officer unlocked Garrett's handcuffs. The special agent pushed the door open and she was shoved inside. Stumbling, she heard the door lock behind her.

After regaining her balance, she looked around. She stood in a small room, the walls and floor of which were covered with sheet metal. Dominating the room was a large chair that reminded her of the old electric chairs from the nineteen-thirties. The far wall had been covered in plexiglass, from roughly waist-high almost to the room's top. In a small room behind the plexiglass partition sat a balding, bespectacled man hunched over a computer terminal. She watched Wilcox and the two officers enter.

Her gaze strayed to the ceiling. A robotic arm with needle-like fingers and tubes running into a small black case attached to the arm's frame dangled over the chair. A series of air vents also decorated the ceiling. She frowned a little. Then her eyes widened. Those weren't air vents—they were gas vents. If the machine determined she was zot, she would be gassed right here in this room.

"Sit in the chair, please," a nasal voice came over a pair of loudspeakers in each corner over the plexiglass wall. "All the way back." Garrett swiveled her head. The technician at the computer terminal was giving her a hard, cold-eyed stare. He was the one who'd spoken. She walked to the chair and sat, scooting backward until she could go no further. Her feet didn't reach the floor.

"Place your arms on the armrests, palms up."

She did so. As she watched, a pair of cuffs emerged from the armrests and snapped over her wrists. Inspecting them, she noticed they were made out of thin strips of silver, gold, copper, pearl, and cold iron. *Not taking any chances…weres can't change and elves can't use their glamour.*

Then she looked closer. Her heart leapt into her throat and her breathing quickened. At the cuff's bottom, on the side closest to her, was a thin strip of dull silver metal. *Oh, no—spelled steel!* Spelled steel renders a witch powerless. Panic threatened to overwhelm her. A second later, the voice of reason cut through her fear. *Wait…just wait. Check the spell on it.* She concentrated. The spell's power was weak—it must have been cast a long time ago. She couldn't break the spell because she wasn't the witch who'd cast it but it was weak enough that she, with her mage's powers, might be able to override it. Assuming, that is, her powers were working at the moment.

Through the loudspeaker, Garrett heard the technician clear his voice. She looked up. His stare was just as cold as it had been earlier. "The robot will take blood from the fingers of your left hand and feed it into the analyzer. The results will come up on the screen in front of me. It will only take a minute. If you are human, you will be free to go. If not, you will be executed." He paused. "We will begin…now."

The robot's elbow hinge squeaked. It's needle-fingered arm lowered. She watched it come closer and closer to her hand, trying to resist the urge to curl her fingers. Then the needles plunged into her fingerpads. It hurt. *Sjo hominum, sjo hominum, sjo hominum,* she mentally chanted. A moment later, another wave of panic flashed through her. Would she be able to override the spell? Would her magick desert her now, in her moment of need?

Taking a deep breath, she watched her blood being sucked up into the tubes attached to the robot's digits. A few seconds later the robot arm withdrew, its needles leaving tiny spots of blood on her fingers. She watched the man behind the plexiglass. As he stared at the computer screen, she could see its colors reflected in the technician's eyeglasses.

After about ten seconds, the technician looked up with hatred in his eyes. "She's—" Then the screen's reflection blipped out and returned a moment later. He frowned. "Wait a minute." He started fiddling with the machine.

"What happened?" Wilcox said.

The technician shook his head. "I don't know. We have to do this again."

The robot's arm dropped. Its needle-fingers stuck her in the same place, this time hurting her even more. After what seemed like forever but was less than five seconds, the needles withdrew. The technician stared at the screen then looked up and goggled at her. "The GST machine first read her as a zot but then it changed to human. This reading shows the same. Not only is Miss Larkin human, she's about as pure a human as they come."

Garrett almost cried in relief. Her magick had worked. The cuffs unlocked and slid back into the chair's arms. "We won't hold you any longer, Miss Larkin," she heard Wilcox's voice over the loudspeakers. "One of the officers will escort you to the door." She watched him turn to the technician. "Get that machine looked at. We don't want to make any mistakes."

She scooted out of the chair and headed for the chamber door. There was no knob on the inside. She waited. A moment later, the door opened and the policewoman with the flinty eyes stood before her, holding her purse. The woman handed it to her. "This way," the officer said. She turned and began walking along the corridor, opposite of the way they'd come in. The heels of the officer's boots thumping on the floor sounded thunderous.

They reached the door. The policewoman opened it and practically shoved her outside. The door slammed shut.

In a daze from her brush with death, Garrett stared at it a moment. Then she turned. Even in her befogged state, she knew she had to find a cab to take her back to the theater. The building would be locked so she couldn't get her clothes, but she could at least retrieve her car. She swiveled her head left and right. No cabs in sight. Maybe she could go to one of the nearby hotels and catch one. She looked down at herself. Wearing just a cloak, robe, and flip-flops, and with dried cold cream caked on her face, she wondered if a cabbie would even take her as a fare.

She started to walk. She hadn't taken five steps before Basile's limousine slid up to the curb. He jumped out of it. "Garrett," he shouted. He ran the ten feet separating them and swept her into his arms. "Oh, Garrett, you're all right."

Garrett looked up at him with wide eyes. "Take me home," she said, her voice sounding shaky and far away to her ears. "Take me home, Basile."

"Of course, of course." He walked her to the car and helped her inside. Then he climbed in. He took her into his arms again and held her tight. She buried her face into his chest. Neither spoke as James pulled away from the curb and drove off.

In moments, it seemed, they'd arrived at her little house. Basile exited first and then helped her out of the car. His arm around her, the two made their way up the steps. Reaching the front door, she stared at it, then remembered she had to unlock it first. Digging into her purse, she found her keys. After isolating the right one, she fitted it into the lock and turned it. The door swung open and she stepped inside.

Basile was right behind her. He shut the door. "Garrett, I—"

She turned. "How did you find me?"

"James followed the car from the theater." He seemed to look her over. "Garrett, what did they do to you? How did you get away?"

Garrett told him. "And then they just threw me out into the street." Something in the retelling snapped her out of her daze. She burst into tears. "Basile, I was so scared. I thought I was going to die."

He took her into his arms again. "Shh, shh…you're home, now. You're safe." Holding her close, he slowly twisting from side to side while stroking her hair. She cried for what seemed like hours.

Presently, Garrett lifted her face. She looked at the cold cream her tears had rewetted smeared on Basile's coat. "Oh, no—look what I've done."

Basile glanced down and smiled. "Coats can be cleaned, Garrett."

She stared up at him, her eyes still full of tears. "I-I know you have things to do, Basile, but would you…will you stay with me tonight? I just don't want to be alone."

Still smiling, he hugged her tighter. "No one could drag me out of here. I'll tell James to pick me up in the morning. Meanwhile, why don't you make us some tea?" Letting go of her, he pulled out his cell phone and started punching numbers.

Garrett walked on unsteady legs into the kitchen. Stopping at the sink, she wet a dishcloth and wiped the remaining cold cream from her face. Then she crossed the small room, passing by the stove with the kettle on it without a second glance. After what she'd been through tonight, she needed something much stronger than tea. Reaching the counter, she opened the cabinet above her head and took out a bottle of Courvoisier. Then she took out two snifters.

Basile walked into the kitchen. "We're not going to have tea?"

She turned. "I need something stronger than tea."

He crossed over to where she stood. "Here—let me." He poured the cognac, then handed her a snifter. "A toast—to the brave and beautiful Garrett Larkin."

"I don't feel exactly brave and beautiful right now."

"Ah, but you are. You kept your head, and that was what kept you alive." He took a sip of his drink.

Garrett drained hers and held out her glass for more.

He chuckled and poured it full. "That should hold you for a second or two."

She raised the glass to her lips and drained it again.

He chuckled a second time. "Shall I pour you another?"

She shook her head. "I've had enough."

Basile took her hand. "Come. Let's go sit in the living room." Together, they walked out of the kitchen.

In the living room, he set his glass on the low coffee table. Sitting close on the sofa, she lay her head on his chest and he draped his arm around her shoulders. Neither said anything for a long while. Presently, she lifted her head. "Thank you," she whispered.

"For what?" he whispered back.

"For being there for me."

Basile gave her a squeeze. "No thanks needed, Garrett. I'm just glad I *could* be there for you."

She lay her head on his chest again. Minutes passed in silence. Then she took a breath. "Basile?"

"Yes?"

"I…I love you."

He didn't say anything at first. Then she felt him kiss her hair. "Yes."

Garrett smiled for the first time since her ordeal had ended. "Yes," she whispered. She closed her eyes. The cognac was doing its work. Still smiling, she drifted into sleep.

CHAPTER 31

In the late afternoon of February second, Melera, Parker, Kurt, and Garrett, travel cases in hand, stood before a thick, wooden door of a house perched on the edge of a rocky outcropping. The sun's rays slanting over the mountaintops indicated it would be dark soon. Melera watched Kurt reach for a large, U-shaped piece of black metal attached to an up-ended rectangle that looked to be made of the same material. He lifted and banged it twice. Its sound reverberated through the air.

The door opened almost immediately. She looked down at the smiling, short brown man with tightly curled white hair who stood in the doorway. His teeth were as white as his hair. "Come in, come in," he said, sounding excited. He moved out of the way to let them enter. Standing next to Parker in the foyer, she took a discreet look around. The house was ancient, no doubt about that. It even smelled ancient. Her other senses told her this was a peaceful, happy place—a place where trouble could not enter. It made her feel peaceful, too.

"Welcome, welcome," the short brown man said. He greeted Kurt and Garrett with hugs. Then he took Parker's large hand into his smaller ones and patted it. Lastly, he turned to her and looked her up and down. "So this is our space alien."

"Yeah," Parker said. "Feodor, this is Melera."

She smiled, already liking this man who radiated such goodwill. "Hel-lo."

"Melera, welcome." He peered into her face. "Such beautiful eyes. I love the way they sparkle and seem to spin." Parker had told her that Feodor already knew about her so she didn't bother to disguise her golden eyes as the human-looking, dark amber ones.

"Come into the kitchen. I know the four of you must be hungry after your long trip. It may be easy to do but misting takes energy, especially when you've got someone else along."

Parker licked his lips. "You know me, Feodor. I'm always up for eating."

Feodor laughed.

Melera's eyes widened a fraction. His laughter was fascinating—so hearty and joyful.

"Well, come along then. Before Parker eats us all." Feodor laughed again. He turned and headed deeper into the age-old house.

The four followed, led by Garrett, then Kurt and Melera. Parker brought up the rear. The five entered the kitchen. Food, a lot of it, lay on a scarred wooden table that, to her, looked as old as the house. Melera could tell who would sit where just by looking at the spread. On a platter, there was a stack of raw steak slabs for Parker, a carafe of blood for Kurt—fresh, her nose told her—a plate holding a mound of assorted vegetables for Garrett and for her, a plate holding another slab of steak— this one cooked—and a smaller mound of vegetables. A tray of cut fruit and assorted cheeses lay in the table's center.

Her mouth watered. She hadn't realized it before leaving Parker's house but she was ravenous. The four took their places at the table. From the corner of her eye, she watched Garrett bow her head as if in prayer, then pick up her fork and begin eating. Kurt poured himself a goblet of blood and sipped at it. A contented-looking smile appeared on his face. Parker attacked his pile of steaks with gusto. Melera picked up her fork and knife and cut a piece of steak. It wasn't quite as rare as she liked it but it was close enough. And the seasonings were superb.

"Melera, I hope your meal is all right for you," she heard Feodor's voice. She looked up. The older man appeared a bit anxious. "I wasn't sure how you liked your steak, so I just took a chance."

She swallowed her morsel and smiled. "Is good, Fe-o-dor. Very good, yes." She thought Feodor looked relieved.

During dinner, she watched Parker, Garrett, and Kurt talk and laugh as if there was no trouble between them. Feodor regaled them with stories of his youth. Even Kurt took part, telling tales of what life had been like six hundred years ago when he'd been alive.

Melera speared a piece of fruit and popped it into her mouth. *I love it here. So serene.*

Yes, but do not let your guard down, her czado said. *We never know what might happen.*

I don't think Fe-o-dor would let anything happen. Can't you sense his power?

Of course. But Fe-o-dor's power may not be enough to counter any trouble that might arise.

You think something's going to happen?

I sense nothing. But that does not mean something will not occur.

Pawty-poopah, as Pawkher would say.

Perhaps. But this pawty-poopah is the reason you are still alive.

"Melera," Feodor's voice sounded, bringing her back into the moment. He was smiling. "So. Tell us about your galaxy."

She did so. Rather than try to speak in her broken, halting English, she spoke Toro, letting Parker translate. She told them about what her life had been like on Xia'saan, about their communal lives, and growing up as the rough equivalent of an Earth princess. She told them stories of some of her adventures, on planets inhabited and uninhabited. She told them a little about the war now consuming Maqu but left out huge chunks of the tale, like about her battle fleet and her capture and torture as Beloc's prisoner. She mentioned nothing about her czado.

Her audience appeared rapt. When she at last fell silent, Feodor peered at her. "There is much more about yourself that you are not telling us, cherie. I sense great power in you…a power perhaps greater than my own." Then he shrugged. "But we are all entitled to our little secrets, non?" He smiled and clapped his hands. "Off to bed, you four. You need your rest. I'll let you figure out your sleeping arrangements."

Garrett tried to stay behind and help Feodor clean up but he waved her away. "Don't fret, cherie. I'll have this finished in no time." He winked. "Ah, the advantages of being a mage."

The four left the kitchen and trooped into the foyer where they'd left their travel cases. After some discussion, it was decided that Melera and Garrett would share one room and Kurt and Parker would share the other.

Parker cocked his head. "Is that okay with you, sweetheart? I mean, we can always——"

She smiled. "Is ohh-kay, yes." Sneaking a glance at Garrett, she thought the other woman didn't look so sanguine about it but she said nothing.

For almost a week, Melera did nothing but relax. She didn't think about the Vst, breaking her father's code, or Beloc and his starlegions' presence on Earth. It was as if she lived in a bubble and the outside world had ceased to exist. Through Parker, she met the local alpha wolf who made her, like Parker, an honorary member of her pack. The five of them talked about the tryst and while she still condemned Garrett's methods, she could understand and appreciate the nobility of her quest. Even Kurt earned her grudging respect as a fellow warrior after she'd learned about his exploits in a war hu-mans called World War II, spying for the faction called the Allies.

"Never would have thought that of you, Kurt," Parker had said, eyeing him. "I'd have thought you wouldn't care."

Kurt had smiled. "It wasn't entirely altruistic, dear Parker. The war left a lot of vampires homeless. Because of my exemplary war record, my construction company was awarded a number of choice contracts. So I secretly rebuilt many a colony's warren beneath the cities. Because of that, the Masters and Mistresses of those cities are forever in my debt."

Parker snorted. "Figures."

At the end of the week during dinner, Feodor announced it was time to try out his new spell. "We will work it the day after tomorrow. That means tomorrow we fast, non?" He smiled at Parker. "I know it will be difficult for you, mon ami, but trust me, you will not starve."

Melera almost laughed at the stricken look on Parker's face. She turned to Feodor. "Me watch, yes? Or me there be bad for you?"

He shrugged. "I don't see why not. From what Garrett tells me, our brand of magick doesn't work on aliens, which means your energy makeup is different. The spell will probably work as if you are not even there."

On the appointed day, the five gathered in Feodor's library. Feodor telepathically taught Parker, Kurt, and Garrett the magickal chant. After that, they slipped behind a hidden door in the library that led to a cave below the cottage. Reaching the staircase's bottom, Melera looked around. Although much smaller, the cave was not unlike the one on Ekahn, an uninhabited planet in Maqu and one of the many hideouts she'd used while on the run from Beloc. Stepping over to the cave's wall, she traced her fingers along the rock, feeling its roughness on her skin.

"Melera, come here," she heard Parker's voice. "Come look at this." She turned. Alone now, she hadn't noticed the others leave. Following the sound of her lover's voice, she walked into the next room. Parker stood next to what looked like a pit with multicolored wisps of energy radiating from it.

"You ever seen one of these before? It's a vortex. Pretty, isn't it? That blue color?"

Frowning, Melera stared at the pit. "Is not just blue. Is many colors." She looked up. "You not see tsem?"

Parker, Kurt, Garrett, and Feodor stared at her in seeming wonder. "No," Parker said.

She gave a little shrug.

"You've seen one of these before, haven't you, cherie?" Feodor said.

She turned. "Yes, many time. Many planet in Maqu have tsem. Is energy from planet core." She smiled. "Now me know why me feel so good. And me all-er-gic to Dirt, too. Me have not see-gar all week. You lucky you be here, Fe-o-dor."

Feodor smiled back. "There's been a mage living in this spot for two thousand years. Probably longer." He looked at the other three ranged about the cave room. "We need to get started. Give me your robes and step into the vortex, please."

Parker, Kurt, and Garrett complied. Feodor turned to Melera. "Sit anywhere you like."

Melera sat cross-legged on the floor at the cave's entrance. From here, she had a view of the entire room. She watched Feodor lay the three's robe on a nearby rock and then take off his own robe. Facing them, he held his hands in the air. "Now. Begin."

Parker, Kurt, and Garrett raised their arms and touched hands, finger pad to finger pad. They began to chant words that sounded to Melera like "beji mo naret tayra." As she watched, their auras manifested. When she saw the irregular splotches in the glow surrounding each, she understood. It was one thing for Parker to say he was a vampire. But now, with that big red stain obviously belonging to Kurt in his aura, she saw that he really *was* a vampire. Judging from the green blotch in Garrett's aura, the mage, she surmised, must have a lot of Parker's werewolf traits— maybe more than she was letting on. And Kurt had a smaller splotch of blue and even smaller green dots in his red aura. She also noticed that his aura seemed as if it had been torn in places.

Feodor began to dance. Swaying at first, his feet beat on the floor in a rhythm that she, even with her musician's training, found hard to follow. Then he started beating his chest with his left hand in a third rhythm, which was soon followed by his right in a fourth. That he was able to keep the various beats going without error impressed her.

"Gayara merito prasnat," he began in a sing-song voice. "Coshina limio neropata." As he sang, his voice ranged up and down the scale, from highs she hadn't thought possible from a Dirt male to lows that sounded more like growls. That impressed her, too.

The vortex's energy changed. Instead of swirling about, it shot straight up toward the ceiling. It began to vibrate. She watched what looked like three cracks form in the glowing force. The cracks widened and the power's tendrils began to spread downward like the petals of a flower opening until Parker, Kurt, and Garrett were surrounded. The energy pulled at the three's auras. The red in Parker's aura flowed toward Kurt. The green in Garrett's aura flowed toward Parker and the blue in Kurt's aura flowed toward Garrett. The tears in Kurt's aura lessened.

By now, Feodor had stopped beating his chest and singing, though his feet maintained their rhythmic thumping. Hands held chest high, he began rubbing them in a circular motion. He started pulling his hands apart. In the space between them, Melera watched a white glow appear and grow brighter. Feodor pulled his hands further apart and the white light grew in size. It formed itself into the shape of a ball. After it had reached a diameter of about a foot across, Feodor threw the ball into the vortex's middle.

The result was spectacular. Though it made no noise, the ball burst in a flash of light, not unlike the one that accompanied her entrance into the Void. She put a hand up to her face. After the spots before her eyes cleared, she saw the ball's energy crackling around the three like lightning, so bright it almost obscured their auras. It was mesmerizing.

From the corner of her eye, she saw Feodor stumble and fall to his knees. Then he toppled, falling face-first to the floor. In a second, Melera was on her feet and reached his side in two bounds. Rolling him onto his back, she peered into his face. His skin looked grayish. Remembering what Parker had taught her about Dirt people's physiology, she felt for his pulse. It was rapid. His skin was cold, too. She snatched his robe from the rock where he'd left it and wrapped him in it. Then, picking him up, she cradled him in her arms.

We need to get him upstairs, her czado said.

She closed her eyes and pictured the library in her mind but nothing happened. *Open the portal.*

The cold might kill him.

Waiting for me to run upstairs might kill him, too. Open the damned portal.

She pictured the library again and skipped. Opening her eyes, she noticed that Feodor's skin looked even grayer. It was colder, too. She laid him on the sofa. Looking around, she spotted an afghan draped over a nearby chair, snatched it up, and swathed him in it from head to toe. Then she sat on her knees and waited. She watched the color slowly return to Feodor's face. He opened his eyes and looked at her. "What happened?"

"You faint. Me bring you up here."

He nodded. "I need some rejuvenating tea. Go into the kitchen and look on the top shelf to your right. It's the third jar from the end."

Melera obeyed. Running into the kitchen, she located the jar and filled the kettle. It took her a minute to figure out how the stove worked— Parker did all the cooking—and after she had, she put the kettle on the burner. Soon the water was boiling. She took a mug from a rack next to the stove, dumped in a measure of tea and poured water over it. Then she returned to the library.

By the time she'd done so, Feodor had worked his way out of the afghan and was sitting up. She handed him the tea. He took a sip. "Ah."

Melera sat on her knees again and watched Feodor take another sip. She stared at him, her senses pinging. "You dying, yes?"

Feodor nodded. "Slowly but surely. My power is failing but my body is failing faster."

"Tsen why you do tsis?"

"Because if I don't, Parker and Garrett will go mad. You see, it hasn't manifested yet but their individual auras are at war. Parker cannot be a werewolf and a vampire at the same time. Garrett cannot be a mage and a werewolf. And Kurt..." He shook his head. "Kurt may not go mad but in his severely weakened state, someone is eventually going to challenge him to a will contest and he will lose. He will die twice."

She looked down and nodded. "Me see." Then she looked up. "You use vortex to be alive, yes?"

"It's the only reason I am and still have power." Feodor fell silent a moment. "You must not tell the others I am dying. If this spell did not work completely, I will have to create another. If they know my state, they may not agree to it. I will not allow that to happen."

Melera gazed into his kind brown eyes. "Me not tell, yes."

By now Feodor's tea had apparently cooled because he drained the cup. "We'd better get back to the cave. I need to see what's happening."

"You finish spell?"

"Once I threw the ball of energy, my part was over. Now I have to see how it's affected them." He stood and swayed a little. She caught his arm. "I'm all right, cherie. Come."

He started for the hidden staircase. Her grip on his arm tightened. "Me have faster way." She closed her eyes, pictured the room in the cave with the vortex and skipped them. Once there, she let go of Feodor's arm.

He smiled. "Handy, that."

She smiled back but said nothing.

Feodor turned to the three standing in the vortex. Melera could see that the lightning had abated until it was just wisps of light circling their bodies.

"The spell is almost finished," he said.

The two watched the white light dissipate until it had disappeared. The three sections of the vortex began to rise, column-like, until it once again pointed at the ceiling. Then the column collapsed and the vortex's energies return to their natural state. Parker, Kurt, and Garrett's individual auras disappeared.

The three stopped their chanting. Eyes blinking, they stood as if in a daze. A few minutes later, they seemed to come to their senses.

"You may step from the vortex now," Feodor said. "Come. Put on your robes. We will go upstairs and I will give you a report."

After their robes had been donned, and with Feodor in the lead, the five walked up the stairs. In the library, Melera, Parker, Kurt, and Garrett ranged themselves in the chairs while Feodor sat on the sofa.

Feodor looked at Parker, Kurt, and Garrett in turn. "We are not there yet, mes amis, but we have come much closer." He turned to Kurt. "You still have a big streak in of blue in your aura. However, the tears have closed considerably. You do not yet have all your powers. Or if you do, they will be weak. But they are there."

Melera watched Kurt reach over to the small table and push a bowl of fruit off its mirrored base. "Well, let's test it right now." He picked up the mirror and held it up to his face. "Hmm…a little fuzzy but I can see my reflection." He put the mirror down, plucked an apple from the bowl and bit into it. He chewed, swallowed, and immediately choked. Managing to dislodge the piece of fruit stuck in his throat, he stared at the morsel in his hand. "Not yet, I suppose," he muttered.

Feodor turned to Parker. "You still have a good deal of Kurt's aura mixed with yours, but it is much less. I would say you will need blood"—he shrugged—"perhaps once a week but the blood lust will not take you. You will still be able to mist, too." Parker nodded.

"And as for you, cherie," he said, speaking to Garrett, "you have far less green in your aura. Your wolf, while still there, is too weak to come out on its own. Your mage's powers should be greater and less erratic."

Melera thought she looked relieved.

Feodor stood. "Time for bed," he announced. "You are leaving tomorrow and after today's spell, you need your rest. And I need mine." He turned and headed for the library door. The four followed him out. At the top of the stairs, Feodor bade everyone goodnight. "I will see you at breakfast." Then he entered his bedroom.

Melera, Parker, Kurt, and Garrett looked at each other. Parker let out a little sigh. "Guess Feodor's right. Time to hit the sack." He paused. "Though I could use a snack."

Melera held out her arm, her wrist face up.

Parker laughed. "No, sweetheart—not that kind of snack."

She lowered her arm and smiled. "Tsen we go now. Goo-night."

"Goodnight," the others chorused.

Melera turned. Taking one last look at Feodor's bedroom door, she followed Garrett into their shared room.

CHAPTER 32

For the next ten days after returning from France, Kurt, Parker, Melera, and Garrett met at his penthouse every other night or so. Feodor's spell was still settling and while Melera looked on, the three tested their abilities on each other and traded anecdotes about how their mixed-up powers were affecting—or not affecting—them.

"Do you still put yourself under stasis sometimes?" Kurt asked Parker while picking up his glass of wine.

He shrugged. "It's happened three times since the first time we went to Feodor's but now it's not nearly as strong. I mean, I can move and all. It just feels like I'm slogging through mud."

"Has it happened again on a job?"

"No, thank God."

Kurt leaned over, picked up a cheese knife, and cut himself a piece of brie from the wheel on the low table.

Parker's eyebrows rose. "Hey, you can eat."

Kurt smiled. "I've been doing some experimenting on my own. I can only eat soft foods, but it's a start." After depositing the morsel on his small appetizer plate, he passed the knife to Garrett. "More cheese, my dear?"

She took the knife. "I'd love some."

"So how's your wolf these days?" Parker said.

Garrett spread the cheese on a cracker. "She's there but as Feodor said, she's very weak. I get little headaches from time to time. Nothing major, though. She also talks to me but it's easy to block her out." She peered at Parker. "Does your wolf talk to you?"

He rolled his eyes. "All the time. Sometimes I can't get him to shut up."

The four laughed.

Kurt had noticed that ever since they'd returned from France, much of the tension that had defined their relationships with one another had largely melted. Before their trip, he wouldn't have imagined the four of them in the same room without being at each other's throats. Especially Parker—his hostility toward him and Garrett had been palpable. *But now… I wonder if it's because we got to know each other somewhat when we were in France. Familiarity might breed contempt but it can also breed friendships.* He stole a glance at Melera. During the week they'd spent at Feodor's, he'd come to understand just how much Parker loved her. He was still jealous of their love but he knew they belonged together. He lowered his eyes. *If I destroy Melera, I'll destroy Parker, too. I just can't—won't—do that to him.* A pang of sadness lanced through his heart. *Well, if we can't be in love, maybe we can at least be friends.*

Suppressing a sigh, he shook off the feeling and put his plate on the table. "All right—let's get to work. Garrett, I probably can't put a stasis on Parker and I know it won't work on Melera, so that means you're the lucky one. Do you mind?"

She nodded. "What do you want me to do?"

"Just stay where you are." Kurt concentrated for a second, then directed a blast of power in her direction. "Now. Lift your right arm."

Garrett didn't move.

"Nod your head."

She still didn't move.

"Roll your eyes."

Garrett stared straight ahead.

Elation zipped through him. His stasis power had returned. Maybe not all of it—Parker still had some—but enough. Kurt sent out another blast of power in Garrett's direction, lifting her out of her immobility.

She shook her head. "Whew. That was scary. Wanting to move, but not being able to…" She peered at him. "Is that how you capture humans for your meals?"

He smiled. "No, we do that by hypnosis. Only regents have the stasis power. It works on everyone—" he glanced at Melera— "everyone from Earth, that is." He looked at Parker. "What about your feeding habits?"

"Feodor was right—once a week. And no blood-lust." Parker raised his brows. "What about you?"

"I haven't had to feed since we left France. I don't know when the hunger might strike again but I'm going to hold out for as long as I can." The room fell silent for a moment. Then he smiled again. "I may not be as lucky as you are to have a blood cow like Melera at my beck and call but I do have a blood bank."

Parker's expression turned startled. "You—"

Kurt's smile widened. "That's right. I read your mind. One of my other powers that have returned. My remote viewing is better, too."

"What about your mage powers?" Garrett spoke up. "Have you tested them?"

"Haven't had the chance." He shrugged. "But I suppose we can see if I can still make witch light."

Garrett looked alarmed. "Uh, Kurt—"

"Fear not, Garrett. This time I know what I'm doing." Turning his hand palm up, he stared at the center of his hand and flipped his mental toggle switch. The magick laser beam shot straight up from his palm. A second later, he switched his mental toggle off. The light disappeared. Kurt looked at the ceiling. A splotch of black marked the spot where the laser had burned the paint. "See, Garrett? Only a scorch this time. Nothing to worry about." He looked at Parker and Melera to see their mouths hanging open. His face broke into a smug grin. "Pretty impressive, hmm?"

"Whoaa," Parker said.

"Yes," Melera said. "Very—what you say?—im-pres-sive."

Silence reigned for about ten seconds. Then Parker stood. "Well, I've got a job in the morning, so we'd better get going."

Kurt rose from his chair. "Of course. Let me get your coats." He walked to the closet and retrieved Parker and Melera's outerwear. "Here you are."

While they shrugged on their coats, he turned to Garrett. "Should I get your coat, my dear?"

She nodded. "I should leave, too."

Kurt pulled her cloak from the closet and helped her into it, holding her purse so she could slip her arms through the sleeves. They stepped over to the private elevator and he pressed the call button. The doors whisked open.

She stepped inside the cab and looked at Parker and Melera with a small frown. "Aren't you coming?"

Parker grinned. "No, we have our own way of getting about."

Kurt smiled. "Thank you for coming tonight. I think we've all made a lot of progress. Hopefully, Feo will be able to work out another spell to make us whole." He saw the expression on Melera's face turn thoughtful but ignored it. "So, shall we say the night after tomorrow, at nine?"

"Sure," Garrett said.

"Wonderful. I'll see you then. Goodnight." He pressed the button again and the doors whisked closed. "As for you two, I take it you'll be here?"

Parker nodded. "Yep. See you." He watched Melera close her eyes, then closed his own. A blast of frigid air enveloped him. When he opened his eyes, the two had disappeared.

Turning from the elevator, Kurt crossed the room and sat in the chair he'd occupied. Leaning back, he looked at the ceiling and stared at the scorch mark left by his beam of witch-light. Since returning from France, he'd tested what powers he'd regained over and over, not just on Garrett and Parker, but also on his human and zot servants, his vampires, and even unsuspecting humans on the street. Some of his powers were weak and some almost nonexistent but with the powers he did have, he was confident he could carry out his plans for Henry Wu. His lips stretched into a mirthless smile.

It was time to call Li An.

Two days later, Li An materialized in the middle of Kurt's office underneath his nightclub. "So why am I here, Kurt?" she said without ceremony, smoothing her embroidered silk dress.

Choosing to ignore Li An's rudeness, Kurt rose from behind his desk and smiled. He gestured to one of two comfortable chairs in the middle of the room almost facing each other. "Please, have a seat."

Li An walked over to the nearest one and sat. "You've done some redecorating. What happened to the chaise?"

"Oh, it's in storage. After seventy years, I decided was tired of it."

"I see." Li An tilted her head. "I'll ask again, Kurt. Why am I here?"

Kurt sat in the chair across from her. "I owe you an apology, Li An, for throwing you out and threatening you last November. It was completely uncalled for. Just because I was angry did not give me the right to behave the way I did."

She gave him a severe look. "That's true."

"So, to make up for it, I've got a special treat for you. But first, a glass of my finest." He leaned over and pressed the button on an intercom resting on a side table. "Julie, we're ready."

The door to the office opened fifteen seconds later and Julie stepped inside, bearing a silver tray with two cut crystal goblets of generous proportions. Each glass was filled with blood. She served Li An first, then Kurt.

"Thank you, Julie," he said. "That will be all for now."

Julie dipped her head and left the room.

He lifted his glass. "Let me propose a toast. To our colonies, long may they be."

"Hear, hear," Li An said.

Kurt took a sip from his glass while watching Li An. Her brows rose. "This is delicious."

"Yes. Fresh from the vein. No anti-coagulants." He smiled. "And then I added a smidgen of my secret seasoning. My version of the Bloody Mary."

Li An nodded once and took another sip.

They drank in silence. After their third glass of Bloody Marys, Kurt cocked his head. "Li An, would you like to meet the servant who's been so generous with his blood? He's wonderful—one of my best servants. I think you might even like him."

Li An raised her brow. "I'm surprised he's still conscious."

Kurt smiled. "Oh, no, I'm sure he is." He turned in his chair and pressed the intercom's button. "Simon, Gregory—would you bring in our donor, please?"

A minute later, the door opened and a human, head hanging and supported by the two vampires, was half-dragged into the room.

He smiled again. "Li An, meet Henry Wu."

Henry's head snapped up. His eyes bulged. "Mistress, please," he cried, his words slurred. "Please, they're—"

Kurt raised his brows. "Oh, so you two know each other, hmm?"

Li An's lips tightened. "I've never seen this human in my life."

His smiled died. "Come, come, Li An. I know exactly who he is and why you sent him here. Somehow, you figured out I had attempted to make a tryst and you think my powers have deserted me." His brow rose. "I'm happy to say they have not. Think fast!" He slashed his finger through the air.

Henry's head shot off his neck and sailed across the room. Blood spurted from the stump. Kurt waved his hand and the spurting stopped.

Li An caught Henry's head in both hands. Lips tight, she stared at Henry's face. *Mistress*, the head mouthed. Then Henry's eyes glazed over.

Kurt watched Li An's expression turn furious. She leapt to her feet. "How dare you kill one of mine?" she shouted.

"How dare you send a spy to my colony," he said, his tone pleasant.

She glared at him. "This means war, Kurt!"

He shrugged. "Fine. But don't forget who started it." His lips stretched into a small smile. "I think our little visit is over, wouldn't you agree?" Then he chuckled. "Don't worry about Henry's body. My justborns will be happy to have the leftovers."

Li An bared her teeth at him. "I will get you for this and everything else you've done to me, Kurt. I know what you do. The bloodwine, stealing from your blood bank, the mirrors. You may be doing everything you can to hide it but you are weak. Your hold over Seattle is even weaker. And I will see that you lose it."

The Mistress of Shanghai dissolved into mist and was gone.

CHAPTER 33

Kurt stared at the spot where Li An had stood seconds before. "Please take what's left of Henry to my justborns," he said without turning around to the two vampires holding Henry's body. "It's time for them to feed." He heard them leave the office.

"Kurt," another voice said a moment later. He turned. The speaker was Daniel.

"Did you hear?"

"Of course. She was shouting loud enough to wake the dead."

Kurt chuckled. "We *are* the dead, Daniel. Or have you forgotten?"

Daniel rolled his eyes. "You know what I mean."

He smiled but said nothing.

"What about Simon and Gregory?" Daniel said. "They heard Li An."

"I've already erased their memories."

Daniel's eyes widened. "You can do that?"

Kurt nodded. "One of my powers that returned after our last visit to Feodor."

Neither vampire spoke for a minute. "So," Daniel broke the silence. "We're at war with the Shanghai colony. How will that work out? From what I've heard, Li An's vampires outnumber us by at least twenty-five to one and that was when we were at full strength. Don't we need a battle plan or something?"

"We have one. Several, in fact. But I don't think we'll need them. There hasn't been a pitched battle between vampire colonies in well over two hundred years."

"Why not?"

"We'd have to fight on unclaimed territory and there's precious little of that left in the world. Even the wild country has been claimed.

The regent in Fairbanks has claimed the North Pole and its environs. No one's challenged him on it, so I suppose it's his."

"What if Li An sends an invasion force to Seattle?"

"Unlikely. Her vampires would be disadvantaged since they don't know the city or speak the language. Plus, they'd have to face all the other zots living here. It might be a matter between vampires but I can't imagine anyone taking kindly to an invasion on their home turf." He shook his head. "All our war really means that if any of mine show up in her territory, Li An has the right to kill them with impunity. It's the same for me." He winked. "Just stay out of Shanghai and you'll be fine."

"All right." Daniel peered at him. "But don't you have a lot of business dealings there?"

"Plenty. But I'm not worried. I've buried my interests under so many corporate layers, it'd take a genius a hundred years to figure it out."

"A hundred years is nothing to Li An."

"Yes, but she's not a genius, either." Both vampires laughed.

Daniel sobered. "She might have a genius in her colony."

Kurt shrugged. "She probably does. But even if she or one of hers figures out the corporate structure, there's nothing she can do about it short of challenging me to a will contest. And I don't think she'll do that."

"Why not?"

"Because despite her bluster, she's really not sure if I'm weak or not. She's not going to take the chance of my inheriting Shanghai if she loses a contest. Not after she worked so hard to hold on to it."

"Let's say she goes batty and challenges you. Kurt, you're stronger than you were before but you're not strong enough to take on another regent."

Kurt gave him a little smile. "Maybe not but I have a number of little tricks up my sleeve, as the saying goes."

"Like what?"

"This." He held up his hand and flipped his mental toggle switch. The laser shot out from his palm. He flipped the switch off and turned to Daniel.

Daniel stared at the scorch mark on the wall with saucered eyes. He looked at him. "You got any more tricks like that?"

Kurt grinned. "A few."

Daniel gave his head a small shake. "All right."

Kurt's grin faded into a smile. "Don't worry, Daniel. This will all work out. Everything will be fine."

CHAPTER 34

A week after Henry Wu's death, Beloc sat at one of the rear tables in Craddock's, one of Seattle's finer seafood restaurants, nursing his drink while waiting for his dinner.

The 'bot surgeons had sewn his third eye shut to make his disguise and it itched. He resisted the urge to scratch it. Doing so always gave him a headache.

He took another sip of his drink and stared into the glass's honey-colored depths. He liked this beverage Terrans called "scotch." It had a smooth taste, mellow with a hint of something he couldn't identify. *I'll have to take some with me when we leave.* His eyebrow twitched. *If we leave.*

Beloc set his drink on the table and let out a little sigh. His search for Melera was going exactly nowhere. His legionnaires were combing New York City. She didn't seem to be there. The same with Chicago. And Los Angeles. *Maybe it's time I expanded the search. That place called Miami, Florida, maybe?* His lips tightened. He really didn't want to pull his legionnaires out of New York City, Chicago, or Los Angeles. She could always turn up there at some point and he needed his people on the ground.

Picking up his drink again, he swirled the scotch around in the glass and wondered if his instinct about choosing Seattle as a hunting ground had been wrong after all. Seattle was a large city, true, but not nearly as large as the others he'd targeted. If he'd been right, in a city this size, his legionnaires should have found her by now.

He looked around the restaurant. From the corner of his eye, he noticed a woman with yellow hair staring at him. He made a small grimace. This wasn't the first time he'd been stared at by Terran women. It seemed that everywhere he went, he'd catch one or two or even more of them looking him over. If he made eye contact, some looked away but others didn't. They stared right back. *So bold. At home, they'd never stare like this. Women should keep their eyes lowered.*

His meal arrived. He liked this "salmon steak." He understood salmon was some type of animal Terrans called a "fish," and that it lived in water. Whatever it was, like the scotch it too had a smooth, mellow taste, albeit slightly oily.

Beloc dug into his meal, savoring the salmon's flavor. He noticed the woman was still staring at him. *Let her stare. She's never seen a man eat before?*

He took a bite of fish and thought about JL8762. The legionnaire's disappearance continued to worry him. He didn't care about the legionnaire but he did care if the Terrans had caught him. He'd read about the place called Area 51, where the American military housed captured aliens. He'd also read that it was a hoax but that didn't mean much. Great God Aerpolis knew he had any number of secret compounds where he kept his special prisoners, usually high-ranking officials of the various planetary governments with important information to impart, once he'd tortured it out of them.

Beloc finished his salmon and frowned a little at the vegetables. He wasn't fond of the edible plants but vegetables were something Terrans ate regularly and he'd do whatever he had to do to blend in. He speared one, a long, green stalk with what looked like a closed flower on one end and cut it with his knife. He popped the morsel into his mouth and chewed, trying not to make a face as he did so.

He thought about JL8762 once more. *If he's been caught, he won't have much to tell them. He's just a guard. But he could tell them where the prison ship and the fleet are anchored. From what I've read about their space capabilities, there's nothing the Terrans can do about that but it would put the rest of my legionnaires on this planet in danger of being captured. Well, I could always signal them to abort the mission.*

Beloc had just put down his knife and fork when his waiter appeared and took away the remains of his meal. The Jahannan warlord rested his elbows on the table for a few minutes. His primary stomach felt as heavy as a kukli ball. His primary would digest part of his meal and then his secondary stomach would take over. Given his big dinner, he wouldn't have to eat again for at least another two days.

He sat back in his chair, toying with the idea of having another scotch before leaving. As if he'd read his mind, his waiter appeared bearing a glass of scotch on a silver tray. Beloc smiled. "How did you know?"

The waiter's lips twitched. "Compliments of the lady, sir."

"What lady?"

"The lady sitting at the table by the window, sir." He made a minute gesture with this head.

Beloc looked. It was the table where the woman with the yellow hair had sat staring at him. But she was gone, now. He turned to the waiter and smiled. "Very nice of her. But she's apparently left the restaurant. Too bad I'll never get the chance to thank her."

"She also asked me to give you this, sir." The waiter proffered a small, stiff rectangular card.

Beloc took it. The front of the card was blank. He turned it over. There was writing on it. *Call me anytime,* it said. Below that there was a telephone number.

He looked up. The waiter wore a small smile. "If I may be so bold, this isn't the first time this has happened, sir. Correct?"

Beloc made a small grimace. "Correct. Happens all the time."

"Enjoy your drink." The waiter gave a short bow and left his side.

Beloc looked at the card with its message and turned it over to the blank side. *Interesting—all of the women who've given me their numbers have signed their names. Wonder why she didn't?* He gave his head a minute shake. It didn't matter. He wasn't going to call her.

He gripped the card and had started to rip it in two when a familiar tingling feeling flooded his secondary stomach. He turned the card over and over as if maybe it had some new information to impart. It didn't. *Keep the card,* a small voice echoed inside his head.

Beloc thought for a moment, then slipped the card into the inside pocket of his suit jacket. He finished his scotch. Signaling the waiter, he paid his exorbitant bill and left the restaurant. He started walking. At the next corner, he stopped and pulled the card out of his pocket. He stared at the message and the number again.

He nodded once and slipped the card back into his pocket. He'd call her. Not tonight, not tomorrow, and maybe not even next week. He'd make her wait. He was sure he knew what she wanted to talk to him about—she wanted to "get to know him," as the Terrans say. His lips tightened. These brazen Terran women needed to be put in their place.

But he would call her.

CHAPTER 35

Spring had come to Seattle and Garrett had never been happier. It wasn't just that the air had warmed, though she was grateful for it. The real reason she felt so happy was she'd found the love of her life. Basile Roche was everything she'd ever wanted in a man. He was loving, attentive and romantic. He was the dom she'd always dreamed of. She'd trust him with her life.

Oh, she still loved Kurt. She would always love Kurt. But Kurt couldn't—or wouldn't—give her what she needed. Basile was not only her lover but her friend. Best of all, because of him, the terrible burden she'd been carrying had been lifted from her shoulders. She fell into a reverie, remembering.

Basile had come over one night, after returning from one of his many business trips. "I have something for you," he'd said.

Garrett had smiled. He always brought her little gifts from wherever he'd been. "What is it?"

Basile had smiled back. "This." He took out a small box from his suit jacket's inner pocket and opened it. Reaching inside, he pulled out an exquisite silver necklace with a delicate, intricately wrought medallion hanging from one end.

She'd caught her breath. It was one of the most beautiful necklaces she'd ever seen.

"Come here," he'd said. "Let me put it on you."

She'd obeyed. Stepping closer, she'd turned so that he could fasten the piece of jewelry around her neck. He'd just closed the clasp when a terrible burning sensation began in her chest and spread along her neck. She was on fire.

Garrett screamed and fell to her knees. "Take it off, she cried. "Take it off—please!"

A moment later, the red-hot burning sensation had stopped. Garrett rose to her feet on shaky legs and looked down. A bright red spot, starting to blister, decorated her chest. Two red lines, also blistering, sprouted from the large red spot. She could still feel their heat but not as intensely as before.

"What happened?" Basile had nearly shouted.

Tears had filled her eyes. She'd thought enough of her werewolf tendencies had been erased by the last spell-casting Feodor had done.

"What happened?" Basile had repeated.

She turned.

He'd gasped, his worried look turning frightened and horrified at the same time. "Oh, Garrett—what did I do to you?"

Garrett hadn't known what to say. She opened her mouth and made a snap decision. She took a deep breath. It hurt. "Come. Sit on the couch with me."

Basile had followed her to the sofa and they sat. She'd looked into his eyes. "I'm going to start at the beginning. This might take a while."

She'd begun by telling him about her apprenticeship to Feodor, about finding the book that contained the tryst spell and the Eall Tholia spell and what it could do. "The spells would have changed how humans felt about us. Zots and humans would finally be able to live in peace. That's what I'd wanted. It's still what I want."

Then she'd told him about her long, frustrating journey to find just the right combination of zots and how she'd finally found Parker and Kurt in Seattle. She'd told him about the revolution and the riots. "We knew we had no choice. We weren't ready to cast the spells but to stop the massacre of our kind, we had to try."

She'd taken a deep breath. "The tryst spell went wrong. We should have merged into each other but we didn't—not completely, anyway. Now we all have a piece of one another within us." She paused. "I've gained some of Parker's power. I'm part werewolf. We've been working with Feodor to separate ourselves, but"—she gestured at the necklace Basile still held—"we obviously haven't separated enough."

"Why did the necklace hurt you?"

"Silver is an anathema to werewolves. It burns. Steel and any other metal won't hurt a werewolf. You can even use a gun but a regular bullet won't cause much damage. That's why you need silver. A silver bullet, a silver knife—anything silver will hurt a werewolf and enough silver will kill one." She paused again. "That's why the necklace burned me."

Basile had dropped the necklace on the table and had then taken her into his arms. "I'm so sorry, Garrett."

She'd looked up at him. "Why? You didn't know."

He'd given her a squeeze. "I'm sorry this happened to you. I'm sorry for what you've been through and what you're still going through. I don't know what but I'll do everything in my power to help you."

A small smile had appeared on Garrett's lips. "There is one thing you can do."

"Anything."

Still gazing into his dark eyes, her smile died. "Be more than just my lover. Be my friend."

"Yes. I will." Then Basile leaned down and had given her a deep kiss. After ending it, he stood. Taking her hand, he'd pulled her to her feet. "Let's go upstairs." They hadn't let go of each other until they'd reached her bedroom.

Back in present, Garrett drove along the downtown street feeling almost as light as the breeze tickling her nose coming through the open window. Basile was off on another business trip but he'd be back tonight. If he wasn't too tired, maybe they'd play out a scene. She shivered in anticipation.

Reaching the Stohlman Theater, she entered the parking lot, found a space and shut down the car's engine. She got out and looking around to make sure no one was watching, skipped to the back entrance. The theater would be opening soon for the spring season, and there was much to do.

She opened the door and her light mood clouded. A small frown appeared on her face. She hadn't heard from Feodor in weeks. He'd said he was going to the Paris repository but surely he would have been back by now. She'd called the cottage but there'd been no answer. *I hope everything's all right. I can't go to Paris—not right now. Maybe he'll call soon.*

With that thought, she walked along the hallway, heading backstage.

Parker hadn't noticed winter had given way to spring.

He wasn't home much these days. He was too busy having the time of his life. He spent most of his time either at Melera's home base or on her corvette, zipping around the solar system. By now, they'd visited every planet and a few of the planetoids beyond. They'd even landed on Pluto. The only times he'd returned to Seattle was for the new moon pack meetings and the full moon hunts.

Melera had taught him everything about her ship and had shown him how to carry out all manner of repairs. She'd deliberately break something, like a computer server or the replicator, and have him fix it. Her lessons included repairs requiring a spacewalk, too.

The only thing that had marred his vacation was Melera's seizures. She'd had two of them. But now that he and his wolf knew how to help, it wasn't as bad as the first time they'd witnessed it.

Right now, Parker lay in bed with her, staring at the pockmarked ceiling. He sighed. His earthly duty called. The new moon was four days away and he had to get back to Seattle for the meeting. While he'd been gallivanting around the solar system, Tran had been handling the day-to-day matters. Their cover story was that Parker was away attending to affairs concerning his inherited farm in Iowa. So far, it was working. No one had questioned his absence. But the monthly meeting was something he couldn't miss.

He looked down. Melera lay in his arms, dozing. She'd been up for most of the night, trying to crack her father's symphonic code. He remembered their conversation about it not long after he'd arrived at her base for the second time. She'd told him the code could be solved any number of ways but only one solution was correct.

He'd cocked his head. "How do you know you're on the right track?"

She'd given him a wan smile. "I don't."

"Then—"

"I grew up with my father's music. He was a composer. Taught me to write music, too. So I've got a good guess as to what he might do. Better than anyone else, anyway."

"Wouldn't a computer be able to solve it?"

She'd shaken her head. "Too many variables. It would take years."

He sighed again. He sincerely hoped she was hitting the right solution. He'd seen her after a code-cracking session. Sometimes, the look in her eyes…it was if she was hanging on to sanity by a thin thread. God knows what would happen to her mind if it turned out she was wrong.

Parker poked her a couple of times. "Melera? Sweetheart, wake up."

"Mhm?"

"We have to go home. The new moon will be here soon."

"Mhm. Ohh-kay." She started to get up.

He pulled her back down. "Not right now, baby. You need to sleep. Maybe tonight."

Instead of answering, she snuggled closer to him.

Parker kissed her hair and turned his face back to the ceiling. Not for the first time, he wondered how he could get out of being alpha of the werewolf pack without dying. A werewolf who wanted to be alpha challenged the incumbent to single combat and they fought until one of them was dead. If someone challenged him, he would gladly throw the match but he certainly didn't want to die while doing it.

Maybe Melera and I could just disappear. His lips tightened. No, that wouldn't work either. If an alpha died of other causes or became incapacitated, the beta automatically became alpha. Problem was, an alpha who hadn't won the position through combat was subject to be challenged. Tran was a formidable wolf in his own right and could probably kill any of the other First-ranked wolves who might challenge him. But if Parker left, he'd be leaving Tran to fight for his life who knew how many times. That wouldn't be fair.

Besides, his business was suffering. His prolonged absence had caused a number of his clients to hire other programmers. If he kept this up, he wouldn't have a business left. It wasn't that he needed the money. The farm provided him with enough income to live comfortably and then some. But he'd promised his grandmother he would work for a living and not rely on the farm's income to meet his needs. So there wasn't much he could do.

He made a decision and sighed. Starting with the new moon meeting, his little vacation from life was over.

A few hours after Parker said they should leave, Melera still lay in his arms pretending to be asleep. She hadn't said anything when she'd come to bed but she'd finished her work on the code.

She was scared. Right down to her toes.

What if it isn't the right solution?

You will never know if you do not try it, her czado said.

I know but—

If it is not the correct solution, you will just have to try again.

I don't know if I can. You saw the toll it took on me.

You forget that you are a warrior. An elite among elites.

Yeah, well, even I have my limits. My seizures, breaking the code—it's just too damned much.

Her czado said nothing for a minute. *When do you plan on making the transmission?*

After Pawkher's meeting, I guess.

You are stalling.

Absolutely.

Parker stirred. "Sweetheart, we should go." He untangled himself from her and got out of bed.

She looked at him. "I need to have a bath, first. I stink."

He sniffed. "You do not."

"Do so."

Parker smiled. "Okay, you stink. Go get your bath."

Melera rolled out of bed and headed for the bathing room, feeling Parker's gaze on her back as she walked across the cavern floor. After traversing the short tunnel, she entered the bath. She crossed the room to the washer and inspected the hoses for leaks. There weren't any. She stepped into the stall and shut the door.

Her cleansing ritual didn't take long. Not long enough, anyway. She returned to the cavern. Parker was watching her. "All clean?"

She nodded.

"Good. Can we go now?"

"Yes." Melera walked to her clothes rack and was ready in minutes. Then she walked to her siitheer and pressed a button. A small polyhedron popped out from a hole next to the instrument's pulls. She put it in her pocket.

"What you got there?" Parker called from across the small camp.

She looked up. "Nothing. Let's go to your house."

Parker's lips twisted. "Sweetheart, how many times do I have to tell you? It's our house. You and me."

She gave him a small smile. "Yes, Pawkher." Turning, she started for her ship, Parker right behind her. They walked in silence. Reaching it, they boarded and made their way to the compact bridge. Melera sat in the command chair while Parker sat in the second's chair. They made a pre-drive check. All systems were ready to go. She activated the forward viscreens.

Melera was just about to fire the drives when she reached over and placed her hand on Parker's arm. "Pawkher, when's the new moon?"

"Four days away."

She took a deep breath. "I finished the code."

Parker's face lit up. "You did? Wow, sweetheart, that's great! When do you want to try it out?"

She bit her lip. "It'll be two days. Twenty-four hours out to the transmission point, twenty-four hours back. You'll still be in time for your meeting."

"Hell, yeah. Let's go."

Melera drummed a tattoo on a square indentation on the console. The ship's four drives rumbled. "Kyle, take us out."

The AI took control of the ship, turning it so that it faced the exit, now a solid rock wall. She heard the hum of the disruptor powering up. A moment later, the mountainside dissolved. The drives roared. Kyle steered them through the opening and then they took off.

Twenty four hours later, the corvette floated in deep space, far from the central solar system. "We're here?" Parker said.

Melera nodded. She reached for the polyhedron she'd left on the command console and picked it up. Her hand began to shake.

He took it from her. Leaning over, he dropped it into a small hole on her left. Then leaned back in his chair and smiled. "Now we wait."

An hour passed and they were still waiting. Melera despaired. Her ship's communications worked like her transmitter and receiver back at her base. The fleet should have received the message immediately.

"Maybe it's on a different frequency," Parker said.

Melera shook her head. "This is what my father gave me." A tear trickled down her cheek. Then she screamed, leapt from her seat and started banging her head against the ship's bulkhead. "It's wrong, it's wrong, it's wrong!" she wailed in Xia'saan. "I can't do this again. I can't!"

The next thing she knew, Parker had clamped his strong arms about her. "Kyle," he yelled over her screaming. "Hold her!"

Through tear-filled eyes, she saw Kyle materialize next to him. Stepping behind her, it grabbed her arms and pinned them behind her back. Parker grabbed her by the head. "Shut up, sweetheart," he shouted in her face. "I want to try something."

Melera stopped her screaming. She watched Parker sit in the command chair and lean forward. "Scan and transmit." A small square on the viscreen brightened. Colors swirled inside it. Thirty seconds later, the screen flashed tan. At the same time, myriad blue dots appeared on the viscreen. Parker turned to her and grinned.

Her jaw dropped. The transmission frequency her father had given her had been part of the code. The correct frequency was the one she and her father had used for their most private communications—so private even her lost love Ruri hadn't known about it. Her legs went weak. If Kyle hadn't been holding her, she would have fallen to her knees. "P-Pawkher," she whispered.

Parker rose from his seat and took her from Kyle. She sagged against him, buried her face into his neck and sobbed. He held her tight, rubbing her back.

"Yes, sweetheart," he whispered into her hair. "You did it. You found the fleet."

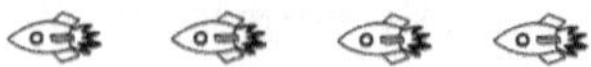

The first thing Kurt saw when he walked into his office beneath Last Chance was the folded black parchment trimmed in red lying in the middle of his massive mahogany desk.

He stopped and stiffened. His throat tightened. If his face could have paled any further, it would have done so.

Daniel ran into him from behind. "Kurt, what—"

"Will contest, Daniel," Kurt said after his throat had loosened. "Someone has challenged me to a will contest." He strode to his desk and dropped into his burgundy leather executive's chair. Picking up the parchment, he unfolded it and scanned its contents.

"Who?" Daniel said.

"Giorgio. A city-less vampire regent." He crumpled the parchment and threw it across the room.

Daniel frowned. "I don't know Giorgio."

"No reason why you should. Giorgio is looking to be a Master. He roams the world, staying with the regents of various colonies, always poking around for a weakness so he can challenge them to a will contest. So far, he hasn't found one."

"Why doesn't he just challenge someone outright?"

"Giorgio's a new regent. He hasn't fully grown into his powers yet and won't for another two hundred years. But he's impatient. He wants a city and he wants it now." He paused. "And he wants mine." He slammed his fist on the desk. "Li An's behind this. I just know it."

"Can't you simply decline?"

Kurt shook his head. "If I did that, I'd forfeit my domain. It would be the same as if I'd lost the contest."

"Where's the contest being held?"

"Moscow."

Daniel frowned. "Moscow? Why Moscow?"

"The Master there, Alexei, owes me a number of favors. He's been reluctant to pay them back. Because he's so graciously allowing the contest to take place on his territory, he knows Giorgio will never call in those favors if I lose."

"So when's the will contest going to take place?"

Kurt stared at his executor. "Tomorrow."

CHAPTER 36

On the outskirts of Moscow, inside a cavernous concrete chamber, Kurt lay on his back on the floor of the ring set up for the will contest. A former storeroom, it was deep in the bowels of what used to be a Soviet-era administration building. When the Soviet Union had crumbled, the building had been left to do the same. The visible portion of the building had been razed long ago, the upper basement filled in and a park built in its place. Only a few ancient humans and the vampires knew about the bunker-like warren in the former building's sub-basements.

He stared at the ceiling lights. Arms crossed behind his head, one leg bent and his other leg resting on his knee, anyone watching him would think he was daydreaming. He wasn't. His body thrummed with fear. What if Giorgio killed him? His vampire strength had returned but he was not as strong as a full regent. At least there was no shape-shifting allowed in a will contest. He'd gotten some of his shifting abilities back but they were feeble. He wanted to jump to his feet and pace. But that would show he was nervous and nervousness was a sign of weakness.

My one advantage is that I'm so much older than Giorgio. I've fought hand-to-hand in several wars. I'm sure I have far more experience in combat than he has.

The murmuring of a hundred voices rippled through the room. Giorgio had obviously arrived. Every vampire regent who'd been able had come to see the mighty Kurt fight—and maybe lose—to the upstart newcomer.

He rolled his head to the right and almost burst out laughing. The two's attire couldn't have been more different. Giorgio wore a high, white lace collar, paired with an elaborately embroidered, slashed green satin doublet with matching breeches. More lace spilled over the tops of his wide-cuffed, two-inch heeled boots. All that was missing were the cape and feathered hat. He looked like a wealthy seventeenth-century pirate—which he had been, while alive. But the fifteen-inch, needle-pointed wooden stake he held was no laughing matter.

In contrast to Giorgio's flamboyant costume, Kurt wore a skin-tight, full-body spandex suit. The material was slick, to make him hard to grasp. There was no extraneous material for an opponent to grab hold. A long, slim pocket had been sewn into the suit's right leg. Aside from that, if it hadn't been for the boots he wore with their hard rubber soles, he might have been on his way to an aerobics class.

He got to his feet and picked up his own sharpened stake. "Let's get this over with, shall we?" he said, trying to sound bored.

Alexei stepped in front of the crowd. Moscow's Master wasted no time with pleasantries. "We are here to witness the will contest between Kurt, Master of Seattle, and Giorgio," he said, his deep, booming voice echoing about the cavernous room. "The only rule is no shape-shifting is permitted. The contestant who shifts forfeits his life." He paused. "Let the contest begin."

The room turned dead quiet. Kurt bent into a defensive crouch. Giorgio did the same. They circled one another looking, he knew, for a weakness. He transferred his stake to his left hand. So did Giorgio. Kurt noticed the expression on the other's face. It was minute but some of his cockiness had faltered. *He's right-handed. Hmm…maybe that's something I can exploit. Force him to fight left-handed.*

Giorgio sprang at him, his stake raised. Kurt stepped to the side and the other flew past him. Muffled laughter came from the spectators. Giorgio hit the floor and rolled to his feet. Giving Kurt a ferocious glare, the young regent's expression had turned from cocky to murderous.

Giorgio rushed him. Instead of backing away, Kurt slipped his weapon into his pocket. He stepped forward, grabbed Giorgio's right arm and flipped him. The young regent's stake flew out of his hand. With a clatter, it slid across the smooth floor. Whispering swept through the big room.

Kurt dove for the fallen stake. Giorgio did, too. They reached the weapon at the same time and grabbed it. A tug of war ensued. Giorgio won. Kurt jumped up and tried to spring backward but he was too close. Giorgio's arm shot forward, the stake aimed for his heart.

He twisted to the side but not before Giorgio's stake raked his breast, tearing the fabric of his suit. Pain ripped through him but he didn't cry out. That would be a sign of weakness. He glanced at his chest. Though his wound bled, he was relieved to see it wasn't much more than a scratch.

He looked up. Giorgio smiled.

The young regent rushed him again. Kurt executed a forward flip, landing just behind the other vampire. Giorgio whirled. He was now close enough for Kurt to drive his stake through his heart. He lunged. But Giorgio was faster. Blocking Kurt's move, he swung at his weapon. The blow connected. A good six inches of Kurt's stake broke off and skittered across the floor.

Eyes wide, he stared at his stake in horror. The crowd cried out in disbelief. It was a clean break, meaning the stake had been sawn in two and then glued back together. He could see traces of the sawdust which had been mixed with the glue to hide the break. Only a close inspection would have revealed the tampering.

He looked up a second time. Giorgio was grinning, now.

Gripping his stake, Giorgio's arm shot forward again. Kurt, dropping his now-useless weapon, caught it and pushed back. Giorgio increased pressure. He watched the stake come closer and closer to his heart. There was no question about it now. Giorgio was stronger than he. Much stronger. He let go of the stake and immediately executed backflip. The toes of his boots connected with the underside of Giorgio's chin. The young regent went down.

Kurt sprang. He'd no idea what he'd do, given Giorgio's strength, but he was determined to wrest the stake from him. But Giorgio had other ideas. He thrust out with his weapon. Kurt had just enough time to change his trajectory and fell to the floor on his back.

Before he knew it, Giorgio was sitting on top of him, the point of his stake digging in his chest. Giorgio bore down. Kurt could feel the weapon sliding through his body and his blood flowing. He didn't feel his fangs emerge. Agony consumed him. If he didn't do something and fast, in seconds he'd be twice dead.

With Giorgio hunched over him, Kurt did the only thing he could do. He slammed his hand against Giorgio's chest and flipped his mental toggle switch. The laser beam tore through the young regent's heart, incinerating it.

Giorgio's fingers uncurled from around the stake. Eyes wide with seeming disbelief, he fell forward. Kurt managed to shift his torso to the left, lest the other's weight drive the stake the rest of the way into his heart. Giorgio landed on his shoulder. Squeezing his eyes shut, he bit his tongue to keep from crying out. In less than a minute, the young regent had disintegrated into dust.

Kurt slowly sat up. The last time he'd felt such pain was while he was being tortured in his own dungeons. Gritting his teeth so as not to scream, he pulled the stake out of his chest. Blood poured from the hole. Even as he watched, the bleeding slowed and then stopped.

He brushed Giorgio's ashes from his shoulder. He tried to stand and almost didn't make it. It was even more agonizing than sitting up. But he refused to show his vulnerability. He forced himself to his feet. Upright, he swayed a little, feeling woozy and numb. He barely felt his fangs retract.

"You violated the law, Kurt," Alexei's voice boomed. "Your life is forfeit."

Kurt turned and stared at him. He shook his head and almost fell over from dizziness. "I did not shift and you know it. Besides, you saw what happened. My stake had been tampered with. Someone wanted me to lose. I simply defended myself in the only way I could."

Alexei stared back with narrowed eyes. Without taking his gaze from Kurt's face, he addressed the assembled vampires. "Fellow regents. What say you?"

The crowd babbled. "Kurt won fairly," a voice shouted. "Giorgio cheated," came another voice. From the corner of his eye, Kurt saw most of the vampires nodding.

A howl pierced the cavernous room, heard even above the vampires' babbling. Like an arrow, a body flew over the heads of the regents, headed for Kurt. It was Li An, a sharpened stake in one hand. Rage twisted her beautiful face. "You will pay for what you did," she screamed. "I'll kill you myself!"

Before Li An could reach him, he aimed for her heart and flipped his toggle switch. The laser beam struck her square in her chest. She fell to the concrete floor inside the ring, a smoking hole where her heart had been. The stake rolled out of her hand.

The shock in the room was palpable. Kurt and the regents stared at Li An's body and kept staring as it crumbled into dust. Then all the vampires began talking at once.

"Silence, please," Alexei boomed. The big room quieted. He turned to Kurt and gave him a smile that didn't reach his eyes. "The regents have spoken. You are the winner." He paused and glanced at the pile of ashes that was left of Li An. "And, according to the law, Li An's Shanghai colony is now yours."

Kurt nodded but said nothing. That little speech he'd given had taken almost all the strength he had left. He wasn't sure he could speak without his voice cracking. He turned and stared Li An's ashes.

"Thank you for coming," Alexei said. "Let us hope we will not have to witness a will contest again."

A few minutes later, he felt better. The wooziness in his brain had stopped. But he was exhausted. And his chest hurt.

He looked up. All of the regents had left, even Alexei. Then he looked at the hole the stake had made in the fabric of his suit. He grabbed one edge of the torn fabric in each hand and pulled. A ripping sound echoed through the storeroom. Inspecting his wound, he could see it was healing. Tomorrow, there wouldn't be even a scar to evidence his ordeal.

Staring at it, he thought about his close call with permanent death. In his mind's eye, a montage of his life as a prince and a regent appeared. He saw his cruelty and the fear it had inspired. *While I lived, my subjects were terrified of me.* He would randomly pick a peasant or even a courtier, throw him in his dungeons and torture him. *And I did the same thing as Master of Seattle. Pick a random vampire and slowly pound a stake through his heart. Or throw him outside to die in the sun. As for other zots…no one is safe from me.*

The montage ended. His lips tightened. *My rule turned out exactly as Machiavelli had said it would.* He'd been, and was, a tyrant. His people had hated him. So did his vampires and the rest of the zots. *When I was human, I probably would have been assassinated, maybe poisoned. Or overthrown. As a regent…I don't know. But I'm sure someone would find a way.*

His jaw set. *No more.* He would gain back his colony's and the other zots' trust and respect. *And I'll start with——*

"Kurt."

He turned and frowned in surprise. Daniel walked toward him.

Where did he come from? Only regents were permitted to attend will contests.

"I sneaked in," Daniel said in answer to his unspoken question. "No one noticed."

Kurt raised his brow. "You were lucky. You know what would have happened if you'd been caught."

A half-smile stretched Daniel's lips. "Yep. I'd be twice-dead." He sobered. "Kurt, I had to come. You're my friend. The only friend I've ever really had."

Kurt smiled. Here, at least, was one vampire who trusted and respected him, and even liked him. "I understand." His smile widened into a grin. He linked Daniel's arm in his. "Come. Let's go home."

The two dissolved into mist and headed back to Seattle.

CHAPTER 37

Two nights after Kurt's will contest and after the pack's new moon meeting, Parker, Garrett, Kurt, and Melera conferred in Parker's great room, debating whether they should go to France. Garrett hadn't heard from Feodor and she was worried. "This isn't like him not to stay in touch. I haven't heard from him in at least six weeks."

Kurt raised his brow. "So you're saying we should just show up on his doorstep unannounced? Rather rude, don't you think?"

Parker frowned. "Yeah—we can't just barge in there."

She looked from one man to the other. "You don't understand. What if something's happened to him? What will happen to us then?"

Kurt cocked his head. "Ah, so that's what you're really worried about. Breaking the tryst spell."

Parker watched her delicate hands clench into fists. "No, that's not what I'm worried about. I'm worried about Feodor. You don't know him like I do. And I'm telling you—not staying in touch isn't like him."

He nodded. "I think Kurt's right. You're worried about the tryst."

Garrett threw up her hands. "Fine," she spat and stalked toward the kitchen. She shoved the door open and walked inside. The door swung shut with a bang.

Parker turned to Melera. "What you think, sweetheart?"

She shook her head. "Me not in tsis."

"Aw, c'mon. I'm just asking for—"

The doorbell rang. The three looked at each other. "And who might that be?" Kurt said.

Parker shrugged. "Dunno. Probably Tran." He walked to the front door and opened it. A homeless man stood on the porch. His clothing was much too warm for the weather. The hood of his jacket was pulled down, obscuring most of his face. He frowned. "Can I help—"

The next thing Parker knew, he was staring down the barrel of a gun. He held up his hands. "Whoa, whoa," he said and took a step back.

The homeless man stepped over the threshold. His gun never wavered from Parker's face. "What is this?" he said. That was when he noticed the homeless man smelled odd. Then he knew.

The homeless man took another step toward him. He stepped back. Lifting his gaze from the gun, he looked up to see more of the homeless pour into his house. They spread out in the great room, opposite of where Kurt and Melera stood. By his count, there had to be thirty of them, maybe more. And they were all pointing guns at him.

The homeless man who'd pointed his weapon at him on the porch walked over and joined the others. Parker walked backward until he stood next to Melera and Kurt. They now faced the crowd of homeless people. His great room stank of many different odors, and none of them familiar.

He decided to play along. "Who are you? What do you want?"

No one answered.

A handsome, impeccably dressed man of medium height stepped through the doorway. "We—or rather I—want Melera."

From the corner of his eye, he saw Melera's jaw tighten. She said nothing.

"Beloc," he said through his teeth. "How did you know she was here?"

Another person stepped through the door and stood next to Beloc.

Parker's eyes widened. "You bitch," he roared.

"I had to do it, Parker," Mandy shouted back. "You—it's just like last year. Because of *her*"—she stabbed her finger at Melera—"you've abandoned the pack. Again!"

"I told you—"

"Don't give me that bullshit about the farm. I called your uncle— you were never there!"

Parker heard the kitchen door open. "I heard shouting," Garrett said. "What's happening? What's going on?" She reached the spot where Melera, Parker, and Kurt stood. In his peripheral vision, He saw her wide smile. "Basile," she said, sounding delighted.

Melera snorted. "Basile? Hah! Is Beloc."

Garrett looked at Melera then turned and stared at Beloc. "Basile, is this true?"

"Yes, Garrett. It is. I am Mag Beloc, Jahannan warlord of the Akkad Protectorate. And I've come for Melera."

No one spoke for a minute or so. "So it's been about her all along," Garrett said in a small voice. "It was never about me."

"I'm afraid so."

Her face reddened. Tears sprang from her eyes and poured down her cheeks. She ran over to Beloc and looked up at him, her expression pleading. "B-but you said you loved me."

Beloc gazed down at her and slowly shook his head. "I've grown fond of you, Garrett. Very fond. But I never said I loved you."

She slapped him, hard. "You bastard!" she screamed. Sobbing, she turned her back to him and clapped her hands to her face.

"I suppose I deserved that," Beloc said, his voice soft. He stared at the back of her head. Then he looked up. "Come quietly, Melera. Even you can't take on thirty-six of my best legionnaires. Especially when they're armed and you're not."

"No," Melera said through her teeth.

Beloc grabbed Garrett's arms, twisted them around her back and slammed her against him. "Then I propose a trade. Melera for Garrett. If Melera doesn't come with me,"—he paused—"I'll kill Garrett."

"Go ahead," she said in a broken voice. "I don't care."

"Of course you do," Beloc said, his voice soothing. "Do you want your friends to live out their lives as cripples?"

Parker stared at her. "Jesus fuck, Garrett—how much did you tell him?"

Her lower lip trembled. "Everything."

Parker looked at Kurt, who rolled his eyes.

"Enough," Beloc said. "Well, Melera?"

Melera didn't answer for a long while. "If me go wits you, we all go, yes? You fleet, too?"

Beloc smiled. "You're hardly in a position to make deals but…yes. No one will be left behind."

Her lips tightened. "Tsen me go."

"What?" Parker shouted. "Melera—"

She stepped over to him. "Pawkher. Me you listen to, yes?"

He opened his mouth but closed it. Then he nodded.

Melera took a deep breath. "Me Fe-o-dor tell what happen if you not make spell. You and Gharrett be cray-zee. Can-not be werewoof and vam-pire for you, said he. Can-not be mage and werewoof for Gharrett. Khurt be weak, maybe die in will contest. So need you Gharrett to make spell, yes?"

"But—"

She put a finger to his lips. "Pawhker. Is best way. You need Gharrett."

"But Melera, I need you!"

Her golden eyes filling with tears, she cupped his face in her hands. "Forget me not," she whispered and kissed him, hard.

He stared at her for a few moments after she pulled away. "Never," he whispered over the lump in his throat.

Beloc sighed. "This is all very touching but we really must go now."

Melera blew out a long breath. She turned and squaring her shoulders, walked over to Beloc. "Me ready."

He released Garrett and gave her a hard shove. She stumbled over to Parker and fell into his arms.

The Jahannan warlord smiled. "Good—" He stopped. "Oh. I almost forgot." Whipping a pistol from his pocket, he turned and shot Mandy in her chest at point-blank range.

The smell of charred meat filled the air. Mandy stumbled backward a few steps, looking surprised. Then she crumpled to the floor.

Beloc's smile widened. "I despise traitors." In the next instant, he, Melera, and the rest of the legionnaires disappeared.

No one said anything for a full two minutes. Parker felt Kurt's hand on his shoulder. "Parker, I'm so—"

He shoved Garrett out of his arms. "Okay. I'm outta here."

"Where are you going?" Kurt said.

"Going after Melera."

Kurt frowned. "How?"

Parker gave him a feral grin. "I know three things that Beloc doesn't. One, I know where Melera keeps her ship. Two, I know how to drive it. Three, I know where her fleet is." He sobered. "That's why I have to hurry. I have to rescue Melera before Beloc finds out she knows, too."

"I'm going with you," Kurt said.

"Me, too," Garrett said in a strong, firm voice.

Parker turned. Her eyes were still puffy and red from her crying but her look was resolute. "Wait, wait. Do you two have any idea what you're getting into?"

"Do you?" Kurt said.

"Yeah, I do. Look, this isn't going to be a walk in the park. Beloc travels with a whole damned fleet. I might not make it back."

Kurt set his jaw. "All the more reason for us to go."

Parker cocked his head. "Why are you two so interested in Melera all of a sudden?"

"It's not so much Melera as it is the tryst," Kurt said.

Parker rolled his eyes. "Listen—"

"No, you listen. If something happens to you, I'm not spending the rest of my life as a cripple. I've already been through one will contest and I'm not going through another. So if you die, I die, too."

Parker turned to Garrett. "And you?"

"Same thing. I heard what Melera said. Do you really think I want to go mad?" She gave him a half-smile. "Besides, I *want* to snatch her away from Beloc. It's not the best payback in the world but I'll take it."

Kurt gave him a meaningful look. "Bottom line, Parker, is that we need each other."

Parker let out a breath and nodded. "Okay, fine. Kurt, you take Garrett and I'll take Mandy."

"What are you going to do with her?" Garrett said.

"Drop her into the Sound. The weresharks will make sure there's nothing left."

Kurt frowned. "Hardly a fitting burial for your freya."

Parker's lip curled. "She doesn't deserve better." He walked to where Mandy's body lay and hefted it over his shoulder. He turned. Kurt had Garrett's hand in his. "We ready?"

"Yes," Kurt and Garrett said at the same time.

"Then let's go."

The four dissolved into mist and left Parker's house. Flying high, when they were over the Sound, Parker let go of Mandy's body. She materialized and fell. Parker heard a faint splash. There—that was taken care of.

So where's Melera's ship? Parker telepathically heard Kurt's voice.

San Juan Islands. One of the deserted ones.

Good choice, I should say.

Yeah. Close enough for her to skip to Seattle, too.

How far can she skip?

About two, three hundred miles.

They flew on. After a few hours, the islands appeared beneath them. Some had houses that were lit against the night. Other islands were dark. Parker flew to one of the smaller, dark ones. *We're here.*

They descended to the ground. On materializing, he looked around. Trees covered most of the starlight and given the new moon, it was almost impossible for him to see, even with his wolf-sight. *Damn.* "Kurt. How well can you see?"

"Well enough. Why?"

"I can't. Not enough light. Can you see her ship?"

"Yes."

"Guide me. I need to get close to the nose."

Parker felt Kurt take his hand. They started walking. Then he saw it, a looming hulk darker than the night. "Okay. I'll take it from here."

He roamed his hands over the corvette's side, looking for the hatch's manual opening mechanism. He stepped further to his right and then again. After taking his third step, his fingers found the square indented into the ship's skin. He drummed the tattoo Melera had taught him in the square's middle. It lit up and he heard a click. The hatch door swung down.

Light flooded the area where they stood. He jumped on the boarding ramp and ran to the inner hatch door, Kurt and Garrett right behind him. He heard the outer door close. He drummed a tattoo on another small square beside this door. This square lit up too and the door swung open. The three ran through it. Then the second door closed.

Parker barreled toward the compact bridge. "Kyle," he yelled. "We're leaving. Run the check!"

"Yes, Parker."

"We're going to the bridge," he shouted to Kurt and Garrett over his shoulder. "Follow me!" Without waiting to see if they were doing so, Parker ran for the lift. He saw it was level with the main deck. But there was a faster way. Without breaking stride, he leapt, caught the edge of the bridge deck and hauled himself up. On the bridge, he reached the command chair in three bounds. He settled in and started doing his own pre-drive check.

"Kyle's perfect," he heard Melera's deep voice in his mind. "But you never know."

Parker tightened his lips. *We're coming for you, sweetheart. Just hang on.*

Behind him, he heard the sound of the lifts powering down and then Kurt and Garrett's hurried footsteps. "Kurt, you're here." Without looking up, he pointed to the second's chair. "Garrett, there's a jump seat behind Kurt." His gaze swept the heads-up display on the viscreen one last time. All was well. "Viscreens on bubble." The bridge disappeared and except for the console and their seats, it seemed like they floated in mid-air. "Kyle, we're ready. Stealth shields on."

The powerful vibration from the ship's drives revving up made Parker's insides quiver. A moment later, his stomach lurched and the blackness outside disappeared. Stars became visible. Now that they were on their way, he felt his tight shoulder muscles loosen a bit. He let out a minute sigh.

Please, God—let us get there in time.

CHAPTER 38

Garrett had always been a stargazer. Away from Earth, with no lights, no pollution, and no air filtering the starlight, the stars seemed to blaze. With the viscreens showing space all around her, she felt as if she floated among the bright pinpoints. She smiled the tiniest bit. *So beautiful…and from the best seat in the house.*

"Parker, do you have a plan for getting Melera out from Beloc's clutches?" Kurt said. She turned her attention to the two men.

Parker grinned. "Nope."

Her jaw dropped and she leaned forward. "You don't?"

"Well, do you have any idea where we're going?" Kurt said.

"Of course. But it'll take a good while to get there. Plenty of time for Kyle and me to figure out a plan."

Garrett frowned. She'd heard him yell out for this Kyle when they boarded the ship. "Parker, who's Kyle?"

He turned his head but didn't look at her. "The ship. Or, more accurately, the ship's AI." He smiled. "Wanna meet her?"

"Sure. Yes," Garrett and Kurt said at the same time.

"Kyle, show yourself," Parker said.

A black figure with glowing red eyes appeared behind Parker. "Kyle, this is Kurt"—he pointed to his right—"and this is Garrett," he said, pointing at her over his shoulder.

"Hello," Kyle said.

"Yes, well…hello, Kyle," Kurt said. "A pleasure to meet you."

"Likewise, Kurt."

Garrett stared. "Uh…hi, Kyle."

The AI inclined its head. "Garrett."

Parker shifted in his seat. "Kyle, give me a chance to get something to eat and then we can talk about how we're going to rescue Melera."

"Very well. We make the jump to hyperspace in forty-five minutes." The AI's physical manifestation disappeared.

Silence reigned on the bridge. "How do you know Kyle's a she?" Kurt said.

Parker shrugged. "I think of the ship that way. You know, like a fine sports car."

"Ah. How is it that she speaks English?"

"I taught her."

"Then how come Melera can't speak English?" Garrett broke in.

Parker shrugged again. "Dunno. We tried the translator on her but it didn't take. Probably because of Beloc's tortures. She told me they fucked around with her brain a lot."

Garrett's eyes widened. "Tortures?"

She watched Parker's lips tighten. "Yeah, Garrett—tortures. That's another reason to get her out of there as soon as possible—before Beloc has a chance to put his hands on her again."

Garrett sat back, horrified. *All of those nights Basile and I spent together in a scene…and those times he got too rough…he tortured her…oh, Mother… that—*

"I'm hungry," Parker said, interrupting her thoughts. She looked up to see him patting his stomach. "I'm going below. You guys can stay up here if you want."

"I'll come with you," Kurt said. "I'd like to see the rest of the ship."

"Me too," she chimed in.

"Okay, then. Come on." Parker rose from the command chair and walked toward the lift. Garrett and Kurt followed.

Reaching it, she eyed the platform. "There's not room enough for three."

"No problem," Parker said.

The next thing she knew, she'd been swept into Parker's strong arms. He and Kurt stepped on the lift and they rode down to the main deck. During their ride, she remembered the halcyon days when he'd been in love with her. Sure, it was the result of a spell but he'd been so happy. Sweeping her in his arms like this was something he'd loved to do. And she had to admit, she liked it, too. Sadness and regret washed over her. *I doubt if he'll ever care about me again.*

"Here we are," Parker said. He stepped off the lift and set Garrett on her feet.

She looked around. On the way in, she'd been too focused to notice but the deck's walls and floor were a uniform, featureless, and slightly shimmery gray. She looked up. Even the ceiling was the same.

"Rather bleak, hmm?" Kurt said.

Parker grinned. "Not really. Here, let me get us something to eat and I'll show you." He turned to her. "You hungry?"

"N…" She thought for a moment. "Actually, I am."

He turned to Kurt. "What about you? Some brie, maybe?"

Kurt sighed. "Sounds delightful, but I'm going to need a little something more than brie."

"I can take care of that, too." Parker walked to a bank of what looked like three cabinets. Garrett followed. Each cabinet, she noticed, had what seemed to be a blank black panel next to it. She watched his fingers play over the panel on two of them. Turning, he jumped a little at seeing her.

"Sorry. Didn't mean to scare you."

"S'okay."

One of the cabinets dinged. Parker opened one and retrieved a plateful of round patties about a quarter-inch thick.

Garrett inspected them. "What are these? They look like veggie burgers."

"They are."

She frowned. "How—"

"These are replicators. Make anything you want. I can whip up all sorts of alien dishes. I loaded them up with Earth food so I wouldn't get too homesick."

She eyed him. "Since when do you eat veggie burgers?"

He smiled a little. "Melera likes them," he said, his voice soft.

The second replicator dinged, saving her from having to reply. She turned and walked over to where Kurt stood. She felt a little foolish, just holding her plate.

"Here's your brie, Kurt," Parker called.

Kurt walked to the replicators and took the plate Parker proffered.

Parker rubbed his hands. "Okay. Now we need someplace to eat."

He walked to the far wall and opened a small door. Garrett would never have known it was there.

"What are you going to eat?" Kurt said.

"Let me get the enviro together and then I'll make something for me," Parker said without turning around.

She frowned. "Enviro?"

Parker turned. "Environment." He went back to his fiddling. "Here we go. This is a good one."

The deck went dark for a second. When Garrett could see again, the gray walls were gone. She looked around. Where the walls had been was now a vista, the likes of which she'd never seen. Teal-colored grass carpeted the ground. She stood under a stand of trees with yellowish trunks and pink leaves. Mountains in the distance seemed to glow a deep, ruby-red color. Under a peach-colored sky, the air was fragrant and a warm breeze tousled her hair. Before her was what looked like a wrought iron table with three matching chairs.

She looked around. "How—"

"It's a holosensory projection," Parker said.

"Where are we?"

"Trani. An uninhabited planet somewhere in Melera's home galaxy."

"It's beautiful," Kurt said.

Parker looked at him. "Is, isn't it? And you can walk, too. Melera and I hiked to the mountains, once." He shrugged. "Anyway, I thought we'd eat out in the fresh air." He peered at them. "Unless you'd rather go someplace else?"

"No, no, this is fine," Garrett and Kurt said almost at the same time. She pulled out a chair, her plate of veggie burgers in hand. Kurt joined her with his plate of brie. "Just give me a minute, and I'll get us some utensils," Parker said. He left them.

"I would never have imagined such a place," Kurt said.

"Me, neither."

At that moment, Parker returned with a bowl of what looked like bloody beef cubes in one hand and forks in the other. He handed a fork to her and Kurt. Then he sat down and joined them.

"What's that?" Garrett said around a mouthful of veggie burger. "Beef?"

Parker shook his head, then swallowed. "It's gnulia. Looks like a cow." He speared a forkful of meat. He started to bring it to his mouth but stopped. "Sorta."

"Does it taste like beef?" Kurt said.

"Nothing like it."

They finished their meals and followed Parker to a stand of tall bushes. "Here," he said. "You can put your dishes and utensils in the recycler." He grabbed a fistful of branches from one of the bushes and pulled to reveal the recycler's yawning abyss. They dumped their dishes inside. Parker let go of the branches. Garrett heard a faint whirring sound.

"Now for Kurt," Parker said. He stepped over to a sparkly rock wall Garrett hadn't noticed and pulled on one of the rocks. It opened. She saw it was one of the replicators. He programmed it and pushed the "on" button. Less than ten seconds later, Garrett heard a chime. Parker opened the door, reached in, and took out a glass of red liquid. "Here you go," he said, handing the glass to Kurt.

Kurt took it and upended the glass. His eyes widened. Then he let out a whoop. "My goodnish. What *is* this shtuff?" He ran over to the table and chairs and danced around them, singing in German at the top of his lungs. A few minutes later, he fell to the ground. He didn't move after that.

"Oh, shit," Parker yelled. He ran over to where Kurt lay, Garrett right behind him. He knelt beside him. "Kurt. Kurt! Wake up!"

She pushed him aside. "Here, let me try something."

At that moment, Kurt's eyes opened. They looked bleary. "Parker, what the hell did you give me?" He placed a hand on his forehead, grimaced, and slowly sat up.

"I'm sorry," Parker said. "I didn't think. That was Melera's blood." He squinted at Kurt. "How do you feel?"

"I have a terrible hangover. And vampires can't get drunk. Not on alcohol, anyway." Kurt chuckled. "It's rather funny—I haven't been drunk in well over five hundred years."

"Well, I can pop open a vein—"

"No need. I'm not hungry anymore. But the next time, please do."

"Parker, we will make the jump to hyperspace in three minutes," Kyle's voice sounded around them.

"Okay, Kyle." He turned to the others. "We'd better go."

Garrett helped Kurt to his feet. He swayed. Slipping her arm about his waist, she held him a little tighter. "Melera," he said, his voice low. "Full of surprises, that one." In the next moment, the Trani vista disappeared and the deck returned to its gray, shimmery color.

The three proceeded to the bridge. She slid into the jump seat behind Kurt. Once again, she marveled at the stars all around her.

"Hyperdrive engaged. Making the jump in five seconds," Kyle said. "Four. Three. Two. One. Jump."

The stars disappeared. To Garrett, it was disconcerting. Where there had been pinpoints of light, now there was nothing but blackness. "What happened to the stars?"

Parker turned. The bridge's soft green glow lit him from behind. "We're in hyperspace, not normal space. We're somewhere else. The usual laws of physics don't apply here."

Garrett gave a minute shrug. She knew nothing about physics. *Well, as long as Kyle knows what she's doing. And Parker too, I suppose.*

A moment later, she realized she was tired. "Park, where do we sleep?"

He rose from his chair. "Come on. Back to the main deck."

"I'll just stay here," Kurt said.

Parker looked at him. "Sure? Not much to see. I can create a separate enviro for you if you want."

Kurt shook his head. "Maybe later."

"Suit yourself."

Garrett rose from the jump seat and followed Parker to the lift. They said nothing as they rode to the main deck.

"How do you want to sleep?" Parker said after they'd reached bottom.

She frowned. "Huh?"

He smiled. "Guess I should have been clearer. I can put you in a classic bedroom, a couch strewn with flower petals, a—"

"I'll take the classic bedroom, please."

"Good enough." He walked over to the enviro control. He mumbled to himself for about twenty seconds and then a wall with a door set in its middle appeared, closing off part of the deck.

He gestured toward the door. "There you go. It's all ready for you."

Garrett walked to the door, leaving Parker where he stood. She turned. "Park, I just wanted to say…I mean…" She took a breath. "Look, I'm sorry for what I did to you, Park. It was wrong but all I wanted was…" Her gaze searched his face.

Parker stared at her, impassive.

She shook her head. "I guess I'll see you tomorrow."

"Sleep tight." He headed for the lifts.

She watched him for a few moments, then turned back to the door. She took a step forward and the door seemed to melt. Stepping inside her bedroom, she looked over her shoulder. The door reappeared. Then she took in her surroundings. It was spartan but it looked comfortable enough. And it was quiet, too. She shed her clothes, placed them on a nearby chair, then stepped over to the bed. She crawled under the sheets. After arranging them to her taste, she turned on her side and gazed at the wall.

You have much to atone for, Sister, she heard Feodor's voice in her mind.

Garrett tightened her lips. *Yeah, Feo—but will they let me?*

CHAPTER 39

Kurt sat in the second's chair, staring at the entropic blackness showing on the viscreens. Most cannot, but a few vampires can remember bits and pieces about the rebirthing process. Kurt was one of them. He remembered being insanely hungry all the time. And he remembered the deep, utter darkness. Much like what he was seeing now.

He heard Parker walking on the deck behind him but didn't turn around. "Garrett all tucked away?"

Parker slid into the command chair. "Yep."

They sat in silence for a while. "How long will we be in hyperspace?" Kurt said.

"About thirty-seven hours."

"May I ask where we're going?"

Parker nodded. "The edge of the solar system. The border to interstellar space. That's where Melera's fleet is."

"Why—"

"Part of the plan, Kurt. Part of the plan." His lips tightened. "I just hope we have enough time."

Kurt frowned. "When did you come up with a plan?"

The wolf smiled. "While we were eating. I still have to talk to Kyle but I think it'll work."

They fell silent for several minutes. Parker turned. "Before we left, you said something about being in a will contest. What happened?"

Kurt told him. "So now I'm not only the Master of Seattle, but I'm also the Master of Shanghai."

"That must give you a thrill. The Master of two cities?"

He shrugged. "It's an enviable position to be in, but I wouldn't call myself thrilled by it."

Parker frowned. "Why not?"

"Because, dear Parker, there's nothing like staring death in the face to persuade one to rethink one's priorities."

"And your priorities are?"

Kurt looked down. "Regaining those things that were lost to me."

"Huh?"

Kurt looked up and waved his hand. "Too complicated to get into. Suffice it to say that I'm going to do my damnedest to get them back." He gazed into the other man's eyes. "You're one of the things I lost, Parker." There was a second of silence and then his brow quirked. "Or maybe you're one of the things I never had."

Parker gave him a dubious look. "You know you're not making sense, right?"

Kurt laughed. "No, I suppose not." He turned and stared at the viscreens. "Do you remember when we met?"

"Sure. I was just a couple of years out of college."

"What did you think of me then?"

"I thought you were an arrogant ass. Why?"

"I was quite taken with you. You were smart, easygoing, funny—really, a joy to be around." Kurt turned. "I fell in love with you, Parker. I still love you."

Parker didn't respond for quite a while. "Yeah, I remember your saying something to that effect while we were casting the tryst spell." He shook his head. "But if you love me, how could you have done what you did to me? You put me through hell, Kurt."

He nodded. "I know you won't believe this but I really didn't want to. But Garrett's proposition—I wanted to be a prince again, Parker. A true prince, with Seattle as my princedom. Like I had when I was alive."

"So you were greedy for absolute power."

He nodded again. "And that greed won out over everything—including my love for you."

Neither said anything for a few minutes. Then Parker looked up. "Kurt, are you jealous of Melera?"

He smiled. "Of course."

The wolf's eyes narrowed. "You didn't have anything to do with—"

"No. That was Mandy's doing." He paused. "There was a time when

I would have done anything to destroy Melera. You're in love with her and she made a fool of me, not once but twice. But having seen you two together…" He let out a sigh. "Destroying Melera would destroy you too, Parker. I couldn't do that to you."

Parker smiled. "Melera's a pretty tough cookie, Kurt. It wouldn't be as easy as all that." He stood and stretched. "I'm going to get a little sleep before I talk to Kyle. You want me to set up an enviro for you? Nothing much going on up here."

"No, I'm fine. This blackness makes it easier to think."

"Okay." Parker started for the lifts. "See you in a couple of—"

"Parker."

The wolf turned.

Kurt stared at him. "Do you think you could ever forgive me?"

Parker stared back but said nothing. Then he took a breath. "I don't know, Kurt." He stepped on the lift and went below.

Kurt looked into his lap, thinking on all that had transpired between him and Parker since the latter had arrived in Seattle. *I don't deserve it but I want and need his forgiveness.* He looked up and gazed into the darkness. *And I will do whatever I have to do to get it.*

CHAPTER 40

The trap was set. Now all they had to do was wait.

Forty-two stealth-shielded battleships belonging to Melera's fleet had been positioned in a tight spiral before the wormhole. When Beloc's prison ship and its escort arrived—assuming they weren't too late—the vessels would be inside the spiral. Or so Parker hoped.

He recalled the conversation he and Kyle had while planning their assault. "Do we need so many ships, Kyle?" he'd said. "Wouldn't one or two or ten be enough?"

He'd have sworn he'd seen Kyle smile. "You have no concept of the size of Beloc's ship. It is as big as a large asteroid. About thirty-five of your miles long, with its own armaments. And do not forget about his escort. We must hit them hard and fast so we can make our escape before his fleet has a chance to recover."

Parker had nodded. "Okay. But what makes you think they'll stop before going into the wormhole?"

"The wormhole is filled with an unknown type of energy which causes a ship's electronics to fail. They must be specially shielded before making the transit. For a ship the size of Beloc's, that will take time."

"Oh. So why can't they shield them before they get here?"

"Because the shields interfere with the ships' normal operations." Kyle had paused. "When Shen'zae Tarq first came through the wormhole, his electronics failed. The drives stayed connected just long enough for him to exit. His ship was inoperative for two days before he was able to bring the electronics online."

Parker had frowned. "How do you know this?"

"Shen'zae Tarq's AI told me."

He'd stared at Kyle with wide eyes. "You guys talk to each other?"

"Of course. That is how I am going to get you into Beloc's prison."

Now, sitting in the command chair aboard Melera's ship, Parker ignored the itching from the gravity boots he wore, as well as that from the wide neck collar beneath his form-fitting, black suit. He was nervous enough to bite his nails—something he never did. For relief, he turned to examine the wormhole. There wasn't much to see. The wormhole's perimeter was surrounded by a halo, the light from the stars bent by the hole's twisting space around it. He could see a lone star shining bright on the other side. Any other time, he would have been awed that he was staring at another galaxy. But right now there was only one thing on his mind.

Please, God—let this work.

"This is like something out of a movie," Kurt said, sitting in the second's chair.

"Yeah—I think I saw it three or four times," Garrett said from the jump seat.

"Mm," Parker grunted.

All was quiet for about five minutes. Then Kurt's arm shot forward. He pointed at the viscreens. "There they are," he said, sounding excited.

"Yee-haah," Parker yelled. The prison ship and its accompanying fleet had emerged from hyperspace inside the spiral made by Melera's battleships. He jumped to his feet. "It's showtime." He zipped his suit closed. "Kyle, you ready?"

"Yes, Parker."

"Then let's do it."

Parker ran for the lift and rode to the main deck, then ran for the hatch. He stopped at the door. "Te'po." A golden aura enveloped him. The force field would protect him from the ravages of space's vacuum without having to use a spacesuit. By taking shallow breaths, the field would give him about seven minutes of air before it dissipated. But he wouldn't be outside that long.

A small thump let him know they'd landed on the prison ship. "We are as close to Torpedo Bay 774821 as I could place us," Kyle said. "You will have two minutes to get to the bay. The ship's AI will turn off the bay's force field. You will have five seconds to enter—"

"I know, Kyle, I know. Just open the hatch."

Nothing happened.

He rolled his eyes. "Please?"

The door swung open.

Parker stepped inside. Blowing a small breath, he waited for Kyle to open the outer hatch. A second later, the ramp swung down. He was out like a rocket. Calling on his wolf-strength, he sprinted across the prison ship's hull, his only thought to get to the torpedo bay in time.

When he was a short distance away, he saw the bay's force field slide open like a curtain. *Oh, shit!* Dismay washed through him and his steps faltered a bit. He was too late.

Keep going, his wolf growled softly. *We'll make it.*

His wolf's words gave him new resolution. He put on a burst of speed. The curtain-like force field was just starting to slide into the closed position when Parker leapt. The field's power grazed the soles of his gravity boots. He hit a solid surface on his shoulder, rolled a few times and ended up on his back.

By now he was breathing hard. He worked to still his body. The last thing he needed was to run out of air while there wasn't any in the torpedo bay. A few seconds later, he heard a whoosh. From talking to Kyle, he knew what it meant. The bay was filling with air again.

When the whooshing stopped, Parker unzipped his suit partway and manually turned off the collar's force field. He breathed in the sweet-tasting air, reveling in the feel of his lungs filling up. Then it dawned on him. *Jesus fuck—I'm lying on top of a goddamned live torpedo! What if—*

His wolf-hearing caught the sound of machinery working. It was coming from the doorway. Parker misted and rose to the ceiling, spreading himself out so as to be less noticeable. He watched two technicians—at least that was what he assumed them to be—enter the bay and walk along a raised walkway toward the bay's force field. He waited until the technicians' backs were to him, then sped out the door.

Parker immediately plastered himself to the ceiling and spread out again. The corridor was filled with people. Judging from the plasma rifles they carried, some were legionnaires and the rest, he assumed, were more technicians. *Don't look up, don't look up, don't look up,* he chanted as he slowly made his way along the corridor's ceiling. He counted the vents as he passed. When he'd reached the ninth one, he zipped inside.

Now he was in an air duct. He stopped and brought up in his mind the schematic diagram he'd memorized of this portion of the ship's ducts. He knew from Melera's earlier accounts of being Beloc's prisoner that she wasn't being held with the prison's general population. Beloc would have her tucked away on one of the higher decks, special ones reserved for high-ranking officials who might have information about the rebels he could use. Melera had also told him it was on these decks where most of the torture chambers were located.

Getting there from where he was on one of the lowest decks wouldn't be easy. The ship's ductworks were like a maze. Still, Parker was confident he could navigate his way through them. He moved forward. Smaller ducts branched off from the main duct in which he now floated. He turned at the fifth duct and floated a short way until he came to a vertical duct. He misted upward.

He kept going, duct after duct, turn after turn, when the ship shuddered. Then it shuddered again. Deep in the prison ship's innards, he faintly heard the alarms. *Right on time.* He knew what was happening. Melera's fleet had started its barrage. Not only that, all of the doors to the prisoners' cells had been opened, adding to the mayhem. Her cell door, though, had remained shut. He didn't need her wandering around in the confusion. But he was certain that every prisoner on the ship would be out of their cells by now, doing whatever it is newly freed prisoners do. The guards, overwhelmed by the horde, would be calling for reinforcements, cutting down on the number of ship's personnel available for fighting the bombardment.

Parker had gone three-quarters of the distance to the duct where he'd make his next turn when he saw a wall of smoke coming his way. *Fuck!* He had to get to the tertiary duct before the smoke arrived. If the smoke caught up to him, the duct where he floated was too small for him to materialize and feel his way forward. Like a misty spear, he sped toward the smoke. He made the turn just as the smoke reached it.

But he wasn't out of trouble yet. The constant pounding of the fleet's cannons was producing more smoke. The smoke that he'd barely beaten to the duct was now behind him, denser than it had been before and gathering speed. Parker flew faster, trying to put some distance between him and the smoke. It wasn't working. The smoke rolled closer and closer. Just when it was about to overtake him, he arrived at the vent for Melera's cell. He dove through it. The smoke followed.

"Melera," he shouted after he'd materialized. The cell was filling fast with smoke as well as an acrid, fried wire smell. It was hard to see, too. "Melera!"

A body slammed into his, knocking him off balance. He staggered back. "Pawkher," Melera cried. "I knew you'd come!"

By now the cell was so filled with smoke he couldn't see a thing. His eyes watered and he coughed a few times. "Yeah, well, right now we need to go. Get us out of here." He hesitated. "Please." There came the familiar blast of mind-numbing cold and then they were on the corvette's bridge. The prison ship shuddered and rocked beneath them.

"Kyle," Parker yelled. "Take us to the nearest ship!" He heard the drives powering up. They took off. Only then did he let himself relax. He sank into the command chair, bringing Melera with him. Closing his eyes, he let out a heavy breath.

"Melera, how wonderful to see you again," Kurt said.

"See you is good, too, Khurt."

"Hi, Melera," Garrett said. "Welcome back."

"Tsank you, Gharrett. Is good be back, yes."

Eyes still closed, Parker gave her a little squeeze. "Did Beloc do anything to you, sweetheart? Anything I need to kill him for?"

She chuckled. "No, Pawkher. He leave me 'lone. Tsink me he wait until back to Maqu we get, yes."

"Good." He opened his eyes. Kyle was doing an expert job of dodging the plasma fire from Melera's battle fleet and Beloc's escort. He focused on the escort. Some of the ships that had accompanied the space-going prison had been annihilated. All that was left were floating chunks of twisted metal. Other ships had maintained some integrity but they were good for nothing but the graveyard. He smiled. His plan had worked and he'd come home with his prize.

From the corner of his eye, he saw movement. He turned his head. "Shitfuckhell," he shouted.

Melera jumped in his lap. "What, Pawkher? What it is?"

He pointed to his left.

"Sheetfookhail," she yelled and jumped to her feet.

"What are you two going on about?" Kurt said.

"Javelins," Parker said. "Like fighter jets. They've found us." He looked up at Melera. "Sweetheart, you take the starboard cannons. Skip us if you can." She ran for the lifts. "Kurt, you're on port—"

"Parker, unlike you, I've no idea how to operate the weaponry on this ship."

"It's easy," he said, his words rushed. "Trackball controls the cannons' position. Button number one controls the angle. Button number two is for firing. Go!"

"All right," Kurt said, sounding doubtful. He rose from his chair and hurried for the lifts where Melera was waiting. Parker heard her murmur something to the vampire but he didn't have time to wonder what.

"Kyle. Since Melera's going to be skipping us, I'll take the ship. You take the tail guns."

"Yes, Parker."

"What about me?" Garrett said.

He pointed to the second's chair. "You sit tight." Reaching up, he flipped a switch on the secondary console, activating the ship's intercom system. He slipped his hands into the biointerface port. It glowed, and in a second, he was nervejacked into the corvette.

"Everybody ready?" he said.

"Yes, Parker. Yes. Yes." Kyle, Kurt, and Melera said at the same time.

Parker gritted his teeth. "All right, here we go. Hang on, 'cause it's gonna be a helluva ride!"

CHAPTER 41

The javelins swarmed around them, moving so fast Garrett had a hard time tracking them with her eyes. Between the bubble-like view on the viscreens, Melera's constant skipping them through the Void, and Parker's maneuvering the ship, her brain couldn't get a fix on anything. It made her dizzy. The ship's juddering from the shields absorbing the hits they'd taken didn't make her feel any better.

Parker was a remarkable driver, she had to admit. They'd taken a lot of hits but they would have taken a lot more if he hadn't been able to weave the ship through friendly and enemy fire.

"Kyle," Parker said, his tone conversational. "Talk to the fleet. Tell them to deploy the drones. Get these javs off our ass."

"Yes, Parker," Kyle said.

She was also impressed that he was so cool and calm under so much pressure. Faced with what they were facing now, she wasn't sure she could do it. But then, he was no stranger to being under heavy pressure. The job of wolf pack alpha wasn't an easy one. He'd turned out to be a fine alpha but even so, she knew his heart wasn't in it. He'd only landed the position after she'd goaded him into challenging Darrylon Slade, the old alpha, to a death-match. After that, he'd simply done what he had to do.

Like me. I did what I had to do. Except it all went to hell.

"Garrett," Parker said. She looked up just in time to see him do a belly-roll past a javelin that had fired on them. The shot missed by inches, it seemed. Then the scene abruptly shifted. Melera had skipped them.

"Look to your right. There's a big square that's lit up. See it?"

Her gaze swept over the right side of the console. She wondered why he was asking since she could see the heads-up display on the viscreen. Maybe it was just to give her something to do. She did feel pretty useless while everyone else was busy fighting for their lives. A moment later, she spotted the large square. "Yes."

"What color is it?"

"Umm… She hesitated. "It's kind of this bluish-green color."

"So it's not bright blue."

"No."

"Okay."

He didn't elaborate and she didn't inquire further. But there was something she wanted to know. "Park, is it my imagination or are the jav drivers really bad shots? I mean, we should be dead right now, shouldn't we?"

Parker rolled the ship to port and smiled. "They're not trying to kill us. They're trying to cripple us."

"Why?"

"Melera's fleet. Beloc knows it's here and he needs Melera and Kyle to communicate with it."

"What about the rest of us?"

His smile widened into a grin. "We're dead meat."

She said nothing.

"Kurt, how you doing down there?" Parker said.

"Oh, as well as can be expected, I suppose," Kurt's voice came over the intercom. "I just shoot at anything that moves."

"That's the rule."

Garrett watched Parker drive through the swarm. Melera skipped them when she could and when she couldn't, she'd tell Parker. In response, he'd play a game of deep-space chicken with whatever javelins were facing them. They always veered off—if Melera or Kurt didn't blow them up first—but it was still nerve-wracking.

A trio of javelins loomed before them. "Pawkher, no skip room," Melera's voice sounded.

"Okay, sweetheart." He charged the trio. Two turned chicken and altered course. But the third didn't. Neither did Parker. He bore down on the smaller craft as if he intended to ram it.

Garrett gripped the seat of her chair. On the viscreens, the javelin grew bigger and bigger, and bigger still. At the last minute, Parker rolled to starboard. She saw a green orb shoot from the javelin's belly.

"Fuck!" Parker yelled. He dove the corvette but it was too late. An alarm jangled. She heard and felt a bone-shaking bang. The bridge disappeared in a spectacular burst of light. She felt a brief sensation of flight and then something hard smashed against her head. Stars skittered across her vision. She lay on the deck, trying to figure out what had happened. Then her nose caught the harsh smell of burned insulation and she remembered. Adrenalin surged through her, banishing the pain in her head. She struggled to her knees, coughing against the dense smoke enveloping the bridge.

"Park," she screamed. "Parker!"

There was no answer.

Blinded by smoke, Garrett crawled in the direction she hoped would take her to the bridge's console. The interior fans kicked on and in seconds, the smoke had been sucked out. Her eyes widened. Parker lay crumpled on the floor against the console. She jumped to her feet and ran over to his inert form.

"Parker," she cried and shook him. He didn't move. Then she noticed his badly burned hands which were already healing. She shook him again. Parker's eyes flew open. "Garrett," he said, his voice dreamy. "Wha—" Then he came fully awake. "Shit!" Pushing her out of the way, he leapt to his feet and slid into the command chair.

Taking her seat in the second's chair, she watched him manipulate the controls with his burned hands, wincing in obvious pain. The viscreens came up first. She gasped. Despite the drones picking them off, javelins circled around them like a pack of hyenas. And they were awfully close.

"Melera, Kurt, Kyle," Parker shouted after he'd restored the intercom system. "You guys all right?"

"Yes. Yes, Parker. Of course," Melera, Kyle, and Kurt said at the same time.

"Good. Let's take out some more javs."

He turned to her. "The heads-up display is gone. What color is that big square now?"

"Orange-red. More red than orange, though."

"Damn."

She peered at him. "What?"

He shook his head. "That last shot basically wiped out our shields.

Another hit or two and we'll be at their mercy."

She bit her lip. It looked like there was no way out. Then she had an idea. Years ago, she'd watched a mage like her magickally jumpstart a computer with a burnt-out motherboard. "Same principle," he'd told her with a shrug. "Flesh or plastic, a body's a body."

And a computer's a computer, isn't it?

Garrett leapt from her seat and ran for the lift.

"Where are you going?" Parker called.

She didn't answer. Reaching the lift, she jumped on the platform. Parker had given her and Kurt a tour of the ship while they were in hyperspace and she had a pretty good idea she'd be able to tell which computer controlled the shields. "The one that's blasted," she muttered.

She reached the drive deck. Just as she'd thought, there was one computer that looked like it had exploded. The cabinet doors hung open at a crazy angle. Most of the indicator lights had gone dark. Smoke wisps still rose from the areas that had burned. She ran over to it. Not caring that the wires were still hot, she grabbed in each hand all of the ones that had been ripped from their sockets.

She frantically searched her memory for a spell she could use and settled on a restorative spell. *Mother, please let this work...*

Garrett concentrated for about ten seconds, marshaling her magickal energy. Starting in her solar plexus, the magickal force traveled throughout her body. Her head and legs grew heavy. Then the rest of her. When she'd reached the point where she thought she'd sink through the deck, she started chanting. "Kaelle si vis. Kaelle si vis. Kaelle si vis."

She was too engrossed in her spell to notice the lights on the computer panel that had been dark had started flashing.

CHAPTER 42

Parker stared at the shield power gauge. He'd done this often since that disastrous hit, willing the square to turn even yellow but no such luck. This time, though…

"What?" he shouted. The square shone bright blue.

"Pawhker, what happen?" Melera's voice came over the intercom.

"Dunno, but we have shields again." He looked around. There were fewer javelins than there had been before but there were still a lot of them. He glanced up. The nearest battleship was tantalizingly close.

Parker tightened his lips. "Okay, everybody. I'm going to make a run for it. Melera, skip us when you can. Kyle, tell the ship to open the bay and keep hammering on those javs."

"Yes, Parker."

He turned the corvette and aimed it for the battleship. The bay doors slid open, revealing a bright rectangle. He revved the drives, watching the gauge ripple through the rainbow and more until it held steady on aqua. He nodded once. Any higher and he'd blow them. "Let 'er rip," he muttered.

Angling the nose upward, Parker drummed a tattoo on a medium-sized circle under the aqua light. The ship shot forward. The javelins followed. He dodged the streaks of plasma coming from the battleship. Melera, Kurt, Kyle, and the drones were doing their part but there were still too many javelins to destroy every one. The corvette was hit again and again but as long as the shields held, he didn't care. He glanced at the gauge. The shields were holding.

After what seemed like hours, they'd made it behind the curtain of plasma fire raining down on the javelins. Those that tried to follow were obliterated. Eventually, the fighters backed off, milling about like angry hornets. But Parker knew there was nothing they could do, now.

He powered down the drives, hoping to slow enough so as not to overshoot the bay. He needn't have worried. The battleship caught them in its tractor beam. Their ship seemed to stop even as its drives still blasted away. He shut them down. The battleship hauled them into the bay. He looked at the viscreens. The javelins were still out there. Then the bay doors closed, cutting off his view.

Parker slumped in the command seat, exhausted. He stared at the burnt-out biointerface port without seeing it. A feral grin spread across his face.

Fuck you, Beloc.

Melera, Parker, and Kurt met on the compact bridge.

"I can't believe we did it," Kurt said.

Melera frowned. "Where Gharrett is?"

"Right here," came a soprano voice.

The three turned as one. Garrett stepped off the lift and joined them.

"Where've you been?" Parker said. "You left just after the shields blew. Where'd you go?"

She smiled. "Down to the drive deck. I got the shields back up."

Melera's jaw dropped. "Tsat you? How you do tsis?"

Garrett turned. "Magick. Sometimes being a mage comes in handy."

Melera picked her up and twirled her around. "You save us," she shouted. "We need shields, or we lose fight!"

Parker enveloped her in a bear hug. "Melera's right. Without those shields, we'd all be in Beloc's prison by now."

"Speaking of Beloc," Kurt said, "is there somewhere we can go to see how he's faring?"

"Kyle?" Melera said. "We want go bridge. You help, yes?"

"Yes, Shen'zae." The AI fell silent for a few seconds. "The ship will take you to the bridge, now."

The four descended to the main deck. Kyle let down the boarding ramp. They ran toward a set of doors on the near side of the huge docking bay that whisked open just as they reached it. They stepped aboard and the doors closed.

"Why do we need Kyle to help us with the ship?" Kurt said.

Melera shrugged. "AI know us not. Do nutsing we say unless Kyle ask."

He frowned. "How come it obeys Kyle?"

She shook her head. "Not obey. Just do as Kyle ask. If it want not, will not."

Kurt's eyes widened. "So we're at the mercy of an AI?"

"Guess so," Parker said.

The cab stopped and the doors whisked open. The bridge was huge. But even from where she stood, Melera could see Beloc's prison ship was in trouble. The four hurried to the forward viscreens. Despite the mayhem going on outside, the cavernous deck was silent.

The barrage from the battleships surrounding the truncated tetrahedron had meanwhile continued. Massive explosions rocked the prison ship from stem to stern. Melera stared at the stricken vessel. Memories flooded through her. Beloc torturing her with his zaprod, a foot-long laser he used to burn holes in prisoners' flesh. Except for her. Knowing she was a self-healer, he'd impale her with it even in her most delicate areas. She remembered his penchant for dropping her naked into a room with thirty or more prisoners. He'd watch her fight them off. She always managed to kill at least ten or twelve but in the end, there were just too many. *And afterward…*

"Do you want us to destroy the ship?" a deep voice boomed in Xia'saan, breaking into her thoughts. The voice, seeming to fill the bridge, belonged to the ship's AI.

Melera didn't hesitate. "Yes."

"Very well."

"What was that about?" Kurt said.

"Battleships destroy Beloc's prison."

"But they can't," Garrett cried. "There are innocent people on board!"

She turned. "Prisners is galaxy scum. Better off dead. And nobody in-no-cent work for Beloc."

"What about the other prisoners? Like you?"

"Is too bad. Tsis happens in war."

Melera turned back to the viscreens. Now, instead of just cannon fire, she saw the fleet had loosed the torpedoes. It didn't take long. Five minutes later, Beloc's ship seemed to burst. A blaze of white floodlit the deck. She shielded her eyes against it.

"Hold on," she said and grabbed the railing in front of her. In her peripheral vision, she saw Parker and the others do the same.

"Why do we need—" Kurt said.

The ship rocked, hard enough so that she nearly lost her grip. Pieces of debris flew at them and thumped against the battleship's shields. The rocking subsided. "What was that?" Kurt said, sounding awed.

"Shock wave," Parker said.

Beloc's ship was gone. Only a few chunks of metal floating aimlessly about told the story of the prison ship that had been there.

No one said anything for several minutes. "Do you think he made it out in time?" Garrett said in a small voice.

Melera knew she was thinking about Basile and not Beloc. It didn't matter. Even she didn't think Beloc was dead. "Prolly. Beloc is…" She turned to Parker. "You have word, yes?"

Parker seemed to think a minute. Then he looked up. "Resourceful. He can figure out a way to get around any problem."

She turned to Garrett. "Yes."

"Well, we'd better get out of here before the AI kicks us out," Parker said.

The four crossed the bridge to the elevator and boarded. "Please take us to Kyle," Melera said in Xia'saan.

The elevator doors closed.

Melera stood on the battleship's observation deck watching the last of the fleet pass through the wormhole. Kyle had brokered an agreement between her, Parker, and the ship. The AI, whose name was Nyv, now counted the two as its masters.

"Nyv, you gave the Vst the coordinates for finding the fleet, right?" she said in Xia'saan.

"Yes, Shen'zae."

She winced. "I'm not…" Tightening her lips, she shook her head. This was Kyle's doing. The AI had told Nyv who she was and it would call her Shen'zae no matter what she said.

The observation deck's doors whispered open. She didn't turn around, knowing it was Parker. His footsteps came closer and then he was standing next to her. "I watched from the bridge. So that's it." He took her hand.

"No."

From the corner of her eye, she saw Parker peer at her. "Sweetheart, what's wrong? You seem——"

"Now, Nyv."

A cluster of torpedoes headed toward the wormhole and exploded against its perimeter. The hole seemed to waver, then slowly collapse in on itself until nothing was left but a bright new star. Moments later, the star winked out. No trace of it remained.

Parker placed his arm around her shoulders. "Oh, honey, I——"

She still stared at the viscreen. "I had no choice. Beloc would have come back. You know that. And Dirt would be in trouble. Again."

"That's Earth."

"Whatever."

Neither one said anything for a long while. "But you've just closed yourself off from Maqu," he said, his voice quiet.

She shrugged. "There's nothing there for me. No home, the Vst and Beloc want to kill me…" Turning, she wrapped her arms around Parker's neck and rested her head on his shoulder. She thought about her father. She'd broken his code, found the battle fleet, and just now had sent it off to the Vst. Her promise to him, on which she'd given her ka, had been met. For the first time since the war began, she was free—truly free. *A new galaxy…and a new beginning.* She raised her head and laughed as joy flooded through her.

Parker looked surprised. "What's up, sweetheart?"

Melera grinned. "Let's go. Let's go to y——" She caught herself. "Let's go to our house, now."

He swept her off her feet and kissed her. "Yes," he said after pulling away. "Let's go to our house, now."

CHAPTER 43

Not long after returning to Earth, Melera, Parker, Garrett, and Kurt stood on Feodor's doorstep. Melera watched Garrett reach up, lift the large black ring and knock twice.

The door opened a few minutes later. "Ma Déesse!" Feodor cried. He looked at Garrett. "Where have you been? I've been calling and calling—"

She grinned. "We were—"

"Out of town," Kurt finished for her.

Feodor peered at him. Then he looked sideways at Melera. "Out of town, eh? Well, I imagine that's accurate enough." He shook his head. "Come in, come in," he said, stepping back so the others could enter.

The four filed into the cottage. Feodor looked at each of them in turn. "I'm sorry. I wasn't expecting you so I don't have anything prepared for you to eat."

Parker smiled. "That's fine. We ate before we left."

"Bon. But I can at least get us some wine." He gestured to his right. "Go sit in the library." Turning, he started for the kitchen.

Garrett followed. "I'll help."

Feodor nodded and the two walked deeper into the old house.

Parker stepped over to the library's doors and opened them. The three entered. Melera and Parker made themselves comfortable on the sofa while Kurt sat in one of the wing chairs. No one said anything.

Presently, Feodor and Garrett returned each bearing a tray with glasses filled with wine. Garrett handed out the wine to the others and then took a seat on the wing chair across from Kurt.

Feodor pulled up a side chair and faced them. "Mes amis, I have created another spell. I had to go to Paris to do it. The repository there has books even I don't have." He paused. "I am hoping this one will work."

Parker's lips stretched into a half-smile. "Third time's the charm, right?"

Feodor smiled back. "That's what they say."

While Feodor explained the spell, Melera kept her gaze on the old mage. To her, he looked older, his face more drawn. It was so minute, she doubted the others noticed. She wondered how often he went down to the cave to rejuvenate.

"So we will spend our usual week realigning our energies," Feodor said. "Then we will try out the spell." He seemed to notice that they'd all finished their wine. He clapped his hands. "And now, to bed. You need your rest."

Garrett yawned. "Feo, what did you put in this wine?"

He grinned. "I cast a mild soporific spell." Then he looked at Melera. "I suppose it did not work for you."

"No, but a little tired me is," she lied.

"Good. I will leave you to make your sleeping arrangements. I will see you in the morning." He walked to the open library doors. "Goodnight." He left the room.

The four walked into the foyer, collected their travel cases and followed Feodor upstairs.

Garrett reached the top of the staircase first. "You want to do what we did the last time?"

Parker shrugged. "Sure. What about you, Kurt?"

"Fine with me."

The two men entered the third bedroom, leaving Garrett and her in the hallway. Melera would rather have slept with Parker but decided it didn't matter.

Garrett picked up her bag. "Come on, Melera. I'm getting really sleepy." She walked to the second bedroom and disappeared inside.

Melera stood in the hallway, staring at Feodor's closed door. The other three didn't know what had happened to the old mage the last time. She wondered if he would survive this time.

A week later, they were ready to cast the spell. Feodor led the four down the staircase and into the caves. Parker, Garrett, and Kurt shed their robes and entered the vortex. Like the last spellcasting, Melera took a seat on the floor in the opening between the two cave rooms.

Feodor took off his robe. "All right. Get into position."

Standing close, the three formed a triangle. Instead of touching finger pads, they took each other by the wrist.

"Are you ready?"

"Yes," they chorused.

"Then let us begin."

As Melera watched, Feodor began a slow chant that sounded like "musa kayra musa." The three's auras appeared. Then the colorful vortex divided itself into three parts. The first section enveloped Parker, the second Garrett, and the third, Kurt. Feodor's chant changed. Now it sounded more like growls and screeches. He began to dance, his feet stomping on the dirt floor. His arms pushed at the air, then flailed about, and went back to pushing. His torso undulated. A second or two later, sparks flew from his body. While the sparks popped, his body started to glow with a bright white light. In the midst of it, she could barely see Feodor's outline.

The old mage stumbled and fell. Without thinking, Melera jumped to her feet and ran to him. From what she could tell, he was unconscious.

What do I do?

Put him in the vortex. That should revive him, her czado said.

But the spell—

Do it.

Melera hefted Feodor's body and stepped over to the vortex. She pushed him inside. To her surprise, he passed through Kurt and Garrett's clasped wrists as if he was a ghost. He got to his knees and stood upright. Melera knew it was the vortex holding him up since his head still hung down to his chest.

Feodor's body began to spin, slowly at first, then faster and faster. She knew this was the vortex's doing, too. She watched the white light invade Parker, Garrett, and Kurt's auras until it seemed that all of them were glowing white.

Feodor's head snapped up. He'd come to. He began a chant, different from the one before. The sparkling white light grew so bright that she had to shield her eyes. With slow, backward steps, she walked back to the cave entrance and sat. A moment later, the light seemed to explode. She hid her eyes again. Only after the cave had darkened did she uncover them.

Parker, Garrett, and Kurt lay sprawled. They appeared to be unconscious. Feodor stumbled out of the vortex and leaned against the rock that held their robes. He looked haggard.

Rising to her feet, Melera walked over to him and placed her arm around his shoulders. "You ohh-kay?"

"Non." Feodor gave her a weak smile. "But I will be all right. The spell was a little too much for me." He sighed. "Thank you for putting me in the vortex. How did you know that was the next part of the spell?"

She shrugged. "Me not. Seem like right tsing to do."

Feodor nodded and stood. He swayed a little. She reached out to steady him but he waved her away. He picked up his robe and put it on.

She turned and looked at the three still floating in the vortex. They hadn't moved. She turned back to Feodor. "Now what?"

"We wait. They will wake up soon."

A minute or two later, Parker, Garrett, and Kurt woke. The three sat up, bleary-eyed.

Parker shook his head. "Anybody get the number of that truck?"

Feodor chuckled. "I imagine you all feel that way. Come. Let's go upstairs and I'll tell you how it went."

The three slowly got to their feet. One by one, they stepped out of the vortex. Feodor handed them their robes. After they'd covered themselves, the four followed him out of the room.

In the library, Feodor sat in one wing chair while the rest ranged around him. "Your auras are not completely free of one another but we did the best we could."

Kurt groaned.

Feodor smiled. "Cheer up, mon ami. It is not all bad. The tears in your aura have closed. I imagine you now have your full regent's powers back. There are a few tiny spots of green in your aura and a tiny streak of blue. So you may have a little witch power left but I doubt it."

Kurt looked like someone had just handed him a much-wanted present. "Well, let's test it." He walked to the window, opened it, and held up his hand. The laser shot from his palm and then winked out. Grinning, he returned to his seat.

Feodor stared at him in obvious shock. "Ma Déesse, what was that?"

Kurt winked. "My version of witch light. It burns, too. It's come in handy a couple of times."

Feodor gave his head a little shake. He turned to Parker. "Yours is similar—a little bit of blue and a small streak of red. That means you will no longer have to feed."

Parker smiled. "But maybe I can still do this." He dissolved into mist for a second or two, then rematerialized. He laughed. "Good. That comes in handy, too."

Feodor turned to Garrett. "And you, cherie, have a smidgen of red and a little streak of green in your aura. I should think you will have a craving for meat every now and then."

Garrett shuddered. "Uck."

The old mage looked at each of the three in turn. "Most of all, these little bits and pieces mean you still have a psychic connection with one another. Not much, but it is there." He paused. "But there is one more person in this room who needs healing."

Everyone turned to stare at her. She pointed to her chest. "Me?"

Feodor nodded. "Your aura—it may be different from ours but it is still an aura. And yours is riddled with holes. I suggest—"

"But you magick work not on me."

"I didn't say anything about using magick. The vortex is full of healing energy and it might heal you."

Parker squeezed her hand. "Sweetheart, it's worth a shot, don't you think?"

"Me…" Then she nodded.

"Bon. We will try tomorrow."

Melera stood before the vortex, looking into its depths with trepidation.

Feodor touched her shoulder. "Hand me your robe, cherie."

She unwound the sash from her waist. Slipping the robe from her shoulders, she handed it to him.

"Now step into the vortex."

She obeyed. Like the others had said, it felt springy against her bare feet. She looked up. "What me do now?"

Feodor smiled. "I don't know."

Not knowing what else do, she bounced on the energy. When she'd tired of this game, she looked around the cave. Parker, Kurt, and Garrett hovered in the doorway, watching with wide, expectant eyes.

Five minutes passed. Nothing. "Fe-o-dor, me not tsink—"

A streak of unutterable pain slashed through her head. Melera screamed. She fell to her knees and then prone, writhing in agony. None of Beloc's tortures were even comparable to what she felt now. Tiny needles, thousands of them it seemed, threaded through her brain. She screamed again and again, clutching and clawing at her head. Finally, mercifully, she fainted.

When she came to, the first face she saw was Parker's. Eyes wide, he stared at her, looking anxious. "Sweetheart, are you all right?"

She didn't answer at first. "Me know not," she croaked.

He settled at the edge of the vortex and pulled her into his arms. They sat that way for a long time. Then she heard another voice.

"Cherie." Melera peered around Parker's arm. Feodor stood close by, holding up her robe.

Parker helped her up. On her feet, dizziness overcame her and she started to sway. He steadied her. His hand on her elbow, she stepped over to Feodor. The old mage helped her into her robe. "Come. To the library."

Parker carried her up the stairs. Reaching the library, he lay her on the couch, then sat at one end and put her head in his lap.

By now, Melera felt much better, though weak. She looked around. Kurt occupied the side chair. Garrett sat in the wing chair. Both stared at her but said nothing.

Feodor, sitting in the other wing chair, smiled. "Now how do you feel, cherie?"

"Diff'rent. Me know not how, but…"

"Well, let me tell you that it worked. Your aura has completely healed."

Parker stroked her cheek. "Hear that? No more seizures. Beloc can really go fuck himself now."

"Yes." She smiled. "And maybe Kyle learn me talk good Ink-lees, too."

She fell asleep to the sound of the others' laughter.

CHAPTER 44

Kurt, Parker, Melera, and Garrett stood in the foyer of Feodor's cottage, their travel bags littering the floor. Except for Garrett's.

Kurt gave her a surprised look. "Garrett—you're not coming with us?"

She shook her head. "I think I'll stay for a while. I...I have a lot to learn."

"About magick?"

"Yes, but more important...about being a mage."

At that moment, Feodor rounded the corner obviously having come from the kitchen. He glanced at the bags on the floor. "Bon. But before you leave, I would like a word with Parker." He looked up at the wolf. "Into the library, please?" He turned and opened one of the library doors.

Parker followed, looking puzzled. Feodor shut the door behind them.

No one said anything for a few minutes. "So, Melera, what do you plan to do when you get back to Seattle?" Kurt broke the silence.

She grinned. "Me have to know Dir"—she seemed to catch herself—"Earts ways." Her grin faded into a smile. "Is good me have Pawhker to learn me."

"Do you think you two will go traipsing around the galaxy again, ever?"

She stared at him as if he'd asked a particularly silly question. "Yes."

"Kurt," Garrett broke in.

He turned.

She licked her lips. "I'll ask one more time and then I won't ask again." Her gaze was steady. "Do you—"

Kurt smiled. "My dear, I already have."

She bowed her head. "Thank you," she whispered. Then she looked up. "I love you. You know that, right?"

Kurt nodded. "And contrary to what you might think, I do love you, Garrett. I just can't give you what you want and need."

Her lips tightened a little. "I know."

The door to the library opened. Feodor emerged, with Parker trailing behind. The wolf wore an odd expression. He stopped in front of Garrett.

She frowned. "Park, what's——"

Parker didn't answer. Kurt watched him lift her from the floor and hold her in a tight hug. He kissed her cheek and set her down. "It still hurts, Garrett." His voice was husky. "It will always hurt. But I understand." He gave her a small smile.

Garrett gazed into his face. A single tear trickle along her cheek.

"And you, cherie," Feodor said. Kurt turned his head. The old mage was talking to Melera. He walked over to her, picked up her hand and patted it. "You must come visit us, soon. You have much to teach me, non?"

She cocked her head, a tiny frown creasing her brow.

Feodor smiled. "I want to learn how to—what did you call it?—skip."

She laughed. "Yes. Me do tsat."

Feodor nodded once. "Bon." He looked around with a big smile. "And so we have said our good-byes and until we meet again, please take care of yourselves."

Kurt picked up his bag. Parker picked up his and Melera's. "We will, Feodor," Parker said. He and Melera misted and slipped under the door.

"And the same to you, my friend," Kurt said with a smile. Giving Feodor and Garrett one last look, he too misted and was on his way.

A month later, Kurt stood at the window on the top floor of his downtown office tower, looking at the construction below. Much progress had been made since last November. Two of the office towers had been rebuilt and the third would be finished in a few weeks.

The door to his office slammed open. He whipped his head around.

"Hey, Kurt," Parker said, striding over the threshold.

His lips tightened. "Parker, when are you ever going to learn to knock?"

Parker grinned. "Afraid I'll catch you in flagrante delicto?"

"My, what big words you know."

The wolf laughed.

He glanced around. "Where's Melera? I hardly ever see one of you without the other."

"Oh, she's at home, trying to figure out how to run the dishwasher."

Kurt smiled. "Domesticating her, I see."

Parker snorted. "Domesticate Melera? Right. Easier to domesticate a crocodile."

Neither man said anything for a few minutes. "So," Kurt broke the silence, "what brings you here?"

"Well, I was just thinking over what Feodor and I talked about in his library."

"What did you talk about?"

"Forgiveness."

Kurt said nothing.

Parker shrugged. "So anyway, I was on my way home and thought I'd see what you were up to."

A long silence ensued. Kurt was about to open his mouth when Parker spoke. "Kurt...I can't say I can let bygones be bygones but I'm willing to try." He stepped closer to the window and stuck out his hand.

Kurt took it. "Friends?"

"Fuck you, asshole."

His eyes widened. Parker grinned, and they both laughed. When their laughter subsided, Parker let go of his hand. "I'd better get back. See if I still have a kitchen." He turned to leave.

"Parker," Kurt said.

The wolf looked over his shoulder.

"Stop by anytime. Bring Melera. Maybe we can have lunch or something."

Parker smiled. "I'll do that." Then he left.

Kurt walked to his desk and sat in his black leather executive's chair. A small smile appeared on his lips. His new relationship with Parker wasn't what he would have wanted but he'd take what he could get.

Still smiling, he pressed the intercom button on the telephone. "Julie, get me Shanghai."

FOREVER BOUND

Roxanne Bland

Kurt, world-renowned as the greatest vampire regent who'd ever unlived, leaned back in his float chair and contemplated driving a stake through his heart.

He sighed. Rising from his seat, he walked to the window in his office on the top floor of his commercial tower building and looked out. One of the few vampires who could walk by day, he saw it was bright and sunny as the days usually were now that the meteorological bureau had control of the weather. Every so often, the bureau would allow rain to fall during the daytime but when it did rain, it was mostly at night.

He looked down. On Track Seven, air cars, five abreast and stacked eight levels deep, hovered in orderly rows before the traffic coordinators. The coordinators, one for each level, hung motionlessly as if suspended from invisible wires. He waited, willing one or more of the driverless cars to go haywire and run the coordinators over or maybe crash into each other. Create a little mayhem. But none of them did.

Careful, now. Keep thinking like that and they'll pack you off to the re-education camp. His lips tightened. These days, any sign of aggression on the part of anyone—exotic or human—was met with a trip to the camp. If the re-education program was unsuccessful, the person was never seen again. He'd heard they were shipped to a special island in an unspecified location to live out their days, presumably in uninhibited aggressive behavior. It was Kurt's opinion that they were executed. Usually, though, the re-education was successful. But he'd seen some of those who'd returned. It was his opinion that they'd been lobotomized.

Kurt's thoughts turned to Parker Berenson, alpha of Seattle's werewolf pack—when there had been a Seattle—and Shen'zae Melera, his space alien love. He thought about them a lot, these days. They'd met as enemies but had parted as friends. *Six hundred years, and I still miss them.*

He looked over his shoulder at a lock of hair floating in an environmentally controlled shadow box. The hair had belonged to Garrett Larkin, a mage with Seattle's now-defunct Balthus coven. He blinked. *And Garrett, dead for almost as long. Despite her atrocious manners, I miss her, too.*

Kurt sighed again. *There's noth—*

The door to his office whisked open. He whipped his head around, ready rip out the intruder's throat—re-education camp be damned.

His jaw dropped instead.

Parker strode over the threshold. "Hey, Kurt, you fucking asshole."

Melera was right behind him. "Hel-lo, Khurt."

Speechless, he gave his head a hard shake. "What…how?" he said after he'd found his voice.

Parker smiled. "We were in the neighborhood and thought we'd drop by to see how you're doing." He looked around the office. "Nice digs you've got here."

"But—"

"But what?" Melera said.

"How did you find me?"

Parker laughed. "Easy. We still have that psychic connection from the tryst, remember?"

"Ah. Of course." Kurt looked the two over. "It's been six hundred years since you left. How is it that you're still alive? And you…you haven't aged."

"Neither have you," Parker said.

"But I'm dead." Frowning, he squinted at them. "Are you…?"

Melera chuckled. "We're very much alive."

"Then—"

"The miracle of the vortex, Kurt." Parker's smile widened into a grin. "Remember Feodor, the old mage who helped us break the tryst? And the vortex below his house?"

"Of course."

"Well, we found an uninhabited planet full of them. That's where we made our home base. Whenever we start feeling our age we just go home and rejuvenate."

Melera nodded.

The office fell silent for a few moments. "So…how've you been?" Parker said.

"Oh, fi—" Kurt shook his head. "To tell you the truth, I've been thinking about suicide."

Parker's mouth fell open. "What?"

Melera looked just as stricken as Parker. "Why?"

"My dears, I am twelve hundred and forty-one years old and bored out of my skull. The world has much changed since you left. Zots like us are no longer pariahs. Humans have learned to get along with one another. We have one world government. Disagreements are resolved amicably by a panel of arbiters. Peace reigns over the Earth."

Parker frowned. "That's a good thing, isn't it?"

"No. There's no excitement. Nothing to get the blood going. Every day is the same. No surprises. And everyone is so damned agreeable all the time." He shrugged. "I'm tired of it, that's all."

Now it was Melera's turn to frown. "But I tsought you wanted to live forever."

"I do. But not like this."

The office fell silent again. No one spoke for several minutes. Kurt saw Parker and Melera look at each other. Something unsaid passed between them.

Melera turned. "Come wits us. We can guarantee your life won't be boring."

He smiled. "My dear, I'd just be a third wheel, as the ancient saying goes. I—"

"What's this?" Parker pointed to the shadow box.

"A lock of Garrett's hair," he said. "She gave it to me when she left the United States for France. Back when there *was* a United States and France, that is."

"Why did she leave?"

"To take care of Feodor." He cocked his head. "When he helped us with the tryst, did you know he was dying?"

Parker looked surprised. He opened his mouth but Melera beat him to it. "Yes. I promised not to tell."

Kurt nodded. "Anyway, after Feodor died, she stayed on."

The big office was quiet a third time. "Well, I have an idea," Parker broke the silence. "Why don't we clone Garrett? Then she can come with us, too. Surely after all this time you guys can do that."

"Yes, but I gave my word I wouldn't."

"Why?" Melera said.

"She died about fifteen years after the war between the nationalists and the one-worlders had spread over the globe. She said she didn't want to live in a world at war."

"But—" Parker said.

"Oh, I know. The world has changed. But a promise is a promise, hmm?"

Parker's lips stretched into a sly smile. "Didn't you tell me once regents weren't known for keeping promises?"

"I certainly did. But—"

"So why don't you break your promise?" Melera said. She raised her brow. "Tell her we made you do it."

He didn't answer at first. He thought about a life gallivanting around the galaxy with his friends—on a battleship, no less. Discovering new worlds. Maybe meeting aliens. It would be new, it would be exciting. And like Melera had said, he'd never be bored.

Kurt looked up. "All right. I'll do it."

"So where do we get her cloned?" Parker said.

He smiled. "My dear Parker, I own cloning parlors all over the world. In fact, there's one in this building."

"Let's get to it, then."

Kurt walked to the shelf holding the lock of Garrett's hair in its box. Picking it up, he turned to the others. "Ready."

The three left the office. A hundred and seventy-six floors down, they stepped off the elevator into a tastefully appointed receiving room. Kurt walked up to the human receptionist. He could have used a robot or android and saved the money he paid staff for this function, but he'd learned through trial and error that people—zots and humans— preferred to be greeted by the living.

He smiled. "I'd like a cloning appointment, please."

She consulted the holographic calendar floating over her desk. "I'm afraid we don't have an opening until October. If I might have your name and other information, I can make an appointment for you then."

Kurt faked a crestfallen look. Her expression turned sympathetic. "What's your name, sir?"

He smiled again. "Masters. Kurt Masters."

The receptionist's eyes looked like they'd pop from her head. "Uh, Mr. Masters...um...let me see..." She consulted her calendar again. "There's an appointment available in fifteen minutes. Will that do?"

Kurt beamed at her. "That'll be fine."

"Motherdammit Kurt, you promised!"

Scowling, Garrett stood before him in a robe, her waist-length hair still dripping wet from the tank, fists on hips.

He tried to look apologetic. "I'm sorry, my dear. But I was forced to do it."

"By who?"

Kurt pointed.

He watched Garrett's jaw drop. Her eyes widened until they were like saucers. "Parker! Melera," she cried. Smiling, he looked on as Garrett ran over to the two and tried to embrace both at the same time. After a minute, she stepped back. "You said you were leaving Earth for good. What are you doing here?"

"Well, we want to ask you something but we should go to Kurt's office first," Parker said.

"Miss Larkin," a voice sounded. Kurt turned. An android technician stood in the doorway behind the receptionist. "Please come with me. We need to test you to make sure all is well."

Garrett stamped her foot. "I'm fine, can't you see that?"

"Miss Larkin, please come with me."

Kurt watched her eyes narrow. "Didn't you hear what I just said?"

"Miss Larkin, please come with me."

Kurt almost laughed. She obviously had no idea the tech wasn't human and would repeat its request until she obeyed. Scowling a second time, she opened her mouth but he spoke first. "My dear, go with the technician, please. It's standard procedure. And you wouldn't want me to be sued, would you?"

Garrett crossed her arms. "Hmpf." Then she sighed. "Oh…all right."

A half-hour later, Garrett stepped through the doorway wearing street clothes. She looked down at herself. "These clothes are weird."

"Fashion tastes have changed considerably in the last half millennia, my dear."

Garrett looked up. "Guess so." She swiveled her head left and right. "Come on. Let's get out of here before they poke me again."

They boarded the elevator and zipped up to the office tower's top floor. During the short journey, Kurt explained to her a little of what had happened in the world between her death and resurrection. "Six hundred years," Garrett said, her voice full of wonder. "I've been dead for six hundred years."

"Not anymore," Parker said.

Inside his office, Kurt retrieved a bottle of wine from his desk drawer, popped the cork and decanted it into four crystal goblets. He picked up his glass. "A toast—to the four musketeers." They each took a draught from their glasses.

Parker lowered his goblet, looking confused. "Shouldn't that be the three musketeers?"

He shrugged. "Who's counting?"

Garrett took a sip of her wine. "So what did you want to ask me?"

Parker and Melera glanced at each other. "Garrett," Parker said, "we want to know if you'd be willing to come with us."

She frowned. "Come with you where?"

"Exploring the galaxy."

Her eyes widened. "You mean—"

"Yes."

The office was silent for a long while as she sipped her wine, seeming to think it over. She finished her drink and twirled the stem of her goblet between her fingers. "Well…I don't see why not. I mean, it's not like I have any ties here, now." She looked up and grinned. "Yes. I'll come." She looked at the three of them in turn. "So when do we leave?"

Parker smiled. "How about now? Oh, wait." He turned to Kurt. "Don't you have to, you know, get your affairs in order?"

Kurt shook his head. "It's already done. If anything happens to me, Daniel gets everything. All I have to do is call."

"Daniel—your executor in the colony, right?"

"Not anymore. No colonies, now. Colonies, packs, covens, or whatever, were broken up when we were granted equal rights after the world government took over. We were told that since killing zots had been made illegal our means of protection and survival were no longer necessary." He paused. "Anyway, just give me a minute." Closing his eyes, he sent a telepathic message to Daniel. Five minutes passed before he opened them again. He looked at the others. "All set."

Parker grinned. "Then let's go."

Melera held out her hands. Parker took one and Kurt took the other. Garrett stepped forward and held her by the waist. He knew what was about to happen. Melera was going to skip them through the Void, the nothingness between here and there. And then they'd be on her spaceship, hurtling through the cosmos.

Kurt smiled. *Forever...*

TO MY READERS

Hello, and thank you so much for reading *Invasion* and its companion short story, "Forever Bound!"

Invasion is the sequel to *The Underground.* For the most part, *Invasion* was fairly easy to write—after the action in *The Underground,* I knew exactly where to go next. The hard part was figuring out how to get there! I wrote "Forever Bound" because I didn't want anyone to think I was finished with Parker, Melera, Kurt, and Garrett. Exploring the galaxy? There's loads of trouble out there for our four heroes to get into—and trust me, they will!

I'd love to have you along on my writers' journey! To hitch a ride, just join my email list at http://www.roxannebland.rocks. You can stay updated on my works-in-progress, enter contests for nifty swag, and don't be surprised if I ask for your feedback on a project! More than that, by signing up you'll get a FREE copy of my ebook *The Final Victim,* a companion tale to the dangerous world of *The Underground,* where the drama unfolds from the elven point of view. What's more, *The Final Victim* is exclusive, available only from me, and I can provide it in .epub, .mobi, or .pdf formats! If *The Final Victim* piques your curiosity about *The Underground,* the ebook is available from Amazon, Barnes & Noble, Kobo, Smashwords, and similar outlets, or get it in print from your favorite bookstore (including Amazon and Barnes & Noble)!

One more thing—please consider leaving a review of *Invasion* on the platform where you purchased it, on your favorite readers' website(s), or recommending it to a friend.

Thanks again for your support!

Roxanne Bland